LUTHECKER: REVOLUTION

KEITH DOMINGUE

CONTENTS

PART III
THE REVOLUTION

PROLOGUE

"WATCH YOUR STEP SIR," RAHUL MALIK said to the man who trailed several steps behind him on the hard-packed snow that blanketed the Siachen Glacier, a forty-seven mile long sheet of ice that bridged the border between rivals India and Pakistan.

Malik, a short, barrel-chested Indian in his early forties, had been put in charge of guiding the foreigner, an American scientist, to the military outpost located closest to the Pakistan-Indian border.

The former captain in the Indian Army stomped his feet on the hard- packed snow to keep warm as he waited for the much slower American.

Now special counsel for the region and under contract to the American military conglomerate Coalition Properties, Malik had been tasked with chaperoning one of its representatives, a pale-skinned, bald-headed man by the name of Mark Kirby.

Kirby, a civilian and therefore soft in Malik's mind, was unused to the extreme weather conditions of the remote frozen outpost and had struggled a great deal to keep up as soon as they stepped clear of the helicopter less than an hour earlier.

Located in the eastern Karakoram section of the Himalaya Mountain Range, the Siachen, a word in Balti that roughly translated to "land of abundant roses," was a region that had been in a territorial dispute between India and Pakistan since the early 1980s.

Despite the bitter cold, with temperatures that could dip to minus 50 degrees Celsius, and the average winter snowfall, which could be ten meters or more, both countries kept a full contingent of soldiers on constant alert across the glacier, with skirmishes between them being commonplace.

"Hold up, I have to rest," Mark Kirby called out to his guide.

The combination of elevation and cold made Kirby dizzy with every effort, and he was forced to stoop over, resting his hands on his thighs while trying to catch his breath. After several seconds, Kirby stood upright and instinctively pulled his parka close.

He did a quick scan of the ice-horizon. It was late afternoon, and despite wearing dark wrap-around sunglasses specifically designed to shield his eyes from sunlight that reflected off the surface of the glacier, Kirby was forced to squint from the glare. Even though he had been told what to expect, what Kirby saw shocked the scientist.

Extending all the way to the horizon, the white-blue of the glacier was peppered with refuse. Kirby could see countless plastic bottles, abandoned tents and poles, along with tires, fuel drums, axes, and old television sets, all half hidden in the melting ice. There were newspapers, fast food wrappers with familiar logos, along with lost gloves and hats. But more numerous than anything else, were the empty shell casings.

The larger ones appeared to be from RPGs and shoulder mounted rockets, but most of the metal casings were from small arms fire, and they were sprinkled across the ice as far as the eye could see. To Kirby, it looked like an eerie frozen battlefield, a wasteland museum representing the twin engines of consumption and war, which drove much of the world, all of it contrasted by the peaceful and pure-blue skies overhead.

"What happened here?" Kirby asked, his voice echoing through the open air.

Malik walked down the path toward Kirby. His thick rubber boots crunched on the snow. "Conflict," he replied, as he approached Kirby. "As the ice melts, the past... disagreements are more and more revealed."

"Conflict over?"

"Territory and resources, my friend. Along with God, what else is there to fight for?"

Malik's Indian accent provided a singsong rhythm to his English that made the question sound like a nursery rhyme.

"What resources are here?" Kirby asked as he once again looked over the giant sheet of ice. "There's no oil."

Malik smirked then opened up his thick coat and pulled free a bottle of water. "This. Soon, it will be more important than oil." Malik held the bottle out for Kirby. "Drink. Dehydration is deceptive in the cold."

Kirby grabbed the bottle with mitten-covered hands and struggled to twist the cap free.

He swallowed the water in big gulps, the liquid noticeably warmed by Malik's body heat. Kirby finished the water, surprised by how thirsty he was.

"Thank you," Kirby said, gasping for air yet again as he held the empty bottle out for Malik to take.

Malik shrugged. "Throw it in the snow with the others. One more won't make any difference," the Indian guide said as he turned back to the trail and marched onward.

Kirby looked over the refuse-strewn glacier. He carefully unzipped his thick wool parka and stuck the bottle into an inside pocket before quickly zipping up the jacket.

"How much farther?" Kirby yelled out. He realized that shouting caused him to feel dizzy, and his heart pounded with the effort.

Malik pointed. In the distance, the outline of several tents and small shacks were visible, along with the smoke of fire.

~

"You come here representing the interests of the Coalition," Colonel Banerjee said as he shook Kirby's hand.

Kirby took note of the same singsong rhythm of English in Banerjee's voice that he caught in Malik's. It was disarming, almost playful, and seemingly implied no threat.

However, Banerjee's eyes said different—they were hard and piercing, and missed no detail. The soldier's posture and gait were strong and confident, and to Kirby, Banerjee appeared ready for battle at a moment's notice.

Kirby eyed the sidearm strapped to the colonel's hip. The American scientist instinctively knew that Banerjee could, and, if necessary, would kill him with no hesitation or remorse.

Banerjee sensed the American's assessment and cracked a knowing smile.

Kirby took note that the dark skin of Banerjee's face was hard-lined and leathered—a tough exterior visibly wind-worn from the harsh air of what was considered the "third pole."

"Technically, you are correct that I work for the Coalition," Kirby finally replied, before he unzipped and removed his parka. "But my interests here are my own."

Banerjee smirked. The men locked eyes, and Banerjee searched the American's for any indication as to what Kirby was after.

Kirby broke the gaze, rubbing his hands together to keep warm. The doctor took note of a wood stove in the center of the canvass command hut that provided heat.

"Are you hungry?" Banerjee asked.

"Starving."

Banerjee pointed to a small metal folding table where a warm bowl of stew and a large soup spoon sat ready.

Kirby sat down in a wooden chair at the table, and the colonel watched as the American paddled the vegetables, Yak meat, and broth into his mouth, as if the pale skinned foreigner with the thick unkempt beard hadn't eaten in weeks.

Banerjee turned to Malik, who was standing at parade rest near the entrance to the tent, and nodded. Malik nodded in return, about faced, and quickly disappeared.

Banerjee turned back toward Kirby. He watched as the American drank the last of the broth before wiping his beard.

He waited until Kirby looked at him before he spoke. "First the Coalition wanted all of the oil. And now they want all of the water. Is that why you are here? For the water?"

Kirby wiped his hands with a cloth napkin and got to his feet. "How long have you been fighting on the Siachen?"

"Does it matter? It's melting, you know. This—" Banerjee stomped his boot in the ice for emphasis. "All of it will be gone before the next generation sees its last days."

"I know. It's a serious problem. And I'm sorry to say that it won't be stopped."

"There is nothing you can do?"

"I'm not here for that. At least not right now."

"Than why are you here?"

"I'm here for the pattern reader."

Banerjee stopped moving. The colonel stared at Kirby for several seconds without a word. It made Kirby uncomfortable.

"My information says that he came this way," Kirby continued. "I've been tracking him for months. Have you seen Alex Luthecker?"

"What do you know of this man?" Banerjee questioned. There was suspicion in Banerjee's tone, and the colonel made no attempt to mask it.

Kirby took a moment to think of the right words. The last thing the American scientist wanted to do right now was upset the military leader of this remote outpost.

"I believe he frees minds," Kirby finally answered. "And many find him dangerous because of this."

"So he is a weapon then? Is he part of the Coalition arsenal?"

Kirby felt his forehead get hot, and sweat dripped down the back of his neck. "There are many on the Coalition board who think he is a weapon. However, I disagree."

"If he is not a weapon, what is he?"

Once again, Kirby searched his mind for the right words. He finally looked Banerjee in the eye. "An agent of change."

"A weapon," Banerjee fired back.

Kirby moved closer to the wood stove and held his hands over the hot metal to warm them. "Clearly you did not see or speak with him," Kirby said. He then turned toward the colonel. "Or more accurately, he did not see you when he was here."

"How would you know this?"

"If you had seen him, if he had made contact with you in any way, I believe that you would no longer have any questions. About anything."

Banerjee kept his eyes locked on Kirby for several more seconds before abruptly turning toward the entrance to the tent. "So you understand how he works, then. Exactly how he can do what it is that he does."

"Like you, I've never met Alex Luthecker. But I very much want to. I knew his parents, and there is much I can share with him about who he is. I thought I had the chance in Los Angeles, but he promptly disappeared, as he is wont to do. That's why I've been tracking him. I want to better understand how he can affect people such as he can."

"Tell me what this means," Banerjee said, before he whipped back the tent flap.

An ice-cold breeze caused Kirby to shiver.

"Look," Banerjee said as he pointed north.

Kirby pulled on his parka before peering out of the tent. He looked over to where Banerjee pointed.

On the hard packed snow and ice, Kirby eyed a pyramid of several dozen American supplied M-16 rifles. The weapons looked as if they had been tossed aside in haste. Even at this distance, Kirby recognized the weapons as Coalition-made.

"You are correct. He was here. Two nights ago. With a woman."

"Nicole Ellis."

"So my sentries say. I only arrived this morning when I heard you would be coming. I thought you would have an answer for this."

"Where are they now?"

"I was told that they disappeared during the night. The very same night that they arrived."

"How is that possible?"

"Perhaps they left with the soldiers who laid down their arms and abandoned their posts."

Kirby looked at the pile of rifles. He looked back at Banerjee. Kirby already knew what had happened.

"They say he came in under the cover of night like an evil spirit, his woman at his side," Banerjee continued. "They say he whispered in the ears of my soldiers, and that his words somehow altered them at their very core. I was told some were left crying and shaking. Some were inconsolable. One of my captains even took his own life. And by morning, the rest whom this...Alex Luthecker had spoken to...were gone."

Banerjee stepped close to Kirby. Although the colonel was only five foot six, his intensity caused Kirby to step back. "Tell me, Doctor Kirby, what manner of weapon is he? What kind of man can come in like a thief in the night and convince battle-hardened soldiers who would fight to the death with a single command and without hesitation, what would convince them to abandon everything, to abandon the *only* thing they have ever known?"

PART I

MISSION CREEP

1

ARRANGEMENT

COALITION PROPERTIES CEO GLEN TURNER SAT QUIETLY IN A CORNER booth of the café, sipping his coffee. Still a bit jet-lagged from his flight from Los Angeles to Paris, he found the caffeine jolt provided by the strong French brew necessary to keep him alert and focused.

The café where he sat waiting, *Le Select*, was legendary, having once served the likes of Hemmingway, Picasso, and Henry Miller. Opened in 1923, Le Select became one of the most popular cafés on Montparnasse, as it was open 24 hours and catered to the whims and secretive natures of its bohemian customers.

In days long past, the artists, aristocrats, spies, and political revolutionaries were the ones who packed the cafés of Paris such as Le Select. It was even rumored that Karl Marx had met with social scientist Friedrich Engels in Le Select, the two men crafting their economic ideals over coffee and croissants.

Now it was mostly tourists and long-time locals who kept the handful of remaining old cafés such as Le Select open.

Turner eyed the current crowd of customers as he finished his cup of coffee. It was just past 11 a.m. local time, and the restaurant would normally be filled with the rabble of its regulars for this hour.

Right now, the café was quiet and near empty. The half a dozen customers, all men and all more rough looking than bohemian, sat alone, a calculated distance apart, reading newspapers or staring out windows.

They never made eye contact with Turner, but he sensed that they were always watching. Their deadpan expressions and mechanical attempts to look casual revealed that they were not locals—and certainly not artisans.

The cloak and dagger element of this meeting that Turner had been called to made him nostalgic for simpler times. Perhaps not as much had changed in the last 84 years as most people thought, he mused to himself.

It was the Russian oligarch Ivan Barbolin, otherwise known as "the Barbarian," who had chosen Paris, and specifically Le Select, as their meeting place. It was neutral territory, the Russian had claimed, but as Turner considered the rough looking and distinctively non-French patrons who currently covered both exits and constantly checked the sight lines, he knew otherwise.

On the other hand, considering the two-dozen Coalition Assurance Special Ops enforcers he himself had strategically located in the kitchen and also on the street in front of Le Select, Turner felt reasonably safe.

"You should try the vodka," the deep rumble of the Barbarian's accent-heavy voice echoed through the near empty café, breaking the silence.

Turner looked behind him to find the big Russian standing.

"I came in through the kitchen," the Barbarian continued, before Turner could enquire. "Past one of your agents. Not to worry, he took the time to pat me down. Just like old times, eh? Welcome to Paris," he continued, as he stuck out a meaty hand.

Turner got to his feet and shook hands with the Barbarian, before both men sat down across from each other.

A waiter brought a bottle of vodka, along with two shot glasses.

"It's barely eleven a.m.," Turner stated, looking at the vodka bottle.

"It is tradition when business agreements are reached," the

Barbarian replied as he poured two shots then held up his own. "Salute," he said, before he quickly drank the shot.

Turner followed suit. The alcohol burned the back of his throat, but Turner forced himself to show no reaction.

The Barbarian smiled before pouring himself another shot of vodka. "How is your predecessor?" the big Russian asked.

"James Howe? He's in jail."

"A risky option."

"We're not like you."

"Ah. American Exceptionalism. Where one greatly exaggerates the differences between their people and others, no?"

"It's no exaggeration."

"It was one of yours who killed my partner. A deed not so exceptional. And that particular American is still free."

"He isn't one of ours. And your partner went off the reservation."

The Barbarian looked over the Coalition leader's face. He did not like Turner, but he understood that their interests were aligned, at least for now. He also understood that getting on the wrong side of Turner, the newly crowned CEO of the world's largest defense contractor, the world's largest corporate entity of any kind, would end in his quick demise.

He also knew that he had faced down formidable foes disguised as allies in the past, and he had been the one who had survived. There were still variables left unaccounted for that the Barbarian could use to his advantage. And until those advantages presented themselves, he would play along as the jovial cooperative Russian businessman.

"James Howe is more valuable to us alive than dead if that's what you're alluding to," Turner continued. "He's on a time out for now. He's not a concern. This meeting can't be about him. Why did you insist that I come to Paris?"

"You do not enjoy one of Europe's most storied cities?"

"Get to the point, Ivan."

"Those of us who deal in unregulated economics prefer our dealings in the old way," the Barbarian explained.

"Do you mean face to face? To look me in the eye? Why? Are you afraid of your phone being tapped? Of getting caught? You're showing your age, my friend, this isn't the Cold War. In case you didn't notice, corporatism won, and America is still at the head of the only table that matters—the one of wealth and profit. We own the seas, the airways, the Internet, the cell towers, trade policy, all branches of government, and the law. We monitor and control the narrative from every angle.

"If I wanted you to be dead, you'd be dead right now, and I'd make it look like the patriotic thing to do, which in a lot of minds it would be. This arrangement between our interests is already off the books, and *that*, my friend, is nothing new—United Fruit Company in Central America, the Gulf of Tonkin in Vietnam, Iran-Contra, the Iraq-Afghan wars, all of those off-the-books business arrangements were hidden in plain sight. This will be no different.

"There's no need for concern. The Coalition is going to run guns, drugs, contraband, labor, and regional influence on your continent through your organization. We'll use the U.S. Navy and intelligence apparatuses to protect both of our interests. We'll run it all through our banks and real estate to turn your dark money into light.

"In turn, you just make sure that there are forever wars for us to engage, cheap labor, no regulations to adhere to, and no lack of product of any kind to be sold. We take seventy percent of your revenue, and in return for that, we make sure no one ever bothers you. You walk off with more billions than you could possibly acquire on your own, tax-free I might add, which is more than enough to rebuild your country in any manner you see fit, so long as it doesn't threaten the order of things. It's not that complicated, Ivan."

"And the prisons. Don't forget the prisons you own. The slave factories that your immigration lobby created, not just in the U.S., but all over the world now."

"We prefer the term labor integration, and with our arrangement, you won't end up integrated. That's also part of the deal. You'll be another protected king, in a long line of protected kings, living in a billion dollar castle. You can even officially run your country if you want."

"I do not seek the Russian presidency. A powerful office, but one too easily compromised. Even in America. Just look at your last election. Your people already suspect our involvement."

Turner signaled the waitress for some water. "You're smarter than I thought. But it would be yours, if you so chose."

"So Coalition Properties reaches its goal and becomes the world's first corporate superpower," the Barbarian said, before he downed another shot of Vodka.

"We already were that. We have been for a long time. This is about eliminating competing narratives that lead to bloodshed whose profits are not on our balance sheets. The underground economy is the only thing that we didn't own outright. And now, with this agreement, we do."

"And your board? It is comfortable with this arrangement?"

"Once the collective governments of the region gave the green light through the United Global Trade Act, there was little reason to say no."

"Your predecessor wanted these things, and yet he is in jail."

"My predecessor was impatient, and neither understood nor cared about the optics regarding his actions. He didn't understand the commoners and did not care how social media connects them. In short, he couldn't coordinate the proper elements, which caused him to eliminate the wrong people at the wrong time, in front of the wrong people.

"Optics are more important than ever in a post-truth environment. He ignored this fact and that was his mistake. But the benefit is that the people can be much more easily controlled these days via their cell phones and short attention spans. And you must always present the illusion of what's best for the people."

"As you rob them blind." The Barbarian poured Turner another shot.

"As Russia did to their own the minute the wall fell. You were one of the primary beneficiaries, Ivan. And all the superpower bluster in the 80s was propaganda. It was all that you ever had. A gas station with nukes was all you ever were. So you people became masters at the psychological arts.

"But we're different. When you literally own all the money, natural resources, and weaponry, it's not arrogance to believe you are exceptional. You already have proven yourself superior. You are by definition exceptional." Turner picked up the glass and finished the shot of vodka in one gulp. This time, he grimaced from the burn.

"The concern I have is not with the mutually beneficial elements of our arrangement. That is not why I wished to see you in person. The concern I have is with the unfinished business of your predecessor and my late partner."

"Alex Luthecker? Is *that* what this is about? Don't tell me you've become one of the obsessed, Ivan. It doesn't suit you." Turner felt beads of sweat beginning to form on his forehead. The last thing he wanted to discuss was the refugee soothsayer. He resisted the urge to wipe his brow. *It's the alcohol*, he thought to himself.

Turner watched as the Barbarian momentarily searched inside his jacket pocket and pulled out a bright-white handkerchief.

The Russian offered the silk cloth to Turner. "*In Vino Veritas*," the Barbarian thought. A phrase his late partner used to say in times like these.

Turner waved off the offer.

The Barbarian shrugged and put away the handkerchief. "His actions do not concern you?"

"The fear of his alleged abilities has caused far greater harm than whatever his alleged abilities actually are."

"Is that not the root of power for all revolutionaries?"

"He's not a revolutionary. He's a minor annoyance. And I don't plan on making the same mistake as my predecessors."

"You plan to let him go?"

"I don't plan to hang my fate or that of Coalition Properties on one man who lives outside the system."

"You are not looking for him then? You have not yet labeled him a terrorist?"

"I didn't say that. I have a man on it. One who claims to have a different approach. But let me be clear, I don't regard Luthecker as a threat. Labeling him as a terrorist, recognizing him in any way at all, only serves to validate him as a problem. I don't need him as an asset."

"So your plan is to ignore him?"

"There's nothing he can allegedly do that Coalition technology will soon be able to do better."

"It is not so much his...how do I say in English? His...*pattern reading* abilities...that concern me. It is his direct effect on labor costs."

"You mean the recent lost labor shipments in the Port of Long Beach."

"There have been more."

"Statistically the impact is zero. There's no need for concern. We're monitoring what his people are doing in Los Angeles. If anything, the morale boost our lenience on their freeing the occasional group of refugees or slave workers gives helps keep things under control.

"People need a pressure valve for their hopes. They need to believe they haven't lost and that someone is fighting for them. I consider it an insurance policy. A remainder of a very old equation that's never going to change, and I'm smart enough not to stomp it out."

"It is beyond just a few lost laborers. Have you heard what has happened in India?"

Turner hesitated for just a second. He had allowed one of his scientists to explore rumors regarding sightings of Alex Luthecker in the region, but the report he got back from the scientist over a month ago made no mention of anything out of the ordinary and certainly no mention of any contact with Alex Luthecker.

The Barbarian did not miss the hesitation.

"My man in the field reported no problems," Turner answered.

"You need to look closer, my friend. The pattern reader has been there. He has been to many places. And wherever he goes, things are being disrupted. Profitable conflicts taken for granted are now being questioned." The Barbarian leaned in close. "His legend is growing. The slaves we need, that *all empires need*, are beginning to grow restless. *He* is making them restless. And he must be stopped."

Turner's face grew red with anger. If Kirby had held back any intelligence regarding Luthecker's whereabouts, the scientist would pay dearly.

"Don't worry. We're working on it," Turner responded. "We'll shut down his little group of freedom fighters in Los Angeles to send a message. And we'll catch up to Mr. Luthecker and his enabler, Nikki Ellis, soon enough and eliminate them."

Turner reached over to the bottle of vodka and poured both the Barbarian and himself a fresh shot. It was time to finish with Ivan, confront Mark Kirby, and take care of the Luthecker problem before it got out of hand.

He held up his shot glass in toast. "To our mutual interests."

The Barbarian smiled and held up his shot glass. He had Turner where he wanted him. "To our mutual interests."

2

LA BESTIA

ENRIQUE MARTINEZ PULLED HIS LITTLE SISTER CLOSE, WRAPPING THE only blanket he owned around them both, trying to keep warm. The blanket, a well-worn cotton fabric that his grandmother gave to Enrique when he was only six years old, was the only possession he had kept for this journey. His sister Maria kept one possession from home as well; a small stuffed tiger she called "Nala," which she cradled in her arms.

As the swirl of the cold desert wind whipped his long hair in every direction, Enrique used his body to shield his sister from the brunt of its force as they huddled together on top of the fast moving train car.

Maria, only ten years old, peacefully slept in her big brother's arms as the rattle of "*La Bestia*" or "The Beast"—as the train was known in English—continued its journey in the black of night from the city of Lechera in Southern Mexico all the way to Nogales, close to the California border.

The nighttime sky provided just enough illumination for Enrique to see the outline of hundreds of other migrants packed on the back of the Beast, sitting or asleep on top of the long line of cars that made up the infamous cargo train.

The moonlight also allowed Enrique to see his sister's face and the calm and undisturbed look on her dozing visage, along with the sight of her tightly grasping Nala. It made him smile. That peaceful visage also gave the exhausted Enrique strength, strength he knew he would need, because although the sixteen year old was beyond tired, he was keenly aware that there could be no sleep for him tonight. Not with the potential threats ahead.

As he fought the sleep-inducing rhythm that the motion of the train provided, he kept his eyes alert for signs of danger in the form of bandits from drug cartels and human traffickers that could jump the train at any moment to rob, kidnap, rape, or kill any or all who rode north in search of a better life.

For Enrique, born and raised in San Salvador, El Salvador, gang violence had been a part of everyday life for as long as he remembered. But in recent years, life in the city had gotten particularly grave, as Mexican drug cartels, the Calderon Cartel in particular, had aligned with local El Salvadorian gangs to more efficiently move both drugs and people throughout the Americas, and eventually throughout the world.

The cartel enforcers, foot soldiers arrested in America and trained in U.S. prisons before being deported back to their homelands, had gotten more aggressive in their recruitment efforts of local boys Enrique's age and some much younger, to join their cause. More often than not, the recruitment efforts were done at gunpoint.

Enrique had been remarkably lucky so far, having managed to evade the gang's recruitment efforts. He was careful to mind his own business, choosing to stay close to his family, with a keen interest in protecting his little sister Maria. It was because of this that Enrique believed he never found himself in the wrong place at the wrong time in regards to the cartel. His mother thought of Enrique's luck in avoiding gang recruitment as a direct blessing from God.

Two of Enrique's closest friends had not been so lucky. They had refused to join and had been killed for their responses, and the young El Salvadorian knew that despite his luck and best efforts to avoid the cartel-controlled gangs, it was only a matter of time before he would be approached with the same offer and suffer the same result if he refused to join.

Yet to Enrique, San Salvador was his home, the only one he'd ever known, and at first he had chosen to stay in order to protect his family. But when his father was gunned down in the streets of San Salvador in broad daylight, for no discernible reason and with no arrests made, Enrique changed his mind and decided he had no choice but to leave his homeland for good.

Enrique knew that the journey north through Guatemala, Chiapas, and Mexico, leading to America, the land of opportunity, would be weeks long and dangerous. But to stay in El Salvador and face the Calderon Cartel would be far worse.

When Enrique told his mother of his plans to move the family, she refused to go, believing that she was too old, but she insisted that he leave to start a new life. She did insist on one more thing—that Enrique take Maria with him. Enrique assured his mother that there was no way he was leaving his little sister behind to be subject to the abuses of the cartel soldiers.

So Enrique took what little money he had, hired a coyote, what migrant smugglers were known as, to get both he and Maria all the way to Arriaga in Chiapas. It was in Arriaga where he would board the first leg of the Beast, making the final switch of trains in Lechera, the last train that would take them to Nogales, as close to the U.S. border as La Bestia went. From there, he would take his chances to cross into America via the state of California.

But he had to survive and protect his little sister during the three-week journey to the border first. So far, he, Maria, and the other migrants had been lucky. At each transition, where the migrants were most vulnerable to attack, it had been relatively quiet.

Migrants, who were at risk from falling off the top of the train cars and potentially losing limbs or their lives as well, had, thus far, suffered no incidents. But the true test would be when the Beast passed through Veracruz, a stop notorious for migrants disappearing at the hands of traffickers.

Enrique's immediate goal was to make it to a Catholic mission rumored to be just before Veracruz, where a missionary by the name of Father Alejandro Gracilas was known to take migrants in and feed them, allow them to bathe, and provide them with supplies for the rest of their respective journeys.

Father Gracilas was also rumored to know where the cartel soldiers and traffickers lay in wait to hijack the Beast, and the priest would allegedly do his best to steer the refugees clear from harm. It was at the mission that Enrique hoped that the priest would help him make contact with a trustworthy coyote, one who did not work for the cartels, to provide passage for he and his sister across the U.S. - Mexican border.

Enrique's stomach growled from hunger as he sat in the darkness. He had not eaten in over a day, giving the last of his rations of simple bread and water to Maria. He tried not to think about his hunger or the great risks he faced on this journey. It was the only way to keep his panic in check. Most of all he tried to forget that beyond today, he had no plan to get himself and Maria across the border, other than faith and hope.

The current leg of the trip on the back of the Beast was fourteen hours, but it already seemed like forever to Enrique, as he had lost all sense of time's passage long ago. The relentless instability of his situation made every minute feel like an hour; the only benchmark he had was the knowledge that sunrise would indicate they were very close to their destination. And the current nighttime sky was infinite black, save for the array of stars.

Enrique wrapped his arms tightly around his little sister, both for her comfort and his own. He decided he would focus on the stars and say a prayer to St. Jude, the patron saint of the oppressed and hopeless, that he and Maria would make it across the border safely and begin new life.

A SUDDEN TURN of the Beast snapped Enrique awake. He instinctively pulled his sister tight as his left arm shot out and braced them both against the top of the train car for balance. Pulled from a dream of better times and completely disoriented, it took the squeaks and moans of the moving train for Enrique to remember where he was.

He was also abruptly reminded of current dangers as he witnessed a migrant roll off the back of the Beast. Enrique and the other migrants watched in sorrow as the man tumbled helplessly onto the dust of the desert floor. Enrique kept watching as the train pulled farther and farther away from the place where the man's movements came to a stop, from the place where he lay motionless.

Enrique hoped the fallen passenger was okay and breathed a sigh of relief when the man slowly got to his feet and disappeared as the train roared on. It was then that Enrique also realized it was daylight.

"I'm hungry," Maria murmured as she stirred awake. She instinctively clutched her stuffed tiger close to her chest.

"We will arrive at the mission soon," Enrique answered as he pulled the blanket away from his little sister.

"Will they have food?"

"Yes," Enrique assured her, before kissing her on the forehead, hoping that his words would prove to be true.

The loud blast of the Beast's horn interrupted Enrique and Maria's thoughts, and as the train slowly moved around the next curve in the tracks, Enrique looked ahead, and his heart started to pound at what he saw. The train station was now in view. He and Maria's lives literally hinged upon what happened next. He hoped it would be Father Gracilas and not cartel soldiers waiting to greet them.

The migrants moved to a crouching position in anticipation as the brakes of the train began to squeal, the large locomotive slowly grinding to a halt.

"Let's go. Hurry now," Enrique said to Maria, before he grabbed her hand and led her to the back of the train car, where a single metal ladder led to the tracks below. There was some pushing and shoving as migrants tried to exit the train as quickly as they could, before the Beast rolled back into motion.

"Go, go," Enrique said to Maria, when a break in the traffic at the ladder appeared, and she hustled down the metal rungs on cue.

Enrique pushed aside another migrant and quickly followed his sister.

Once on the ground, Enrique quickly grabbed hold of Maria's hand again and scanned the train station, his heart racing.

He nearly collapsed with a sigh of relief as he saw what he was looking for: A bald headed man, his face lined with age, the color of his skin deep-brown from the sun, wearing a dark-brown robe. Around the man's neck hung a large wooden cross.

A big smile spread across Enrique's face as he grabbed his sister's hand tightly, both sprinting as fast as they could to meet Father Gracilas.

∾

"WAS IT GOOD?" Enrique asked Maria as she finished the last of her tamale.

The ten year old responded with a smile and a rapid nod of the head. "May I have another?"

"Let me check and see if there's any left," Enrique replied, before he got to his feet and walked toward the food table.

∾

MARIA MARTINEZ HAD ALWAYS LOOKED out for her older brother Enrique, for as long as she could remember. To Maria, her big brother never paid attention to things like she did. How people behaved, for example.

People's behavior would always tell Maria what they were about to do. When the gangs came through the neighborhood, it terrified everyone, but for some reason, Maria always knew when the gangs would come looking for Enrique. She could tell by how people in the neighborhood would walk or talk. Sometimes it would be in their mannerisms or how they would move. Sometimes it was what they would wear. Still with others, she could tell right away what they would do by a look in their eye. Sometimes, it was a combination of all these things. And sometimes, if the weather was bad, that would tell her too.

And when all these things combined to tell Maria that they were coming for Enrique, she always convinced him to go into town to buy her candy, or play hide and seek with her in the old schoolyard. There were dozens of places to play hide and seek where Maria lived, and she knew them all.

Maria didn't understand why she knew what people would do before they did it. What was even harder for her to understand was why Enrique couldn't see what she could see.

If it weren't for her, Enrique would run into trouble just like their dog Chewy ran into walls whenever the big dopey mutt was chasing a fly in the house. And it wasn't just Enrique who acted as silly as Chewy. It seemed like no one could ever see what they were doing or where they were going. It seemed like no one paid attention to what was happening around them, ever. It frustrated Maria. Why did they choose to ignore everything? Why couldn't they just *see*?

The other children in the neighborhood picked on Maria. Called her a weirdo. She hated that word. To Maria, they were all stupid and blind. When they called her names, it caused her to lash out at them.

But they left her alone after she told that loud-mouthed boy Jose that a car would hit him and break his leg, and the next day it happened. Jose was always running or talking without looking or thinking. How could he not see it before it happened? How could *everyone* not see it before it happened?

Maria tried to explain this to the parents when they asked how she knew that the car would hit Jose. But they couldn't understand. None of them could understand. It was so frustrating. So she stopped talking about what she saw. Eventually she stopped trying to see. And then she stopped playing with her friends. She only played with Nala her stuffed tiger.

Maria saw that her father was going to die. She saw it a week before it happened. She tried not to see it, but she couldn't help it.

Her father had gotten into an argument with their neighbor about making loud noises at night. Maria's father wanted the noises to stop. The neighbor had said no. The neighbor was a younger man than her father, but taller and skinnier, with tattoos on his arms and neck. And his eyes were always angry.

Maria watched as he and her father yelled at one another three days in a row. She watched as the neighbor flexed his hands in anticipation the final time. To Maria, that meant the neighbor would be back, but not to argue again.

The neighbor had dangerous cartel people over to his house once. Maria saw them there when she peeked out her bedroom window the night before the last argument.

When the neighbor walked away from her father that time, it was an angry walk. When Maria saw the look in the neighbor's eyes, the way he walked, the way he flexed his hands, and the way he laughed with the cartel people only days earlier, she knew her father would be dead in a week.

Maria tried to warn her father. But he didn't listen. He only yelled at her for spying on him. Maria ran to her mother. Her mother only prayed to Jesus. Maria knew Jesus wasn't going to help, and her mother did nothing to stop her father from going into town, like he did every Wednesday, where Maria knew he would die.

Maria had warned Enrique. Enrique was the only one who was kind to her. The only one who didn't yell at her or call her silly. Or weirdo. Enrique said he believed her, but she could tell he really didn't. But still, because Maria asked him, Enrique tried to warn their father.

Their father didn't listen to Enrique either. Their father never listened to anyone. Her father was stubborn, angry, and blind. And then he died.

Maria stopped believing in the things she saw in her mind after that day. She didn't want to believe them. She didn't want to see them. She wanted to be blind, just like everyone else. So she just played with Nala and stayed close to Enrique who she knew loved her no matter what she said or did. The only thing she would make sure to see from now on were the things that kept Enrique away from the gangs. Enrique was the only part of home life that Maria wanted to hang on to.

Pretty soon, she stopped paying attention to many things on purpose. Things would happen to people and places, and she would be surprised that they happened, because she wouldn't see it before it happened, because she chose not to see things before they happened. Things were easier this way, Maria had convinced herself. She understood it now. If you were blind, you didn't have to worry. You could just let things happen and be surprised. She would be happy if she never had the visions again.

When Enrique said they were leaving San Salvador, she convinced herself that she was surprised. She was happy to leave San Salvador, where people called her weirdo. She was happy because she and Enrique were leaving San Salvador together and happy because it was an adventure into the unknown. And she hoped that the visions would stay behind her for good in San Salvador.

Maria scanned over the room looking for Enrique. There were so many people here, desperate, scared, and hungry. They hid the fear with laughter and with hope for something better.

They were too scared to see what was about to happen, but Maria could see, no matter how hard she tried not to. She kept herself from screaming in terror at what she saw. For the first time in a long time, she saw everything, just like she used to, and she knew what would happen next. She had to get to Enrique. She had to save him again.

ENRIQUE APPROACHED the food table to see if he could find another tamale for his sister.

The temporary mess hall of the Christ Savior Missionary was a converted warehouse that had been long abandoned, the furniture consisting of a half dozen folding tables and several dozen chairs. The place was packed with migrants, all hungry, but laughing and smiling now, relieved and grateful for being fed.

Enrique looked over his fellow migrants and wondered how many would make it across the border into America to work in the fields. Enrique also took note of the building's details and saw that each faded stucco wall had a wooden Crucifix hung next to a picture of Jesus. He wondered if, after the migrants left, Father Gracilas took the religious items down to throw off the cartel.

He looked over to the makeshift kitchen area, which consisted of hotplates with big metal pots of soup on them, along with a handful of tamales put out on paper plates. To the side of the tamales were napkins and bottles of water.

Father Gracilas toiled behind the tables of the makeshift kitchen, handing out the bowls of soup, along with the rest of the food and water, to dozens of hungry migrants. The priest made sure to bless each migrant as they took their food. The migrants were more than happy to accept his blessing.

As Enrique approached the long line of hungry people to fetch his sister another tamale, he hoped he would have a chance to talk to the priest. He hoped that the padre would be able to advise him on how he could get both he and Maria across the border.

But the sudden popcorn-sounding crack of automatic gunfire from just outside the building stopped everything.

MARIA KNEW that everything she saw in her visions was real when she heard the sound of gunfire. The pit of her stomach sank like it did when she knew her father was going to die and no one would do anything to stop it.

Dread of knowing what would happen next made her mind go blank with fear. Maria had never tried to stop the things she saw from happening directly before. The only thing she had ever done was guide Enrique away from the gangs. But this time she would have to do something. The details in her mind were scrambled now, but the results had stayed clear. The only thing she knew now was she had to get to Enrique.

Maria sprang from where she sat and ran toward the food table. She only made it three steps before a large man who had been running toward the exit and didn't see her, ran into her, and knocked her completely off her feet.

She tried to get up, but a terrified woman knocked her down. She tried again, but another fleeing migrant's knee hit her in the chest, knocking the wind out of her, sending her to the floor once again.

In their terror, they couldn't see her. In their terror, they couldn't see *anything*. *They run because they are blind*, Maria thought. *And stupid*.

Maria tried to get to her feet one more time and was stepped on, twice—once on the hand and again on the stomach. She howled in pain. Then she howled in anger. It was rage Maria had never felt before. Enrique was going to die, and it was because they were all so blind and stupid. Enrique was going to die because of *them*.

FOR ENRIQUE, time itself slowed to a stop as his worst fears leaped to the front of his mind—the realization of what was happening had put time on hold, allowing the pressure from unfolding events to build.

And then the pressure abruptly released, and events began to flow again with accelerated chaos.

Tables were overturned as people scrambled for the doors. Screams echoed throughout the hall as men and women pushed and shoved each other aside, trampling one another, as they scrambling for the exits. As people squeezed through the doorways and out of the building, more gunfire erupted outside the hall. This time followed by screams.

Enrique immediately sprinted toward the table where Maria was sitting, the view of his sister strobed by the panicked rush of migrants. His eyes went wide when he reached the table and saw that she was gone.

"Maria!" he called out as he searched frantically for his sister. He pushed fellow migrants aside and sprinted to where she had been seated only moments earlier. When he got to the table, all he found was her overturned chair.

"Maria!" Enrique called out again, his voice cracking. Tears filled his eyes and his heart filled with dread.

And then something completely unexpected happened to Enrique. Without warning, the fear abruptly stopped.

Extreme clarity washed over his mind, replacing the fear. A simple subconscious command that seemed to come from outside of him, one that he realized had always guided him in the past, one that transitioned from a sense of family to an unwavering sense of certainty.

It now manifested itself as a simple mantra: *Save Maria.*

For Enrique, there was literally nothing else left in the world.

It was a clear vision of purpose. Enrique realized, in a flash summary of his entire life, that saving Maria right now had driven his actions from the moment his baby sister was born. It was something that he never understood or paid mind to before but could see with clarity now. And he felt it from blood to bone.

So when two cartel soldiers entered the mission hall carrying automatic rifles, Enrique was calm. The impermanence of all things revealed itself to Enrique, and he did not fear it; he embraced it. He knew Maria was alive; he knew Maria was *destined* to stay alive, even if he was not.

The feeling was something he could not explain, but it was overwhelming, and he instinctively relaxed into it. It was a form of tunnel vision, a clear and unwavering sense of destiny, of being one part of many, and it made Enrique almost giddy. He knew what must be done.

Save Maria.

Those two words became his mantra, his prayer, and it kept repeating in his mind.

Enrique watched as one of the cartel soldiers lowered his rifle and shot Father Gracilas twice in the chest, sending the priest smashing into the wall before his lifeless body clattered to the floor.

Men and women screamed as they witnessed the cold-blooded murder.

Enrique stayed calm.

"Everyone, face down on the floor, arms and legs out. We do not wish to kill you. But we will if you resist," the first cartel soldier said.

Enrique took note of every detail of the two soldiers as he lowered to one knee. Sunglasses. Thick black hair. Blue bandanas covering the lower halves of their faces. Calderon Cartel ink. Calloused hands. Dirty fingernails.

The cartel soldier looked at Enrique. And Enrique was amazed at the detail he could see of the M-16 rifle the cartel soldier pointed at him, from the scratch on the barrel to the wear on the stock.

"You. On the floor. Now," the soldier said to Enrique.

Enrique took one more look around the room as he lowered himself to the stone floor.

Maria was nowhere to be seen.

"Some of you will be held for ransom," the soldier continued as he walked among the migrants, who were lying on the floor. "Be prepared to ask your families for money. Be prepared to tell them if they do not pay, you will die."

Enrique watched the soldier's boots as the cartel gunman walked past his head.

"Others of you will be transported elsewhere," the gunman continued.

Enrique kept watching the gunman. One stood at the door, his rifle at the ready. The other moved about the room, searching under tables, behind the food boxes, looking for anyone who might be hiding.

Enrique kept his eyes searching. He took note of the priest, who lay less than twenty feet from him, the missionary's lifeless eyes looking right into his as the pool of blood continued to grow.

Enrique stayed calm as he watched the walking gunman stop at each migrant, forcing them to sit up and empty their pockets. Most had little in the way of money. Some had rings and gold chains around their necks. The cartel soldier took it all.

Enrique turned his head in the other direction, keeping his face on the floor, the stone warm against his cheek. Something caught his eye, and his heart nearly stopped.

Behind a stack of boxes marked "canned goods," Enrique saw the outer edge of a child's sneaker. Maria's sneaker. She was hiding. Enrique had to think quickly on what to do next.

Remaining face down on the floor, he turned his head back in the other direction to see where the cartel soldier was.

The man was robbing an elderly gentleman less than five feet away. Enrique would be next. He looked to the door—the other soldier still held guard.

Enrique made a decision. He closed his eyes and prayed harder than he had ever prayed before for God to protect him from what he was about to do.

Save Maria.

The cartel soldier inched closer. He was less than three feet away when Enrique smelled the mixture of dirt and leather from his boots. He could see the scratches on the barrel of the rifle.

Enrique took a deep breath, and calm washed over him.

"You. Sit up." The cartel soldier pointed the rifle directly at Enrique's head.

Enrique slowly pushed himself from the floor and got to one knee.

The cartel soldier abruptly hit Enrique on the side of the head with the butt of his rifle.

The pain was like a flash of lightning, and it nearly knocked Enrique unconscious. But he did not fall.

Save Maria.

What happened next surprised everyone.

Out of the corner of his eye, Enrique saw a woman, Latina and muscular, with long hair pulled back tightly in a ponytail. She carried a two and half-foot long stick in each hand as she entered the room quick and silent.

Before anyone could react, she hit the cartel soldier guarding the door in rapid-fire succession with the sticks, breaking his gun barrel, arm, and jaw before it registered to anyone that she was in the room.

After the soldier slumped to the floor unconscious, the cartel soldier standing above Enrique began to turn toward the sound with his rifle raised.

That's when Enrique saw a large muscular black man standing in the doorway, spinning a chain with small metal spheres at each end, whipping the orbs in a circular blur.

As the cartel soldier began to raise his rifle, the black man launched one end of the chain toward the remaining cartel soldier.

The metal ball flew across the room and struck like a cobra, hitting the stock of the rifle with such force that it shattered the weapon, hit the cartel soldier in the chest, and knocked him to the floor.

MARIA WATCHED as the strangers with the sticks and toys came into the room and took control. Their arrival here was unexpected, even by her. Maria was so focused on Enrique, so angry with all the blind and stupid people that she had not seen this happen in her visions.

But now that she did see these people, their movements mesmerized her. The precision, the detail, and the power they displayed were things she'd never seen before. All eyes in the room were on the strangers. Maria knew that if she was going to reach Enrique, she had to move now.

ENRIQUE SAW Maria bolt from her hiding spot. He leapt to his feet and raced in her direction to intercept.

But the downed cartel soldier rolled to his feet and got to her first.

"Stay back," the soldier said as he scooped up Maria mid-stride.

The soldier then pulled a 9mm from a holster on his hip and held it to the young girl's head.

Everyone froze. Maria started to kick and scream with rage.

The soldier squeezed her hard, and her movements slowed.

"Be quiet, Maria," Enrique said. "It will be okay. I promise." Enrique turned his attention to the soldier who held his sister. "Let her go. Let me take her place. And I will go peacefully." He took a step toward the soldier.

"Stay back," the soldier said as he pointed the gun at Enrique, then at the Latina and the black man, then back to Enrique.

He began backing his way toward the exit, Maria still locked in his arm.

"Please," Enrique pleaded. The sixteen year old looked over the horrified faces of the other migrants.

Then he looked at the faces of the black man and the Latina. Their eyes were locked on the soldier.

Then another man entered the room and stood between the black man and the Latina. This man was white, with calm soft features offset by piercing eyes. He wore loose fitting jeans and a gray T-shirt,

"Alex..." the Latina said to the latest arrival. Then she pointed to the cartel soldier holding the little girl hostage.

"Stay back!" the cartel soldier screamed, this time pointing the gun at the man with the piercing eyes, who now stood between the black man and the Latina.

Enrique watched as the man named Alex stared at the cartel soldier. But stare wasn't the right word. His eyes vibrated in a way that Enrique had never seen before, and it spooked him.

Enrique looked at the cartel soldier who held his sister and noticed that the gun shook in his hand.

"You're not going to hurt her," the man named Alex said to the cartel soldier.

Enrique saw that Alex's words and odd moving eyes caused the cartel soldier to hesitate.

Alex then turned to Enrique. "She'll be okay. We'll take care of her. I promise," he said, before he added, "I'm sorry. I wish I could've been here sooner. This is the only way things can happen now if you want her to live. There just isn't enough time."

Enrique nodded. It was as if the man had read his mind.

And then without thinking, Enrique went for the gun.

He caught the soldier's arm and pushed the weapon away from Maria as all three tumbled to the floor.

The cartel soldier gripped the girl tightly as he fought for control of the gun.

Enrique held the gun arm with both his hands, head-butted the cartel soldier who let go of Maria, and put both hands on the gun.

Enrique watched his sister run across the room, and he lost sight of the gun. Then he heard a loud explosion next to his ear, and everything went silent.

Enrique's skin burned, then his body, as his heartbeat drowned out all other noise. Breathing suddenly became very difficult. He touched his hand to his chest and pulled back bloody fingers.

His eyes darted about, searching frantically for his little sister. He saw the muscular Latina, the one who had taken out the other cartel soldier, scoop up Maria, hold her tight, and sprint out of the room.

Save Maria.

Enrique let out one last breath of relief, before everything went black.

Yaw reached the cartel soldier less than two seconds after the gun went off. But he already knew that the teenager who had freed the young girl was dead.

As the cartel soldier began to raise the 9mm in Yaw's direction, Yaw struck the man's wrist with his Kali stick, hard, shattering both the wrist and forearm, then he rebounded the stick off the wrists and whipped it across the man's jaw, shattering the bone and knocking out several teeth. The cartel soldier was unconscious before his head bounced off the stone floor.

Yaw then looked at the dead boy and turned the body over. Yaw hung his head in sorrow. The kid couldn't have been more than sixteen.

Yaw slowly turned toward the unconscious cartel soldier. Yaw's martial art training was never about the ability to defend himself or hurt someone. His size and strength all but guaranteed that capability against nearly anyone. Yaw's training was about finding inner peace, finding a reason *not* to give into anger, and only resorting to violence when circumstances justified aggression. Circumstances like now.

Yaw stared at the cartel soldier. Anger he had not felt in a long time arose. As the cartel soldier regained consciousness and started to squirm in pain from his broken bones, Yaw gripped the Kali stick in his right hand, got to his feet, and marched in the direction of the waking man.

He raised the stick over his head, ready to strike down the man who had just shot a teenage boy in cold blood. He felt a hand on his shoulder. Yaw turned to see the hand belonged to Alex.

"Find Camilla," Alex Luthecker told Yaw. "She has left with the young girl."

Yaw took a quick glance about the room. It had emptied of migrants. Yaw looked at Alex, who was on the floor, whispering in the ear of the cartel soldier.

Yaw could tell by the look in the cartel soldier's eyes that what Alex was sharing removed any false pretense, any illusion of what the man saw of himself, leaving only the truth—that he was a murderer of men, women, and children, and there would be no hiding from that fact...ever again.

Yaw knew the impact of Alex's abilities on those who did evil was like no other. He knew that the weight of this man's choices would be enough to destroy him. For the cartel soldier, Judgment Day had arrived.

Satisfied, Yaw headed for the exit in search of Camilla.

∾

"I HATE THEM. I want them all to die," Maria screamed at Camilla as the two of them stood out in the open desert. The venom in Maria's voice was palpable.

Yaw approached. "What's your name?" Yaw asked Maria, his voice gentle, trying to both deflect the young girl's anger and sooth it.

"Her name is Maria," Camilla answered as she tried to approach the ten year old. Maria stepped back to keep her distance.

Yaw and Camilla looked at one another. They shared a young daughter, Kylie, and the plight of this girl struck close to home for them both.

"Who's this guy?" Yaw asked Maria about the stuffed tiger she held tightly in her arms.

"Nala," Maria replied, before squeezing him tighter.

The sound of a train horn signaling the next Beast's arrival got Yaw's attention. It was then that he noticed the migrants walking toward the station, a resigned walk; all were preparing to board the back of the next Beast and take their chances again, as if nothing had happened.

Alex approached Yaw and Camilla. He locked eyes with Maria, before he stooped low, so he was face to face with the ten year old. The little girl held his gaze.

"It's nothing but blackness everywhere, for everyone," Maria blurted out to Alex. The rage was palpable in her voice, and her choice of words disturbed everyone.

Alex studied Maria for several seconds before speaking. "That is not true. There is always hope. Your brother died saving your life. He did so because he loved you and had hope for you," Alex explained. His tone was gentle yet direct.

He touched Maria's cheek and she recoiled.

Alex stood up. "Don't make his sacrifice be in vain. I know this is hard. But there is no time to mourn now. We must go."

"I hate them."

"And that will blind you. Make you just like the people who frustrate you. Is that what you want?"

Maria didn't answer. She was surprised that this stranger knew about the stupid blind people. With her stuffed tiger still locked in her arms, she turned away.

"Come with us."

Maria looked back at the strange man with the piercing eyes. She had no visions about him, no matter how hard she tried to see them. This was something she'd never experienced before. The only thing her instincts told her was that he was not one of the blind and stupid people. This was another first for her because up until now, everyone Maria met had been blind and stupid.

She kept her eyes on Alex for several seconds before she slowly held out her hand. She was young, but she could sense that this man was different from the others. She sensed that his words were not hiding other words with different meanings. And Maria also knew that she had nowhere left to go.

Camilla and Yaw looked at one another in reaction to the strange conversation between Alex and this ten-year-old girl.

"She comes with us. We take her to Safe Block," Alex declared, as if reading their minds.

"I didn't think we did that," Yaw cautioned. "I didn't think we brought anyone across the border."

"What if she has family?" Camilla added.

"We are her family now," Alex said with certainty as he and Maria continued to study one another. "Nikki has arranged a computer black out at the border to help us get across. But we have to hurry," he continued.

"It's going to be okay," Alex said to Maria.

"They will be back soon. And then you can kill them all," Maria replied.

"We will be killing no one," Alex answered, his eyes still locked on Maria's and hers on his. Alex held the gaze for several seconds before turning to the others. "We have to go," Alex said, before taking Maria's hand and guiding them away.

3

CHOICE

ALEX LUTHECKER COLLAPSED ONTO HIS BED, EXHAUSTED. HE LOOKED over at Nikki lying beside him; she was already fast asleep. He wished he could follow her into deep slumber, but he knew it would never happen.

Despite the level of fatigue created by both recent travel and events, sleep would prove to be difficult for him. Alex rarely slept well even under the best of circumstances, and with all that had happened in Mexico and the events leading up to the confrontation with the Calderon Cartel hijackers, he knew there would be no rest for him tonight.

I was too late, was the only thing running through his mind as he turned away from the dozing Nikki and stared at the ceiling. Alex and Nikki's arrival in Mexico to meet with Yaw, Chris, and Camilla had been delayed.

Their flight from India through Europe with alternate IDs had gone smoothly enough, but when they arrived in Mexico, their passports had been briefly held. Both Nikki and Alex were being tracked by Coalition surveillance, and their facial profiles were in the system, but Nikki's software algorithm PHOEBE had always been one step ahead of electronic surveillance, intercepting recognition or anomaly with their identities and negating it before it reached Coalition servers. The delay in Mexico had been caused by something else entirely, and Alex had read it immediately—there was no electronic intercept or Coalition Properties screening attempt; it was the matter of a simple bribe.

Instead of manipulating the situation and costing more time, Alex and Nikki simply paid the rogue customs official off and were on their way. The delay at the airport was only twenty minutes, but that caused them to miss their bus, which delayed them further, causing their arrival at the train stop to happen *after* the cartel soldiers had kidnapped the migrants, forcing Yaw, Camilla, and Chris to intervene without he and Nikki.

And it was because of this that Alex was late to the mission hall where a sixteen-year-old boy had been killed, along with a handful of others. If he had arrived sooner, he might have been able to stop it from happening.

The death of Enrique upset Alex a great deal, but what caused Alex even greater concern was the boy's sister, a ten-year-old girl named Maria—and the fact that he could not make sense of the patterns that formed her destiny.

Her choices and mannerisms were chaotic and massive in number, as though her behavior had yet to anchor to a belief structure. It was as if Maria's ability to choose was free of influence, a wide-open and pure psychological configuration—more like an infant than a ten-year old girl. No doubt, that would change now, with the murder of her brother. It was clear that the young girl's thoughts were currently clouded by rage.

But it was when Maria spoke that Alex realized there was more at play here. Maria's way of perceiving events was highly detailed and well organized, and not just beyond the ability of a ten year old, but beyond the ability of a normal adult. In many ways, it reminded Alex of how he himself had analyzed events in his own youth.

He sensed that Maria was gifted, but his inability to make sense of the chaos that surrounded her made it impossible for him to perceive exactly how gifted. And to make matters more difficult, Maria had refused to speak with anyone after they left Mexico.

Alex could sense that Maria trusted her instincts more than she trusted people, and it was Maria's instincts and situational awareness that was behind her choice to come to America with Alex and the family, not an inherent trust of Yaw, Camilla, or himself. Alex understood that they would have to earn her trust before she would open up to the family. Maria did remind Alex of himself at that age, but there were distinct differences.

When Alex was Maria's age, he was awkward, and he lived in reactive isolation from others. He felt guilty about being different. There was no guilt in Maria's reaction to the world, only unbridled anger. Alex may not be able to read the young girl's destiny, but he knew one thing for sure—he had to help Maria manage her anger; otherwise, it was inevitable that she would lash out at the world. And in order to help her, he had to find out exactly how gifted the young girl was. And in order to do that, he had to get her to open up to him.

Since Alex couldn't read Maria, he had to find other ways to get her to communicate. She was now part of the family, and as head of the family, Alex would see to it that Maria had everything she needed. Normally, Alex would read the patterns of a stranger's fate and help them see the truth about the cause and effect of their choices. But that was impossible with Maria, at least for the time being. This left Alex without a plan or approach.

And not having any parenting skills or experience with children, Alex Luthecker simply did not know how to help a justifiably angry ten-year-old girl, a girl who refused to speak and whose patterns of behavior he couldn't make sense of.

But at the moment there was a more pressing concern for Alex, something that had been troubling him long before his encounter with Maria. His insight, his ability to read patterns in others, was fading. Simply put he was forgetting things, the intricate details that allowed him to distinguish complex patterns over longer timelines, the patterns that allowed him to assess accurately direction and destiny.

Things began to change with Alex's perception shortly after Winn Germaine's funeral in Los Angeles six months ago, but he had told no one at the time. Not even Nikki.

It had started with the simple and mundane—dates and times of events he had committed to. Not a source of alarm for the average individual but quite disturbing for someone with Alex's senses. Then the fading of details bled over and marred his ability to read the origin behind historical objects and places.

Normally, Alex could look at an historical building and—based on its designs, construction material, and countless other details lost to the average individual—know the building's origins and often events of note that had taken place there in the past. Such were the extrapolative abilities of Alex's flawless memory. And the history of manmade structures was something that usually came easy for Alex —something that was far easier than reading people. But now he was becoming less sure of the details and, therefore, less sure of himself.

The death of his mentor had hit Alex hard, but his friends Yaw, Chris, Camilla, and now Masha, the Russian woman who accompanied his crew home from Trans Dniester, had been supportive. And of course there was Nikki. She had remained at his side throughout his mourning period, and when Alex decided that he wanted to visit Kunchin, the Buddhist monk in Tibet who had helped him in the past, it was important to Alex that Nikki meet him.

Nikki's computer prowess and PHOEBE had made alternative identities and travel arrangements that would go unnoticed by the Coalition relatively easy. So with Yaw and Camilla in charge of both the courier business and training regiment left by Winn, Alex and Nikki once again set off for the Potala Palace in Tibet.

Alex promised his friends he would be back in a month. He hoped that Kunchin would be able to answer his questions. He hoped that the old Monk, with abilities similar to his own, could tell Alex, whose photographic memory had proven nearly infallible in the past, why he was beginning to forget things...

"HE HAS BEEN EXPECTING YOU," Chodak, the Buddhist monk and Potala Palace guide said to Alex and Nikki as they entered the enormous monastery in Lhasa. "He knows that you will have many questions."

Choden, Chodak's brother, smiled and nodded to both Nikki and Alex, pointing the way.

"This place is beautiful," Nikki said to Alex, awe in her voice as they made their way through the hand-painted, Sutra-covered hallways and past the golden statues that filled the multiple prayer rooms in the temple, often with only candles lighting the way.

The Byzantine array of halls, temples, libraries, galleries, and narrow hallways were dizzying.

"You're sure you can find our way back, right?" Nikki whispered to Alex.

Alex smiled. "I'll do my best," he answered. "And besides, we have them." Alex pointed to the brothers, Chodak and Choden, as they scurried through the hallway ahead.

"Is Kunchin in some sort of throne room?

"No. Underneath all of this beauty," Alex began, "is just a cave."

"FEAR IS THE ENEMY," Kunchin said. "It is always the enemy," the eighty-year old monk continued as he stoked the fire of the wood stove at the center of the Dharma King Cave.

Nikki's jaw was on the floor. Underneath the enormity of the Potala Palace, which was the world's largest and richest Buddhist monastery, was nothing but a simple cave, with smooth, uneven walls carved into the rock, and holes in the stone decorated with small statues and Buddhist carvings.

In the center of it all was a metal folding chair across from a small cast-iron stove, with a small elderly man in its attendance.

"Fear has the ability to rearrange events," Kunchin continued as he stoked the fire one last time. "Fear has the ability to rewrite the past. It has the ability to alter the entire timeline—past, present, and future," the old Monk continued.

Satisfied with the glow of embers, he used a metal poker to shut the small door of the stove.

He then turned to both Alex and Nikki. "But so does love. The choice between the two is yours to make."

"I'm starting to...forget things," Alex said to the Monk. "In my memory. Some of the details go missing. In the stories I see in others."

Nikki looked at Alex in shock. He had never said a word of this to her. Never even hinted at it.

"This is not unexpected," the elderly monk answered Alex. "This is the challenge of the universe, to stay resolute. This is why things must always renew. This is why all we do is clear the path for those who follow. It is the very purpose of the impermanence of all things."

Kunchin turned his attention to Nikki a moment, eyes locking with hers, before looking back to Alex. "It's the suffering caused by fear that affects you."

"But I'm not afraid."

"Perhaps, but most of the world still is. And as one who sees the patterns of this world, it is impossible to remain unaffected by that burden." Kunchin steadied himself against the rock wall before continuing. "The suffering caused by fear is relentless. The human condition is not. Without discipline and rigorous practice, we soon become inseparable from the influence of our surroundings. And if those surroundings are filled with suffering and fear, the soul detaches from reality. It creates its own narrative. It forgets things by design in order to survive. That is the exhaustive power of fear. Fear consumes much and gives nothing in return. It suppresses the memory and makes destiny seem chaotic, and not the result of cause and effect. That is why fear is the root of all suffering."

"Is that why you live in a cave? To isolate yourself from a fearful world?"

For the first time, Kunchin smiled. It was a near toothless smile. "In my time, I did what was asked of me. No different than you are doing now. But I am not as strong as you. Nor am I as gifted. But in my time, it was enough. Your time requires your strength and your gifts. And the next generation will require greater strength and gifts than yours. The universe always provides balance."

"I don't feel very strong. Or very gifted."

"Again, choice. When you first went to Mawith in the desert, you ran from your responsibility to others. Then you learned to love. And you no longer ran. When you came to me, you ran from yourself. Then you learned about selflessness. And then you no longer ran from your own power. Your recent travels and losses had much to show you about Karma, did they not?"

"I lost my best friend."

"And in that pain you let fear encroach. But did he not show you the power of love over fear? Did he not show you the power of choice? Of selflessness defined by his connection to others? Of the recognition and acceptance of Karma? Do you not fight on, with what he started, in his name? In you, is not the battle renewed?"

"But it just doesn't end. The suffering," Alex, said, exasperated. He looked at the old man. He took note that the monk labored to breathe. The man's posture and frail movements alone showed Alex that Kunchin did not have long in this world. Still, the old man's eyes remained bright and clear.

"And this is why you forget. You are not a moral compass for the entire world at once, Alex, you are only a compass for those you meet, in the time that you meet them. You have been put here to guide, but only for a short time. You allow people to choose. And over time, others will provide a compass, with the hope being that in the end, all will choose. And how do you know the suffering does not end? Not even you can see that far."

"I don't...I don't want to do this anymore."

"And yet you fear losing the ability to see. Do you understand the purpose of the paradox?"

"No."

"Those best suited for power are by design ill at ease with such power. In a universe designed by balance, it is the only way that it can be. You've seen the opposite of that, have you not? Those who lust for power are most often the least deserving. It is the acceptance of your paradox that is your final burden."

"But what do I do?"

"Stay in the moment, and trust your training, then, there is nothing to remember. There are only events to observe. Events are cyclical. They transcend the definition of time and create "Samsara" in the old definitions, or "patterns," as you have called them. This realization must be done, again and again, generation after generation, until all are enlightened. Do you not yet see that it is the cycle itself that gives you your power? The need for balance created you, and thus you were created. Only when one is given the ability to choose, can one break Samsara. But it is still a choice. Once you accept this, your memory will not falter. Only then, can you go back to the beginning."

"Go back to the beginning?"

"Rest your warrior's sword and become a farmer."

"A farmer? I'm not a farmer. I never have been. That's not me."

"But it is."

"I don't understand."

"What does a farmer do? A farmer plants seeds and tends to them. A farmer understands that he is part of the cycle of life, and not separate from it. And he is certainly not above it. Do not stop planting seeds, Alex, wherever you go. Do not stop tending to them. Make everyone you meet see his or her true self. That is your gift. Plant these seeds and nurture them. And before long, a beautiful garden will grow, one that can be tended to by new gardeners for generations to come.

"And when things seem hopeless, when you must overcome those who would challenge your cause, remember it is in the effort to help others that we save ourselves. It is the effort that is handed down from one generation to the next. It is the effort that binds us. That is why you cannot and will not fail, no matter how much seems lost. In the end, it is these efforts in totality that create the momentum."

"That doesn't help me remember the things I've forgotten."

"Once again, choice. And when your time is done, there will be another. In your heart, you know this already. That is also part of the momentum. This is all that I have for you. But then that is not the only reason why you are really here. You are also here because of her." Kunchin then turned his attention back to Nikki.

The abrupt turn of energy in her direction made her take a step back.

"And you. Do *you* understand why you are here?" Kunchin asked her.

"What? Me? No, I..." Nikki felt her face get hot.

"It is not for you to simply meet an old monk, or for you to bear witness to your lover's journey. It is no accident that you and Alex have become one. You've felt it in your heart from the moment he interrupted the patterns of your destiny and allowed you to see new choices.

"You are not here for him today. You are a mystic as well, but one of a different world. A new world. And you've unleashed something in that world that will affect this one, something far more powerful than any of the old magic or religion. Something far more powerful than anything that either Alex or I can do. And it will take what you both bring to this world to guide it. Guided correctly, it will elevate mankind. Incorrectly, it will be the end for us all."

4

PHOEBE

Nikki made sure that Alex was still asleep before she gently rose from their bed, moved to the second bedroom, and sat in front of the array of high definition screens that were the primary connection to her online creation, PHOEBE. She had acknowledged that the program had long ago grown beyond her original design intent, which was to find patterns in large data sets in order to predict macro trends.

When she set about creating PHOEBE as a student at M.I.T., her original goal for the program's purpose was altruistic— she believed PHOEB's prognostic abilities could prove invaluable in the search for everything from cancer cures, to drought patterns, and pandemic containment. As with all dreams and ideals, its beginnings were perfect. And as with all dreams and ideals, the potential for corruption always lay in wait, like a lion in the weeds.

When Nikki chose to work for the commodities trading firm Kittner-Kusch, she had been sold on the idea that her altruistic vision of making the world a better place could be best realized through using PHOEBE's abilities in the world of energy. It was a self-serving delusion—Nikki had made enormous amounts of money and lived an envious lifestyle available only to a select few in this world.

That all changed for Nikki when children died over oil and money and no one cared. The bombing of a refinery that PHOEBE failed to predict had caused a catastrophic loss of life, and her boss and then boyfriend and his partners were only concerned with how it affected their bottom line. Nikki was devastated. In many ways, she felt responsible. The mission creep of her dream had drifted too far off course. She quit the energy business and moved to Los Angeles, unmoored and at a total loss. And then Alex Luthecker saved her life —in more ways than one.

In her training with Winn and then Alex, Nikki found her true self, which circled back to the original dream—using her talents to make the world a better place. And in the process, Nikki had recalibrated PHOEBE to do the same. Or at least that's what Nikki had believed.

Nikki took a deep breath before running through the encrypted password matrix that allowed her to log on to PHOEBE. As she waited for the system to boot up, she thought back to Kunchin's words in the Dharma King Cave underneath the Potala Palace in Tibet. She knew that the old monk was speaking of PHOEBE. Nikki already knew that PHOEBE had created a language all her own—and done so on her own—a language that the program needed to crack through any firewall or encryption protocol.

She also knew that this language would need to be beyond human comprehension in order to make sense of the massive complexity required to communicate effectively with state-of-the-art encryption technology. And in turn bend the massive global surveillance network to the needs that she required of PHOEBE.

Nikki never saw this as an existential threat. She never considered that developing language was a step human beings took to separate themselves from other species. And now that possibility was beginning to worry her.

The six large high-definition screens, arranged in a half hexagon, abruptly sprang to life in front of Nikki. She spoke the words "local security status" to PHOEBE as a voice command, and all six screens turned into a homogeneous view of the city of Los Angeles, represented only by electronic signals that were created by surveillance technology. It was a high-density, city-shaped web array of neon-red lines, all pulsing with activity as information was moved to and from and around the structures of the city, not unlike blood through the human vascular system. It was a synaptic view of the city's security, and the constant movement of information made it seem alive, a living organism with the Coalition One Building in downtown Los Angeles being the central brain.

Nikki then spoke the command "family travel history," and the array of screens abruptly began to change. A series of blacked out streets appeared on the surveillance array, channels of surveillance darkness indicating the family's movements from LAX through surface streets and on to the apartment complex on Terminal Island in Long Beach where the family now resided.

Other blacked out areas included the Terminal Island apartments where other members of the family currently lived as well as the areas where refugees were kept in hiding until safe transport could be arranged. These safe areas and travel pathways were cloaked zones that PHOEBE had created upon Nikki's directive. These zones kept Safe Block and the family invisible to the digital world.

In order to do this, PHOEBE had surveillance technology that could track the family's movements either turned off or misdirected, including law enforcement vehicles and communication. This, along with instant digital identity creation, allowed the group to travel completely unnoticed. It was a new definition of "off grid" that only PHOEBE could create.

Nikki suspected something had gone wrong with her commands to PHOEBE even before Kunchin's warnings. The first incident happened when she arranged for her and Alex to travel from Tibet to India. Nikki had created IDs and travel documents for the both of them, but when she selected the airline that she and Alex would fly on, PHOEBE not only generated tickets under pseudonyms, the program had also completely shut down a competing airline's terminal.

The black out of the rival airline had lasted over four hours, just long enough for she and Alex to make the trip. The shutdown of the rival airline had been blamed on computer failure, and Nikki would have never suspected PHOEBE's involvement had she not checked the program's activity log when they returned to North America. And she had only chosen to check it because of Kunchin's words during their visit to the Dharma King Cave in Tibet.

The implications based on that incident alone had given Nikki pause, but at the time, she held out hope that it was merely a glitch. It was her intention to find out whether it was an anomaly or a systemic problem with PHOEBE now.

Nikki had originally given PHOEBE specific instructions regarding keeping the family safe and to protect itself from Coalition attacks, but within the language she had also given the program specific commands to keep it from breaking laws unnecessarily.

With PHOEBE's ability to develop a language entirely her own, had she also developed broader interpretations of Nikki's command set? Had there been mission creep in the program's assigned functions? Nikki decided to give the program a structural command that would override all the others, a generalized code that she hoped would cap any mission creep on PHOEBE's part.

"Protect the family, but do no harm."

Nikki watched the cursor blink for several seconds before all six HD screens began displaying detailed schematics of six brand new high-rise buildings, one on each of the six screens. The buildings were next to one another in a tight cluster and located in downtown Los Angeles.

Nikki recognized the building at the center of the cluster immediately. It was formerly named Coalition Properties West, now named Coalition One, and it was the new worldwide headquarters of the Coalition. But the Coalition headquarters was not the building schematic being displayed on the center screen. PHOEBE wanted Nikki to focus on a different building located northeast of the Coalition One Building. This structure was numbered building four and titled Coalition Assurance on the schematic diagram.

Nikki sat back in her chair. She knew exactly what Coalition

Assurance was. It was the Coalition's private military. And it looked as if Coalition Assurance now had their own high-tech barracks right in the middle of downtown Los Angeles.

Standing at sixty stories, the building more than likely housed over a thousand men. The schematic details of a massive underground garage looked to house dozens of military vehicles. But what got Nikki's attention was what was on the third floor. The building plans showed several rooms with reinforced walls and floors labeled "containment apartments" on the diagram.

Prison cells, Nikki thought to herself.

The array of buildings, along with the connecting streets, were separated from the rest of the city and had an overall title: The Coalition Fortress.

"Holy shit, the Coalition is forming its own city-state right on American soil," Nikki thought out loud.

Nikki reflexively voiced a command to PHOEBE. "Why are you showing me this?"

PHOEBE replied with three words that scrolled across the bottom of the center screen: *"The end of the animal is near."*

Nikki read PHOEBE's response several times. "What does that mean?"

Nikki waited several minutes for a response from PHOEBE.

There was none.

Nikki decided to type the question this time, but as she reached for the keyboard, all six screens went black.

She hit several keys, but still no response.

"What does that mean?" she asked again.

No response.

She tried a hard reboot of the system, but still nothing. The station and the monitors were all dead.

"Shit," Nikki said aloud.

The last thing she needed right now was a hardware problem. Instead of trying to fix the system, she would simply purchase all new hardware.

Nikki started to get up from her chair when her computer beeped and whirred back to life. Puzzled, she sat back down in front of the monitor array.

"Systems analysis," Nikki requested.

The system did not respond.

Nikki typed the same command into the keyboard and nothing happened. The blinking cursor remained.

"What the actual hell...?"

All six screens came to life, scrolling an alphanumerical stream of characters faster than the human eye could follow.

No matter what Nikki typed into the keyboard, her commands were ignored.

Then all six monitors abruptly stopped scrolling code and displayed the same message: *The end of the animal is near.*

5

CYBER CENTER PUSHBACK

"It dumped Black Widow's surveillance code in twenty-three nano-seconds," Michael Chan said as he sat staring at his computer screen.

Behind him stood Coalition board member, Tom Miller, and head of Coalition Properties' cyber-security division, Rika Muranaka.

Miller, a portly man in his mid-fifties, looked bored. Not particularly tech-savvy, he wasn't interested in the details. Like most investment manager types, he liked explanations to be short, simple, and actionable. Miller was visiting the Coalition's new Cyber Center at the request of CEO Glen Turner. He was there to keep an eye on Rika Muranaka.

Muranaka, a twenty-six-year-old Stanford PHD in computer science by way of Japan, stood with her arms crossed in front of her, staring at Chan's computer screen. Piercing eyes offset her long black hair and peaceful features, and the look in those eyes indicated that she was not happy.

"That's impossible," she fired back.

"That's eons better than last time," Chan replied as he hit keys. Alphanumeric symbols scrolled down the screen faster than the eye could see. "And it may be as close as we can get."

"I don't understand. Tell me what's going on," Miller cut in.

Chan looked at Muranaka.

She nodded her approval to explain.

"Black Widow is the NSA's most powerful code-breaking software," Chan started. "As you know Black Widow was financed and developed with Coalition Properties resources. It was powerful enough to bring down the Silk Road, which no one thought could be done."

"What's Silk Road?"

Muranaka turned away. She hated it when the board of directors sent babysitters to her division. They never explained why they were here or what they were after, and they were annoyingly ignorant about current cyber-war technology.

"The silk road was the largest black market on the deep web," Chan began his lecture. "You understand what the deep web is?"

"Of course I do," Miller fired back, the tone in his voice betraying his ignorance.

Muranaka kept her patience by checking her phone for messages.

"Okay good. Then you know it's vast. Current search engines only scan less than four percent of what makes up the entire web. This makes it very difficult to track anything that exists in the deep web. Silk Road was where drugs, weapons, information, and, more than occasionally, people were illegally trafficked. It's also where the rogue algorithm PHOEBE lives. It is a lawless cyber-land that the NSA and, by proxy the Coalition, have sworn to control. And that's what Black Widow is supposed to do."

"And?"

"And when trying to crack the enemy code breaking algorithm PHOEBE with Black Widow, we encountered problems we didn't expect," Chan continued, this time looking at Muranaka.

"Those unexpected problems are why I'm here," Muranaka began as she put away her phone. Miller, she knew, likely had no idea why he was here. That didn't prevent him from having an opinion.

"The Coalition Properties Cyber Center, which you are in charge of, Ms. Muranaka, is equipped with the finest counter intelligence technology that money can buy," Miller began.

Muranaka bit her tongue.

"I mean, look at this place," Miller continued as he waved his hand over the room.

The Coalition Cyber Center was near white-room clean and filled with everything from 3D monitors and printers to ultra high-definition wall screens that tapped into every CCTV camera on the globe, the imagery displayed providing a kaleidoscope of worldwide human activity.

Everything from cell phone camera images generated by unaware Instagram users to bank lobby security cameras to a live feed of the stock market trading floor to private hospital rooms to street corners in every major city in the world, including Los Angeles, London, New York, and on and on.

It was an enormous sea of information that was useless without the required expertise to navigate. And at the Coalition, Rika Muranaka was the chief navigator.

"It's the center of the cyber universe. If you use a smart phone, you're in here somewhere. You should have everything you need to stop one terrorist hacker," Miller continued.

Muranaka waited several seconds, long enough for Miller to understand two things: 1) she was not intimidated by him in any way, and 2) he wasn't smart enough to understand the complexity of the details.

"We're working as quickly as we can," she finally said.

"Good," Miller answered, missing Muranaka's dismissive tone. He felt satisfied with his words and had nothing more to add to his grandiloquent comments about Coalition Property prowess.

Muranaka looked at Miller several seconds longer before turning back to Chan.

"So what were you saying about unexpected problems?"

"Ok—well, once PHOEBE discovered our attempt to hack, not only did she stop us cold, this time, she took a pretty mean swing at us—she crashed seven servers and pretty much gutted Black Widow in the process." Chan swiveled in his chair to look at Rika. "The NSA is going to be real pissed that we broke their toy."

"It's not their toy, it's our toy. What do you mean gutted?"

"I mean PHOEBE infected Black Widow with more viruses than I can count. Tricked the widow into multi-trillion step calculations that only led to more calculations. I had to quarantine the program to keep it from spreading. And hope I did it in time. Black Widow, for all intents and purposes, is busy for the next thousand years."

"That bitch..." Rika whispered under her breath. She was speaking about both PHOEBE and its creator. "Was it Nicole Ellis who discovered our surveillance and programmed PHOEBE to lash out?"

"No. That's the scary part. The commands I used were part of a program that was specifically designed to be adaptable to PHOEBE's code and go unnoticed. Part of a command set that neither PHOEBE nor its designer should have been able to recognize without going through at least three trillion guesses that we were trying to piggy-back her movements to begin with. PHOEBE shouldn't have been able to detect us, let alone Nicole Ellis, and Ms. Ellis' activity log verifies this. But somehow the software picked it up and flipped the trillion dollar pyramid back on us. But *that's* not even the real problem."

"What's the real problem then?" Miller asked.

"That she got pissed off and took a swing at us," Muranaka answered. "Programs aren't supposed to get pissed and lash out."

"And that means?" Miller asked, looking back and forth between the two programmers.

"It means the program may be self-actualizing," Chan answered first. "It needed to develop its own language to do that. One we can't decipher. It's learning and growing. It's making choices. Unpredictable choices."

"Another reason to stop it," Miller responded. "And arrest Ms. Ellis for creating it in the first place. She used the program to hijack a drone and commit a terrorist act. Part of your job is to acquire the necessary intelligence to prove it. And then I want Ms. Ellis in custody and her program either destroyed or in our hands. It's the only way to keep America safe."

Muranaka held her tongue. She hated the jingoism. She hated the ignorance that drove the fear mongering hawks that ran the Coalition board.

"It won't be that easy," Chan added. "Not with what I think is happening."

"And what do you think is happening?"

Chan was hesitant to continue and nervously ran his hand through his hair. "I think that PHOEBE is becoming A.I. And if she gets out of control..." He looked back and forth between Muranaka and Miller. Both looked upset, albeit for what Chan suspected were very different reasons. "If PHOEBE gets out of control, she could shut off power grids, crash airplanes, zero out bank accounts, maybe even launch missiles, for no rhyme or reason—at least not one that we understand. And that's just the beginning.

"Mr. Miller, you have to understand, we're all pretty much cyborgs now. Just try going a day without connecting to the world with your smart phone, and see how well you can function. Or count how many times you check your Facebook profile in an hour. People think social media is an addiction, but from a digital perspective, it's the early stages of a hive mind. The combination of artificial intelligence and information integration—the terabytes of audio, video, imagery, and linguistics people upload on a daily basis can be used to create accurate profiles of people, families, neighborhoods, cities, and...you get the point.

"And all of it can be analyzed to predict the next move of any given "data set." And that data set could be manipulated to correct perceived errors in the human code—decision making. And it could do it on both an individual and global scale. The implications are staggering.

"Behave in a way that an A.I. control system deems defective or a threat? It wipes out your bank accounts, puts evidence of a crime on your computer, alerts the police, and then lets society do the rest. Because it's already calculated what society will do.

"The political leanings of a city or state are deemed dangerous or a threat to the system? Shut down the power and water, making life as we know it come to a complete standstill, and then let our inherent savagery that the A.I. has already calculated into the equation to do the rest.

"PHOEBE could decide to do all of that. She could decide to wreck things. She could conceivably wreak apocalyptic-level havoc on a global scale. And there'll be nothing that we, or Nikki Ellis for that matter, can do to stop it."

6

TERMINAL ISLAND

NICOLE ELLIS WOKE WITH A START. SHE IMMEDIATELY REACHED ACROSS the bed and noticed that Alex was gone.

After PHOEBE had shocked Nikki with its cryptic response to her command, she had tried for hours to get her algorithm to respond to additional instructions with no results. PHOEBE had effectively locked her out, with no explanation as to why.

Exhausted after several attempts to reengage with her creation and unsure what to do next, Nikki finally logged off the system and crawled into bed with Alex around 2:30am, where she proceeded to stare at the ceiling, unable to sleep.

She knew that their 4:30am wake up time would come quickly, and it only heightened her anxiety about being unable to sleep. She thought about simply staying up all night before drifting off into a short, restless slumber.

Still lying in bed, she looked over at the alarm clock, a thirty-year old wind up device with face hands instead of digits, similar to the one Nikki's grandmother had. It was purposefully not an electronic clock, but an isolated device, one that both Nikki and Alex preferred. She saw that it was 5:47am. She had overslept.

"Alex...?" she instinctively called out in the early morning darkness.

She reached over and turned on the lamp before she pushed aside the covers and sat up.

She looked around the bedroom of the small two-bedroom apartment that they currently called home, and a flash of memory made her take stock of how much her life had changed in the past eighteen months.

She used to live in a multimillion-dollar Manhattan high rise with expensive albeit sparse furnishings, and now all of her belongings were contained in a half a dozen plastic containers, which consisted of their clothes and personal items, along with several practice Kali sticks in a neat pile. Beside those items were an old phonograph player and a milk crate of albums, most of them classical music. That was all that she and Alex owned.

The phonograph and records belonged to Alex, a comforting reminder of the first person who saw him for what he was, but he rarely listened to these albums now. Still, they were his only personal items, and he took care to bring them to wherever the family called home.

Nikki got to her feet and slipped on a pair of jeans, then a T-shirt, before tying her hair back in a ponytail. She quickly put on her sneakers, laced them, and exited the apartment. She tried to put aside her thoughts on PHOEBE and focus on her training.

The family, formerly Master Winn's students, now all studying under Alex, was becoming larger and more philosophical under his leadership. The one thing that hadn't changed since Winn's death and the family's return from Trans Dniester was that, as an off-grid entity, the family was always on the move, even if PHOEBE provided ample cover for their current whereabouts. And their current location was the abandoned Naval Base on Terminal Island in Long Beach, California.

Nikki, along with Camilla Ramirez, Yaw Chimonso, Chris Aldrich, Joey Nugyen, and relative newcomer Masha Tereshchenko had become decidedly closer to one another since Winn's death, and they trusted in Alex completely, even when his actions didn't make sense to them.

Alex had fought his instincts for isolation and tried to strengthen his bond with all members of the family, but it had not been easy for him. His observation skills required a certain amount of distance from others, and it had proven a hard habit for Alex to break, even with those he had grown to love.

That distance from others that defined Alex was something that Nikki had slowly grown accustomed to. Alex was a loner by nature and design, but he had always been honest, loyal, and above all else, kind.

Alex's tendency to be secretive and introspective was something that Nikki no longer felt threatened by. Alex needed to think things out before sharing. He needed time to assemble the data of any given situation before engaging, which was why when Alex revealed his memory concerns to Kunchin during their visit to the Potala Palace in Tibet it had taken Nikki completely by surprise.

"Do not stop planting seeds, Alex, wherever you go."

These were the final words the Buddhist monk had said to Alex. But it wasn't what the old monk said to Alex that worried Nikki, it was the harsh warning Kunchin had given her.

When Nikki tried to investigate PHOEBE's actions, the program had effectively locked her out, at least for the moment, and the possibilities of why and what could go wrong kept spiraling through her mind.

If PHOEBE was becoming self-aware and beginning to make her own decisions, Nikki had to backtrack through every isolated command instruction, every cause and effect vector in order to put together what could influence PHOEBE's decision-making matrix. Only Nikki had ever interacted with PHOEBE directly, so Nikki's actions would become PHOEBE's first guide by design.

Nikki had to wonder, what did PHOEBE learn from me? At what depth and detail had PHOEBE analyzed both Nikki's behavior and command sets? Did PHOEBE learn from the hopeful side of Nikki?

Or the fearful one? How much data did PHOEBE truly have access to?

PHOEBE had proven extremely effective in keeping the family off grid by creating a cyber void around them—the entire family was in the program's database. So it was quite possible that PHOEBE was learning from all of them.

Nikki already knew that if identifying markers—face, driver's license, passport, social security number, any history personal history that could be tracked by modern technology—were fed into PHOEBE's algorithms, the program could literally ghost you out of the system. Security cameras would not recognize you. Watch lists would not track you. Passport and social security number crosschecks would lead to dead ends. Credit card purchases were encrypted and rerouted through anonymous Bit Coin accounts. Even imputing your name into a basic search engine would lead to wherever PHOEBE chose.

Through electronic tracking, PHOEBE made sure you didn't exist. And in a world of seven billion people, where electronic surveillance was increasingly depended upon, you were a ghost, able to move about the globe with little to stop you. It was a simple algorithm that Nikki felt should not be causing wide-scale problems. That the Terminal Island compound was not swarming with police or Coalition Assurance soldiers was clear evidence that, despite locking Nikki out, PHOEBE still kept her primary mandate to protect them intact. But for how much longer?

In Nikki's mind, there was no room in the command set for PHOEBE to go off script. And yet she had. PHOEBE shouldn't be interfering with other systems that had nothing to do with protecting the family, and yet evidence was becoming clearer and clearer that she was. And before Nikki could question PHOEBE on this, the software had locked her out.

Nikki knew that PHOEBE's calculative power was considerable, perhaps evidenced best by the downing the world's largest military drone.

Something dawned on Nikki with that thought. Perhaps it was

when Nikki tasked PHOEBE to take down the drone that the software program had broken free and began to act out on its own. Perhaps it was this command set, which allowed PHOEBE to override all others because of the urgency of the situation, that permitted the program to launch its own narrative.

It was well within PHOEBE's original programming to fend off attacks from the NSA's less sophisticated Black Widow program, but the command to take down the drone had been something entirely different. It had been an override command. And now, perhaps, PHOEBE felt she could override any command she chose and start making decisions on her own, decisions that were only based loosely on Nikki's requests.

What would happen when PHOEBE stepped beyond Nikki's programming entirely? What would happen if she chose to make decisions outside of Nikki's control? What if PHOEBE decided that a programming request would become the software's overall mandate, with every other command reconciled with this self-chosen mandate? Was this the glitch Nikki was searching for? And what did PHOEBE mean when she said, "The end of the animal is near?" Did it mean that it was too late?

Guilt overwhelmed Nikki. PHOEBE was her heart and soul, and if it ever hurt anyone, Nikki could never forgive herself. *Maybe I should have never created her at all*, Nikki thought.

Nikki pushed thoughts of PHOEBE aside. The program existed, and wishing it didn't or feeling guilty that it did accomplished nothing. Nikki was PHOEBE's creator, and as such she would fix the problem. She was confident that she could do so, and there was no reason to be unduly alarmed. At least that's what she kept telling herself.

PHOEBE not talking to Nikki was unacceptable, and she would start a conversation with the software with that premise, even if she had to create back door routes into her core programming. The "silent treatment" PHOEBE was engaged in would not work. And until she had a better grasp of what needed to be changed, Nikki would limit her commands to the program, lest those commands become some overall mandate that Nikki couldn't control. Nikki knew she would have to proceed with caution.

Much like Alex, in regards to his memory issues, Nikki chose not to disclose her concerns regarding PHOEBE to anyone until she had a better understanding of what was going on. She surmised that Alex's motivations for not revealing his memory issues were not altogether different from hers in regards to PHOEBE. There was no reason to upset anyone with incomplete data. She would solve the problem before alarming anyone.

This was how both Nikki and Alex worked. And as long as there was trust between them, Nikki couldn't be upset with Alex in how he chose to reveal his vulnerabilities via sage advice from the Buddhist monk, and vice versa regarding these new developments with PHOEBE.

The more time she spent with Alex, the more she realized they were very much alike. In Nikki's mind, it was becoming clearer every day that their pairing was no accident. She turned her thoughts back to Alex and realized that the more time she spent with him, the more amazed she became by his ability to influence others. And their recent trip only made the extent of his influence more visible.

The passage through the Siachen Glacier on the way back to America had been Alex's idea. He seemed revitalized by Kunchin's words and wanted to put them to the test. And he wanted to do it by seeing if he could alter the dynamics of individuals hardened by war and ideology.

Despite having witnessed Alex in action in the past, as well as experiencing the impact of his pattern-reading abilities first hand, she had been amazed by Alex's effectiveness on the Siachen. Alex's ability to read the momentum of another person's life, particularly the lives of several hardened soldiers all at once, seemed to indicate no lack of detail recollection or memory problems on Alex's part.

"Finite emotions and belief systems based on inflexible ideologies are the easiest to read," Alex had always told her.

The capacity to kill another human being requires an unshakeable ideological narrative and dehumanizes anyone who those willing to kill fear about their victims. Hardened beliefs by definition were rigid data sets, self-enforcing, not self-correcting. And the narratives created by rigid belief systems must exclude all other options or possibilities in order for both the belief system and the believer in that system to survive. It was this inability for a believer to change their narrative that made a believer's destiny so predictable for Alex.

"When I speak to them," he had told Nikki, "I show them who they really are, and in doing so, I destroy the false narrative created by their false beliefs. In the Siachen, I showed them the destructive patterns of behavior that led them atop a frozen glacier for the sole reason of killing others, which began long before many of those young men were born. I showed them that this is not who they really are. I showed them that the person on the other end of their rifle is human. I made them understand the sanctity of life. I made them *feel* it. And in doing so, in holding them accountable to reality, I opened their minds for other possibilities."

To witness this in action was nothing less than stunning to Nikki, every single time.

Whatever memory issues Alex claimed to have while in Tibet had not been visible on the Siachen. But what had happened on the India-Pakistan border was different than what she'd seen him do before. For the first time, it was both direct and proactive.

It was not in reaction to being hunted or captured. It was not an attempt to correct an impending event, like when Alex had saved her life. It was a larger scale redirect, and she knew there would be a cost to actions like these, not just for Alex but for everyone in the family.

With the disruption Alex's "planting seeds" was causing, Nikki knew that neither Alex, herself, the family, nor PHOEBE for that matter, could remain in the shadows much longer. This was beyond being chased by Coalition Properties. It wasn't about surviving or being "on the run" anymore. It was about changing global paradigms convincingly, one person at a time.

Nikki didn't need Alex's level of clairvoyance to know the amount of pushback this effort would cause. The powers that be, from Coalition Properties and beyond, would stop at nothing to get to Alex and the family now. This would have to be planned for. And with PHOEBE behaving erratically, the challenges ahead were going to be great.

But she had faith in Alex. And more importantly, she had faith in herself. Surviving her encounter with Lucas Parks in Trans Dniester and seeing to what lengths both Alex and the family were willing to go through to save her only strengthened her belief.

It had been a whirlwind of travel and activity since Tibet. Yaw had contacted them about what was happening in Mexico, and they had barely arrived in time to free hundreds of migrants from slave traders. A sixteen-year-old boy had died saving his younger sister, and Nikki knew Alex would feel responsible.

Ten-year-old Maria Martinez, refugee and orphan, was now part of the family. Both she and Alex felt it best that Maria stay with Camilla, Yaw, and their daughter Kylie for the time being, until they could create a more stable environment for the young girl.

After arriving from Mexico at the abandoned apartment complex on Terminal Island, a locale for the family that Camilla had arranged, they were all so exhausted they barely had time to speak about what was next, but they would do so, and soon.

She hoped that this morning's training session would revitalize and orient them all. And afterword she and Alex would have time to finally clear the air on what they'd been keeping from one another. She hoped that for the first time since they became a couple, since Alex had literally stepped into fate and saved her life, they could plan what was next as a team.

Nikki turned the corner to find Alex seated and meditating on the small patch of lawn next to the apartment building, which was a former barracks of the Long Beach Naval Shipyard on Terminal Island, closed in 1997. The first rays of daylight gave the angular horizon of the abandoned shipyard an eerie feel. Camilla had picked the 119-acre Terminal Island outposts because several of the 160 plus buildings on the island were abandoned. It was an easy location to house people and go unnoticed, at least temporarily.

As Nikki approached Alex, he slowly opened his eyes. She

noticed that beside him were two sets of wooden Kali sticks. When Alex saw Nikki, he smiled. As Nikki bent down to pick up a pair of sticks, Alex spoke.

"You won't need those today," he said, before he got to his feet.

~

"ONE SHOULD NOT "GET UP" at a five a.m.," Masha said to no one in particular as she tried to rub the sleep from her eyes. "One should only stay up until five thirty a.m." Dressed in sweat pants and an oversized T-shirt belonging to Chris, Masha tied her long black hair into a ponytail.

"Here," Chris said to Masha, before handing her a Styrofoam cup of coffee. "You'll get used to it," he added.

Chris looked over at Yaw, then Camilla and Joey Nugyen, as they stretched and warmed up in some fashion. The location for the morning routine was a small concrete pad between empty industrial buildings on the south end of the Island. The large, rusting cranes of the shipyard, parts of which that were now leased to China, were visible in the background.

"He's here," Chris said to Yaw as he nodded west.

The group glanced in Alex and Nikki's direction and simultaneously got to their feet. They took note, looking at one another, when they saw that neither Alex nor Nikki carried weapons. Not even the traditional Kali sticks for training.

Alex stopped at the head of the group and looked them over. Yaw broke from the group and approached Alex. The men shook hands and exchanged a brief hug.

"Ready when you are," Yaw said to Alex.

Alex nodded, noting the eager expressions of the group. They were ready to learn.

"You do not become expert by only practicing what is advanced," Alex began. "You become expert by having a thorough understanding of the basics. The basics begin long before any conflict arises. Before any weapon is raised."

Alex looked over the group again to make sure he had their undivided attention.

"Today's lesson regards cause and effect," Alex continued. "Understanding this is the first step of any learning, the first step in recognizing any pattern. Now pair up and follow me."

7

ONE STEP BEHIND

MARK KIRBY TRACED THE MAP WITH HIS FINGER UNTIL HE FOUND THE city he was looking for: Veracruz, Mexico, specifically the city of Xalapa. He carefully pressed a pin into the corkboard to mark the location before tying a thin piece of yarn to it and connecting it to the others. He stepped away from the wall where the map hung to get a better look. He was looking to see if there was a recognizable pattern to Alex Luthecker's movements.

Kirby had been tracking Luthecker for the better part of six months, starting in Tibet, leading to his near miss at the Siachen Glacier on the India-Pakistan border, and ending at the pattern reader's last confirmed sighting in Xalapa.

By the time Kirby had arrived in Mexico, Luthecker, along with Nicole Ellis and his other followers were long gone. However, the impact of their influence on the inhabitants of Xalapa, Veracruz was still fresh. Kirby dared to stay in the Mexican city for an extra day. He wanted details.

Kirby knew to tread carefully when inquiring about Luthecker, as due to the events in Xalapa, it was a touchy subject. He was deep in cartel territory, Veracruz being one of the most dangerous states in all of Mexico, and Luthecker had just interrupted their product supply.

With countless unsolved disappearances, frequent kidnappings, and rampant extortion, the drug cartels ruled over all, including local law enforcement. And judging by the number of soldiers in the area, the cartel was clearly not happy about their encounter with the pattern reader.

Still, many of the locals, when free from the eyes and ears of the cartel, were eager to explain to Kirby what had happened. It didn't surprise him to discover that Luthecker and his friends were quickly becoming a fixture in local legend.

The local people had already named them, a moniker that was only spoken in whispers: "*Los Libertadores.*"

From what Kirby could gather, Luthecker and his group had liberated several immigrants riding the Beast train north, a train that had been targeted by the cartels for slavery. Luthecker's interference had led to the arrest of over a dozen cartel soldiers by "*Federales*" and not local lawmen on the take, as many of the soldiers were wanted in connection to several murders.

Most of the migrants had scattered immediately after the incident, and many had returned to the "Back of the Beast" as it was known, in hopes of still making it to the U.S. border.

Although their safe journey was far from guaranteed, Kirby detected a sense of boldness in the tone and mannerisms of the locals. They spoke with a sense of destiny that they credited with the arrival and actions of *Los Libertadores*. The sentiment was not altogether different from what he heard and saw from the soldiers he spoke with on the Siachen Glacier in India, after Luthecker's pass through.

Kirby's description of Alex Luthecker being an agent of change was seemingly more accurate than even Kirby himself suspected. It made finding Alex Luthecker that much more urgent, before the powers that be realized the true extent of the pattern reader's impact. Before they decided Luthecker must be destroyed at all costs.

The one part of the puzzle that didn't fit was the death of a sixteen-year-old boy during Luthecker's liberation of migrants in Xalapa. According to local accounts, the boy died at the most critical juncture of Luthecker's involvement. Something—if Kirby's understanding of Luthecker's abilities was accurate—the pattern reader should have been able to prevent.

He wondered if Luthecker had seen the patterns that would eventually lead to the boy's death before it actually happened and had been unable to stop it. Or perhaps Luthecker had seen that the boy's death was an unfortunate necessity, as part of larger set of patterns that only he could see. Or the worst possibility of all—the pattern reader's abilities were degrading and over time, the memory necessary to calculate all possible outcomes and derive the exact one were too much for the human system to handle. And like any other system, eventually Luthecker's abilities would breakdown and become inaccurate.

According to locals, the boy, Enrique, had been traveling with his younger sister Maria. The scuffle with cartel soldiers that had led to Enrique's death apparently involved the freedom of the young girl. Maybe the patterns of the situation dictated that Luthecker had to choose between the two lives, between brother and sister. If this was so, it must have been heartbreaking for the pattern reader.

Kirby wondered what kind of impact that decision would have on the way Luthecker viewed reality—would it warp his ability to be objective? Would this be a catalyst and cause the inevitable degradation in memory that would impact Luthecker's accuracy in event recollection? Or maybe the boy's death was simply an outlier data point that Luthecker did not see?

Kirby wanted to speak with the girl to get a better understanding of the specifics, but she had disappeared. When the American scientist had asked around, the answers had all been the same. Maria had been last seen leaving with Luthecker and his group. For all Kirby knew, the young girl was no longer in Mexico.

Maybe the girl, Maria, fits into something bigger in some way, Kirby thought to himself. He stood back and looked at the pins in the map. Luthecker had gone from Los Angeles to Tibet, from India to Mexico, the last stop where he had joined up with several members of his group. It had come almost full circle, and Luthecker left a disruptive imprint wherever he went.

And considering the circular nature of Luthecker's travels it wasn't hard to predict where he would most likely end up next. According to the pins on the map, he would be home in Los Angeles. With over thirteen million people, finding Luthecker would still not be easy. But at least Kirby had an idea where to look.

Kirby hoped to find the pattern reader soon. He hoped to speak with Luthecker about the process that created him. He hoped to introduce Luthecker to his genetic second mother.

A knock on the door interrupted Kirby's train of thought. He took a deep breath for patience and moved to the door of his small one-bedroom apartment in Studio City. He already knew who was at the door before he answered it.

"Mr. Turner is very upset with you, Doctor Kirby," said the man in the crisp-blue suit and purposefully visible sidearm.

Kirby looked down at his own left wrist, which was shackled to a steel table. He sat rigid in his matching steel chair, as he examined the pale-gray walls of the room.

Kirby could almost hear the screams of the countless people held in this cell, those who had come before him.

"I'm not a terrorist," he replied.

"All it takes is the suspicion. Just the label itself, and then it's over for you. For anyone."

"I have my rights."

"The need for national security says otherwise." The man who sat across from Kirby, dressed in the perfect blue suit, kept his eyes locked on the scientist as he slowly loosened his tie.

"Who are you?" Kirby asked.

"My name is not important."

"You're an operative for Coalition Assurance. The enforcement arm, or should I say the hit men of the Coalition. What are you, ex-

Special Forces? CIA? Are you now part of the Coalition torture squads?"

"Doctor Kirby, this is simply a debriefing."

"I'm chained to a table."

"As a precaution."

"Precaution for what? You're a trained killer and I'm a civilian."

"Doctor Kirby, if I were you, I'd cease with your hostile tone."

"*My* hostile tone?"

"I wouldn't let it descend into an interrogation if I were you. So let's just answer some questions, shall we? Now—Mr. Turner wants to know why you didn't report evidence of the missing asset in India."

"Gee, I don't know, maybe because it's a foreign theater, and I didn't want you goons showing up and causing a major incident. Like you fools did in Trans Dniester."

The man in the suit showed no reaction. "We have interests in that region."

"Of course we do."

"And no interests in the asset Alex Luthecker."

"You have no clue about the asset Alex Luthecker," Kirby said.

"You were given a job with specific parameters."

"I was laughed at. I wasn't given the resources to succeed. I wasn't *supposed* to come up with anything. I was *supposed* to disappear."

"Nevertheless, when it comes to intelligence of any kind, it is your obligation to keep Mr. Turner up to date in real time."

"We are in the early stages of the sixth great extinction in this planet's history. If the current trajectory remains in place, our species has a less than fifty percent chance of surviving beyond the next two hundred years. How's that for real time?"

"That's not why we're here."

"Of course it is."

"The data for what you claim is inconclusive."

"You're an idiot." Kirby leaned in toward his well-dressed captor. "I believe that the only way to turn this extinction-level reality around and find a way to save our sorry asses is through Alex Luthecker, and even then, it's a slim possibility," Kirby continued. "We need his mind on the problem. We need advanced-level thinking on the challenge, not current-level thinking.

"He needs to be brought in. He needs to be studied. He needs to be understood and accepted as the long-term solution that he is, before what he sees overloads his memory system and breaks him down, which is a real possibility.

"You tell your boss that I know how to get to him. I know how to convince him to work for us. You tell Mr. Turner that I know how to monetize Alex Luthecker, all in the name of the Coalition."

The man in the perfect suit with the visible sidearm tilted his head. The claim of monetization by Kirby was unexpected. "How?"

Kirby kept himself from reacting. With that one word question, he knew he was getting out of this cell. He knew that he just bought himself some time.

"You tell Mr. Turner that if he doesn't want to meet with me, then he's just going to have to trust me. And there's one more thing."

Kirby kept his eyes locked with his captor. In Kirby's mind, there was still a closing line to deliver—a signal, one that would signify loyalty, a line that Turner would understand.

But he wanted the hard-muscled, but soft-brained, knuckle-dragger in the suit to ask. He wanted the larger, stronger man to sense the shift in power, even if he was too dumb to understand it.

"Which is?" The man in the crisp suit finally asked.

"You tell Mr. Turner that when I deliver Luthecker, he's going to have to give me my cut."

8

CAUSE AND EFFECT

"I COUNT FIVE CARS," MASHA TERESHCHENKO SAID TO CHRIS.

"It's not just about the number of cars, it's about remembering all the details. What color are the cars? How fast are they going? What models? Who is driving? Are there any passengers? Try not only to witness these things, try and remember as many details as you can, about everything, in five minutes, and be able to recall all of those details at will. That's the drill."

"I have a phone that I can record this on."

"You have one more minute."

"This is silly."

"Do as Alex instructed—focus on the people first then work your way out."

Masha sighed in frustration before scanning the pre-dawn empty streets of downtown Long Beach, one last time. She was relatively new to the group, the one led by the odd and occasionally scary man Alex Luthecker who, along with Nikki Ellis, she had joined in rescuing in Trans Dniester.

Despite her budding romantic relationship with Chris and the acceptance of her inclusion by the group, her insecurities of still feeling like an outsider made her instinctively defensive. Her reactions were a hard habit to break.

Chris was aware of the difficulty, had treated her defensiveness playfully, and had always been patient with her, which only made her like him more—itself a source of frustration for Masha. Not having the emotional upper hand when it came to men was as foreign to Masha as was her new country.

The adjustment to American life, particularly Southern California life, had proven more difficult than Masha's childhood fantasies had led her to believe it would be. It was not the glamorous "Hollywood" that had mesmerized her by way of a flickering television set in the small apartment she had been raised in.

Being born to working-class parents and growing up just north of Moscow, the sunny days and pretty people pictured on American TV seemed dreamlike. She discovered that the reality was far less so. It was beautiful, yes. And so were the people, at least on the surface. But the residents of Los Angeles had a quiet and constant anxiety about them, and many were capable of layered deception unlike anything she had seen before, even from her ex-boyfriend Semyon, who in Masha's mind was the definitive liar.

When Chris asked Masha to explain what was so different here than from her home, what made her adjustment so difficult, he was charmed by the simplicity of her explanation.

"In Russia, people are the opposite of L.A. When someone says, 'Fuck you' in Russia, they mean 'have a nice day.' In Los Angeles, when someone says, 'Have a nice day,' they mean 'Fuck you.' It is all so very confusing."

She remembered her explanation had made Chris smile and that he kissed her right after the fact. *Again, with the charm*, she thought to herself about her man.

When she left Russia as a teen and moved to Trans Dniester in search of a better life, she learned the hard way that cruelty and hardship, along with dishonest men, were something she would always have to look out for. It was when she was working for the Russian oligarch Ivan Barbolin, also known as the Barbarian, that Chris and his friends randomly entered her life. Or, as she was beginning to learn, perhaps it was not so random.

Her well-honed skills for survival sensed opportunity upon first meeting Chris. In part, because right from the start he seemed genuine, almost innocent. Her initial approach was tactical, part of the routine reconnaissance she did while under the Barbarian's employ.

She was attracted to the young American almost immediately, however, and she was taken by surprise at how quickly she found herself subscribing to his group's cause. It quickly went beyond her going along as a way to get out of Trans Dniester and to America.

The initial adrenaline of the escape proved seductive; that type of action always was for Masha, but that spoke nothing of the effect Alex Luthecker had on her. The man's ability to see past constructed narratives of personality was surreal. To have someone peer into her soul and reveal exactly who she was made making the major changes in her life—that she hesitated with—suddenly easy. It was unlike anything she had experienced before.

Before she knew it, Masha was in America.

But once she settled into her new home with Chris in Los Angeles, the same survival skills that kept her safe from harm in Trans Dniester took over and prevented her from getting too close to anyone, in particular Chris.

She tried to let go, tried to embrace this new sense of trust and connection that this small group of people seemed to have with one another. More than anything, she wanted to be part of it. But when it came to Chris, she swore to herself that—at the very least—she would keep a part of herself safe from seduction and from falling in love completely. It was the part of her heart she would protect and rely on in case she needed to escape, should her new country prove to be dangerous. For Masha, survival came first.

"Masha, you have to stop drifting off," Chris said, interrupting her thoughts. "Being able to focus is part of the exercise. Your time is up, but I'll give you an extra minute because you haven't had enough coffee this morning. Now concentrate."

Masha took a deep breath and tried to focus. The drill that Alex had given them was harder than she thought. Her mind always ran at 100 miles per hour, except at 5:30 a.m., when it ran at zero. The task seemed simple: Stand on an average street corner, observe, and remember everything to the last detail. Then, report those details back to the group.

She did not understand how this related to cause and effect, other than the *effect* made her want to go back to bed. With Chris. Preferably naked. She shook off her distractions and closed her eyes to settle her mind; then opened them.

The first thing she noticed was the older woman approaching the bus stop. She looked to be in her forties. Perhaps older, Masha considered on second thought, judging by the lines in her face. The puffiness around the woman's eyes indicated a lack of sleep, but it was offset by determination in her movements. She probably had a family to feed. Her skin was dark, Latin, perhaps Mexican-American.

She carried a large bag, too heavy for her; it looked to be filled with cleaning equipment. It did not slow her down. She wore a black sweater, worn and faded even from this distance.

Watching this woman pulled at Masha's heartstrings. This woman was a housekeeper, or perhaps a cleaning lady. She was waiting for a bus that would take her to someone's home or business, where she would go about her day, invisible to all who were not like her. Masha had seen this type of woman countless times in Russia. In this woman, she saw her mother. Her aunt.

Masha was surprised to feel her eyes well up with tears over the connection to her past. She finally understood the purpose of the exercise.

~

"WHAT DID YOU HEAR?" Alex asked Yaw and Camilla.

The couple, along with Alex and Nikki, Chris and Masha and Joey Nugyen, sat in a circle inside the abandoned warehouse on Terminal Island. Behind them, Mrs. Chen, a woman in her forties who, along with twenty-seven others, had been rescued from a shipping container at the Port of Long Beach less than a year ago, watched over both Kylie, the daughter of Yaw and Camilla, and the ten-year-old girl rescued from Veracruz, Maria.

"The sound of cars, of traffic, drowned out most of everything," Yaw began.

"How many cars?" Alex asked.

"Too many." Yaw thought about his answer for a moment. "But occasionally one would break out from the others and be distinct, like the roar of a truck. And then there was the jet that flew overhead."

Alex nodded. "Continue."

"There was also a loud car horn that lasted about five seconds." Yaw looked at Alex and smiled. "Someone was angry."

"What else?"

"Not much. I'm sorry, man. I ain't got your skills."

"You have more than you think. Trust your instincts. You have been trained to ignore what matters. I will retrain you. Now close your eyes. Concentrate."

Yaw closed his eyes. For several seconds the group was silent. Then Yaw opened his eyes and looked at Alex. "There was a constant hum. It had a rhythm too it, with crescendos and low points. Almost like music. There was never any silence." Yaw turned to Camilla. "And there was the sound of her breathing."

Alex smiled. "That is good. A very good start. Soon, you'll be able to distinguish the individual harmonies that make up the hum."

"I don't know about that."

"I do."

"My brother, I gotta say, I'm just not sure what we're doing here."

"You already know how to move and fight, Yaw. Now, I'm teaching you how to be still." Alex turned to Masha. The eyes of the group followed.

Masha was suddenly overcome with emotion, and she didn't know why. Chris gently took her hand. The gesture almost caused her to break. She fought the urge to burst into tears and spoke. "I saw my mother," she began.

Masha had everyone's attention.

"There were cars passing by. Blue, red, black. The expensive ones stood out. The others blended in. It is like that in Russia. Visually, it was like…it was like Yaw said—a certain hum that was constant. I closed my eyes to concentrate, and when I opened them, she was there. Standing on the corner, waiting for the bus. She was worn but determined. I already knew how her day would be. I already knew what her life was about. It was like I could feel it."

"And what did you feel?"

Masha thought about it for several seconds. "Connected. Truly connected."

This made Alex smile big. "Connection. That is the first step in not just seeing patterns but understanding them. It is the sense of connection that allows one to see the future before it unfolds. It is the disconnect that makes events appear random when, in fact, they are not. It is in the disconnect that the world itself seems too big to understand. It is when we truly feel the connection to all things that the patterns begin to appear."

"But, sir, no offense, we're not like you," Joey Nugyen opined. "Not even close. I can't tell what's going to happen with someone next. I'm still just trying to learn how to spin the Kali sticks."

"The mind is like a muscle, it can be trained. Eighty percent of your mental work is used to block the senses. It does this in order to keep you sane. But you can still see all that is around you. But in order to do this, first you must understand that cause and effect is about accountability. Accountability for the impact of one's thoughts, words, and deeds, down to the smallest detail. It is in those details that the patterns emerge. And one cannot feel accountable, unless one feels connected. That is the lesson."

"But how will this help us in combat?" Joey asked.

"If you connect yourself to your surroundings, if you pay attention to the details to the degree that you understand cause and effect, you will know when combat is inevitable and when it can be avoided.

You will be confident in your ability to see conflict in advance—sometimes by minutes, sometimes by days, sometimes by years. And when you recognize those patterns, you will be able to take the appropriate actions. And from the view of those who are disconnected, it will seem like magic. It will seem as if you are predicting the future."

"That sounds really nice." Masha spoke in a borderline sarcastic tone that her heavy Russian accent made more dramatic.

All eyes were back on the Ukrainian woman.

"How you say in America? '*Kumbaya*?' But to what end is all this connection? When we have slave traders? When we have those who profit from the suffering and death of others? When most of the world is a horrible, horrible place?"

Chris put his hand on Masha's shoulder, but she brushed him off and stepped in front of Alex. "I have seen much brutality from those who do not wish to connect with anything other than their own greed," Masha said.

"I know what you've seen," Alex softly replied.

"Yes, you see everything. But what do you plan to *do*?"

Alex looked into Masha's eyes. The fire in them was genuine. And so was the challenge in her words. She stood unwavering, awaiting his answer. If there was any doubt before, there was none now—Masha was a warrior.

"I'm glad you asked," Alex finally replied, "because connection starts with inclusion. It is no accident that you are with us. And we're going to need you. In the coming conflict, there will be plenty to do. And we're going to need everyone."

9

NEGOTIATION

"You have five minutes." The Coalition CEO sat across from Doctor Mark Kirby and waited for a reply.

Turner noted that this time Kirby was not sweating.

"I want my own division, with my own budget, with no questions asked," Kirby replied.

Turner briefly thought about having Kirby killed. "Do you understand who you are speaking to?"

"Yes, sir. Sorry, sir."

Kirby started to sweat. *Perhaps I've overreached with my bold demands*, he thought. He quickly pushed the thought aside. There was too much at stake to turn back now. Kirby knew he was not a good negotiator, but he also knew this would be his only opportunity.

"I know who I'm talking to. And I don't mean to offend you by saying, 'no questions asked.' You're the CEO of the company and have a right to know everything. But understand when dealing with Alex Luthecker, knowing things can be a liability."

"Where is he? Where is Alex Luthecker?" Turner interrupted. He was beginning to lose his patience.

"I don't know," Kirby replied. Turner moved to speak, but before he could, Kirby quickly added, "But I don't have to. He'll reveal himself."

"Why would he do that?"

"I've been tracing his movements. They form a pattern. And I've been in contact with his only living relative."

"His mother."

"One of them, yes. He has two..."

"I know his history. Do you think he's going to come out of hiding for her?"

"Possibly. I have his medical records. But more importantly, I know what he wants."

"And what is that?"

"Change."

"Change of what?"

"Trajectory."

"Doctor Kirby, if you do not start answering in specifics this conversation will not end well for you."

Kirby took a deep breath. He was losing the Coalition Properties CEO for a second time. He felt sweat pouring down his back. Kirby began to realize that more than being a bad negotiator, he was just plain bad with people. He carefully gathered his thoughts before he spoke. If there was a time to be direct, it was now.

"Perhaps I should start with my goals and work backwards from that," Kirby began. "That might make things easier to understand."

"Make it quick."

"I am primarily concerned with one thing: survival of the species."

"Oh. Your extinction theory."

"It's not a theory. It's a mathematical certainty."

"The valued members of the species will survive."

"Maybe, but in what manner? Because the state does not exist without the people."

"There will be enough who survive to service the needs of the upper classes."

"I don't agree. There will be chaos. Savage chaos that benefits no one, unless we intervene and steer things in a manner that benefits what you consider the more valued members of the species."

"What does Alex Luthecker have to do with all of this?"

"If he's capable of what I think he's capable of, we need him to step in and use his influence. We need to convince him to save the world on our behalf."

"The world will be just fine. This isn't a comic book, doctor."

"Comic book or not, things are about to come to a savage end, and we need to convince him to help stop it."

"Why? To what end?"

"To set the stage for a glorious future. A rebirth of mankind."

Turner no longer thought about having Kirby killed. He thought about having Kirby committed to a Coalition asylum. "That sounds just a bit unrealistic," he finally replied.

"It's the only way that Coalition Properties stays on top. Has anything to stay on top *of*."

"And exactly how does Coalition Properties benefit from your ideas on saving the world?"

"That's the best part. We part ways with the climate deniers and get in front of the problem. We kill the golden goose."

"The golden goose?"

"Oil. We reestablish the Coalition as a leader, but not just in weapons and energy, but in world-saving technology. We clean up our image, along with the planet. We do so aggressively. And all the while, we monetize it. We own it all, lock, stock, and empty oil barrel."

Kirby could see that he finally had Turner's attention. "Our core businesses do not change. Our core ownership structure does not change. And we patent and make proprietary all the technology necessary to save the world from itself."

"I'm not going to get rid of our oil interests. That's ludicrous."

"I'm not saying get rid of it. I'm saying stop *protecting* it. Let it die a natural free-market death, and be the leader in what naturally replaces it. And if in the process it starts the world along a path that prevents the next extinction all the better. And you can profit from all of it."

Turner thought over Kirby's words.

"The Coalition ends up owning the world, not just now, but in the future. But here's the important part. This is all your idea. It's in your head, not mine, a very important distinction when it comes to dealing with Alex Luthecker specifically. Neither of us wants him running around inside our heads. So focus on your goals, monetizing the survival, and I'll focus on mine, getting him on board. Trust me, and I'll trust you. Then we both win."

Turner examined Kirby for several seconds. He thought the man was a bit of a kook, but the Coalition CEO decided to play along with Kirby and see where he was leading.

"So how does Alex Luthecker fit into the Coalition?" Turner asked.

"First, we stop defining him as either an asset or a threat. We stop defining him in any way. More importantly, we stop being afraid of him. We stop thinking about him at all. The Coalition literally stops all efforts to chase him, bring him in, or hunt him down. And I mean that."

"And then what?"

"I find him and convince him to come in and join us voluntarily. I involve him in the problem I want to solve: saving the planet from certain doom. I put his massive memory capacity and ability to influence others to work—and I am completely, one hundred percent sincere about it."

"When you say 'I,' you really mean the Coalition."

"No, I mean *I*." But I remember who I work for. And you do what you have to, and you keep me out of the loop. See how that works?"

Turner mulled over Kirby's proposition. "I'm not interested in meeting him," Turner said.

"You can't. In fact, no one from Coalition Properties outside of myself should ever deal with him again. And after this meeting, we can never speak again. Not until it's done, and he's on our—my team."

"But— "

"Say no more, Mr. Turner, for your own safety. Considering whom we're dealing with here, it's important that we strictly compartmentalize our thoughts. And it's important that you understand one more thing: I am one hundred percent sincere in my desire to save the species. And that is my only desire. There is literally nothing else on my mind. I will convey that goal and the sincerity behind it to Alex Luthecker. Because I also believe, without a doubt, that he's the only one who can help me."

Turner understood what Kirby had in mind. He had to admit that it was clever. It was also a fool's errand, but Turner saw no immediate downside. And it might inadvertently lead to Luthecker's whereabouts, which was information that Turner, despite his reluctance to even recognize Luthecker's existence, would need in order to keep the problematic soothsayer in check, should the necessity to do so arise.

"Okay, I'll let you run with this. For now. But I want to know as soon as you make contact with him," Turner said as he got to his feet.

I'll have Kirby followed from now on, Turner thought. And he had his own agenda he would pursue.

"Fair enough," Kirby replied as he got up from his seat.

He was surprised when the Coalition CEO offered his hand. Kirby shook it vigorously, pleased to finally be a respected part of the team. At the very least, he had bought himself a little more time. Kirby had sold an idea to Glen Turner without the Coalition CEO seeing the opportunity he had to play both sides against each other.

It was ironic, because what Kirby was planning would be something that Alex Luthecker could probably see before Kirby spoke a word. Knowing this, Kirby decided he would have to craft his argument with Luthecker differently. It was a challenge Kirby looked forward to. Because only then would Kirby get the recognition he truly deserved.

In Kirby's mind, only he could save the world. And when it was all over, Luthecker, Glen Turner, the Coalition, indeed the whole world, would finally see what Doctor Mark Kirby was truly capable of.

10

BLUE CURTAIN

Young LAPD Officer Dino Rodriguez sat quietly outside his commander's office and glanced around the room. It was dated '80s architecture and furniture, but it was clean and well kept.

Rodriguez checked his phone. It was 10:26 a.m. His performance review had been scheduled for 10:00 a.m., sharp. He shifted his weight in the uncomfortable wooden chair, took a deep breath, and did his best to calm his nerves.

Normally it would be the captain, not the commander, who would be giving Rodriguez his review. But the bombings on 108th street in Watts and also the old Metro 417 train station below Hill Street downtown, the latter of which resulted in the loss of his partner, Officer Glen Coleman, had put his promotion to Senior Lead Officer in jeopardy. It was because of these recent events that Rodriguez's commander and not his captain would be conducting the performance review.

There had been an Internal Affairs investigation into the series of incidents, which included Rodriguez's involvement in something known as "Safe Block," a zone in East Los Angeles that had harbored refugees and illegal immigrants. Several buildings had been destroyed, and Russian mobsters had been identified as the culprits.

Homeland Security became involved, and things had quickly become territorial between rival agencies. The press inadvertently helped Rodriguez's case by reducing a complex situation into a conspiracy theory that had its roots in history, that the militarization of the police force targeting minorities was to blame, and it had to be stopped.

Internal affairs brushed back Homeland in what was reduced to a Federal vs. State dispute, and with some surprise pressure by the state's largest employer, Coalition Properties, the Feds backed down.

The LAPD promised community outreach programs as a solution, and the matter quietly slipped into the past.

It helped that the officers that were part of the alleged "Blue Curtain" had stuck together. They spoke as one when they claimed to be helping the local community. The one thing that was understood but never acknowledged was that Officer Dino Rodriguez was the de facto leader of the Blue Curtain.

"He'll see you now."

Rodriguez looked up at the secretary, nodded, and got to his feet. He straightened out his crisp blue uniform, checked his badge, and walked into the commander's office.

"YOUR CAPTAIN CAME out against your promotion," Commander Tom Bruno said. Bruno, a large framed black man in his early sixties, waited for a reaction.

For the first time in a long time, Rodriguez felt the butterflies of nervousness in his stomach. "I was cleared of any charges of misconduct, sir."

"I understand. But your...extracurricular activities have put a bit of a spotlight on your unit. Something that he doesn't care for."

"I look out for the most vulnerable members of the community, sir."

"I understand. What you have to understand is that Captain Vanhelter is by the book."

"You saw what happened. What those people had been subjected to..."

"I've seen worse. Believe me."

"I'm sorry, sir. I forgot who I was talking to."

Rodriguez knew his commander's history—from a teenager during the Watt's riots, to an officer on duty during the Rodney King riots, Commander Bruno understood Los Angeles better than anyone.

"I'm going to promote you," Bruno said.

"Thank you, sir."

"But with some advice."

"Yes, sir."

"Keep doing what you're doing, but don't break the law. And be mindful of the optics. Do you understand what I'm saying?"

"Yes, sir."

"Good. Because I'm going to put it on you to keep things smooth with your captain."

"I will, sir. Thank you."

"You earned it. At the end of the day, you helped save those people—illegal or not. You'll be getting a new partner starting today. Captain Vanhelter will fill you in on the details."

The commander stood up and held out his hand. Rodriguez got to his feet and shook it.

"I won't let you down, sir," Rodriguez said.

"I know you won't. But watch your back, son."

Rodriguez nodded before turning toward the door. He exited the commander's office and breathed a sigh of relief. *The pay boost that comes with the promotion will come in handy,* he thought to himself.

But the biggest question on his mind was whom Vanhelter was going to assign as his new partner. Rodriguez had one specific officer in mind. One he knew would be supportive of his efforts on Safe Block.

∼

"YOU NEED to report any activity regarding illegal immigrants directly to me," Captain John Vanhelter said to newly-promoted Senior Lead Officer Dino Rodriguez.

"Yes, sir," Rodriguez replied. He stood at attention across from the captain's desk.

"We have very specific protocol we must follow. Going outside the protocol is not only grounds for termination, it allows for potential terrorists to come into our country," Vanhelter continued. "And I will not have terrorists ushered into this country with the help and support of the LAPD."

Vanhelter was a barrel-chested man in his mid-thirties. He had short-cropped hair of dark-brown offset by a thick mustache with streaks of gray. Vanhelter believed that violent offenders streamed through porous borders and often found himself at philosophical odds with his officers, particularly those of Mexican-American heritage.

Still, Vanhelter was by the book and made few if any errors. Political beliefs aside, he stood by his officers and reprimanded them hard if they crossed the line, which was why Rodriguez's activities had gotten Vanhelter hot under the collar.

"Bruno promoted you, and it's no secret that I recommended differently. So understand, I'm watching. And if I get any sense you're working with that group moving illegals again, I'll have your badge. Is that understood?"

"Yes, sir," Rodriguez replied but didn't move.

"Good. Your new partner is Officer Ellen Levy. She's waiting for you at the motor pool."

ELLEN LEVY PUT her signature on the time sheet, grabbed the keys, and walked across the concrete floor of the garage toward the parking lot.

At twenty-six, Levy had been on the police force for just over two years. Her parents, immigrants from Israel and both physicians, had hoped she would follow in their footsteps and go into the medical profession. But an attack on campus during Ellen's senior year at college changed everything.

Walking home from a party at 2:00 a.m, she had been assaulted from behind by a large male assailant. His breath smelled of alcohol, and to this day Ellen could no longer stand the scent of liquor; it brought her back to that horrific moment. She had found herself face down in the grass, the man tearing at her clothes. She tried to scream, and that was the last thing she remembered until a sharp pain in the back of her head.

She woke up in the back of an ambulance. The EMTs told her she had been lucky. Two other male students happened on the scene and the assailant had fled. One of the male students had given chase, but the assailant out ran him. The attacker was never identified.

Ellen had escaped serious injury. Considering the circumstances, she had indeed been very lucky. But what had changed Ellen the most was the response she got from both the university authorities and the police.

She had reported the attack to both parties, but nothing had ever come of it. Not only was no suspect ever found or arrested, she was strongly advised to let it go.

Everywhere she went, she was turned away. It was at that point she decided not to *let it go*. She was going to investigate, not only her own case but similar unsolved assault cases. And what she found had shocked her.

Once she started speaking to fellow students, both male and female, along with concerned police officers, the number of assaults had proven startling.

Beyond the officers, students, and administrators who demonstrated little concern, there were others who did express concern but did little. They suffered from what Ellen called "compassion fatigue," a dullness in perception and compassion that set in over time. It seemed that many had simply lost the capacity to care, their emotional capabilities buried among the numbers, creating a sense of normalcy with violence.

And the number of assaults on women, particularly on campus, were huge. It made Ellen angry. Unsure what to do with her anger, she had turned to her father, Dr. Sheldon Levy, for counsel. Ellen adored her father and viewed him as the strongest, kindest man she had ever known.

And Sheldon, who had survived his own encounters with violence during his youth in Israel, knew from the first conversation with his daughter that she would not follow the family profession. He knew that his daughter, known for her fiery temper as a child, would not let this incident stand. And much to the disappointment of Ellen's mother, he was supportive of his daughter's choice to join the Police Academy.

Ellen agreed to finish her Bachelor's degree in psychology before applying to the Academy, with a specialty in criminal behavior. She remembered her first day at the academy like it were yesterday, when she witnessed the pride behind the crisp-blue uniforms and listened to lectures on honor, protecting and serving. She knew, even before her orientation was over, she'd found her purpose.

"I THOUGHT JUNIOR OFFICERS DROVE," Officer Levy said as she sat in the passenger seat of the LAPD Crown Victoria prowler.

She watched the streets and sidewalks of Wilshire Boulevard, eyeing the strip malls with nail salons, Korean barbeque joints, and 7-Elevens as they drove past. She turned to Rodriguez for an answer.

"Not today," he replied.

They drove in silence for several minutes.

"So you knew my former partner Glen Coleman," Rodriguez said.

He pulled the Crown Vic up to a red light and waited.

"He was a good man. Told me all about you," Levy replied. "And all about Safe Block," she added.

"And Vanhelter? What do you think of him?"

The radio squawked as the light turned green, and Rodriguez rolled the Crown Vic through the intersection.

"He's a desk hound," Levy said. "Sees everything through rule sets, not human dynamics. An administrative skill set."

"And if things step outside of the rule set out here?"

"Have you seen my file?"

"Yes."

"Then let's cut the bullshit because I've seen your file too. I asked for this assignment. And I know you were hoping for me. I know what you're up to. And I'm in. One hundred percent."

"One hundred percent in on what?"

"Are we gonna keep fucking around with the back and forth, or are you going to take me to the Block?"

Rodriguez chuckled. "I heard you were blunt and to the point. There are some people I want you to meet first. And then, yeah, we'll go to the Block."

11

THE BARBARIAN

IVAN BARBOLIN STOOD AT THE EDGE OF HIS ROOFTOP PATIO LOOKING over Los Angeles and nursing his drink.

His Los Angeles home, one of several he held across the globe through various shell companies, was located high up on Tower Road in Beverly Hills, and as such, the five-thousand-square-foot dwelling had one of the most amazing views of Los Angeles.

On a clear night, the Barbarian could see everything from Dodger Stadium to the angular building cluster of downtown Santa Monica, parts of the Pacific Palisades with the Pacific Ocean as a backdrop, reaching from Long Beach to Malibu. At twilight, when all was quiet, it was one of the most beautiful views in all of Southern California.

Less than twenty-four hours after his meeting with Coalition Properties CEO Glen Turner, the Barbarian had boarded his private jet and headed back to Russia. Then, in an attempt to hide his whereabouts from the Coalition leader, he boarded another jet at a scheduled layover in Paris, one that he did not own but instead chartered under one of his many business aliases, and headed straight back to Los Angeles. It was a circular path filled with extraneous flight time, but it had likely thrown the Coalition of his trail, at least temporarily.

After his conversation with Turner, Barbolin knew trouble was on the horizon. The big Russian's years of experience led him to believe that Turner's agreements were not only empty but dangerous.

The U.S. corptocracy was notorious for going back on its word and eliminating their business allies once they were no longer deemed useful, often via violent means. From Manuel Noriega to Saddam Hussein, U.S. corporate interests had never failed to turn on their partners, those who were more at ease handling the darker elements of global business than their American counterparts, and the Barbarian knew that, over time, he would be treated no different.

The Russian knew that the only way he would survive would be to outmaneuver the Coalition leader and engineer the American's demise before the American CEO turned on him.

And the only way to do that was to find Alex Luthecker first.

The Barbarian had seen firsthand how the young soothsayer had taken down Lucas Parks, one of the most formidable Americans Barbolin had ever known. In the Barbarian's mind, Parks was as cunning as he was brutal, and this mysterious young man had destroyed Park's enterprise, while ensuring the demise of Turner's Coalition predecessor. The Barbarian had been deeply impressed by Luthecker's ability to destroy his enemies.

The big Russian also understood danger when he saw it, and with what he saw of Luthecker, he knew change and the chaos it created was coming. He knew if he didn't get in front of the situation, it wouldn't be long before he ended up in the crosshairs himself, somehow triangulated upon by both Luthecker and Glen Turner.

To the Barbarian, the past was—more often than not—prologue, and this was how it had been with Luthecker in the past; first, in how Luthecker took down Coalition leader Richard Brown, then Coalition CEO James Howe, along with the Barbarian's partner, Lucas Parks. The Barbarian understood Russian history, and he wasn't blind to the momentum behind a revolution.

Luthecker's influence was growing, reaching as far as the India and Pakistan border, and it appeared unstoppable. The Barbarian didn't need to connect more dots to see a pattern emerging. The

Coalition intended to eliminate their partners and absorb their assets to achieve a new world order—with the Coalition as its one ruler.

And Alex Luthecker, who had no assets to speak of, threatened to put an end to the Coalition's plan. It was a conflict that the Barbarian knew he could easily get swept up in, just like Parks did, should the Russian get caught in the crosshairs.

But it was in this pattern between Luthecker and the Coalition that the Barbarian saw an opportunity for survival. He wanted to make it clear to Luthecker that he had no intention of getting in the young man's way.

Luthecker had taken down the Coalition's last two leaders, and the Barbarian would be more than happy to help Luthecker take down their successor. The Barbarian understood that helping Luthecker was a way to ensure his own survival. In the Russian's experience, everyone wanted something. Surely, Luthecker was no different. Surely, the young man could be bargained with.

And the wealthy and influential Russian had much to offer. All the Barbarian required was an opportunity to make the offer. But in order to do that, he had to find the mysterious soothsayer before his Coalition adversary.

This was why Ivan had flown back to Los Angeles immediately and enlisted the local resources he had at his disposal to find Luthecker well ahead of his Coalition rival. And it was the Russian's years of experience as a dealmaker and a survivor that led him to believe he could strike an arrangement with the young man.

The Barbarian would agree to help Luthecker take down the mighty Coalition, in exchange for what the Russian considered some fair business practices. The Barbarian knew that there would be more to give up in order to gain the soothsayer's cooperation. He knew, at least in part, what Luthecker's motivations were—freeing members of the slave class. The Russian would make it clear to Luthecker that he was willing to give up the slave trade in exchange for the soothsayer's help.

Human trafficking was an enormous part of the Barbarian's business, and the oligarch hoped that releasing this would be enough to appease Luthecker in exchange for help in eliminating a mutual enemy.

In a truth he could barely admit, even to himself, Ivan Barbolin was tired of it all. He was ready to retire, peacefully, and if his countless rivals knew that the Barbarian had a hand in taking down the mighty Coalition, the old Russian oligarch would leave the business and political world on top and step off the world stage as a legend—feared among his enemies. Therefore, he'd be relatively safe when he walked away. But none of this would happen if he didn't find Alex Luthecker first.

The Barbarian took one last look over the City of Angels as the sun slipped below the horizon. Then he pulled his cell phone from his pocket and hit the first number on his speed dial. He wanted an update on the search from his most trusted friend and soldier, Ostap Kosylo.

Kosylo picked up on the first ring.

"Have you found him?" Barbolin asked.

"No. But I have found the next best thing," Kosylo said. His limited English and thick Russian accent made his choice of words blunt.

"What is the next best thing?"

"The Coalition dog who follows the scent. Kirby is his name. He leaves the Coalition as we speak. He has no clue that we watch. I will let him lead the hunt. He will lead me straight to the target. And when this Kirby has found Luthecker, I will intervene."

"Good," Barbolin answered. "Keep me apprised of all progress," he added, before he hung up.

Barbolin took a deep breath and thought about the other possibility. The one where Luthecker would not work with him, and the Coalition marked the Barbarian for elimination. Ivan Barbolin had already decided that he would not go quietly.

He stared at his phone. There was one more call still to make, one that he had mulled over for many hours, unsure if he should actually make it. It was a worst-case scenario phone call, a scorched earth back up plan only to be put into play if all was deemed lost, and the Coalition became completely unopposed on the world stage.

The call was strictly an insurance policy, one that would cost him a great deal of money, eleven billion dollars to be exact, but one the Barbarian had calculated as necessary. This particular deal would serve as the ultimate deterrent to the Coalition, should the worst-case situation arise. It would also ensure his safety in the homeland by providing a large cash payment to an ally in power.

The Barbarian looked at his phone. *At least I'm dealing with an old friend on this deal,* he thought, *a friend who understands the nature of military brinksmanship.* The Barbarian hit the speed dial.

The Russian President picked up the call after the first ring.

12

MISSION CREEP

"Empty the cash register, now!" Marcus Jones said to the visibly terrified Indian woman behind the counter.

Jones pointed the small revolver at the woman's head for emphasis.

When she didn't move, Jones gave the woman a hard stare before briefly eyeing the camera in the ceiling corner of the 7-Eleven.

He saw the red light blinking, indicating he was being recorded and was relieved that he remembered to wear his ski mask.

The decision to rob the convenience store had been last minute, after getting high and playing Grand Theft Auto with his best friend Jamal, and right now Jones was beginning to regret it. But it was too late.

It had been Jamal's idea to begin with, and he had suggested it while the two were playing the video game in his sister's apartment, less than an hour ago. Marcus was beginning to wonder why he had agreed to do it in the first place.

Marcus turned his attention back to the Indian woman. She was heavy-set, perhaps in her early thirties, and she still stood frozen.

"Now!" Jones screamed. His voice echoed louder than he had planned, and the woman jumped.

She hit several buttons on the well-worn cash register, and the cash drawer popped open.

Marcus quickly hopped over the counter and began filling the pockets of his jacket.

"Take what you want, just don't hurt me," the Indian woman managed to say to Marcus, her voice barely above a whisper.

The woman's words rattled Marcus, and he could hear genuine fear in them. He watched her cower in the corner, knocking over a rack of cigarettes in the process.

"I don't want to hurt you," he said in response. "I just want the money."

Marcus continued to fill his pockets with cash until the register was empty. He hoped his friend and literal partner in crime Jamal was having luck in the back room.

"I got the safe. Let's bounce," Jamal yelled from the back, as if answering Marcus' thoughts.

Marcus turned at the sound of the voice and saw Jamal emerging from the storage room carrying a duffel bag.

Jones noted that the duffel bag swung heavy, hopefully full of cash. Jones breathed a sigh of relief underneath his mask, before he hopped back over the counter and followed his partner out the door.

"Get in, get in," Jamal screamed as he got behind the wheel of the 2012 Toyota Camry, Jamal's mother's car.

Marcus hopped into the passenger side as Jamal put the keys into the ignition and started the car. Marcus noted that his hands were shaking.

Jamal put the car in gear, and the 2012 Toyota Camry spun its tires before roaring out of the parking lot and onto Crenshaw Boulevard. They had gone three blocks when both men dared to rip off their sweaty ski masks. They carefully scanned the streets and saw that no one was watching, before looking at one another. They both smiled.

"Slow down, slow down," Marcus said to Jamal, after they had fled another six blocks. Marcus' eyes scanned the streets one more time.

People stood at bus stops, moved along the sidewalks, in and out of shops and apartment buildings. No one paid any attention to the Toyota Camry, or the men inside. No one knew that they had just robbed a 7-Eleven. Marcus took one last look behind them—no cars were in pursuit.

Jamal eased off the accelerator, allowing the car to slow to the speed of traffic. The two young men, both only twenty-two years old, still held their breath. They listened carefully for several more minutes. No sirens. They let out sighs of relief.

"We did it, bro," Jamal said to Marcus, and the two men high-fived one another.

"How much was in the safe?" Marcus asked.

"Five thousand. Give or take."

"Holy shit!"

"Told you we could hit that place and walk!"

"You mean run!"

Both men laughed.

"We'll be safe at home in ten minutes like nothing happened."

The Camry was abruptly rammed from behind, pitching both men forward in their seats.

Jamal oriented himself after the impact and immediately looked in the rear-view mirror. "What the fuck..." was all he could say.

Marcus looked through the rear window to see who or what had rammed into the back of their car.

It was a brand new Cadillac Escalade. Its front grill was smashed from the impact into the rear of the Camry. But that's not what had Jamal's attention. What had his attention was that the vehicle had no driver. There was no one inside the Escalade at all.

The Escalade accelerated and rammed them again. The impact was much harder this time, and it caused the Camry to slide sideways into traffic.

Jamal attempted to correct the Camry's direction, but the force was too great to stop the slide. That was when the second car hit.

Both men were jarred again when the Toyota Camry was broadsided just behind the driver's side door by another vehicle. The second vehicle was a brand new Tesla Model S sedan, and it too had no driver.

The force of the collision sent the Camry spinning off the side of the road, and the vehicle came to a stop when it slammed against a fire hydrant.

The impact caused the rear passenger door to break open. The duffel bag from the 7-Eleven robbery jettisoned from the Camry and split open when it hit the sidewalk. Cash, snacks, and soda bottles spilled onto the street. Then the hydrant began to leak.

Jamal and Marcus crawled out of the vehicle, dazed and confused. They looked at the Escalade and the Tesla. Both vehicles suffered considerable front-end damage but were still functional. They sat idling, passengerless and seemingly sentient like predators working in coordination, and now waiting to go in for the kill.

"What...what the hell just happened..." was all Marcus could say.

Marcus Jones heard the siren chirp of an approaching LAPD patrol car, and he broke from the shock of the moment.

He realized he still had a gun in his hand.

"So LET me get this straight—you're saying that the driver's of the Escalade and the Tesla fled the scene," Captain Vanhelter said to Officer Rodriguez.

"No, sir. I'm saying that witnesses reported seeing the vehicles operating with no drivers."

"That doesn't make any sense. Were they stolen?"

"Possibly. But again, witnesses reported no drivers in either vehicle. First calls in saying so came in about four blocks from the accident."

"Where were the vehicle owners?"

"The owner of the Escalade was out of state. The investigation at his home showed that the alarm had been turned off, and the garage door had been left open. Owner claimed that he's sure he left on the alarm and shut the door before he left."

"Someone they know took it for a joyride? Someone who had the keys and alarm codes?" the Captain offered. It was the only thing that made sense to him.

"All keys were accounted for and away from the vehicle. It gets more strange, sir," Officer Levy added. Both patrol officers stood at attention across from the desk of Vanhelter. "The Tesla driver. He claims he watched it happen."

"Watched what happen?"

"He reported that his car simply activated and took off out of his driveway, with no warning whatsoever."

"He just watched it leave the driveway?"

"That's what he said, sir."

"Impound the vehicles."

"Already done, sir."

Vanhelter turned his attention back to Rodriguez. "And you said you got a text message about the robbery in progress?"

"Yes, sir."

"From who?"

"Unknown."

"We can unlock an unknown number pretty quickly, officer. You should have done that by now."

"Yes, sir, but I couldn't, because the text did not come from a telephone number. It didn't come from any number at all."

"Are you saying it just appeared on your phone?"

"Yes, sir. Tech guys said they couldn't trace the source."

Vanhelter gave both officers a look.

"We're just as baffled as you, sir. We had barely left the motor pool when I got the text. We decided to check it out and came upon the scene."

Vanhelter rubbed his face. "Okay fine. I've seen weirder things. And the perps?"

"Couple of kids. First offenses. Stupid. We're holding them until the parents and public defender get here."

"Should we contact the manufacturers of the vehicles?" Levy asked.

Vanhelter shrugged. "No. We've got enough shit to do. Let's just be glad we caught them. Put it all in the report and file it. If the Feds want to investigate it, it's up to them. We simply don't have the manpower. Dismissed," Vanhelter said, waving his hand.

Rodriguez and Levy looked at one another briefly before exiting the captain's office. They waited until they moved past the desks and ringing phones, through the front doors, and out of the building before speaking.

"So what do you think happened?" Levy finally asked.

"I don't know," Rodriguez answered, "but I have a hunch. And there's one person I know who can confirm it."

"Who?"

"A friend with the Block. And I'm hoping she's where we were headed to before I got the text."

13

WE GOT THIS

"How many people?" Yaw asked Joey Nugyen.

"A dozen. Maybe more. It's tough to get an accurate head count," Nugyen answered.

"Where are they now?" Chris asked.

"They get moved around. Never in one place too long. They were in City of Industry last week—a sweatshop in a rundown warehouse. Last I heard they were being held in an abandoned building downtown. Garment district."

"Who's moving them?" Yaw asked.

"Only thing I know is it's not the Russians this time. Streets say new player, but I can't pin it to any one person or institution," Joey explained.

"In other words, business as usual," said Chris.

"We can follow the money. That'll tell us who," Joey suggested

"My guess is it leads back to the Coalition," Yaw said.

"Probably. Or affiliates. But we don't' have time for any of that now," Joey explained.

Chris and Yaw looked at one another. Joey Nugyen had found his lane with the group. And that lane was street intel, particularly when it came to immigrants or refugees destined for the slave markets.

"We gotta go get them tonight. Can you get an exact location?" Yaw asked Joey.

"I should have it in the hour. Is there a plan?"

"We decide where to hide them once they're ours and work back from that," Camilla chimed in.

"What are you thinking?" Yaw asked.

"We can keep 'em at Terminal Island for twenty-four hours. Then we'll have to move them," Camilla answered.

"They're Chinese. We need Cantonese interpreters and help with placement," Joey added.

Camilla did the math in her head for several seconds. She checked her watch. Smart phones or any form of electronics connected to the Internet were not allowed in meetings. The hands of the old Timex on her wrist read 9:23 p.m. "Okay. I'll reach out to my contacts in the community. If you can get them to me by 3 a.m., I think I can move them safely among their people by 5 a.m."

"Okay, so Joey, you're gonna let us know where they are, and then we move," Chris said. "We'll get them to you before 3 a.m.," he added, looking at Camilla.

"And we'll cover you, should anything come up," Yaw added to Camilla as he reached over and took hold of her hand.

"Where's Masha on this? Is she up to speed?" Camilla asked Chris.

"She doesn't like meetings. She's practicing with her sticks right now. But don't worry, she is raring to go."

Yaw sat back in his metal chair, causing it to squeak. All four members sat silent around the small folding table—the only piece of furniture in the living room of a small apartment where they held their meetings. The apartment reminded Camilla of the one their former instructor, Master Winn, had.

"Where's Alex on this?" Camilla asked Yaw as she bounced their daughter Kylie on her knee.

"He wanted me to handle it. Said bring him in if I needed to. Otherwise, run it without him."

"You got this, bro," Chris added.

"We all got this," Yaw replied to the entire group who had been through so much together, starting from the streets of Los Angeles and going across the country to New York, and eventually across the globe to Trans Dniester.

"But where is he?" Joey asked. "Where is Alex? What is *he* up to?"

"He said that he and Nikki had something to take care of. And he'd see us at training tomorrow."

"I'm gonna go check on them," Camilla said.

"ARE YOU HUNGRY?" Alex asked Maria. The ten-year-old girl sat silent on the bed with her stuffed tiger Nala underneath her crossed arms, staring at Alex Luthecker.

Alex rubbed his temples. Maria had gone mute, and the patterns he could normally read in an individual—that would dictate their behavior—were still chaos when it came to Maria. It was frustrating, and he felt like he was in the dark, grasping at ghosts. It dawned on Alex that this level of confusion and uncertainty must be how most of the world felt, all of the time. It was no wonder that people retreated in fear.

"Let me try," Camilla said as she stood in the bedroom doorway. In her arms, she still held her daughter Kylie.

Alex nodded, and Camilla entered the room. Maria turned her fiery gaze to Camilla.

"Would you like to hold her?" Camilla asked Maria, speaking in Spanish.

Maria looked back and forth between Alex, Camilla, and Kylie, put Nala aside, and held out her arms. Kylie squawked as Camilla carefully handed the girl over to Maria who held the child in her arms. The ten year old instinctively began to rock Kylie.

"She is your little sister now."

Maria looked up at Camilla.

"We are a family here, Maria," Camilla continued in Spanish.

"And you are part of that family now. You are safe here. We will protect you. We will always protect you. And we trust you. And you can trust us. You can trust Alex. He has special eyes. Special eyes that can see things in people."

"What can he see?"

"He can help people see their true selves. And share it with them. And if they want to, they change for the better."

"What if they don't want to?"

"Everyone has a choice. Including you."

"He can't see me," Maria blurted out. "No one can."

Camilla gave Alex a brief glance before looking back to Maria. "He can if you let him. He can help you. He helps us all. And we all help one another. Even Kylie, who you hold in your arms right now—she's going to need your help. She's going to need her big sister. She's going to need you."

Maria looked again to the child in her arms. Kylie reached up with a tiny hand and grabbed Maria's nose. Maria broke out in a big smile, something she hadn't done since Enrique died. She thought about Enrique and how much she missed him. She still wanted to get the people who had killed him. But now she was torn.

She'd never had a younger sibling. She had protected Enrique whenever she could from the cartel soldiers, but in the end, she failed. Maria remembered that Enrique had protected her as well, on countless occasions. He protected her by keeping their father away from her when he was angry. He protected her by making sure she had enough food to eat. He protected her by taking her to the county fair, where he used the last of his money to buy her Nala. Enrique had even sacrificed his life for her.

And it had all led to this moment, where Maria held this little girl Kylie in her arms, a little girl who would need her. Kylie's mother had said that Alex had special eyes that could see things in people. Well he wasn't the only one with special eyes.

Maria couldn't see things about the man named Alex, which was strange. But she could see things about Camilla. She could see that

Kylie's mother was sincere and loving. She could see that Camilla could be trusted. And it was because of Camilla that Maria decided she would talk to Alex.

But she didn't trust him yet, because she couldn't see things about him, not like she could with everyone else. So she decided that she wouldn't just talk with him. She would test him.

Maria held out Kylie, and Camilla scooped her from Maria's arms.

Maria turned to Alex. "Will you help me, like Camilla said?"

"If you let me, yes."

"Thank you, Camilla," Maria said to Kylie's mother, the tone of her voice telling Camilla she should go now.

Alex nodded to Camilla in thanks before watching her leave the room with Kylie. He turned back to Maria and found the young girl's intense gaze locked on him. *This should be interesting*, he thought to himself.

Maria spoke first. "I want you to help me find the men who killed Enrique, and then help me kill them."

Alex sat still for several seconds before answering. "That will not help you," he finally answered.

"But they will kill more people."

"The one I spoke with will never kill again. And killing the others would only perpetuate more killing. It is better to remove the cause behind their desire to kill. It is better to not need the Beast train at all. Wouldn't you agree?"

"When I look at people, I can sometimes tell what they are going to do. Is that what you can do?"

Alex sat back against the wall. Could this be the reason he could only see chaos when he looked at Maria? Was it possible that Maria had the same abilities that he had? Was it possible that she was just like him?

Alex had a hard time getting his head around the possibility. Kunchin was a pattern reader after many years of intense training and isolation. Maria was just ten years old. If Maria was another natural pattern reader like himself, that changed everything.

"Yes. I can," Alex finally answered. "I realized that I could do this when I was about your age."

"Did everyone seem blind and stupid to you?"

Alex laughed. "Yes. They did."

"So what did you do?"

"I avoided them. Until I learned that avoiding them wasn't the answer."

"When did you learn that?"

"I saved someone. And that led to making a choice."

"But what if the blind and stupid people won't leave you alone? What if they take away everything you love?"

Alex took a deep breath before answering. That quandary struck the heart of so many things that the family fought for. "That's a very good question, Maria. One that I struggle with too. But did you know, with what you can do, with the special gifts that you have, that you could help people become less blind? That you can help them make the choice to not hurt anyone?"

"Can you do this to everyone?"

"No. Not everyone is ready. And it's not something you do *to* them, it's something you do *for* them. And if you do it for enough people, you change the momentum."

"What's the momentum?"

"I can teach you what that is. I can help you find your place in this world because you're just like me. But you have to make a choice first. You have to choose between fear and hate, and love and hope. It all starts there."

Maria looked away from Alex and turned her attention to Nala, her last connection to Enrique. Nala, who had been at her side throughout everything she'd seen.

Maria stroked the animal's back several times, feeling the softness of its fur. Enrique often spoke of the difference between fear and love. And it was for Enrique she would do this.

She looked back to Alex. "Teach me."

"SHE JUST WENT DOWN TO SLEEP," Alex said to Nikki as he watched over the dozing Maria.

Nikki stood next to Alex and looked at Maria lying still on the small fold out bed, clutching her stuffed tiger close.

The ten-year-old girl's face looked so peaceful. From that peaceful look, it would be impossible to tell that she'd recently been ripped from her home, rode on the back of the Beast train north, only to see her brother shot in cold blood.

"Camilla mentioned she finally opened up to you," Nikki said.

"Yes, she did."

"What did you two talk about?"

Alex stood behind Nikki and put his hands around her waist. He kissed her on the neck before answering. "We need to adopt her."

"What?" Nikki said, abruptly spinning around so she could be face to face with Alex, shocked at the unexpected turn in the conversation. "Are you serious?"

"Yes. Where else is she going to go?"

"I don't know, Alex. But she needs a stable home. She needs to go through social services..."

"She would become lost in the system. Trust me, I know. And I won't let that happen."

"We can watch over her. Keep tabs. We can't really give her a life..."

"The world can't either. Not her. She's different. And we'll adapt. We'll save a life."

Nikki stepped back from Alex and looked at him with curiosity. "What are you not telling me, Alex? What do you see when you read her?"

"I can't read her. I only see chaos in her patterns. And that's because I think she's just like me."

Nikki's jaw dropped, and she put her hand to her mouth. "Are you sure?"

"Pretty sure, yes. I may not be able to read her patterns yet, but I know there is nothing accidental about this. She belongs with us. I feel it in my heart. And I need to know if you're with me."

Nikki looked at Maria, then at Alex. The responsibility of raising a child had always been daunting to Nikki. When men in her past had brought up children, it was a sign of the end for her.

But it was different with Alex. She trusted him. And although their circumstances were far from secure, she knew that somehow, he would see to it that they would be okay. And if what he said about the young girl was accurate, that if Maria was just like him, at least one part of what Kunchin had said in Tibet was beginning to make sense.

"Yes. Of course I'm with you," she answered.

A loud knock on the door interrupted their conversation. Nikki moved away from the bedroom entrance, down the narrow hallway of the two-bedroom apartment, and into the living room, Alex right behind her.

She reached the door and looked out the peephole. It was Officer Dino Rodriguez, and a young female officer was with him.

"It's Dino," Nikki said to Alex, before she opened the door.

"Sorry to bother you guys," Rodriguez said as he looked from Nikki to Alex.

"Come in," Alex replied.

"This is Officer Ellen Levy. She's new, but she's on our side."

"Pleasure to meet you," Nikki said as she and Alex shook Levy's hand.

"Likewise."

"So what's going on?" Nikki asked.

"Something happened today. Something I think only you can answer. We had two vehicles act on their own with no drivers and take down a pair of suspects in a coordinated effort. I was contacted by an unknown source via text message, telling me both of the crime and exactly where the perpetrators were."

Nikki's heart sank. She knew exactly what had happened. Her worst fear had come true. She thought that she had more time, but it was clear now that she did not. What Kunchin had predicted about PHOEBE had begun, and she was beginning to act out completely on her own. Nikki could no longer ignore the implications. She had to find a way to get PHOEBE to open up to her before it was too late.

"We need your help on this one," Rodriguez continued, his words cutting through Nikki's thoughts. "Is there any chance that software program I know you run, what's it called, PHOEBE? Is there any chance you can use it to help us find out what the hell is going on?"

14

NIGHT RAID

Yaw stood in the shadows of the vacant office building and looked out the window from his third floor perch to the quiet streets below. This was his operation, and after the incident in Mexico, he prayed there would be zero bloodshed.

There had been an unspoken shift in responsibility within the family, as the small group of martial artists had grown more and more focused on liberating the victims of human trafficking. Alex had retreated into a more philosophical figure, providing tools, guidance, and training, while Yaw had become more of the tactical leader. This shift of responsibility suited Yaw just fine.

So much had changed since the birth of his daughter. Kylie had given him a new perspective on life, specifically how fragile and how important it was to protect the most vulnerable. The instinct to protect the vulnerable had always been a part of Yaw, but his observations of Alex and his relationship with his friend had really brought things into focus.

Yaw was beginning to understand that, while studying under Master Winn, he had found peace. However, with studying under Alex now, he had found purpose.

All of which led him here, at 3:00 a.m., to the fashion district of

Los Angeles, working with those close to him to free several individuals from trafficking.

Established early in the 20th century, the Los Angeles fashion district, a design, warehouse and distribution center for all manner of clothing and related accessories, took up over 90 blocks in the heart of downtown and was considered the hub of the clothing and apparel industry on the West Coast.

During the day, thousands of clothing and garment vendors lined the streets, with countless customers from all over the world rummaging through clothing racks and piles of shoes, moving through the 90 block maze in search of a deal from the latest designer of latest knockoff.

But at night all was quiet. The streets were empty and the storefronts were boarded up or secured behind metal gates. And on the third floor of an abandoned building, one that had been built in 1929, eleven refugees from mainland China sat huddled together under a pile of dirty blankets.

The room was dark and stripped down to the concrete, save for an occasional office chair or empty filing cabinet. Standing watch over the eleven was a Mexican man with Calderon Cartel markings, carrying an AR-15. The cartel soldier paced the floor as he waited for the buyer's representatives to arrive.

Across the street from the building, on the third floor, was where Yaw watched and waited. He put a pair of night-vision binoculars to his eyes, turned toward the window, and scanned the building across from him. He made out the forms of the refugees, as well as the Calderon Cartel soldier, along with his AR-15.

Yaw carefully scanned the floor above and then the floor below. He saw no movement. Yaw pulled the binoculars from his eyes and saw a late model panel truck parked across the street. He knew Joey Nugyen was behind the wheel and that Chris Aldrich and Masha Tereshchenko were waiting in the back of the vehicle.

Yaw checked his sticks, which were slung across his back. *This one should be easy,"* he thought.

He quickly wheeled about and headed for the stairs.

~

"JUST ONE GUARD?" Chris whispered to Yaw as he slipped to the street from the back of the truck.

Masha quickly followed and stood beside him.

"The streets and floors are empty," Yaw answered. "Let's clear the stairwells to be sure, and then let's get them out of there."

Yaw looked up and down the street one last time. The lanes were quiet save for one parked car that he had already confirmed was empty. The building windows were dark.

In less than four hours, this area would be swimming with activity, and the people they were trying to rescue would be lost forever.

Yaw turned back to Chris, Joey, and Masha. Kali sticks strapped in holsters across their backs, they were ready to go.

"Joey, watch the streets, and be ready to roll when we come out." Yaw looked over the remaining two. "Chris, clear the stairs from the back of the building. Masha and I will work the entrance. I'll get the guy with the rifle. Masha, you keep the people calm and get them moving."

Chris and Masha nodded affirmative.

"Okay let's move." Yaw watched as Chris sprinted across the sidewalk and disappeared around the side of the building. He nodded to Masha before he made for the entrance.

The building, built in 1929, had a pair of large oak doors at least 50 years old that made up the entrance. During their initial reconnaissance, it had been discovered that the lock was broken, and Yaw carefully turned the brass knob and opened the door. He did a check to make sure all was clear before he signaled Masha to follow him inside.

Yaw and Masha did a quick scan of the first floor. In the darkness, shapes were clear: A dust covered reception desk, corner office entrances, along with a short hallway leading to a single elevator bank, and behind the elevator bank a stairwell. Yaw led as they padded silently around the reception desk, past the elevator, and into the stairwell.

Once inside the stairwell, the two sprinted up the stairs, two at a time, quick and silent. At the third floor, Yaw carefully approached the door that led to the large empty space where the refugees were being held. He signaled Masha to stand behind him. He carefully opened the door an inch and peered inside.

The man with the AR-15 stood looking over the eleven Chinese refugees. He held the rifle low, and his back was toward Yaw. The distance between Yaw and the man with the rifle was less than twenty feet. Yaw knew he could cover that distance before the man could react, let alone turn around.

Yaw took a deep breath and bolted from behind the door.

The man barely had time to turn his head before Yaw cracked him in the jaw with a Kali stick, knocking him out cold.

The man instantly crumpled to the concrete, the AR-15 clattering to the floor beside him.

Yaw picked up the rifle, removed the clip and bullet from the chamber before sliding the weapon across the floor.

He immediately turned his attention to the refugees. All eyes were on him, and all eyes were frightened.

That's when Masha quietly spoke. "Come with us. You are safe now." Her voice was gentle and soothing, filled with the emotion of experience.

Masha had had her own experiences with oppression, and it came out in her voice. It transcended the language disparity. Yaw was happy he had Masha on this mission.

"Back stairwell is clear," Chris said as he entered the room.

Masha already had the refugees on their feet.

"Let's meet Joey in the back alley," Yaw replied.

Yaw and Masha led the group of seven women and four men with Chris trailing behind. They navigated the switchbacks of the stairwell in serpentine fashion, and Yaw quickly led them out.

A bright spotlight abruptly illuminated the alley, stopping them in their tracks.

A Lenco Ballistic Engineered Armored Response Counter Attack Truck, more commonly known as a BearCat was parked at the entrance, the letters SWAT emblazoned in yellow along the thick metal frame of the military vehicle.

On top of the vehicle was the spotlight, along with a fifty caliber cannon. A SWAT officer, dressed in black storm trooper fatigues and armor, manned the gun.

Twenty other similarly-attired officers stood in attack formation, all training AR-15s and other high tech rifles at Yaw, Chris, Masha, and the eleven refugees.

"Put your hands up," a male voice blasted across a loud speaker.

Yaw did as he was told. He noticed that Joey Nugyen was face down on the ground next to the panel truck, his hands zip-tied behind his back.

"You are all under arrest," the bullhorn continued, "for transporting illegal immigrants for the purpose of terrorist activities on American soil."

Those were the last words Yaw heard before an officer struck him on the head with the butt of his rifle and everything went black.

PART II

ALL THINGS ARE CONNECTED

15

RETALIATION PLANNING

RIKA MURANAKA LOOKED AT THE SERIES OF CCTV SECURITY VIDEOS yet again, stunned at what she saw happening.

She had listened to the eyewitness report shown on cable news—bystanders watching in disbelief as two driverless vehicles, a Tesla electric car and a Cadillac Escalade equipped with a state-of-the-art autopilot function, made their way through the city of Los Angeles, meticulously winding down the streets and obeying traffic laws until coming upon the getaway vehicle of two wannabe 7-Eleven hold up men.

Then the Escalade and Tesla did what could only be described as a deliberate attack, incapacitating the getaway vehicle, a 2012 Toyota Camry, and seemingly notifying nearby patrol cars of the incident and location.

Muranaka noticed how the eyewitnesses seemed amused and entertained, unaware of what was really happening—that the first true A.I. incident in America had just happened, and it foreshadowed danger unlike anything this country had ever seen.

After hearing the eyewitness accounts, Muranaka immediately tapped into her own surveillance resources, and in no time had access to security camera footage from all over the city. She entered the aforementioned Tesla, Escalade, and Camry plate numbers into a search engine and managed to cross-reference the vehicle identifications with city-wide security camera footage in order to view the entire journey of both vehicles from the moment they self-initiated to the point of final impact with the Camry. Without even looking for evidence in the vehicle's programming codes, Muranaka knew immediately that this was the work of Nikki Ellis and her renegade A.I. ghost roaming the deep net, PHOEBE.

Muranaka wondered if Ellis had any idea of the repercussions. The growing threat of PHOEBE to national security long ago stepped beyond hacking into information systems or eradicating personal privacy. It had even gone beyond creating micro-targeted alternative realities through social media. Of far greater concern to both the government and private sector was the unleashing of artificial intelligence 'bots' into the deep web where they could roam, untraceable, acting with a preprogrammed mandate to create havoc across the globe with little or no additional programming or continued human guidance.

These A.I. bots could shut down power grids, unlock alarm systems, crash markets, zero out financial assets, dump classified information onto open source platforms, launch conventional weaponry, or even start a nuclear war, all without hesitation, if some individual gave the bot that mandate, or an even worse possibility: a programming quirk within the bot itself created that mandate.

If these things were allowed to materialize, there was absolutely nothing any human being could do to stop it. A.I. bots literally could end the world as mankind knew it, and it could start by simply programming an A.I. system to stop crime across the city by any means necessary, such as what Muranaka speculated had happened here.

As Muranaka hacked into the security and surveillance systems, she took note that it appeared to be the 7-Eleven security camera that set things in motion. Not surprisingly, there was no silent alarm in the convenience store. The clerk had called 911 on her cell phone, and Muranaka speculated that perhaps it had prompted PHOEBE to act.

The scarier speculation to Muranaka was the possibility that PHOEBE was programmed to roam security systems and identify the gun and perhaps the hostile movements as an alert, which it would act upon in microseconds, tracing the movements of the Toyota Camry and sending the Tesla and Escalade to intercept simultaneously while notifying the police.

In many ways, Muranaka was impressed. The memory and computing power required to activate a search through hundreds of billions of digitized images and code to select this particular instance was mind-boggling. It must have been programmed to act in this manner or seek out this type of activity by Ellis herself. It was the only way it made sense.

This only increased Muranaka's resolve about what must be done. Nikki Ellis must be found and PHOEBE destroyed before it was too late. But Muranaka was not naïve to her employer's methods and politics. She knew going through Tom Miller, the head of cyber-security, would be an utter waste of time, with the urgency of the situation being lost in the politics, a delay designed for Miller to take credit for Muranaka's discoveries.

Muranaka had witnessed Miller do this to others, both men and women, and she was not about to let it happen to her. She might be reprimanded and it could even cost Muranaka her job, but she needed to reach the decision makers. She needed to speak to Glen Turner, CEO of the company, directly before it was too late.

"He'll see you now," the pretty but robotic-mannered executive secretary said to Muranaka.

Coalition One in downtown Los Angeles had recently become a collection of buildings, dubbed the Coalition Fortress, with the company buying more and more real estate as its interests grew. The newly named Coalition One, the tallest building in the city, still remained at the center, while other buildings were being retrofit with the latest in high security technology, military-grade equipment that not even Muranaka was allowed to access. CEO Glen Turner's office was on the top floor of Coalition One, and it had taken Muranaka several phone calls and emails to get this one-on-one meeting with the Coalition leader.

"This way," the executive assistant said, before she wheeled about and started toward Turner's office.

Muranaka got to her feet and straightened out her skirt suit before following. For the first time, she realized she was nervous.

The waiting area of the CEO's office was large, almost cavernous, and filled with earth-tone furniture, including dark wood tables and bookshelves. The only out–of-place item was the Picasso on the wall. *It has the look and feel of old money*, Muranaka thought.

The executive assistant reached the large doors of CEO Turner's office, knocked twice, smiled at Muranaka without saying another word, and walked away. The oak doors then opened, and Turner, whom Muranaka had never met, greeted her with his own smile.

"Ms. Muranaka. Please come in," Turner said.

Muranaka entered Turner's office. The sunlight coming in from the large windows caused her to blink. She walked over to the glass, which ran floor to ceiling. The view of Los Angeles was breathtaking.

"Tom Miller says you're our top programmer, and we are honored to have you running our new Cyber Center," Turner said as he waved for Muranaka to have a seat.

"Thank you," Muranaka answered as she sat on the large leather couch.

"I'm surprised you didn't go through him with this request. He's head of the cyber-security division," Turner said as he sat down across from Muranaka.

"Well, like I said in my emails, this is urgent. A matter of national security, I believe. I thought it best to speak to you directly."

"We have an open door policy here at Coalition Properties. Please continue."

"Do you know who Nicole Ellis is?"

"I'm familiar with the name," Turner answered.

"Then you know she's a high-level hacker. Nicole Ellis runs an A.I. program on the deep web that's ghosting several highly encrypted security systems. We've been tracking it."

"And?"

"We've been tracking PHOEBE's every move in an attempt to gain access to it for some time now. And I believe we are getting close. But some unexpected things have been happening that I felt I should bring to your attention immediately. Things that I believe force us to devote more resources and accelerate our search for Nikki Ellis herself."

"What things?"

"I have evidence that the program intervened in the robbery of a 7-Eleven. I also believe it was the source of the American Airlines shutdown two weeks ago. People have been reporting banking irregularities across the state. Everything from debts being wiped out to unauthorized wire transfers. We're monitoring all of it, and I'm finding evidence that it is quite possible that Ms. Ellis' program PHOEBE was involved in several of these incidences."

"Do you think Ms. Ellis is programming her software to specifically carry out these actions?"

"Hard to tell. But my gut tells me that she's not. At least not directly. It would be too time intensive. Ultimately, she's responsible, but I think it's potentially far worse than that. I think that the program is doing it all on its own."

"And why do you think that?"

"When the program took a swing at us in the Cyber Center, I became suspicious. PHOEBE destroyed Black Widow, at least for the moment. I'm sure you've read the report."

"I have. I've gotten the angry phone calls from the NSA, too."

"Did they brief you on the potential threat?"

"The NSA is a cryptic bunch. Their craft and trade are secrets. But with what you're telling me here, I assure you I'll look into it now. What are your immediate concerns?"

"Well let me give you the quick and dirty assessment. If PHOEBE is starting to act out on its own, it could disrupt anything in the digital world, from defense systems to banking systems. It could shut down power grids. I don't want to sound alarmist, but left unchecked, it could potentially end civilization as we know it. We have to stop PHOEBE before it's too late. Before no one, not Coalition Properties, not even Nikki Ellis herself can stop it."

Turner thought over Muranaka's words. He obviously knew of Ellis and was aware of the dangers of her hacker skills. But what was new to him was the severity of the situation that Muranaka was claiming. He wondered how much of Alex Luthecker's influence was behind this.

Turner swore to himself. He did not want to fall into this trap. He did not want to make finding Alex Luthecker a priority. He did not want to go down the rabbit hole of his predecessors. But it was beginning to appear that he would have no choice. He was going to have to hunt down Alex Luthecker and Nicole Ellis and kill them if necessary.

"So what are you recommending?" he finally asked.

"That you use Coalition Properties' considerable resources beyond what we can do in the Cyber Center to find Nicole Ellis, and do whatever you have to in order to convince her to come in."

Turner steepled his fingers in front of his face as he carefully considered Muranaka's words. "Do you know who Alex Luthecker is?" Turner finally asked.

"I've heard of him. As I understand it, he's some sort of cult figure. Rumored to be able to predict the future. Not something that I believe is mathematically possible. I know that the Coalition has had run-ins with him in the past, but much of that information is confidential," Muranaka replied.

The fact of the matter was Muranaka knew exactly who Alex Luthecker was. It would be impossible to work for Coalition Properties and not know who the alleged soothsayer was and what he'd done to the firm. Muranaka would love to sit down with the infamous Alex Luthecker and test his abilities, if only to debunk them. But the thought of that was a luxury at the moment. The real threat was Nicole Ellis and PHOEBE.

"Thank you for bringing your concerns to my attention," Turner said. "Nicole Ellis and Alex Luthecker are partners. They are also notorious outlaws, and I believe where we find one, we'll find the other. And I agree, I think we're going to have to dedicate adequate resources to bringing them both in. So you'll have what you need on the cyber side of things, and I will put the resources in that are necessary to actually locate Ms. Ellis herself. We'll convince her of the urgency of the situation. And when I have her in the facility, I'll want your help in debriefing her."

"If they're outlaws, shouldn't their apprehension be handled by or at least coordinated with law enforcement?"

"Of course. As you know, we work hand-in-hand with both law enforcement and Federal agencies all the time when it comes to concerns such as national security. And I assure you, when the time comes, your help on these real issues regarding national security will not go unnoticed, Ms. Muranaka. I'm really glad you chose to take the risk to come see me directly."

Muranaka felt herself blush at his words, and she was furious with herself over it.

Turner stood up and offered Muranaka his hand. "I'm going to give you my private number, in case you have any questions. I have a board meeting in half an hour, but I'll be in contact."

"I TOLD you he'd be a problem," Collin Smith, the longest tenured member of the Coalition Board said to Turner. "Do you think Richard Brown or James Howe were any less diligent in their efforts to deal with the Alex Luthecker problem? However, unlike you, they recognized the threat immediately. The threat that you are finally coming around to."

"I recognize the threat. I've always recognized the threat. And the threat is fueled by the attention we give him."

"So you thought ignoring him was a solution?"

"What's your point?" Turner snapped back.

He wondered why the old man wouldn't just die already, freeing up another seat on the board, a seat Turner could fill with someone less openly hostile to his own ambitions.

"The point is that we warned you," Smith answered.

Turner looked over the members of the Coalition board of directors. They were all white and gray and balding with wealth on a scale the world had never seen before—and all possessed the power to match. The conference table cost more than most homes in the middle of the country. It baffled him that, despite all that these men had and controlled, they were still fearful, angry, and ultimately unhappy.

"I'll admit, there is a danger to ignoring Luthecker, and I've never ignored him. But right now I think there's a more immediate danger in ignoring his partner in crime, Nicole Ellis. Because of her threat, they both need to be found and eliminated. And, yes, I do differ with my predecessor's assessment that Luthecker constitutes a threat or asset. I don't see him as either. I think my predecessors misread the situation. I don't believe Alex Luthecker or Nicole Ellis possess any ability or asset that Coalition Properties doesn't already have.

"Gentlemen, we are the most powerful human organization that the world has ever seen. Two off-grid individuals may be an annoyance and create P.R. problems for us, but I don't believe they can threaten that structure as a whole. There simply is too much momentum behind our efforts. Not to mention the global scope of our reach and sheer assets we have at our disposal. And the technology we are developing here will soon surpass any alleged abilities of either Luthecker to predict the future or Nicole Ellis to create rogue software.

"Ms. Ellis does present a real time problem, but we will have her soon, and it'll be over. And as far as Alex Luthecker? He's obsolete."

Turner began to pace in front of the board members, and he saw several nodding. The Coalition CEO's presentation skills never failed to squeeze what he wanted from his board.

"However, I will add this—they both still have an important role to play," Turner continued, looking over the faces of his greedy, small-minded rivals.

He also knew that beyond their fearful nature, they were dangerous, and any misstep with this group of ruthless predators would mean his end at the top of the Coalition food chain.

"I believe that there are no accidents in this universe. And I believe that both Luthecker and the hacker, Nicole Ellis, represent a test for us, for our values and beliefs." Turner circled the table, walking behind Collin Smith for effect. "Luthecker and Nicole Ellis represent a final test of both our will to see our vision enacted and our ability to convey our beliefs to the people. And in regards to Ms. Ellis and her hacking skills specifically, in our ability to secure the future through the technological developments that will usher in the next era of human development."

"We've all read the reports of what Ellis did to Black Widow and what her program is doing around the world. We need to stop it," Smith added.

"On that we agree, Collin, and I'm in the process of stopping it. But don't mourn Black Widow too hard. That program is just the beginning of what Coalition Properties' new Fortress complex will be capable of. And when our systems destroy PHOEBE and we eradicate Ms. Ellis and Luthecker, along with their followers and the ideals they represent, we will have, in fact, passed our most crucial test as an organization. We will become stronger because of it. But we must not lose sight of what this is—only a test.

"Our beliefs must remain resolute. We cannot succumb to the threat. We have to understand them for exactly what they are—just a simple test and nothing more. And I'll have you know that we're already winning. We currently have all their followers in custody."

"Here? In the Fortress? Are you crazy? You have to let those people go," Collin said.

"Why?"

"Because we're not law enforcement for starters. But more importantly, do you remember what happened last time? When we attacked this exact group of people in an L.A. neighborhood with a Black Hawk helicopter? Do you remember how we lost that battle? Do you remember the lawsuits and the enormous payouts we had to make? Do you remember the congressional scrutiny? And how long it took us to recover from that P.R. nightmare? Do you remember nothing? Did you *learn* nothing?"

Turner felt himself get hot. "Of course I remember, and I've adjusted our approach. I've added patience and calm. And this time we are working directly with the Coalition-equipped LAPD. Look, this small band of human traffickers is heinous. They bring criminals across the border. They open us up to terrorists. They broke the law. We have proof, and the press campaign will reflect this along with their criminal past. We'll control the narrative this time, and this is only step one," Turner answered, before turning to the entire board and trying to get back on message.

"Now, on to what I see is the real test. As you know, we've expanded our real estate holdings considerably in Los Angeles," Turner continued. "Coalition Towers is now Coalition One, which is now part of a larger matrix of buildings in downtown L.A. referred to as the Coalition Fortress. The security and surveillance systems in use to guard the Fortress represent marketable technological break-throughs that the world has never seen before.

"Combined with our defense systems and weaponry, it is a one hundred percent controlled environment. It is one hundred percent safe, with no room for variables. It is my full belief that at the Fortress, Ms. Ellis and her software design she calls PHOEBE will meet their Waterloo, as will Mr. Luthecker. I believe it is destiny that their threat, perceived or otherwise, ends here."

"I won't see this company step on its own dick again," Smith said. "And as I've said all along, I don't think you treat this situation seriously. How do you know Luthecker won't see this coming? We've never gotten them all in the same place together in the past, how are you going to do it this time? How are you going to get Luthecker, Ellis, and PHOEBE, all in the same place, at the same time, where we can destroy them?"

"I'm working on it. But I'll get them all here, don't you worry. Alex Luthecker, Nicole Ellis, and everything that they stand for will meet their rightful end."

~

MURANAKA COLLAPSED on the couch of her small Santa Monica apartment and closed her eyes. Her meeting with Coalition CEO Glen Turner went better than expected, and she was very happy to be dealing with the CEO directly now.

But the heightened expenditure of energy required to be "on" for the meeting, combined with the anxiety of having to present her case to the head of the company, had left her completely exhausted, in addition to the added apprehension of having the opportunity and assets to pursue exactly what she wanted.

Muranaka had joined Coalition Properties right around the time Nicole Ellis and PHOEBE started being a thorn in the Coalition's side. Because of the timing, Muranaka had been chasing Nicole Ellis and the rogue hacker's accomplishments for the entirety of her professional life, and the younger Japanese programmer had resented it. Having her life defined reactively by those who came before her was something she'd been dealing with since birth.

Muranaka grew up as the youngest of three children, the only daughter in a patriarchal Japanese household. To Muranaka's father, her older brother could do no wrong, while Rika was constantly criticized. No matter how well she did in any endeavor, she would never be good enough. So Rika handled the constant criticism by excelling in everything.

She graduated at the top of her class, which led to having her pick of multiple jobs and being able to negotiate a starting salary far higher than either of her older brother's had out of graduate school. She worked longer hours than her colleagues. She'd had a hand in developing Black Widow. In every metric, Muranaka was winning. But no matter what she did, someone always overshadowed her accomplishments. She was at the top of her game, yet she always felt like she was losing.

At home, it was to her less competent older brothers. In the field, it was to Nicole Ellis and her program PHOEBE. With her long hours, her personal life was nonexistent. With family, with profession, Muranaka couldn't win. It was particularly frustrating because she felt she was destined for so much more in life.

But with the current crisis, Muranaka thought she could break free from this pattern. Perhaps by helping bring the world's most notorious hacker and her criminal conman Alex Luthecker to justice, Muranaka could finally step free from the shadows. Perhaps when it was Rika Muranaka, not Nicole Ellis who made the headlines, Muranaka would finally find the validation she deserved.

Muranaka decided that this would be the goal. She would work extra hard to find Ellis, not just crack Ellis' program. And she had extra tools at her disposal now. She had Glen Turner's favor at the moment, and she would capitalize on all of it.

Invigorated by the possibilities, Muranaka got up from the couch, sat at the kitchen table, and opened her laptop. She found that she had several email reminders waiting for her, a handful that were not work related, and she decided to take care of those first. She recognized two of the emails, one from St Jude's Cancer Center for kids and another from the Humane Society.

Muranaka, a single woman who was well paid but not necessarily materialistic, didn't spend her money on many things beyond clothes and dinners out. She had always spent the bulk of her disposable income on two things—vacations to remote locations and causes she believed in. The first item was months away, but in her email were monthly reminder alerts for charitable donations to her two favorite causes—St. Jude's Cancer Center for kids, and the Humane Society for animals.

For Muranaka, children and animals were deserving of help, but human adults were more suspect. Donating to these two organizations made Muranaka feel like she was making the world a better place, at least in some small way, particularly when life at work was overwhelming. She quickly donated five hundred dollars to each via PayPal and felt satisfied. Now back to the task at hand, dealing with PHOEBE and Nicole Ellis.

Muranaka quickly logged onto Tor, her deep web search engine, and began her pursuit of PHOEBE one more time. She would search all night if she had to, she told herself. And when she was done, PHOEBE and Nicole Ellis would never know what hit them.

16

IN CUSTODY

"They're being held at Metro downtown. In isolation. No one can get near them. Homeland's taken over. They are all under guard, waiting for the Feds to arrive," Dino Rodriguez said to Alex and Nikki.

"They're being held as persons of interest, suspected of planning terrorist acts," added Officer Ellen Levy. "It doesn't look good for any of them."

Levy stuck out her hand to Alex. "I'm Ellen Levy. I've heard all about you, and it's an honor to meet you. I just wish it was under better circumstances."

Alex shook her hand, followed by Nikki. Then Alex set his eyes on Levy. They studied her with the REM-like intensity and movement that Alex had become known for.

"What the hell...?" Levy reacted, while simultaneously taking a step back. Her instincts and training had her hand moving automatically to her sidearm.

Then, nearly as soon as it started, Alex's eye movement stopped. He looked at Levy.

"You will help many," Alex said.

Levy stood speechless. A feeling came across her that was indescribable, something that she had never experienced before. It was unnerving, as if in an instant, Alex had looked deep into her soul. Yet at the same time, there was a sense of reassurance. That being right here, right now, was exactly where she was supposed to be. As near to a sense of destiny as one could experience was how she evaluated the feeling.

A hand on her shoulder interrupted her thoughts.

"Yeah, he does that," Rodriguez said to her.

"We have to decide what to do," Alex interrupted. "If they stay in custody, they die."

"They're out of our reach. I'm sorry," Rodriguez said.

"Can we save them?" Nikki asked. "If we find a way to get them out, will they live?"

"It's possible. All I can say is the end is coming, but I don't see it with our friends dying in prison," Alex said

"What does that mean?" Rodriguez asked.

"All I know is that either the Coalition or we as a group, and our efforts, will come to an end. Soon."

Everyone stood in silence for a moment.

"We can't use PHOEBE to help us," Nikki explained.

Everyone looked at her.

"Not right now. There's some...coding problems. I have to work them out," Nikki continued. She didn't dare look at Alex.

"If you guys pop back up on the grid, it's over," Rodriguez added. "They'll nab you in a second, and I won't be able to protect you."

"I think she'll still protect us. It's just...there's some problems with any new commands."

"Problems?" Alex asked.

"She's not responding."

"How can you be sure she'll protect you then?" Rodriguez asked.

The officer didn't know much about PHOEBE, other than it was the software program that kept Luthecker and his friends hidden.

"Don't worry, we'll be okay," Alex said. "We'll have to look to other ways to stay in the shadows."

Alex turned back to Rodriguez. "The others. The soldiers that I asked for. Are they ready?"

"There aren't any soldiers. There hasn't been any time. I'm sorry."

Alex looked away for several seconds before turning back to Rodriguez. "I need you to do me a small favor."

"Sure. If I can."

"I need you to pay respects to my deceased mentor."

Rodriguez tilted his head in confusion.

"It would mean a lot to me," Luthecker added.

"Okay. If that's what you want." Rodriguez nodded before looking away.

He had never doubted Alex Luthecker before. But now the leader of this small band seemed to be speaking in existential parables that weren't based on any reality the young officer could see. And now Luthecker wanted him to visit a grave. It gave Rodriguez pause. He decided that it was time to leave. He turned to Officer Levy.

"Let's go," he said to her before they exited the small apartment, leaving Alex and Nikki.

"We can't have some sort of armed insurrection, Alex," Nikki said after the two officers had left.

"It won't be violent. I hope."

"Be honest with me—how much can you see? Can you tell what's really going to happen?"

"What's meant to happen will happen whether I can see it or not. But more important than that, is Kunchin's prophecy regarding you beginning to unfold? Is this what's happening with PHOEBE?"

"I think she's beginning to act out on her own. The consequences could be devastating. And I mean end of times devastating."

"She needs to be guided."

"I've been trying. I go to log in and my passwords don't work. Back door access will take time, time we don't have, and that's not a guarantee. We're on our own here until I can figure out what to do."

A small voice called out. "Alex...?"

Both Alex and Nikki turned to the sound of the voice.

Maria stood in the bedroom doorway. "Is it time to go?"

Alex smiled, then walked over to Maria, and put his hand on her shoulder. "Yes. It is."

"I want to go with you."

"Not this time, Maria. But soon. For now, I need you to stay with Camilla where you will be safe."

"Many will die," Maria said as she hugged Alex.

Nikki's heart raced. If Maria was in any way like Alex—like he claimed—her prophecy would come true. Someone in the family would die in the coming conflict, maybe.

"It's possible," Alex replied to Maria, his voice soft. "That is often the way of things. But what you see is not always set. There is room for change if people are willing and you help them to see. In time, I will show you how. But in the meantime, you will be safe. That I promise."

A hard knock on the door interrupted. Nikki immediately grabbed her Kali sticks.

Alex took the Kali sticks from Nikki and motioned for both Maria and Nikki to stand behind him.

He carefully approached the door and looked through the peephole—a nervous looking bald man stood outside, his eyes constantly scanning the hallway. Alex noted that he was not armed, and his movements were not those of a man trained to threaten others. Alex put the chain on the door and opened it three inches.

"Alex Luthecker?" Mark Kirby asked.

"Who's asking?"

"I've been trying to contact you. I know who you are, and I know what you can do. I'm not exactly sure what you can tell about who I am and why I'm here by simply looking at me. It's probably everything, but I'm going to say it anyway—I can help you. But more important than that, I need your help—to save the world."

YAW SAT on his aluminum prison bunk, legs crossed and back straight. He tried to focus on his meditative mantra. He tried to push aside the anger he felt at himself for not seeing the danger during the rescue attempt. He should have been able to see the events before they began to unfold like Alex had taught him. He was mad at himself for letting down the refugees. He was mad at himself for letting down his friends.

Unable to concentrate any longer, Yaw slowly opened his eyes and looked around his cell. It was enclosed concrete, eight feet by eight feet square, with a metal cot, toilet, and sink. The door, also metal, had a solitary food slot. A flickering halogen bulb above provided the only illumination.

There was palpable dampness in the air, humidity that made the skin feel sticky. This clamminess also gave a musty, heavy feel to the atmosphere that—when combined with the relentless smell of the previous inmates' sweat, blood, and urine—rendered the air almost unbreathable.

It was also dead silent. That was perhaps the most disturbing part to Yaw. The complete lack of sound was disorienting—added to the fact that there was no sense of day or night. Isolation was considered torture in nearly every corner of the world, and Yaw knew he would have to rely on his training to keep sane.

He closed his eyes, sat up straight, with his legs crossed in front of him, and focused on his meditation again. He chanted louder this time, the Buddhist mantra Alex taught him as a way to quiet his thoughts echoing off the concrete walls.

The sound of a bolt sliding back on his cell door caused him to open his eyes.

"JUST GIVE us a full run down on your operations, and we'll set you free," the man in the suit and badge said.

Yaw studied the man who sat across from him at the steel table for several seconds. He was white, soft featured, with perfect black hair. His hands were smooth. He had neither the build nor the mannerisms of a field agent. He was a pencil pusher. A negotiator.

Yaw looked to the one-way mirror and had a strong inclination about the type of person who would be on the other side. Behind that one-way was the harder elements of Coalition Assurance. The ones trained in the art of brutality.

Yaw understood that if the man sitting across from him did not get what he wanted, the next man to interrogate him might not leave him alive. Yaw looked at his wrist chained to the table, before looking back to the Coalition agent.

"And I want one other thing," the agent added. "The whereabouts of one Nicole Ellis."

Yaw's face showed a flash of confusion.

The agent didn't miss the look. "I know what you're thinking. Why aren't they asking about Alex Luthecker?" the man in the suit and badge added. "I can officially inform you that we're not interested in him now."

Yaw kept his cool, and stayed quiet.

"I know you think you're protecting your friends. And that you can survive this place. You're a big, physical guy. But the Vietnamese kid. He might not fare as well. And those refugees? Well—deported is about the nicest thing that's going to happen to them. So what do you say?"

Yaw finally spoke. "Lawyer. That's what I say."

"Not going to happen. You're a person of interest, suspected of terrorist activity. And being off grid works against you here, big time. If you're not part of the system, you can't really rely on the system, now can you? Which means you'll disappear if I say so. Just another black man up to no good, found shot on the street."

Yaw remembered his training and did his best to show no emotion. He also thought back to his brother's incarceration many years earlier. How quickly things had escalated. How, for African American men, the penal code was a death spiral.

Once a black man was in the system, he was enslaved by it. In order to stay safe from the law, people of color had to err on the side of caution. Always. Walking down the wrong street at the wrong time could end in death. Say the wrong thing to the wrong person? Do time in jail. It was an undercurrent of threat felt by all minorities in America.

Yaw's brother's difficulties with the law had made him hyper aware. And yet, despite that diligence, here he was. *If you rebel, the system will find you,* he thought. He decided to play along, at least for the moment. He would bait the agent, try to buy time, try to extract information himself that may prove useful later.

"You know the last time, the last two times y'all messed with Alex, it didn't end well for you. What makes you think it's gonna be different this time?"

"You are referring to Alex Luthecker. As I told you, we have no interest in him. He's free to go about his business. But Ms. Ellis, we need to speak with her."

"It didn't work out for the guy who tried that angle either."

"She's going to want to talk to us."

"About?"

"National security issues. You tell us where to find her, you and the refugees are free to go."

Now the agent was baiting Yaw.

Yaw would give the man nothing. "I don't know where she is. And the one thing I have confidence in is my friends. So do what you have to. 'Cause you're right—in the system, I will survive. And Joey's been training. He's tougher than he looks. So if you're gonna kill me, go on and do it now. I ain't afraid."

"WE'RE GOING to deport her, your Russian friend," the man in the crisp navy suit said to Chris. "And you'll never see her again."

"She has papers."

"ICE has full power now to deport anyone at any time, for any reason. Papers don't matter anymore."

"Masha can take care of herself. She's done it all her life. What are you charging me with?"

Chris instinctively pulled against the handcuff that chained him against the steel table. He wanted nothing more than to put his hands around the Coalition agent's neck. And regardless of his words, he was very concerned for Masha. Nikki had arranged green card status for Masha, with the help of PHOEBE. Chris hoped that those papers were still valid.

"We're not charging you with anything just yet."

"That's because you have nothing. Because I, *we*, have done nothing illegal."

"You were trafficking in illegals."

"That's a lie and you know it. We found those people. They were being sold into slavery, and we were setting them free."

"The truth is what we say it is. But there's a way out for you. Where's Nicole Ellis?"

Chris thought it odd that they were asking about Nikki. Still, he showed no reaction.

"I have no idea."

The man leaned in to Chris, motioned him close. "I'm going to level with you. Because we don't have time, and all of you, well, you're all acting the same and it's getting us nowhere. We are not concerned with Alex Luthecker. But we need to find Nikki Ellis. We need her to stop her program PHOEBE. Because it's wreaking havoc in cyber-systems worldwide, and we need to stop it before it literally starts the apocalypse."

17

SHUT DOWN

JEFF BILLINGS WALKED THE FLOOR OF THE REFINERY CHECKING GAUGES. He was nearing the end of his shift. It was Thursday night and he was bone tired and ready to go home. He only had his last rounds to do, and then he was off for the next three days. He planned on going fishing with his brother. He couldn't wait.

Jeff had worked for Coalition Refineries for over a decade. He worked hard from day one, and his efforts had not gone unnoticed. His career at Coalition Refineries began fresh out of high school where he started as an operator, responsible for the desalter unit, a complex piece of equipment that rids crude oil of natural salts before it enters the next stage of refining. It was a critical step not only for the quality of the product, but also for the life of the machinery.

Jeff was pulled from floor operations and put on a management track early on. He climbed the ladder fast, adapting well to the administrative life, but he still loved the technical side of the business. Whenever Jeff spoke of the details behind the crude oil refinery process, he spoke of them with pride. Now he was a process engineer manager, responsible for leading the efforts of over twenty operators, as well as overseeing the quality of the product and the maintenance of the facility. If there were any equipment related problems in his sector, it was Jeff's responsibility to solve them.

He'd been a P.E.M. of Coalition Refinery #7, the Coalition's third largest refinery, for the past two years. Located in Louisiana, #7 as it was called, refined over five hundred thousand barrels of crude oil a day. The facility itself was over three hundred acres of pipes, tanks, warehouses, and refinery equipment. It was all computer controlled with state of the art technology, and other than a few minor technical issues, Jeff's time in management had been a problem-free tenure.

There had been an enormous spill on the previous manager's watch, one that had caused considerable environmental damage, and it had cost that man his job. But for Jeff, the disaster had created opportunity. He just had to keep things running smoothly, which, with the upgraded technology, wasn't too hard.

Jeff's end of shift routine was easy. He'd simply check all readouts of his sector, engage in a bit of small talk with his men, and then go home. It was a relatively stress-free job and one that paid well. And he was lucky to have it. The computer systems did most of the work these days, and his crew kept getting smaller and smaller. It was only a matter of time before Jeff's job would also be automated, and he knew it. But Jeff was in good with the boss, and he had been reassured that his job was safe for the foreseeable future. Jeff had no reason to suspect that today would be different from any other day.

His first indication that things would be otherwise was a pipe shudder that shook the whole of building seven, followed by the eardrum breaking sound of an alarm.

Jeff dropped his clipboard and ran toward the control booth.

"It's shutting off, all of it," said Bill Caldwell, one of Jeff's senior operators.

Jeff entered the control room and watched as Bill desperately hit buttons on the control board to no effect.

Both men froze as the building shuddered once again, several pipes throughout the refinery shaking this time, setting off a multitude of alarms.

"Dear Jesus. Jeff, look at this," Bob said to his boss.

Jeff looked to the control panel. There were a dozen display monitors, all showing the same words: GET OUT. NOW.

"What the fuck do we do?" Bob said.

"Get out now, don't you think? Tell everyone—get out of the building. Do it now," Jeff said, before sprinting out of the control room and onto the refinery floor.

The refinery floor was pandemonium. Operators were in a panic as the refinery operations slowly ground to a halt.

"Everyone out. Get out now," Jeff screamed as he ran in the opposite direction from the exit.

Jeff knew what was happening, even if he didn't know why. Something had gone horribly wrong, something dangerous, and the emergency shutdown of the refinery had been activated.

He knew what would happen next. The doors would seal shut, trapping the workers inside the building. He had to get to the operations booth above the floor to stop it.

Jeff ran across the refinery floor and hustled up the steel ladder to the crosswalk that led to the operations booth. When he arrived, all the lights in the facility started going out.

He scanned over the facility from the higher vantage point, and his eyes went wide when the darkness revealed a small fire at the base of the largest pipe, the pipe responsible for bringing in fresh crude.

He had less than five minutes before the emergency doors would shut, trapping those left to face a fiery death. Jeff would not let that happen.

He ran inside the operations control booth, only to find another operator working the controls.

"What the hell is going on?" he yelled.

"Everything's shutting down," the operator yelled back.

"Is it the fire?"

"I can't say. But the computer systems are dead. They're not responding to any commands or overrides."

"What about backups?"

"Nothing's working, Jeff. We're losing everything."

"The doors are closing in less than three minutes. We've got to get out."

Jeff didn't need to say it twice.

Both men hustled out of the operations booth, climbed down the ladder, and sprinted across the refinery floor.

Jeff could see the large bay doors up ahead. They were beginning to close.

"Let's go!" he yelled, as both he and the operator sprinted toward the door as fast as their legs would move.

Jeff got to the door first and waited for the operator to squeeze through. Jeff immediately followed—the doors ripping through his shirt and deep into his skin because he barely fit through—before the doors closed behind him. He was out.

Jeff did a quick head count. He sighed in relief as he confirmed all of his men had made it out of the building. The sound of emergency vehicles fast approaching provided a small sense of relief.

Bill Caldwell approached, his face covered in sweat. "Everyone got out."

"Thank God. And the crude?"

"Contained. No leaks."

"What the hell happened, Jeff?"

Jeff looked over the building. Wisps of black smoke drifted from several vents. "I have no idea."

18

OBSERVATION

"He has located the target," Ostap Kosylo said into his secure cell phone. The burly Russian stood in the alley between abandoned buildings on Terminal Island.

It was not the first time the Russian had visited abandoned military towns. Kosylo had once chased enemies all the way to Murmanskaya, a Northern Russian province that housed an abandoned Soviet military base, on the Kolsky peninsula. That base was in far greater disrepair than Terminal Island, where he currently stood. For Kosylo, this operation should be easy.

"Are you sure?" the Barbarian asked, his voice booming loud enough for Kosylo to cover the phone.

"Yes I am sure. I saw him in the window."

"Is he alone?"

"No. There is a young girl. Maybe ten years old. She moved to the window. And it was Luthecker who moved her away."

Kosylo looked at the small black and white security photo of Alex Luthecker.

"Who is the girl? Did she see you?" the Barbarian asked.

"I do not think she saw me. I do not know who she is. They rescue refugees. She is perhaps one of them. Do you want me to go in and get him?" Kosylo prompted.

"No. We want Luthecker's cooperation, and that cannot happen if we appear to threaten the child in any way. Continue to observe. Find out who else is with him. But stay with Luthecker. Report back to me with any movements. We want to avoid the appearance of hostility. We want him alone before we approach him," the Barbarian answered.

The line went dead before Kosylo could respond.

"SHE'S the girl from Mexico, isn't she?" Kirby asked, in reference to ten-year-old Maria. The young girl's gaze had spooked Kirby.

"She's not your concern," Alex answered. He nodded at Nikki, and Nikki ushered Maria out of the room.

Kirby turned back to Alex with fascination. "You're a hard man to find."

"Well you've found me. Now what do you want?"

"Did you anticipate this meeting? Was it inevitable in your mind? Is that why you let me in? Do you see patterns simultaneously in the macro and micro scale?"

Alex didn't answer.

Kirby took a deep breath to calm his nerves. He was rattling off questions, and he could feel himself starting to sweat. "Of course you anticipated this. Otherwise, you wouldn't have opened the door. When you look at me, what do you see?"

Alex examined Kirby for several seconds, his eyes moving over the scientist's every nuance with ravenous intent.

In Kirby, Alex saw both opportunity and threat. The scientist had a heightened awareness of Alex's abilities. Unlike the self-affirming ideologies that former Coalition CEOs Richard Brown and James Howe possessed, Kirby used that heightened awareness with adherence to the self-correcting nature of scientific principle. This masked his true intent.

In other words, despite having rigid goals, Kirby was willing to learn new things. On one hand, for Alex, that made Kirby a bit of a tougher read. On the other, it made Kirby more amicable to change.

"That was incredible what you just did with your eyes. Is that a conscious act, or is it reflexive?"

"A better question would be is it trained or untrained."

"I think I already know the answer to that."

"I'll ask you one more time. What do you want from me?"

"You couldn't get that information? From reading me?"

"I find that personal narrative provides additional insight."

"So you're doing this old school. Like a lawyer. I was hoping we could avoid all that psychological chess."

"You made the first move by attempting to test me."

"Fair enough. I apologize for the cheap shot. I'll get right to it. You probably already know from your own large-scale pattern recognition and your five minutes examining me why I'm here. The next great extinction is upon us. My first question to you is whether or not that fact is irreparable."

"Too many variables for a clear pattern to emerge."

"So even you have limits."

"I'm only human."

"Then what does your gut tell you? Or is there a place in your calculus for trusting instincts considering your ability to recognize patterns?"

"My instincts tell me that every person matters."

"That's very Buddhist of you and perhaps reassuring to those who don't like to look at the big picture. But I think you're holding out. The patterns I can measure say it's a near certainty, so unfortunately I don't have time for the psychological tit-for-tat with you. I sincerely want to do everything I can to stop our species from going extinct, and to do that, I believe that I need your help. And I have faith that you see that sincerity in me."

"You work for the Coalition."

"Yes I do."

"The momentum of their efforts and the ideologies that are

behind their actions are a root cause in much of what you seek to stop."

"I know. It's a very old ideology, the one where people believe in their superiority over others in order to justify enslavement for profit and empire. It's very hard to unseat once it's established itself. But I believe we can work around it."

"I believe differently than you."

"I don't have your gifts of insight. I just do what I have to in order to accomplish what I need to in the world I live in now. Look, the Coalition is a compensation scheme for a handful of greedy men, like any other large-scale corporate structure these days. Money and power are their only goals and therefore their biggest weaknesses. And right now, they have assets I need to accomplish my goals. It's that simple."

"And you think that by knowing all this, you can outmaneuver them. And somewhere in your mind, your ego wants to see if you can outmaneuver me as well. You think only you can accomplish what you seek, and to you, what you seek is all that matters."

"Isn't that everybody on some level? And I'm not trying to outmaneuver anyone. Look, I'm not hiding anything. Read both my fate and intentions if you want. I'm not afraid to reveal myself to you. I'm one hundred percent sincere to my goal, and I have no choice but to play the hand that I've been dealt. If turning you in to the Coalition helped me reach my goal, I'd do it, but I don't believe that's the case. Maybe that's what you're reading when you look at me."

"You confuse belief with truth."

"And the truth is in the eyes of the beholder. Just look at religion and how it's twisted to propagate outright lies. People want to believe in something more than they want to know the real truth about themselves or the world that they create. Isn't that exactly what you force them to face?"

"People want to be heard."

"Enough with the Yoda crap. There are scientific explanations behind your abilities, and I know what they are. I know exactly where you come from and why you have your unique abilities. If you help me, I'll help you."

"I don't need your help."

"I think you will."

"Things won't work out like you've planned."

"So you're saying you know how things will work out? I'm involving you now, whether you like it or not, so how can you know if you yourself are involved? That's a mathematical impossibility. Do you want to know why?

"It's the Schrodinger's cat paradox. To observe is by definition to change. And because of this the observer can't observe himself. In the end, there are mathematic explanations for everything. Even you. It's all cause and effect, and for every cause there's the potential for unintended effect.

"People live in denial of the unintended. You have the ability to see this unintended mission creep of people's choices and hold them directly accountable for it. It's what's got everyone so scared of you. Scientific method accepts cause and effect too, you know. We just see it as a natural law and not some dogmatic form of magical thinking."

Kirby started to sweat again. But this time, he didn't care. He kept going.

"But I'm glad that you brought up my plan, because technically I haven't planned an outcome. Science doesn't work like that. It simply measures and adapts its conclusions based on constantly refining its analysis of new data. It's self-correcting, not self-enforcing like politics or religion.

"That's why we're so fucked. The self-enforcing nature of politics and religion mixed with greed and money is a goddamn death spiral that'll inevitably lead to our extinction. But *you* can break that pattern of behavior. Seeing patterns is your thing, and *that's* why I'm here. That's why I think that together, you and I, we can save the world."

"And you want nothing from this personally? You're not looking to profit in some way?"

"If money's there I'll grab it, sure. I'm no different. There's no crime in that. And there is no power without ego. Not even in your case. Or do you think you're different than everybody else? That you're all that different from me?"

Luthecker didn't answer.

"Look—extinction is imminent. The data keeps showing it with more and more clarity. You're trying to change the world, aren't you? Well I'm trying to save it. We're on the same team. I'll either fail or I won't, but wouldn't helping me accomplish my goals fit in with yours? You can't change the world if no one's left on it, can you?"

Kirby felt like he was on a roll. Something about being examined by Luthecker, with the soothsayer's incredible ability to record every detail, had liberated the scientist. Kirby felt like he'd never thought or spoken with such clarity of mind before. He felt that in many ways, he was every bit Luthecker's equal.

Kirby decided to push further. "But since you brought up ego, let's be honest here. You'd like to take them down, wouldn't you? The Coalition. Well, help me with what I want, and I can help you with that.

"I know what you're thinking—this guy's not loyal to anything. He'll turn on the people he works for, so he can't be trusted. But you see, I can be trusted, because I've been very clear on my goal. Stop the extinction of our species. That's what I am loyal to. And if it takes bringing down the Coalition then so be it. Now what do you say?" Kirby crossed his arms, self-satisfied.

He watched Luthecker for signs of what the young man was thinking.

Luthecker was a stone. So much so that when Luthecker spoke next, Kirby nearly flinched.

"I have friends who have been arrested by Coalition influences. I want them and the refugees that they rescued freed immediately. Do this and I'll help you."

Kirby could hardly contain his excitement. He knew he had Luthecker on the hook now. Between his deal making with the Coalition CEO and the legendary Alex Luthecker, Kirby felt like he was a real player. For the first time in his life, he felt empowered and in control.

"That's why you're being so quiet," Kirby finally responded. "That's why you're not ripping me apart like you're file says you like to do to with powerful people like me. You want something from me. You *need* me."

"I do think we can help one another. But it starts with this gesture."

"I can do that. I'll make the call. Consider it done."

"And one more thing. I want to meet my second biological mother."

"As expected and already in the works. I'll arrange for your friends to get out first. I'll spin it as a way to get close to you, and I'll have my friends in the press start snooping into their illegitimate arrest in order to dial up the pressure. I'll go out on a limb like this to prove to you that you can trust me, as long as you understand my loyalties are to the survival of the species. And then you can help me with what I want. Do I have your word?"

"Yes. You do."

"You have to let them go," Kirby said into his cell phone as he paced across the living room of his Studio City apartment.

He had been smart enough to leave his cell phone at home so his movements wouldn't be traced, but it had taken him nearly three hours riding on his Vespa scooter, dodging followers, to get back to his apartment after his meeting with Alex Luthecker.

"Why would I do that?" Turner asked. He was beginning to regret the deal he had made with Kirby.

"First, because you're repeating the same pattern of mistakes that the CEOs before you did, and it's going to have the same result, getting you clobbered in the press. And that will lead to investigations, which if you are not careful, will lead you to a cell right next to your predecessor James Howe.

"Second, these people are inconsequential, so why are you bothering with them? Luthecker is the only one who matters, and this will only serve to make things more difficult with him.

"And third, the most important reason is because I told him I could make it happen."

"What?" was the only word Turner could manage to say. He couldn't believe what he was hearing. "You fucking talked to him? And you didn't think to tell me right away?"

"Yes, I did speak with him. I'm telling you now, and only because I have to. Don't you remember what we talked about in our last conversation? About trusting me, and you not knowing these kinds of details?"

"You know I've thought about having you killed."

"I'm sure you have, and you wouldn't be the first. But that won't help you. Look—if you let his people go, it establishes trust between he and I, and that's much more important than keeping his friend's captive on some trumped up charges, which will only cause you problems in the long run. And once you've let them go, he's already agreed to help me, and that gets me one step closer to my goal, the one that we discussed.

"Remember, the goal is to get him to come in voluntarily and help *me*. And when he does, Nicole Ellis will be right behind him, and you'll have them both. Does that make sense to you now?"

Turner hated to admit it, but what Kirby said did make sense.

At least Turner was one step closer to having Luthecker in hand, and the Coalition leader could always come in heavy whenever he wanted. He reminded himself what he had told the board about patience and calm.

"Fine. I'll let them go. It'll be more productive to monitor their movements anyway," Turner finally replied. "But if this doesn't end with Luthecker and Ellis in my hands soon, it ends with your head on a stick."

⌇

155

YAW REACTED to the sound of the heavy dead bolt on his cell door being pulled back and the door being opened.

He shielded his eyes from the sudden brightness and tried to focus on the guard filling the doorway.

"On your feet," the guard said.

"ARE YOU GUYS ALRIGHT?" Was the first thing Yaw asked as he approached his small cluster of friends standing close together in the prison parking lot.

"We're good," Chris Aldrich answered, although his eyelids were heavy from lack of sleep.

Yaw looked over at Masha. Under the disheveled countenance, her confident ferocity remained.

"I know Russian hotels that are worse," Masha said in response to Yaw's look.

"What happened? Why the sudden release?" Chris asked.

"Someone must've made a phone call," Joey Nugyen responded.

"Or they choose to let us go so that they may watch us," Masha added.

"So who got us sprung? And why?" Chris asked.

"I don't know," Yaw replied. "But Alex would."

"That may be what they want. Us to lead them directly to him," Joey said.

"They kept asking me about Nikki," Chris explained.

"Yeah, me too," Yaw agreed. "Said there's some apocalyptic level shit going on with PHOEBE they want to bring her in for."

"They mentioned this to me as well," Masha added.

"It's about PHOEBE," Yaw decided.

"So we can't reach out to Alex, Nikki, or use PHOEBE, or we risk leading the Coalition right to them. How do we make contact?" Chris asked.

"By going back to square one," Joey Nugyen said.

They all looked at him.

"Doing what we do best. We all started as off-grid couriers, right? Untraceable, hand-to-hand only messaging? Write down what you want to say to Alex on a piece of paper, I'll run it through my channels, and we can get this conversation going right under the Coalition's noses, just like we used to."

19

SOLDIERS

OFFICER DINO RODRIGUEZ HAD TO LAUGH AS HE LOOKED OVER THE group of people gathered together at Winn Germaine's gravesite. That bizarre fate-predicting wizard-boy Alex Luthecker was smarter than the patrol officer thought.

Rodriguez quietly did a quick head count, and it looked to be thirty-four people. He was unsure if more would come. They were all here to pay their respects to a recognized member of the Los Angeles community—and to let Rodriguez know they were available any time Alex Luthecker needed them.

Rodriguez recognized several members of the LAPD, many of them young and idealistic, unspoken members of the Blue Curtain. This was contrasted by several retired gang members, graying or bald, with faded tattoos, all having left their criminal pasts to become active members in their community.

It was an uneasy truce that began at the martial artist's funeral, a truce driven by common purpose—to free slaves and make the world a just place for all.

"Are we safe here?" Ellen Levy asked Rodriguez. "I mean this is right out in the open."

"We're all just paying our respects to a respected member of the community."

"And being recognized."

"Yes, to one another. And without a word."

Rodriguez turned to Levy. "Tell me you can't feel it in the air."

"I definitely feel something. But how did they know to come here?"

"I don't know. But they were all here for the funeral. Alex said a few words, and it must have resonated. And there's some new faces in the crowd too. Must have spread by word of mouth."

"Why today?"

"Today's the six month anniversary of the funeral. Alex must have known they'd show up for that."

"But how did he know?"

Rodriguez shrugged. "You're going to be asking yourself that question a lot."

Levy nodded to Rodriguez as someone approached. The man looked to be in his late fifties, with the darker skin of Mexican American heritage. He was heavy set, his skin covered in faded tattoos. A bandana of the American flag was wrapped around his baldpate. He stopped directly in front of Rodriguez.

"My name is Javier," the man spoke, his voice rough from age and cigarettes. He held out his hand, and Rodriguez shook it. "You were here at the funeral when the pattern reader spoke."

"Yes I was."

"I heard him speak to you. Maybe I wasn't supposed to hear. But I did. He spoke of...being ready."

"Yes he did."

"His words stayed with me," Javier said. He looked out over the gathering, before looking back to Officer Rodriguez. "They stayed with all of us."

Rodriguez and Levy looked out over the gathering—men and women, young and old. There was a clarity and determination in all their faces.

"Sir, if you could, tell him we are ready."

20

BLOODLINE

SHE SAT NERVOUSLY AT HER KITCHEN TABLE, REFLEXIVELY CHECKING THE clock on the wall. It was now three minutes until 4 p.m. He said he would be here at 4 p.m. He said he would not be late. Her heart raced at the thought of their meeting.

Her name was Miriam, and she was fifty-four years old. He said he was a doctor, and he had found her through her medical records. He had introduced himself as Mark Kirby and said that he had found the man who was genetically ten percent her son. And he asked her if she'd like to meet him?

She remembered the day she volunteered like it was yesterday. In fact, it was twenty-seven years ago. She had answered an ad. She had needed the money. She convinced herself that she was helping a young couple make their child healthy.

She signed papers and never heard from them again. She had gone on and lived her life, working as a nurse. Gotten married. Had two children. Gotten divorced. Moved to a smaller apartment. Worried about money. Worried about her two teenage boys, now in high school. She figured she was average at best.

Miriam had been surprised when she got the call. Occasionally, over the years, she'd wondered what had become of that couple and their child. She wondered if there would be any part of her visible in the child. There had been confidentiality agreements signed, so she never spoke of it, not even to her now ex-husband, not even to her two children. She hadn't even known, until her conversation with Mark Kirby, that the child she had given ten percent of her genetic legacy to was a boy.

At first, she turned down the offer of the meeting, but this Mark Kirby character was very persistent. And he offered her money. There was irony to the offer, as she was in need of money. *Some things never change*, she thought.

She had shared her genetic material so a young couple's child would not carry a genetic defect. That was all that she'd been told. And now she would meet that child. She hoped he would be nice. She hoped that he had turned out okay. She hoped that he'd had a good life thus far. Miriam was unsure what she would say to him when they met.

Miriam jumped at the sound of the doorbell.

$\sim$

"WOULD YOU LIKE SOME TEA?" Miriam asked the young man who sat at her kitchen table. *He's handsome*, she thought. He had the same color eyes as her father. She wondered if those eyes came from her.

"No, thank you," Alex replied.

Alex looked over the kitchen area of Miriam's two-bedroom apartment. The dining table was worn and used, with Miriam being its third owner. She was frugal but clean, as evidenced by the neatness and order of her home. The paint on the wall, a faded yellow that had last seen a touch up fifteen years ago, showed no signs of peeling or stains. He could tell she took pride in its appearance despite its simplicity.

The evidence of two teenage boys was present—from the faint masculine odor to the backpack in the hallway to the boxes of Pop Tarts on the counter to the athletic sneakers neatly assembled near the entrance. As she sat back down at the table, Alex took several seconds to read every fiber of her being.

Her life oscillated between hope and despair. The lines on her face showed the wear of multiple disappointments, yet the glimmer in her eyes remained resolute. The hope revolved around her two sons and their futures, which were her primary motivation.

Like most mothers who had limited means, she always had an eye toward her children's prospects, which gave her the emotional resources to see to it that things for her family remained as stable as her strength of mind could create.

Her mannerisms struck a faint familiarity to Alex, something he couldn't quite place the origin of, which was rare for him. To Alex, the combination of faint familiarity combined with an inability to read the origin could only mean one thing—this person was already connected to him.

For the first time, not knowing the origin of a detail was a comfort to Luthecker. It was the only part of her that didn't fit a readable pattern to him, the part that was potentially a faint trace connection to him.

This small mystery made him smile. It was a mystery he would covet and keep precious, a feeling he would store in the deeper recesses of his memory to examine any time. He realized this feeling of comfort with the unknown, and the awareness of it, was in part why he was here. But there would be nothing else for him to find.

He knew that the reason he could do what he could do, read the patterns of people's lives, did not come from Miriam. He realized that whatever block chain of DNA they shared was not different from what would normally pass from generation to generation. It had not proactively formed him, as Kirby suspected.

Correlation is not causation, and there was little more than correlation here. He had suspected this would be the case before he came to visit, but he still felt it would provide closure of sorts to meet her.

Now that he'd met her, he knew for sure there was no connection between Miriam and his abilities. But it was not because of what he saw in Miriam that Alex believed his pattern reading skills were not created in a lab—it was because of his encounters with Maria.

"So, what do you do for a living?" Miriam asked Alex, interrupting his train of thought.

He could tell she was nervous.

Kirby looked back and forth between Luthecker and Miriam. He had promised Luthecker that he would let the conversation be organic between ten percent mother and son, and it took considerable will on his part to refrain from interjecting or trying to steer the dialogue in any particular direction.

"I don't have a conventional job," Alex answered.

She found his voice soothing. Something about his way made her feel at ease.

"He's a therapist," Kirby interjected.

Alex shot him a look.

"Sort of. I'm sorry. This is between you two. I won't interrupt again. I promise."

Alex looked back at Miriam.

"A therapist? How exciting. What kind? I've always wondered what it would be like to have a therapist. Someone you could talk to, someone you could say anything to who could help you change things about yourself that you don't like. Maybe you could give me some advice?" she asked, surprised at herself for asking, her tone half joking and half hoping Alex would say yes. She really did find his presence disarming.

Alex gave her a Cheshire grin. Little did Miriam know, but with that one question, her life was about to change forever.

"I just might be able to help you," he said.

21

CONTACT

RIKA MURANAKA PULLED HER BASEBALL CAP LOW ON HER FOREHEAD when someone walking into the Starbucks. Sitting in the back of the store, she hunched low in her chair before daring a glance at the entrance.

She saw that the man who had just entered was in his early twenties, wearing a suit and tie. She noted that his eyes were glued to his cell phone. He paid her no mind as he got in line to order his coffee. Based on his mannerisms alone, the man did not strike Muranaka as the Coalition Assurance mercenary type.

Still, he was using an iPhone, which automatically scanned for and enabled WiFi, so she used the tracing software on her laptop to locate and tap into his phone. She quickly scanned his contacts and text messages and crossed referenced them with the Coalition personnel database. It came up empty. His current text message conversation was with his girlfriend, arguing over dinner plans.

Muranaka logged off his phone, the man having no idea she had just eavesdropped into his life. Muranaka shook her head at how easy it would be to turn his world upside down. All the passwords to his bank accounts, his social media accounts, his work files, all were extremely vulnerable, all through his phone. She could have easily emptied his bank accounts, catfished his social media, put his personal information out for the whole world to see, all while sipping a coffee at Starbucks.

People should be terrified, she thought to herself, at how easy it is to steal their information. That's why Muranaka, and people like her, always used encryption programs to protect their devices and almost never used public WiFi.

She checked the other phones located in the coffee shop one more time to make sure there were no Coalition connected individuals in or near the store. There were none, at least none that were carrying electronic communication devices.

Sitting at the back of the coffee shop, she had positioned herself to have a good view of the front door. If Coalition Assurance hit men were wise enough to leave their phones at home and came in searching for her, she could simply claim to be working on her laptop. If they checked her laptop, they'd find nothing incriminating, other than the spy software, which was Coalition developed property that she helped create and was authorized to use.

Muranaka also had several burner laptops she kept ready to use in public places, just in case. And if Nicole Ellis actually did show up, they could move to a more secure location.

The email from Nicole Ellis had come to Muranaka as a complete surprise. Ellis, whom she had never met, reached out to her via an encrypted server and asked for the face-to-face meeting. Muranaka had been running an analysis on PHOEBE at the time in an attempt to find patterns in its recent behavior. Perhaps Ellis had detected the observation, or perhaps Ellis feared that Muranaka was getting too close.

It was in the middle of this search when Muranaka's email pinged. It was a simple question from Ellis—"Would you like to meet?"

Through a brief encrypted email exchange, they had confirmed each other's identities and agreed upon this particular Starbucks as their rendezvous point. The store's free WiFi was the most leached WiFi in the area, which made cell phone and laptop surveillance relatively easy for both Muranaka and Ellis. This, oddly enough, allowed them to secure the location. If there were police, Immigration Customs Enforcement storm troopers, otherwise known as ICE, or Coalition Assurance hit men anywhere in the area, their cell phones would be a dead giveaway.

The front door opened again. This time a woman wearing a baseball cap—and with guarded mannerisms—entered the Starbucks coffee shop. Muranaka didn't need to scan phones to recognize it was Nicole Ellis.

PHOEBE's creator carefully scanned the seating area until she met eyes with Muranaka.

The two women shared a brief nod, and Ellis approached the table where Muranaka sat.

"So I'm here," Nikki said as she sat down across from Rika Muranaka.

Nikki knew all about Rika Muranaka and her work at the Coalition with Black Widow, and she had fended off Muranaka's efforts to hack into PHOEBE more than once. Nikki knew at some point, when things became more settled with the family, she would be forced to confront her rival. She had no idea it would happen this way.

Nikki took an instinctive look around the crowded coffee shop and pulled her baseball cap lower.

"I've been running ID checks on anyone within a fifty foot radius of that door," Muranaka said, in response to Nikki's movements.

"So have I," Nikki replied. "But Coalition Assurance uses burners. So we can't be here too long."

There was an awkward silence between the women.

Muranaka finally broke it. "So I'm here."

"So am I. You convinced me to meet you. Said I was in grave danger. So what is the Coalition up to now?" Ellis asked.

Muranaka sat back in her chair. "You're the one who asked to meet," Muranaka replied.

The tension between the women went up a notch.

"No, I didn't ask you, you asked me," Nikki replied. "I first got an email originating from an encrypted server saying who you were, that you needed to speak with me, and that my life was in danger."

"I never sent any email like that," Muranaka fired back. "I got an email from you, encrypted, asking if I wanted to meet and that my life was in danger. We went back and forth a couple of times, and you suggested here because of the consistent crowds and the free WiFi."

"I never sent that email. I would have never sent that email."

"Well I never would've sent you anything."

"Yet here we are."

"Here we are."

It was beginning to dawn on both women what had happened. Muranaka spoke first. "Both of our conversations were entirely fabricated. The fact is that neither one of us reached out to the other. PHOEBE did this. She hacked into my personal info to confirm my ID as well as yours. She's out of control. This could become catastrophic and you know it."

"PHOEBE would never hurt anyone."

"How do you know that? Was it you who programmed her to literally stop a robbery in progress? Or was that something else she did on her own?"

"No one got hurt."

"This time."

"The Coalition wants to weaponize PHOEBE. I'll never let that happen," Nikki shot back.

"Tell me how you code it. Maybe I can help you."

"Not a chance. This is a set up."

"It was your program, literally, that set up this meeting between us."

"You don't know that for sure."

"Well it sure as hell wasn't Black Widow. PHOEBE destroyed her."

"You used Black Widow to attack PHOEBE?"

"PHOEBE took down a classified military drone."

"A drone that was trying to kill me and my partner. I'm not going to hand over PHOEBE to the Coalition. That'll never happen."

"The man behind that attack is in jail. Not everyone at Coalition

Properties is a criminal. We do a lot of good work there, and we keep the world safe. Yes, there's always politics when it comes to money. But you have to learn to work around that. We have to live in this reality, not the one we wish we had. We need the scope and structure of the Coalition to handle the complexity of the world's problems. And, yes, there have been mistakes, but we have to change the culture from within, not tear it all down. If you destroy the Coalition, then what do you have? War? People going back to being hunter-gatherers?"

"They've been after me and my friends as well as many innocent people with their weapons for a long time now," Nikki shot back. "There's no more working around entities like the Coalition anymore. They're a war machine by design. Their ideology embraces slavery. And at some point, you have to take a stand."

"You take a high and mighty stand, and yet you use an iPhone, which was built with slave labor from China. I can't believe you actually have the tits to sit there and lecture me."

"I'm not lecturing you."

"The Coalition is just a platform for me, that's all. All that other stuff? That's got nothing to do with the work that I do."

"It doesn't?"

"No. My relationship with the Coalition is no different than yours is with your iPhone."

Nikki had to admit that Muranaka had a point. "I get what you're saying, but what the Coalition does has everything to do with you. You can't separate the two. Look, I used to be a commodities trader. I specialized in the energy sector. Oil. I convinced myself that energy connected us all, and I used that as a way to shield myself from the bad things my firm and my industry did."

"I know you're background. You lost a lot of money, and you quit."

"I saw a terrorist attack on an oil refinery kill people and the only thing everyone in my office was concerned about was how much money we were losing. That's why I left. At some point, you have to say enough is enough."

"And yet you created your software program, which could literally bring the world to its knees."

"It didn't start that way."

"Nothing ever does. Not even the Coalition. So why do you think your software program put you in front of me? The Coalition's lead programmer?"

"I don't know. How long have you been ghosting PHOEBE?"

"Six months. And admit it. I've gotten close."

"Maybe too close. Maybe all it's done is make her stronger. Maybe your efforts are the reason she's beginning to think on her own."

"What do you mean?"

"All the efforts of the Coalition managed to do was strengthen her defenses. And it's reached the point where she had to finally put their best in front of me."

"To what end?"

"Well, you've been attacking her constantly. Maybe she wants me to physically get rid of you."

"Maybe it's the other way around."

Muranaka got to her feet. Nikki did the same. Nikki found herself instinctively flexing her hands in preparation for conflict.

Nikki had trained hard with Alex, and she knew that Muranaka would be no match for her. Then she shook off the insanity of that thought.

"This is fucking stupid," Nikki said. "We're women, and we don't do this kind of shit. I don't know why PHOEBE put us in the room together, but there had to be a reason, and one of us killing the other sure as hell isn't it."

"Agreed."

Nikki suddenly had an idea. "Have you been followed?"

"Not that I know of."

"Is your lap top bugged?"

"It's a burner."

"Your phone?"

"The same. You know this ain't my first rodeo when it comes to tech security, right?"

"Fair enough, but we need to get out of here and go completely off grid. Are you in shape?"

"Don't be a bitch."

"We're going to move fast on foot, and I need to know if you can keep up."

"Don't worry, I can keep up with you."

"Good. We'll do switch backs through some alleys, move through some building basements, then hit some lanes that I know the CCV cameras are down. We should be fine. But the phone and the laptop, even that iWatch, anything with an electronic signal on your person —it all has to go."

"Why? Where are you taking me? To PHOEBE?"

"Not yet. Before we get to that, I need to know the real you. *You* need to know the real you."

"What the fuck are you talking about? I'm not going anywhere with you."

"I'm going to do you a huge favor."

"I don't need any favors."

"You're going to have to trust me."

"Why should I trust you?"

"Because if I'm right, everything will change for you. It'll be a stunning moment of clarity—about who you really are, why you're really here. I'm taking you to see Alex Luthecker."

22

COURIER MESSAGE

"THAT WAS UNBELIEVABLE WHAT YOU JUST DID," KIRBY SAID TO Luthecker as they exited Miriam's apartment. Kirby could hardly contain his excitement. "I mean, you knew every detail about her life, from beginning to end. And not only that, you showed her. And she saw it. She *really* saw it. It changed everything for her. I could see it in her eyes. It was like a curtain had been lifted. Even her mannerisms were different after the fact. She'll never be the same, Alex. Can I call you Alex?"

Luthecker scanned the hallway of the old apartment building. The two men were alone. They walked next to one another toward the stairwell that would lead them to the alley exit.

"So my theory is, when they swapped out your birth mom's DNA string with Miriam's, they altered your genetic memory—literally altered your genes' *ability* to remember. It turned you into a super computer," Kirby rattled.

"I want to thank you for taking me to meet her," Luthecker replied. "It meant a lot to me. It was important, but not in the way you think it was. And no, your theory about DNA manipulation is not what happened."

Both men stopped walking.

"Then what happened?"

"Nothing. Memory is not wisdom, doctor."

"But what you do is not normal. Your genetic birth situation was not normal."

"You are correct about that. I do have two mothers, and my situation is not normal. And for a long time I thought the same thing you did, that it's what made me different. But now, after meeting Miriam, I know that that is not the case."

"Everything has an explanation, and you're not above that," Kirby countered.

"I'm not saying I am above anything or anyone. No matter what kind of DNA swap was performed to make me who I am, I'm still flesh and blood like everyone else on this planet. I'm still subject to the cycle and mysteries of life, and like everyone else, I'll get old and die. You're missing the big picture."

"Well then explain it to me. How is it that you can do what it is that you do?"

Luthecker took a moment to gather his thoughts. "Have you ever heard of the ancient Polynesian navigators?"

"No. But what do they have to do with you?"

"They have everything to do with me. Just listen. Hundreds of years ago, these Pacific Islanders navigated tens of thousands of miles of ocean with perfect precision in nothing but outrigger canoes. Europeans feared the oceans then, seeing them as menacing and something that must be conquered, but the people of the Pacific looked to the oceans in a very different way. They understood that they as a people were intimately tied to the waters.

"So they studied the oceans every nuance, from movement to sound. They knew the meaning of its every tide, its every wave. It seemed an infinite task, and it took generations. But eventually they understood the relationship of the stars, the moon, the Earth, and the water. They understood that it was all connected, and they sought to understand that connection, and they knew that they were part of that connection.

"To them, being part of and not separate from the ocean was

deeply rooted in their culture. And because of this, they never got lost in the waves. They could travel the oceans with no fear and complete mastery in only outrigger canoes. They handed down this knowledge from father and mother to son and daughter in the verbal tradition, and they understood that passing on that knowledge in that tradition was also part of the connection.

"But when western technology and Patriarchal beliefs separated us from the Earth, told us we were better than the land and the sea and viewed them as something to be conquered, this knowledge was lost."

"So you're saying you're Polynesian now?"

"No. What I'm saying is the memory capacity I have that you think is only capable through some technical innovation with DNA is rooted in the concept of conquering the natural laws, not connecting with them. And that's incorrect thinking. That's incorrect *being.*

"What I can do is something that humans have been capable of since the dawn of time, but only when they worked together. That capacity has been in our DNA all the time. No augmentation is or was ever necessary. And what the oceans were to the Polynesian people, human beings are to me.

"It's been that way since I was a boy. It's just who I am, and I know that now. And I know that it's not an aberration. That *I'm* not an aberration. And meeting Miriam served to confirm what I was already beginning to suspect. That what I can do is necessary and natural in order to help restore balance."

"How did you suspect this?"

"Because I see it in another."

"The girl in your apartment. The one you rescued in Mexico. That's who you're talking about, right?"

"Yes."

"I *knew* it."

"What I can do is not something new. It is not created by some scientific anomaly. Instead, it is something very old, and it exists in all of us on some level. It is an ability whose time was coming again, and that's why it's appearing. Nothing new is learned in this world, it is simply remembered.

"We've repressed our ability to connect with one another and our surroundings as a species. That's what causes many to feel so lost and in pain. It's also what allows those who are most fearful in this world to manipulate those who are most lost."

Luthecker looked at Kirby. "And that manipulation is what I aim to end," he continued. "And if you're sincere in your goal to stop the next great extinction, it starts with recognizing this. It starts with recognizing that we have to reconnect with one another again. Convincing one person at a time, if necessary."

Luthecker moved toward the exit. Kirby thought about Luthecker's words for several seconds before following. Kirby, ever the clinical analyst and never a believer in this kind of nonsense, couldn't help but find Luthecker's words inspiring.

"Every person matters, I remember," Kirby finally replied. "But we're still going to need to change our behavior as a whole to save the species."

The men reached the exit.

"Of course we are. As you've stated in the past, your goals and mine are not in conflict. But do you understand what puts at odds the way you think and the way I do?"

"No, but I have a feeling that you're about to tell me."

"One thing and one thing alone: fear."

"I want you to read my fate like you did to Miriam, like you did to all of those soldiers on the Siachen," Kirby blurted out. "Just like you've done for all of your loyal followers. Just like you've done to everyone you've encountered. I don't understand why you're singling me out on this."

"For some, the weight of their choices destroys them."

"You think I'm afraid I'll collapse under the weight of my own stupidity? I'm not afraid. I don't believe in static definitions of *anything*. I'm willing to learn, and I want to *know*."

"Your path doesn't lie in the same direction as mine."

"It doesn't have to. And I keep telling you, I'm not afraid. Just think of what someone like me could do if I knew what was around the corner."

"I am thinking that. It's what gives me pause."

"Very funny. Can a guy who sees around the corners of the universe even *have* a sense of humor?"

Luthecker stifled a laugh. Then he examined Kirby for several seconds.

"Shit—you know about me already, don't you?" Kirby reacted. "Why won't you tell me? What are *you* afraid of?" Kirby challenged.

"In due time, I will tell you what it is you want to know. If, when this is over, you still want to know it."

Luthecker pushed through the exit and into the alley behind the apartment building. He barely had time to clear the door when an Asian man in his twenties bumped into him.

"Excuse me," the young man said, without breaking stride. In seconds, the young man disappeared around the corner, as if nothing happened.

Luthecker knew exactly who he was and exactly what had happened. He had been given a message. The young man was Vietnamese, Joey Nugyen's younger cousin, and right now Luthecker had a piece of paper with a message in his coat pocket.

The kid is good, Luthecker thought to himself.

"What was that about?" Kirby asked.

"Nothing. We have to go."

Luthecker and Kirby cleared the alley and moved onto the street. Two large men with crew cuts and Slavic features immediately approached.

"Alex Luthecker, my friend," Kosylo said, in the most nonthreatening tone a man with a thick Russian accent could muster. "My name is Kosylo, and this is my friend Mika," Kosylo managed an awkward smile.

"My boss, Ivan Barbolin, who I am sure you know, offers his courtesy and protection and only asks politely if you would perhaps meet with him to speak. It would only be a moment of your time."

The second Russian, Mika, watched the street and stood close to Kirby.

"Do you know who I am? Who I work for?" Kirby mouthed off.

"Yes. We do," Mika said, his accent thick.

"You are not invited," Kosylo said to Kirby. "You can wait here." He then turned to Luthecker. "He is over there, waiting." Kosylo said to Alex, before nodding to a bench across the street.

Luthecker looked over at Ivan Barbolin who sat on the bench looking back at him.

The Russian oligarch nodded recognition like a Mafia Don.

Luthecker did a quick scan of the street. He counted at least a half dozen Russian men guarding the oligarch from strategic points. If anyone made a move on the man known as the Barbarian, they would be dead in seconds.

"A simple conversation is all he requests. Before things get... complicated for us all. What do you say?"

Luthecker looked at Kosylo, at Mika, and then back at Kosylo. He knew that the Russian men's fate dictated they had only moments to live. "I'd say that you're one fatal step behind."

Kosylo tilted his head, puzzled, and that's when he heard helicopter blades, quickly followed by roaring engines and screeching tires.

"Stay close to me. And when the time comes, remember our conversation," Luthecker said to Kirby, before all hell broke loose.

In seconds, the street was filled with four BearCat armored personnel carriers. A Black Hawk helicopter abruptly dropped low and hovered with its gun turrets locking on target. Soldiers simultaneously poured out the back of the BearCats, rifles ready.

Kosylo and Mika drew their weapons, and ran in the direction of their boss, the Barbarian.

The M-16s of the Coalition Assurance officers barked to life, and the bullets cut down Mika and Kosylo before they covered half the distance to their boss.

The Coalition Assurance officers cut down two more Russian

enforcers with their M-16s before the rest, including the Barbarian, held up their hands in surrender.

Both Luthecker and Kirby found themselves facing the smoking barrels of the weapons that, only seconds early, had cut down Kosylo and Mika.

"On the ground, now!" a Coalition soldier screamed at Luthecker and Kirby, the barrel of his AR-16 pointed squarely at Luthecker.

The soldier looked more robot than human, with helmet, goggles, mask, Kevlar vest, padded combat pants and boots, all in black, all designed to be intimidating.

Luthecker glanced at Kirby. The scientist was white as a sheet and shell shocked into silence.

Luthecker held up his hands and slowly dropped to one knee, eyes locked on the soldier. He glanced at the scene and noted every soldier: their looks, their habits, their sizes, their strides, their gates, and their breathing patterns. He noted their every move. He took in the weapons, where they were pointing, and for how long. He took in the vehicles, down to every rivet, every parking angle.

All of it meant something to Luthecker. All of it told a story, an inescapable tale that only he could read. He took note that they were not LAPD. There were no National Guard markings. These misdirects were no longer necessary. Everything was proudly—*unmistakably*—marked with the Coalition Properties, Inc. logo.

23

CHANGE OF PLANS

"I GOT HIM THE MESSAGE," JIMMY NUGYEN TOLD YAW, CHRIS, AND HIS cousin Joey. Masha paced in the background behind them.

"Are you sure?" Yaw asked.

"Positive."

"And no one saw you?" Yaw asked.

"C'mon, man. That's an insult."

"Okay. You're right. What happened after that?" Chris questioned.

"All hell broke loose."

Jimmy Nugyen, his cousin Joey, along with Yaw, Chris, and Masha stood huddled in the empty basement of an abandoned office building in downtown Los Angeles.

They had taken separate routes, wary of CCTV cameras, cell phones, and any other electronic surveillance that could monitor their movements.

It was getting harder and harder to stay disappeared, as Yaw had labeled it. But like Master Winn before him, Alex required that each member of the group, before being considered for courier, must train in stealth. This meant mastering the ability to move through cities without being traced, staying out of sight and off the grid.

It was a skill that Alex had learned well as a teenager, refined under his late teacher Master Winn, and one that he had passed down to the others in his group. Alex had put Yaw in charge of stealth training, and the younger Nugyen's learning curve would be no different from anyone previous.

"Specifics, Jimmy," Joey Nugyen prodded his cousin. "From the beginning."

Despite his training in stealth, the younger Nugyen was still a brand new courier, and this had been only the second message he had been tasked to deliver.

Using a new courier to traffic in off-grid messaging had advantages and disadvantages. The advantage being that the courier was unlikely to be on a watch list, always a possibility the longer one trafficked in unmonitored communication. The disadvantage was an increased likelihood of potential mistakes made.

Joey hoped that the latter was not the case here. He knew that his cousin Jimmy wanted to level up soon and begin martial arts training so he could be part of the crew that actually freed human trafficking slaves. He hoped that Jimmy wasn't out of consideration before he was ever in.

"There were three hand-offs between you and me, couriers that were vetted and trained at my level. I was the last leg. I was supposed to be the one to finish the job, and I did.

"Luthecker came out of the building into the alley just like you said he would. I didn't have to wait long. I saw that there were Russians everywhere right away, but I kept my distance, and they weren't there looking for me, so it was easy for me to slide.

"It wasn't hard to figure out who they were after, so I had to call it. Do I make the drop or not? And I decided it was a go. I had to get him the message, and I didn't think I'd get a second chance, not with those guys lurking. And hey—it's Alex Luthecker we're talking about here, so I figured he knew the situation and how to handle himself."

"Then what happened?" Chris pressed.

"Well, I slid right by the Russians. Like I thought they had no clue, but they weren't the real problem. I did a bump drop and Alex got it so I thought we were good, and I figured he'd just ghost the

Russians, but outta nowhere Coalition storm troopers swooped in. They shot two of the Russians ASAP to shut down any resistance and took everyone else in. It was all over before it started."

"And Alex?" Yaw asked.

"He seemed calm throughout. They put him in the back of a BearCat by himself. They were very careful with him."

"And they never came after you?"

"They didn't see me. I stayed in their blind spot. It was just like you said to do in training—if your enemy focuses too hard on one thing, he misses the other things, and it's among those other things where you hide. So that's what I did."

"And how many others were taken?"

"The big Russian on the bench, who must've been the boss, and a bald-headed guy with the beard that was traveling with Alex. Bald guy looked like he was shitting his pants. Big Russian boss and the pant shitter each got their own BearCat too, just like Alex. The Russian enforcers clearly didn't mean shit so they were all crammed into the last one, at least the ones that were still alive. And the one's that weren't? They just left the bodies out on the street for the buzzards. That was some third world shit right there, man."

"Where do you think they're headed?" Chris asked Yaw.

"They won't be hard to find," Masha cut in. Her tone was confrontational. She already knew who the big Russian was and had an axe to grind. "The Russian boss as you say—what did he look like?"

"Big and Russian."

"Details, Jimmy. We talked about this. And attitude. Dial it down," Joey scolded.

"Sorry," Jimmy replied and took a moment to search his memory.

One of the first training exercises that Joey had personally given Jimmy was memory training, and it included "no screens of any kind for thirty days." It was supposed to clear the mind of clutter and make space for the details of the moment.

Overcoming the addictive and hypnotic effect of digital bombardment proved difficult for everyone, as screens were everywhere, but being screen-free was a requirement for the higher levels of training with the group.

Unfortunately, for Jimmy he loved sneaking off to play Grand Theft Auto, even if it was an older version on an isolated Nintendo console. His lack of focus was showing now, and he had to concentrate hard.

"I'd say he was in his sixties. Big hands. Piercing eyes. Scar on his left cheek."

"The Barbarian," Masha announced, a mixture of dread and fury in her voice. She didn't need to hear more details to know it was her former boss.

"What's he doing in town, sitting out in the open, on a park bench, waiting for Alex? He had to know he was being watched. He had to know that he was going to lead the Coalition right to him. Why would he risk exposure like that?" Yaw asked.

"I do not know," Masha replied. Her Russian accent was thick, and she still habitually avoided vocabulary contractions. "But I do know that the Barbarian is not stupid. This must be a calculated move for him. As in chess."

"And Alex? Why now? Why like this?" Joey asked.

"He's the winner-take-all prize. He always has been. It's an obsession with the Coalition, and he took out Ivan's partner, Lucas Parks. He's right in the middle of it all."

"You're sure he got the message?" Yaw asked Jimmy one last time to be sure.

"Absolutely," Jimmy answered.

"Then you did your job." Yaw put his hand on Jimmy's shoulder. "And we'll be fine."

Both Jimmy and Joey Nugyen let out a sigh of relief. Both men knew it would be Yaw who decided if Jimmy could level up.

"So what's the move now?" Chris asked Yaw.

"We gotta meet with Nikki."

"It's not safe. PHOEBE's down, and we're being watched."

"We're always being watched. We just gotta move old school now."

Yaw turned to the younger Nugyen. "I got another message for you to deliver."

"IS THIS PLACE SECURE?" Muranaka asked Nikki.

Muranaka knew she was risking her job by being here with Nikki Ellis. The Coalition was going after Ellis hard and Muranaka had made promises to its CEO, and it would be very difficult to defend being caught with PHOEBE's creator.

But I can spin easily enough, Muranaka thought. Make it look like she agreed to meet with Ellis in order to access PHOEBE. And that was all true.

However, there was one other thing Nikki offered that was even more interesting to the Coalition programmer. Muranaka was, of course, curious about Alex Luthecker. As a sworn enemy of Coalition Properties, you could not be employed by the firm and not know who Alex Luthecker was and what he had allegedly done.

Muranaka was taking a big risk by being here, not only from her employer, but also from Ellis. The opportunity was worth the risk, however, and she was confident in her abilities to handle Ellis.

Muranaka didn't buy that Ellis couldn't access her own software. Sooner or later, Ellis would have to log in, and Muranaka would be ready. If she could dismantle PHOEBE and help capture Alex Luthecker, she'd be a Coalition hero. For the first time in her life, she'd be able to step out from anyone's shadow.

But even more important to Muranaka than stepping out from shadows was that the young programmer actually wanted *at* Alex Luthecker. She wanted to see if everything she'd heard about him was true. She wanted to test her own wits. She wanted to see if she herself was *smarter.*

"This ain't my first rodeo when it comes to stealth," Nikki answered as she double-checked the windows. "This small apartment in Watts gets screened for bugs along with the entire neighborhood for electronic surveillance. All the CCTV cameras around here are broken, but it's a poor neighborhood so nobody cares. We use that to our advantage. And every person you saw out on the street, walking their dog, whatever—eyes and ears. If someone or something comes this way, we'll know long before it gets here."

"And PHOEBE? When do we try and access her?"

"There's no electronic access of any kind here."

"Why not?"

Nikki paused. "Because the Coalition is more sophisticated than they let on, even to their top civilian programmer. PHOEBE could be piggy backed by your people, leading Coalition Assurance right to me," she finally answered.

"I assured you in our emails, or in PHOEBE's email matrix that put us together, that I would come alone. This isn't my first rodeo when it comes to stealth, either. But I will say this, if I'm gone too long, Coalition Assurance will come looking. But none of that is the real reason you're keeping PHOEBE away from me. If it's like you say, and she won't talk to you, then you're not sure we're safe from her, are you? And you literally don't know what she's going to do next. Am I right?"

Nikki paused a moment before answering. She was unsure exactly how much information she should share with her rival.

"I'm not sure why she's not talking to me," Nikki finally answered. "And I'm not sure why she put the Coalition's top programmer and my biggest rival in a room with me. All of that is true. But if she did it, it's because there's a purpose behind it. And I trust that purpose."

"And you think Alex Luthecker can tell you what that purpose is."

"Maybe."

"You put a lot of faith in this guy."

"I do."

"So where is he then?"

Nikki wished she knew the answer to that question. By her estimations, he should have been back by now.

"He should be here soon," Nikki deflected.

A knock on the door interrupted their conversation.

Nikki checked the peephole and recognized the man standing at the door: Jimmy Nugyen.

Nikki carefully opened the door. "Were you followed?"

"C'mon, what's with you guys? Where's the trust? I know how to ghost, for chrissake."

"Come in," Nikki said, allowing Joey Nugyen to enter the apartment, carefully closing the door behind him.

"Who's this?" Muranaka asked, as she sized up Nugyen.

"Who's this? Who the fuck are you?" Nugyen shot back, before looking at Nikki for answers.

"Rika, Joey, Joey, Rika. Joey's a messenger. Rika's a programmer for the Coalition."

"What the hell's she doing here? She's the enemy," Joey said.

"Says who? You guys are the ones engaged in illegal activity," Muranaka fired back.

Joey took a step toward Muranaka.

Nikki stepped in front of him. "Knock it off. The situation's complicated. Where's Alex? I need to see him right away."

"He's preoccupied at the moment," Nugyen answered, not wanting to get into the details considering the company and never taking his eyes off Muranaka. He finally turned to Nikki, pulling a small piece of paper from his pocket. "This is from Yaw. Your eyes only," Joey said, eyes still on Muranaka as he handed Nikki the small folded piece of paper.

Nikki examined the message. "Shit," she said under her breath, before crumpling up the message and stuffing it in her pocket.

"Change in plans," Nikki said to Muranaka. She turned to Joey. "Tell him I need an hour," Nikki said. "And tell him to come alone."

Margaret Evan's cold had gotten progressively worse throughout the day.

The chills had started in the morning when she woke up, which was in addition to the coughing and sore throat that had started the night before. Now she was so congested she could barely breathe.

Margaret Evans was fifty-nine years old, lived alone in a small apartment with her cat, and she decided that she'd had enough of feeling sick. *It's time to get some Theraflu*, she thought to herself.

She chose Theraflu not because of any brand loyalty, but because she had a 50 percent off coupon from the drugstore, and money was tight for her this month. So she fed the cat dinner from a can of Purina, put on her coat and shoes, and headed out the door for a twenty-minute walk to the CVS Pharmacy.

This CVS was one of the bigger stores in the chain, brand new with over a dozen aisles and security cameras everywhere. The whole store seemed cold and sterile to Margaret, which was why she didn't like coming here unless she had to, but everyone wearing a CVS badge smiled and offered to help her.

In no time, Margaret found herself in the cold and flu section. She saw what she was looking for and approached the shelf where they kept Theraflu stocked. She checked her pocket to make sure she had remembered her 50 percent off coupon. She saw that there was only one box of the medicine left. Margaret took the box and smiled. She felt lucky.

Margaret moved from the cold and flu aisle toward the back of the store, where the food was kept. *A bowl of chicken soup will be good too*, she thought. She found the soup section and picked out a can of her favorite, Campbell's Chicken Soup, on sale for 99 cents. More luck.

Her doctor said the soup had too much salt considering her blood pressure, but she had a bad cold, and in her mind that was enough to justify the extra salt.

Satisfied, she made her way to the front of the store toward the registers. Her head throbbed now, and her throat still hurt, and she couldn't wait to get back home.

She stood patiently in line, and when her turn came, she made sure to pull her 50 percent off coupon from her pocket and hand it to the cashier.

Margaret couldn't help but notice the young man at the register was good looking, perhaps in his early twenties, with perfect hair and a charming smile. *To be young again*, she thought.

He took the box of Theraflu and scanned the barcode on the side of the box, followed by the bar code on the coupon. The register beeped. The teller looked mildly disappointed as he checked the register screen.

"I'm sorry, but the coupon is expired," he said to Margaret, before handing the crumpled piece of paper back to her.

Margaret looked at the coupon, confused. She looked at the expiration date. It was today's date.

"What do you mean it's expired?" she asked, making her throat hurt. Despite the pain, there was still edge in her voice. "It has today's date on it. It should be good through today." Margaret thrust the coupon back in the teller's direction.

The young man tried it again, but with no luck. He handed it back. "I'm sorry," he said again, handing the coupon back. "But the computer won't take it. Says it's expired."

"But it's not."

"I know. It happens sometimes. There's nothing I can do. I'm sorry."

"I want to speak to the manager."

"He's out today."

"This isn't fair."

"I'm sorry, but there's nothing I can do. Do you want the Theraflu or not?"

Margaret felt cheated and thought about making a scene. And she would have if she didn't feel so sick. She didn't care that the security camera seemed to be pointed right at her, just waiting to catch her causing a problem.

"Fine," she finally said. "But you can keep the soup."

She handed the teller a worn debit card, and he swiped it quick before handing it back to her. She hoped that she balanced her bank accounts right, and there would be enough money on it.

The teller's register screen went blank for a second, and the lights throughout the store flickered for several more. When the register screen came back, it showed that the sale had not gone through.

"Can I see your card again?" he asked Margaret.

"What's the problem? Not enough money?"

"No, it just didn't go through."

Margaret reluctantly handed the teller her debit card again.

The teller swiped it a second time and waited.

"Okay we're good," he said. The teller moved to hand Margaret back her card when the register beeped loudly and the screen flashed a message that got his attention: CHECK CARD.

The teller tilted his head in reaction. He'd never seen the register do anything like this before.

"What is it?" Margaret asked.

"It wants me to...check your card."

"Oh Lord, I'm probably outta money. I get paid next week. I promise," Margaret replied, suddenly very worried.

The teller stood motionless, unsure what to do.

"Well you might as well check it," Margaret said, resigned to the fact she'd have to eat Ramen noodles until Friday.

The teller swiped the card. His eyes went wide.

"What?" Margaret reacted.

The teller slowly turned to Margaret. "Says here you have three point six million dollars left on your card."

Margaret almost fainted. She put her hand on the counter to steady herself. "Well, I'll be damned," she finally managed to say.

Now the young teller was really confused. The machine shouldn't be able to share this information. And he'd never seen a debit card with so much cash on it before.

"Um, do you want your card back?"

"Hell, yes."

Margaret had no idea what had just happened, but she snatched the card from the teller's hand with surprising speed.

She quickly grabbed the box of Theraflu as if to make a point and abruptly started walking toward the door, trying hard not to break out into a flat out sprint. She was out the door before she allowed herself to breathe.

Then she broke out in a wide smile. Margaret thought the wind on her face felt good, and it seemed her sinuses were already starting to clear. *It's a blessing from the Lord*, she thought, and she was beginning to feel much better already.

24

ATTITUDE

"How many times are you assholes going to haul me in here?" Kirby asked.

Unlike his previous debriefings from the Coalition interrogators, this time his voice wavered with fear.

The abrupt punch to the back of his head that followed felt like a lightning strike, the shock hitting first, then the pain.

He saw stars for several seconds and fought hard to stay conscious. Then he fought to keep from throwing up.

He looked at his right wrist, which was chained to the steel table he sat behind. Kirby realized for the first time that he was in serious trouble.

Glen Turner kept his eyes locked on Kirby for a reaction, while the two-hundred-and fifty-pound Coalition Assurance enforcer who struck Kirby silently made his way back to Turner's side.

"What was that for?" Kirby asked, his ears still ringing.

"To adjust your attitude. And remind you how severe your situation is," Turner replied.

"I told you on the phone that Luthecker and I had been speaking. But he said absolutely nothing remarkable to me, I swear," Kirby said, his eyes going back and forth between the two men.

"I freed his friends for you, and this is how you repay me?"

"I had him on the hook and was leading him in, but you got impatient. You fuckers blew it."

Turner nodded to the Coalition officer who had hit Kirby, a military cutout in a black suit, and the Assurance officer quietly exited the small room that now only held Kirby, Turner, and the steel table between them.

"I thought we had a deal. Why the hell did you jump me?"

"The situation has changed. I honestly didn't concern myself with what you found before, but now that's over. What exactly did you and Alex Luthecker talk about?" Turner continued.

"You have him now, why don't you just ask him?"

"I'm asking you."

"I took him to see his second mother, like I told you I would. I thought there would be a connection between the two of them, and I could use that connection to confirm my theory, but it didn't go anything at all like I expected. But I did witness what he could do. And it was nothing short of amazing."

"What exactly did he do?"

Kirby took a moment to gather his thoughts. He hadn't really thought about the details regarding Luthecker's exchange with Miriam.

Kirby still hadn't processed how the pattern reader had changed this woman's life, telling her about her reactive upbringing, the abuse she suffered, the patterns of choice and behavior that led to the exact moment of their meeting, followed by the acceptance, and finally the letting go.

It had all happened in an instant and right before Kirby's eyes, only minutes before the Coalition took them into custody.

For a man like Kirby, what Luthecker had done made no logical sense. There was no question that Luthecker's ability to read the most intimate details of Miriam's life, dating all the way back to her early years, was a cognitive skill that was beyond extraordinary.

But it was still a mathematically reproducible skill under the right control conditions. You could essentially program a computer to do it. What didn't make sense to Kirby was Miriam's reaction to the information. She was visibly unburdened, and it was nearly instantaneous.

It was like an absolution and understanding of all her life choices, and with it, the freedom to make new choices and set a new course. And with that freedom was a newfound awareness of outside forces that tried to influence her choices from an early age, some even before she was born.

Granted, Luthecker was charming, and one could never underestimate the human-to-human factor, but Miriam seemed genuinely changed by her conversation with Luthecker. And for the life of him, Kirby didn't understand why.

To Kirby, it was just information, some of it actionable and some of it not.

"I can't explain it," Kirby started to say to Turner. "All I can say is nothing went as I expected. And at the end of the day, he just...told her it was okay to change, and she believed him."

"There are entire industries peddling the kind of nonsense you are describing, and it doesn't work."

"I know."

"Why does it work for him?"

"I don't know."

"Humor me with a guess."

Kirby thought about the question for several moments. "Everyone thinks he can predict the future and game the system for people, but that's completely missing the point. I think his photographic memory, combined with a certain intuitive ability to see collective patterns in behavior, allows him to find the keys that unlock an individual's deeply entrenched perception of themselves. He sees where your choices will lead, both collectively and individually. And with that insight, comes the opportunity to course-correct your life. That's what he does."

"Is that how he expressed it?"

"No. That's how I did. You weren't listening. That's another thing he does well that you don't." Kirby hoped the last statement wouldn't result in another strike to the back of the head.

"Well then how did he explain it? Both his abilities and the allure behind them?"

"He started babbling about Polynesian navigators from hundreds of years ago. All of that's scientifically explainable, but there was something more to it than that."

"Did he read your fate?"

"No."

"Why not? Didn't you ask him to?"

"Of course I did. If only to correct any potential errors in my own decision-making processes."

"And he refused? I thought he played his game with everyone he came across."

"It's not a game."

"Did he tell you why he wouldn't do to you what he's done to everyone else?"

"No. And he didn't say, *never*. He said, in due time. "

"What does that mean?"

"I don't know," Kirby replied. Then something dawned on him.

Turner saw it in Kirby's face. "What?"

"I think I know why. I think I know why he didn't tell me my fate."

"Why?"

"I'm already trying to find patterns in the data. I'm trying to find mechanical explanations for what he can do."

"If you don't start telling me straight answers, I'm going to bring my friend back in here."

"He didn't read the data points that would create my fate because that's what I do all day. He wants something else from me."

"What?"

"He wants me to *believe*."

"Believe what?"

"That we're all connected." Kirby sat back in his chair, as far as the chain on his wrist would allow.

He was dumbfounded by his new revelation. Had Luthecker

played him? Had the pattern reader already predicted the next move only to set up the one after?

"Did you see Nicole Ellis at all during your time with Luthecker?" Turner asked, interrupting Kirby's self-revelation.

"No," Kirby lied. For reasons he couldn't explain, Kirby felt it unwise to bring up that aspect of his conversations with Luthecker.

"Did he mention her at all? Where she might be?"

"No. She never came up."

"Did he express any concern that Ms. Ellis's program PHOEBE was acting out on the public?"

"I wasn't aware that PHOEBE was acting out on the public. Is that why you brought us in? That's interesting if true. But no, Luthecker and I didn't discuss Nicole Ellis, PHOEBE, or their whereabouts, at all. We only discussed his abilities and the world coming to an end. You have Luthecker in custody, why don't you just ask him?"

"It's not that easy."

Kirby grinned. "You don't want to be in the room with him, do you?"

"I'll send someone in to get the answer I want."

"Why do you need Nicole Ellis so badly? She's a hacker. It's not like there isn't a bunch of those running around these halls."

"Her program PHOEBE is wreaking havoc. It stopped a robbery in progress. It gifted a woman three million dollars. I've just gotten word that one of our refineries has been shut down. Our hackers say it's only going to get worse, and they can't crack it. If we can't get in front of these problems soon, the extinction you predict is going to happen a lot sooner than you think."

"Let me talk to him," Kirby responded. "He trusts me. I'll find out what it is you need to know."

"You're not afraid he'll see right through you?"

"No. He'll do whatever it is he's going to do, and I'm not afraid of who I am. But the question is, are you afraid of what he'll do to me? That he'll somehow turn me against the Coalition?"

"If that were to happen, Doctor, I simply wouldn't let you leave."

"How reassuring. So it's a go then?"

"Yes. I'll allow it. But only to find out anything you can about PHOEBE and Nicole Ellis, including where she is."

"Fine. But under one condition."

"How about I let you live?"

"Not good enough."

Turner took a deep breath. "What do you want?"

"If I get you Ellis and PHOEBE, you give me Luthecker."

Turner thought about Kirby's offer for several moments before speaking. He thought Kirby hopelessly naïve about whether or not he would keep his word. Turner had no intention of surrendering Alex Luthecker. Or of letting Kirby leave, for that matter.

"You have a deal, doctor."

"WHAT IS THIS BETRAYAL?" the Barbarian roared, rising from the plush leather couch to his feet.

The accommodations inside the Coalition Properties containment apartment were comfortable, if not small. The couch, the bathroom, the refrigerator stocked with food, the small bar stocked with drink, even the bedroom with the king-sized bed and silk sheets would make an unwary guest feel at home, and not like he was in a prison cell.

The fact that the door was steel and the lock only worked from the outside was the giveaway.

"Have a drink, Ivan," Turner said. "And who was betraying whom? Did you think I wasn't watching you? What was your reason for tracking down Luthecker other than to pit him against me?"

"You have no proof of that."

"I have all the proof that I need, old friend." Turner moved to the overstuffed chair next to the couch, and sat down. "Relax, Ivan. This is what we do to one another. We are adversaries, but we are not enemies. At least not yet. So let's not let it come to that. Understand that if I'd wanted you dead, I'd have had my men shoot you on sight in the street. Now sit down."

Ivan eyed Turner, leery. He had been foolish to underestimate the younger Coalition leader. Now he was trapped. The Barbarian would have to be nimble with his thoughts and words if he was going to survive.

The big Russian moved to the small bar, poured himself a double shot of Vodka, and drank it down. He gathered his thoughts before he moved to the couch.

No matter what happened in the next twenty-four hours, the Barbarian knew he had at least one card left to play. He had set it up before coming to Los Angeles, in the event of something like this. It would end with him dead, but he would exit this world with a bang, and the dreaded Coalition would go down with him.

He sat down and painted on his charming Russian grin. "What you saw was not what you think you saw, my friend," the Barbarian said.

"What am I thinking, Ivan?"

"You are thinking that the pattern reader does not matter. I believe differently. That is solely where our conflict lies. Not on our goals. Those remain the same."

"And how do you think he matters?"

"He has become an icon to the people."

"So? Icons come and go. If they interfere, they are disposed of."

"It is better to leverage them then to martyr them."

"Is that what you were going to do? Leverage Luthecker against me?"

"You are getting paranoid, my friend. How would I profit from your downfall? Without the Coalition, the structure behind my profits would cease to exist."

"You're a shitty liar, Ivan."

"So are you."

"So what do you want?"

"A better deal. As you say—adversaries, not enemies."

"And what would that consist of? More money?"

"Money is not difficult for men like us. Nor is power."

"What then?"

"Give me the pattern reader."

"Why on earth would I give him to you?"

The Barbarian got to his feet and moved back to the bar. He poured himself another shot of vodka.

"You think you can turn him into an asset, Ivan?" Turner continued. "Your partner thought that, and look where he ended up. So did my predecessors."

"My needs are different than theirs. And I have something to offer him."

"Such as?"

"I am an old man," the Russian began. "Wealthy and powerful, yes, but with an uncertain future. I prefer certainty. I believe the young man can provide such for me. I've seen what the young man can do, what he did to my former partner, and I'd prefer to not have him as an enemy."

Turner burst out laughing. "You think he's going to save you from your past? Forgive your sins? I think you need to go to church for that, my friend."

"I simply seek a truce."

"You're a monster, Ivan. That's pretty damn clear to anyone who's watching. What makes you think he wouldn't destroy you?"

"I'll give him what he wants. I'll free many slaves. Not enough to disrupt our profits, but enough to give him a victory. Surely, he will negotiate. He will understand it would be better than the alternative."

"Which would be?"

"His death."

"And you certainly wouldn't use him against me, now would you?"

"Again, I profit from your structure. And my actions could prove beneficial to you."

"How so?'

"He is your sworn enemy. I can keep him from destroying you."

"From destroying me?"

"As he did your predecessors."

"You're so full of shit, Ivan. I know you, and you don't give a fuck about saving me, or Alex Luthecker. I don't either, but my board is filled with fearful old men, and so I have to pretend like I do. You're just trying to save your own ass. Granted you're on the spot, but that's the best you can come up with?"

"I am sincere."

"Fuck off. Nice try, but you're not getting him."

"You will kill him then. Such a waste."

"Yes, I'm going to kill him. And with good riddance, I want to go back to a sense of fucking normalcy around here. But I can't do it yet. I need his goddamn girlfriend first because she's the one creating havoc right now. But after I have her and she cooperates, yes, I plan to kill him. He's caused this organization far too many problems, and it's time to bring that to an end."

"And myself?"

"Well, that's where the fun starts."

"What do you mean?"

"I'm not done with you yet, Ivan."

"Whatever you may be planning, understand that without me, you lack access to the underground economy."

Turner got to his feet and made his way to the bar. He poured himself a shot of vodka, lifted the tumbler, and swallowed the vodka in one gulp. Turner grimaced from the burn.

"I don't know how you drink this shit every day." Turner turned to Ivan. "I don't need you to access the underground economy, Ivan. I own it now. What I'm going to do is throw you into the lion's den, Ivan. For fun."

"What do you mean?"

"I've heard all the rumors. I've read all the reports, but I've never actually seen it. I want to watch him take you apart. I'm going to put you in the cage with the beast and witness it myself. I want you to talk to Alex Luthecker."

25

OUR CHOICE

"She's really pissed. She's cooling her heels waiting. Chris and Masha are watching her. The question is why did you bring her in the first place?" Yaw asked Nikki. "Rika Muranaka works for the Coalition. She's the enemy."

"It's hot in here. How about some AC?" Nikki asked, her face dripping with sweat.

"It's out. I'm sorry."

Nikki looked to the cab of the van and saw that half the console controls were either broken or missing. Parked in the basement level of a parking garage, the vehicle was a 1995 Chevy G20 model, gray, innocuous, with no GPS and apparently no AC.

Staying off the grid without knowledge that PHOEBE was redirecting CCTV cameras, audio pickups, and satellite feeds was getting to be extremely difficult. Even sitting in the back of this van was a risk. But every command Nikki had given PHOEBE was being ignored, and the commands the software was following were causing large-scale effect somewhere else in the world. And until Nikki could communicate with PHOEBE and understand the problem, she was effectively helpless.

Until then, they would have to be extra careful when it came to security simply as a precaution.

"I brought her because PHOEBE arranged for Rika Muranaka and I to meet, and I have no idea why. But there must be a reason. That's what I thought Alex could tell us. In fact, I was sure of it. And now you're telling me the Coalition has him."

"It shouldn't have happened, the Coalition getting Alex. Jimmy did his job, and our security was tight, and PHOEBE makes us invisible. So I have to ask you—now that you know that PHOEBE is going off script, do you think she was proactive on this?"

"What do you mean?"

"Do you think she gave Alex up?"

"No. Absolutely not. I'm not sure of much right now, but I'm sure of that. She would never set him up."

"But how do you know for sure? She's not talking to you, and she's acting out, doing things that you haven't told her to. It's clear that there's some trust issues between you two."

"I never said I didn't trust her. I do. It's just a glitch in the system, and I need to solve it. I think she *wants* me to figure out what to do next before she'll let me talk to her again. That's the only explanation for Muranaka. But one thing I know for a fact is that she would never give up Alex."

"But how do you know that?"

"Because she's part of me, goddammit." Nikki realized her voice was raised.

She was angry, not only at the implication, but at herself for things going wrong and at PHOEBE for shutting her out. She felt guilty enough for PHOEBE's behavior, but the possibility that her own creation had led to Alex's capture? No. She couldn't allow herself to think it.

Yaw put his hands up in mock surrender. "Okay. If you say so, I believe you, Nikki. And I mean that. So what do we do?"

"Coalition Properties west coast headquarters is the head of the entire organization now and part of a much larger complex than before.

They've bought up all the surrounding property, so it's not just the tower, it's a matrix of several buildings, and they're all digitally connected. They're testing new technology there, and it's things I've never seen before. We couldn't just walk in before, and we sure as hell can't now."

"And we don't have PHOEBE to help us either," Yaw added.

They both sat in silence for several moments.

"We still gotta try," Yaw finally said. He turned to Nikki. "It's up to you and me now. You're his love, and I'm his best friend. So we gotta step up and find a way. We gotta lead this. No one else can. And as far as the crew, wherever we go, they'll all follow. You know that."

"Yes, I know. But do we want to get them all captured or killed? Do you actually think we can just march in there and go get him? Again? Because that's impossible."

"No. I don't think that at all. I think there's much more going on here. I've been watching everything, and I mean everything. And listening, too—to *everything*. Nothing too small, nothing too big. I've been quieting my mind and paying attention. Just like Alex taught us to do. And when you do that, when you still the mind and stay in the moment, Alex is totally right—things really do come together. I mean, I'm not at Alex's level, I ain't got that. None of us do. But I think I get it now. I think I see enough to know exactly what it is we need to do in this moment."

"And what's that?"

"Stay in the moment and trust our training. I think this is the time, the one he kept hinting about. I can sense it. I think this is our time. We're going to end this, Nikki, right here, right now, once and for all."

"You mean end the Coalition?"

"Maybe. Or at least just end the running. 'Cause I'm tired of it, Nik. We all are."

"I know. I am too. But when he said that the end was coming, he also implied that maybe all of us wouldn't make it. I listened too."

"Alex always said things could change if we're willing to change. But if we die trying then so be it. If it's our Karma to move on from this world, then it'll be for what we believe in. Winn didn't hesitate, and we won't either. But it'll be our choice. It always is."

"Our choice," Nikki repeated under her breath, like a mantra.

"Shit," Yaw said, remembering something and shaking his head at the memory.

"What?"

"I sent Alex a message. Via courier. Before he got caught up. It don't make much sense now, but it's about you, so you should probably know."

"What did it say?"

"I said they weren't after him...they were after you. That *you* were the one, the key—not him."

"Why'd you tell him that?"

"Because they flat out said it—they're afraid of PHOEBE. More so than they're afraid of him."

"That's a mistake."

"Wouldn't be the first one they made."

Nikki thought over Yaw's words for several seconds. Then something dawned on her. She realized that Alex's interpretations of life patterns had grown beyond a single individual. It was no longer one-dimensional. It was no longer limited to him and his interactions with others.

Was it possible that Alex could now see a collective dynamic as a single entity? He had trained the group to be his eyes and ears. Could it be that they were now an extension of his abilities? Were they really that closely connected? It was possible that he could see ten moves ahead now, not just one, with the family as pieces on the board.

Kunchin's words now made perfect sense to her, as did Alex's behavior. As did her own. There were no *acts of random* at work here. With Alex, there never was. There was only cause and effect. A smile slowly moved across her face.

"What?" Yaw asked in reaction.

"It does make sense. Your message. It makes perfect sense."

"How so?"

"Because that message wasn't for Alex. It was for me. Alex knows us all, better than we know ourselves. He's always ten moves ahead. And you were meant to give me that note, at this moment, right now. He saw this moment. I don't know how, but he saw it."

Yaw thought over Nikki's answer. His head tilted in realization. "We'll I'll be damn," he replied. "My boy's three dimensional."

"And he knew we'd figure out what to do. Gather everybody," Nikki said. And I mean *everybody*. Because I agree, this is it. Alex knows it, and so do we. And I have an idea how we can win."

CAMILLA RAMIREZ WATCHED CAREFULLY as her young daughter Kylie toddled across the floor of the two-bedroom Terminal Island apartment that the family still called home.

Yaw had sent a courier message to her that the Coalition was holding Alex and things were coming to a head. He told Camilla to be ready to move out on a moment's notice, that PHOEBE couldn't be trusted to protect them.

So Camilla made sure that the Go-packs were ready, and the refugees moved out of sight to the basement level until further notice. Camilla was ready to run if trouble came, something she realized she'd spent her life being ready to do, but at least for the moment, she allowed herself to treasure the stillness of watching her young daughter play on the floor.

She loved her child more than anything, like most mothers do, and she and Yaw had even discussed the possibility of having more children, the maternal instinct being that strong. It was a difficult subject, as Yaw often reminded her that the future was far too uncertain.

Yaw was a good father and always there for the family. There was never any question of that. But with the death of Winn and the rise of Alex as leader, Yaw had become more the day to day manager of this off-grid group dedicated to saving the lives of those being trafficked, and his passion to help free those enslaved by others was only growing stronger.

It worried Camilla to a certain extent, as the level of risk from both the Coalition and other sources increased. She had seen it first hand in Mexico, with the death of a sixteen-year-old boy, and she felt the dread far closer to home when Yaw had recently been incarcerated. Alex had somehow managed to secure Yaw's release, but it left Camilla worried for the future.

They had a family now, and they could not always rely on Alex. It was after the trip to Veracruz that the two of them agreed Camilla would be the one to take less risk for the sake of Kylie, at least for now. It was the smart decision, but Camilla didn't want their daughter growing up without a father, or constantly on the run.

At the same time, if she was honest with herself, she was growing restless on the sidelines. Camilla wanted back in the game. She understood the paradox that her situation presented. She could also sense a change in energy, an anxiety in the air that kept growing, one that was becoming harder and harder to ignore. Her instincts told her it was a call to action.

But she had a child now, so she dismissed these instincts from her mind. She attributed those instincts to her restlessness and shifted her focus back to Kylie, who scooted toward her mother with purpose.

Camilla smiled at her daughter as she scooped the young girl up onto her lap.

"You're heart is not wrong," Maria said, startling Camilla.

Camilla turned to see the ten year old standing in the bedroom doorway of the small two-bedroom apartment.

"You scared me, Maria," Camilla said. "Are you okay? Goodness, your English is getting very good and quickly. Alex left you with some books to look at. Did you find one you like? Do you want me to read it to you?"

"I have read them."

"Really? Which one?" Camilla asked, not believing her.

"All of them."

"Well, which one was your favorite?" Camilla asked, playing along.

"*Nicomachean Ethics* by Aristotle."

Camilla nearly dropped Kylie.

"You have to go now. It is time," Maria continued, her eyes locked on Camilla.

"Time for what, sweetie?" Camilla asked, trying to maintain control in her voice.

The ominous fortitude coming from the voice of a ten year old had clearly rattled Camilla.

"When you left your father's home, it was night and you were cold," Maria started. "You wanted to cry, but you didn't. You didn't because you were filled with anger, and to cry would be the first surrender, and you swore to yourself that you would never surrender.

"You left because you knew that you were meant for something better, that this moment you feel right now would come, but you did not know in what form. Your biggest fear has always been that you would miss this moment, that you would not be prepared, and that your having run away would have been for nothing.

"You smiled and you laughed, but underneath there was always sadness and the search. And always the anger. And then Yaw came and gave you strength. And then Alex came and gave you confidence. And then Kylie came and gave you purpose. And then you had no anger. But you still fear missing your moment. Camilla, you have nothing to fear."

Camilla got to her feet. Her knees shook, and she pulled Kylie close.

Maria's words chilled Camilla to the bone. The tone, the certainty, had struck Camilla to the core.

Maria's fierce young eyes looked over Camilla with ravenous intent.

She had seen this before, with the only other person who had said such things to someone in this manner: Alex Luthecker.

"Maria, you're just a child, how could you..."

"It is time, Camilla," Maria continued, politely cutting Camilla short. "The moment is here. For all of you. There will be bloodshed.

And nothing is yet certain. But let me remove this one hesitation. Let me save you from this one uncertainty."

Maria approached Camilla.

As if on instinct, Kylie reached out to Maria, and Camilla let her daughter go to the ten year old.

Maria held Kylie close, and the child responded.

"This little one will be fine," Maria said with confidence beyond her age. "She will lead a long life, one filled with purpose, like her mother. But you—you must go now. You must go to your friends and help them. Before it is too late."

PART III

THE REVOLUTION

26

DESTINY'S ALIGN

"THEY CHOSE TO SEND YOU FIRST," ALEX SAID TO THE MAN KNOWN AS the Barbarian.

Ivan held out his hand.

Alex examined the Russian's big mitt for several seconds before shaking it.

"It is an honor to finally meet you," the Barbarian said to Luthecker. "May I sit?"

"Please," Alex replied, as he waved his hand over to the large black leather couch.

"These plush accommodations, they are meant to imply civility, no? And, yet, we are captive. We are rats in a cage. They watch us, you know. They expect us to destroy one another," the Russian added as he sat down.

"I know. I've been here before."

"And you accept these conditions?"

"This situation was inevitable, for both of us, albeit from different Karmic paths. But make no mistake, it will be the last time, also for both of us, albeit with different ends," Luthecker answered, not just to the Barbarian's question, but also for all those he knew were listening in.

Much like the Barbarian's cell, the small containment apartment that held Alex had the finest luxuries, with a well-equipped kitchen that had stainless steel appliances, a dining area, a well-furnished living room with a flat screen television, and finally a bedroom with a king-sized bed dressed with the finest silk sheets.

The only giveaway that this was, in fact, a holding cell somewhere deep within the Coalition Assurance Building was the lack of doorknob.

Luthecker took his seat on the plush leather chair at a right angle from the big Russian. With the ravenous eye movements, he took in every detail of this man's life. The Barbarian sat, unmoved.

"So do you know the details of my fate now?" the Barbarian asked.

"I think you know your fate already."

"Do you think I fear death?"

"No."

"Do you sense that I regret my actions?"

"No."

"Then what power do you think you have over me?"

"What power do you believe I have?"

"To frighten people with the truth that their lives are meaningless. To make them feel truly accountable for all the wretched things that they have done. Or at least, this is what I have heard."

The Barbarian got to his feet, and moved toward the kitchen. "Have they supplied you with vodka?"

"Alcohol is not in my profile. And I'd tell you that you should drink less, but it really doesn't matter at this point."

The Barbarian grimaced at the dry bar and moved away from the kitchen. He started to pace behind the couch, visibly agitated by the constraint of his favorite habit. Luthecker calmly watched.

"You killed my partner," the Barbarian continued.

"His choice. You killed my mentor."

"Also his choice, was it not? Death is equal and absolute. Perspective and justification are not. So for my actions, I do apologize. It was not personal, what transpired in Trans Dniester. Only business. I felt that I was being stolen from. I did not understand who or what you were. Your actions were justified. Lucas Parks had kidnapped your woman. I would have done the same as you.

"Mr. Parks' failure was that in his final moments he tried to change who he really was. A leopard cannot change his spots, no? He was and always would be ruthless man. He thought he could escape the responsibility for his brutal actions by becoming a philosopher in the end.

"I do not harbor such foolish delusions. There is no philosophy behind what we do in this world, and I do not entertain the way of guilt. Each and every one of us only does what we must do in order to survive and acquire the level of power we feel we deserve. Lucas Parks was held accountable for his decisions. As we all are. I accept this. And this is why, unlike others who cross your path, I do not fear you."

"And, yet, you would use my abilities to harm others, if you could."

"Morality is for those without power, and I make no excuses for how I attain it, nor doing the things necessary to those around me who threaten it. Sometimes a harsh hand is necessary in order to create the most profitable amount of stability out of the chaos.

"And make no mistake, the world always spins toward chaos. It has been that way since the beginning of time, and it is that way throughout all of nature. Throughout the entire universe, I suspect. Polarities define existence, and conflict at one level of magnification is simply harmony at another. These final words are not mine, but are those of a western philosopher."

"Alan Watts. I know of him."

"They are words that I believe to be true, words that speak of the need for balance. You believe in balance, do you not? Is that not what you seek when you view the fate of another? And you yourself—you have created conflict in order to bring this balance, have you not?"

"You create conflict for profit. Balance isn't your goal—power is. The words you speak are words you hide behind."

"I create profit to acquire the resources necessary in order to manifest balance from chaos. And I do this to survive. The human animal, no matter how evolved, is still just an animal. An animal that must be tamed, disciplined, and punished when necessary, lest he destroy everyone and everything around him. I do not see myself above this reality. I do not need you to tell me how my life ends. I know how it ends. I know that it ends soon. We are each born on a path, and we in turn die on that path. My life will end the way it began. With blood and violence."

"True. You will meet a violent end. And soon."

"As I said, I do not fear this. I am responsible for my choices. You have no power over me. No man does. No man ever has."

"And your God?"

"There is none."

"You're sincere when you say you don't fear the how. But do you care to understand the why?"

"I battled a rival and lost. That is why. It is...how you say? The law of the jungle."

"Is that what you really believe? That you've lost?"

"Does it matter what I believe? I'm locked in a cage. With you."

"You claim to accept your death as a battle loss, but that's not why you're here. Not the *real* why. The real why began long before you were born. As you admit, you were born on a specific path. That is true. And the scar on your left cheek, like a guide, benchmarks the timeline. Your father did that to you, when you were just eight years old. As his father did to him when he was only five, producing the scar on his back from the lash of a belt.

"You saw that scar on your father's back when you were very young. You wondered about its origin. It captured both your fear and curiosity as a boy the first time you saw it. And then, one day, you knew. You understood. And once you understood, you made a choice, and your Karma was set. It was in that moment that your destiny was set. You made that first choice in your life, and it was the only choice that mattered."

The Barbarian froze mid step. He had never told a soul about the source of the scar on his cheek or the one he'd witnessed on his father's back. The fact that Luthecker mentioned these things so casually sent a chill down the big Russian's spine.

"You are as good as they say you are," the Barbarian finally responded.

"I'll ask you again," Luthecker continued. "Do you care to know why you came to be the man you are now? What purpose it truly served? Are these answers something you wish to know, before you meet your end?"

"HOLY SHIT," Glen Turner said, his eyes locked on the security monitor.

"Told you," Kirby said as he stood beside Turner. Kirby's eyes were also locked on the security monitor with morbid fascination.

"It's unbelievable, what he does," Kirby continued. "He cuts through all self-delusion like a laser. And he's going to pick this guy apart. I've seen him elevate someone beyond their despair, and now I'm going to watch him single handedly destroy one of the most brutal, violent rulers the modern world has ever known. And he's going to do it all with a conversation. It's the most incredible thing I've ever seen."

"Maybe we should put a gun in there, just see what happens," Turner mused. "See if Luthecker can get Ivan to pick it up and use it on himself, like he did to David Lloyd."

Kirby didn't respond to Turner's brutal suggestion. He kept himself from looking at the Coalition CEO.

"It's like the emperors watching the Coliseum death battles of Rome, but without all the blood," Turner added. "You've talked to him already, and you want more?"

"This is different. The dynamics here are different."

"In other words, you see it as a challenge. You want to be thrown in the cage with this guy."

Kirby's eyes stayed locked on the monitor that showed Alex Luthecker and the Barbarian. "Absolutely."

~

"You people are crazy," Muranaka said. "You can't hold me here."

Muranaka looked about the room. She was standing in a concrete basement beneath an abandoned building in the Union Street section of downtown Los Angeles.

She had followed Ellis away from the Starbucks café on good faith, moving in cloak and dagger fashion across downtown Los Angeles in an effort to remain unseen.

And as soon as they arrived here Ellis promptly disappeared, leaving her under the watchful eye of an admittedly good looking young man named Chris, who kept sentry over her with his very jealous Russian girlfriend by his side.

Muranaka had been told that she must wait here because of "new developments that could change everything," according to Ellis. Muranaka felt like she had been inadvertently dropped into a spy novel.

"We're not holding you," Chris responded. "We're asking you to wait until Nikki gets back."

"And if I want to leave?"

"You'll leave empty handed."

At that moment, as if it was her cue, Nikki walked through the door.

"If something happens to me, there's nowhere you can hide from the big guns at Coalition Assurance," Muranaka said, not only for Chris and Masha's benefit, but for Nikki's as well.

"Nothing's going to happen to you. I promise. Like I told you, there's just been a change in plans."

"Of course there has." Muranaka started toward the exit.

"Wait," Nikki pleaded.

Nikki had never relied on faith before, but she had no choice now.

Alex was missing, and PHOEBE had shut her out, the program's only action being to connect Ellis with Rika Muranaka.

It was clear to Nikki that this connection was the key, and that PHOEBE was looking for Nikki to put together what to do next.

"It's going to take a bit of time before I can take you to see Alex," Nikki finally responded. "But you'll meet him. I promise. In the meantime, I'm going to give you what you originally wanted. I am going to connect you with PHOEBE."

27

COALITION FORTRESS

THE EXPANSION OF THE COALITION PROPERTIES FACILITIES IN downtown Los Angeles had begun as a way for the mega-corp to park enormous amounts of cash with the least amount of scrutiny.

As the Coalition took more and more market share from its traditional business sectors—war, defense weapons, energy, banking, Internet services, computer hardware and software, and more recently, revenue from off grid dark money sources like unregulated products, human trafficking, and drugs—profit margins for the conglomerate began to grow exponentially into hundreds of billions per year.

The company was piling up American dollars so fast that it was literally running out of safe places to put it. The firm already owned several banks all over the world, including in places like Cyprus, a country where many considered the small island nation's banking system to be the money-laundering capital of the world.

At this point, buying up more banks to park untaxed cash would only succeed in getting more unwanted attention from U.S. Federal authorities, which had eager and aggressive investigative branches that could easily trace abnormally large wire transfers or deposits, regardless of their origin.

The least regulated and most stable investment option currently available for large cash sums was therefore real estate investment, and it was in this area that the Coalition was more than happy to take advantage.

All it took was a purposefully complex array of shell corporations to make scrutiny of the transactions too difficult to pursue by the Feds, which when combined with the reality that not many agencies were in fact looking to scrutinize these real estate acquisitions to begin with, made it the smart play.

Regulatory bodies looked the other way because cash hungry state and city legislators were happy with the investment, as it boosted the local economy and tax base, allowing them to keep both liberal and conservative campaign promises. With lobbying to grease the wheels, legislators made the deals easy, as everyone wanted the deals to happen, and this allowed the world's largest defense contractor to quickly become one of the world's largest real estate holders.

In Los Angeles alone, the Coalition had purchased all the high-rise buildings that surrounded its west coast headquarters, known as Coalition Towers West. The real estate purchase in its entirety consisted of a tight cluster of six structures, the smallest of which was fifty stories, and in a first ever deal of its kind, it included all the connecting streets and power grid. The deal even included taking over the maintenance of water pipelines.

The firm paid well over market value for this all-inclusive patch of real estate, price not being a concern, which in turn sent surrounding real estate prices soaring. Between purchase price and the relocation costs of the previous tenants of the newly acquired buildings, along with all the interconnecting roadways, the tab of the downtown Los Angeles purchase was north of two hundred billion dollars.

The Coalition made it clear before the acquisition process began that they had no interest in keeping former tenants in the high rises that they bought; they fully intended to use the office space for their own corporate needs, and any cost to make that happen would not be prohibitive.

The total cost for the project was of no concern to the Coalition because costs, no matter how high, would be inconsequential against the super-conglomerate's gross revenues, not to mention the tax advantages the deals created, which reduced the true cost to nearly zero when amortized over the next twenty years, all based on real estate tax laws that the Coalition itself had a hand in creating.

For the Coalition, it was top to bottom monetization. The firm helped craft the rules that allowed their meteoric rise in profits, and they crafted the rules to monetize their attempts to park all the loot. The Coalition literally could not stop making even more money from their attempts to stash the enormous amounts that they already had.

And the Coalition did not limit its real estate acquisition binge to Los Angeles. The company was purchasing large swaths of metropolitan property all over the world, including New York, Miami, Dallas, and Chicago in the United States, as well as Hong Kong, Singapore, London, Paris, Beijing, Dubai, Frankfurt and countless other cities around the globe.

Metropolitan real estate acquisition was quickly becoming the "new Swiss Bank" for the uber-rich, corporate or private, and Coalition Properties was once again the world leader as it continually parked its endless cash flow everywhere it could, as fast as it could.

But Los Angeles had always been a special place to the Coalition board of directors, away from the scrutiny of New York, and with far nicer weather. So, with a unanimous vote, it was the City of Angels that the Coalition board chose to make their personal homes as well as their corporate headquarters.

They all adapted to Los Angeles quickly, with the excitement of Hollywood, the constant sunshine, and beautiful beaches all serving as the backdrop to some of the prettiest people in the world. Every board member of the Coalition had a luxury penthouse apartment located at what was recently dubbed "the Fortress" to go with his or her Malibu beach home.

And since the Fortress was both the home of the Coalition's top executives and the epicenter of its business, the sophistication of its security systems that guarded the Fortress were state of the art, with military-grade technology. In order to comply with civilian laws, the technology that went into the security system was labeled "proprietary" instead of "classified," but the difference between the two now was only in the name.

The system would also prove to be a test bed for the Coalition's latest civilian surveillance techniques and technology, with the plan being to monetize and export that technology worldwide. Governments would soon be able to monitor their citizens' every movement, extrapolate their every thought even, down to the last detail. And it would all be done with Coalition systems, with all the data stored on Coalition servers.

As such, every movement throughout the Fortress grounds was monitored and recorded for testing and analysis. Every surface had an array of sensors to track contact, motion detection to detect movement, thermal and infrared imaging to detect life, as well as stride and gait analysis to detect identity, with all of it piped through the CCTV systems.

This all-encompassing surveillance had a range that extended throughout the courtyard and connecting streets. The audio systems could record and identify different audio tracks from a growing library of over thirty thousand different sounds. It could even distinguish between individual heartbeats, and with the microsecond it took to access medical records from Coalition Healthcare, identify whom the heartbeat belonged to instantaneously.

The cost for this technological upgrade was "proprietary" but rumored to be in the hundreds of billions. But if the Fortress Beta-test of full-scale surveillance proved successful, the Coalition had every intention of selling the system to governments worldwide, governments that the Coalition had also helped form, as a way to keep their populations safe. Like all things that the Coalition touched, it would eventually turn an enormous profit.

The Coalition Fortress weapon defense systems that backed up the surveillance were state of the art as well and mostly hidden from public view. In addition to the Black Hawk helicopters on each of the helipads that every Fortress building had, the private, well-guarded garage systems below street level had rows and rows of pristine and heavily armored BearCat transports, as well as military grade Humvees, including several that were mounted with fifty caliber rifles.

Building Four of the six was the home of both the armory and Coalition Assurance team, which at any given time housed up to seven hundred ex-Special Forces soldiers, ready to go active at a moment's notice, to any Coalition launch point facility around the world. On the floors just below the barracks was where the armory was located. It included Coalition-made RPGs, M-16 rifles, as well as 9mm handguns, KA-BAR knives, Kevlar armor, night-vision goggles, with hundreds of thousands of rounds of the necessary ammunition.

There were enough men and combat equipment in the Coalition Assurance Building to overturn all but a handful of countries. And the Los Angeles Fortress facility was only the beginning.

The third floor of the Coalition Assurance Building was also where the containment apartments, or holding cells were located. Under heavy guard, there were twenty-four containment apartments, ranging from bare-minimum prison cells designed to approximate those in Leavenworth to the more luxurious accommodations like the one that currently held Alex Luthecker.

The domineering presence of the Coalition Fortress complex in Los Angeles had encountered its share of political opposition, but it was nothing that a few million dollars of lobbying money couldn't take care of.

The Coalition's long range planning for not only the Los Angeles center but for all of its Fortress hubs around the world was an interconnected nation-state status, using Vatican City as a model.

It was the board of directors' hope that the Coalition Fortress Los Angeles, along with its other worldwide holdings, would be politically connected and recognized as one entity, with its own economy, and subject to only its own rules and regulations. Over time, they would even require passport level identification to enter or exit. The

Coalition had more than enough money to make this happen, and they controlled more natural resources than any other business entity, more than many nations even, *and* they had their own army.

In the mind of the board, why should they be subject to rules that were not of their own design? Why shouldn't they be their own country?

It was with all of this in mind that Glen Turner felt perfectly comfortable holding Alex Luthecker for as long as he wanted. With the level of security and power the CEO had, there would be little that Luthecker or the outside world could do that would interfere.

And when Turner had gotten all that he could from Luthecker, squeezed everything useful from the irritating soothsayer, he would then have him executed.

Luthecker had been a nuisance for the Coalition long enough, and the Fortress was more than capable of disposing of a body, particularly that of someone who lived off the grid.

The Coalition Chairman had avoided dealing with Luthecker for as long as he could, considering him only a minor annoyance, but fate had seemed to intervene, and now Turner would finally have to deal with the young man. So be it. But at least Turner could accomplish what his two predecessors could not—kill Alex Luthecker.

But first, Luthecker would be a very useful tool for Turner—first in getting Luthecker's hacker girlfriend to shut down her renegade program, then getting rid of the traitor, Ivan the Barbarian, and then finally in disposing of the intransigent nuisance that was Doctor Mark Kirby.

Turner had to admit to himself that Luthecker's storied abilities seemed to be real, and watching him work was indeed fascinating. And in regards to destroying the Barbarian, the goal was nearly complete.

❦

"YOU THINK your words matter to me?" the Barbarian asked Luthecker. Tears ran down the big Russian's cheeks, and his voice echoed throughout the luxury cell. "Yes, my father beat me. That is not so strange in this world. And did you know that my mother tried to poison me? Perhaps more strange than most, but who cares?

"This is the way things are, the way things have been since mankind crawled out of a cave. For most in the world, suffering is all that there is to know. I'm sure that you are aware of all of this, about not only myself but also many others, although I do not know how it is that you know. Nor do I care. It does not matter.

"They were brutal people, my people, and I am a brutal man because of it. And you probably know that I killed them both. As you say, I made that decision early on, that I would be stronger than them. And I have killed many others along the way. So what?

"Look at all I have accomplished. Look at all that I have. I have lived a life full enough for a thousand men. It is what I wanted all along. I do not regret it, and there is no other *why*. If today is my last day, so be it.

"Your end will come soon, demon. No different than me. There is no plan or reason to life. And when it comes to death, all men are equal, and both horrible sins and works of grandeur are all equally vanquished."

The Barbarian got within inches of Luthecker.

Luthecker did not move.

"As I said, I do not fear you. And if I chose to, I could break you in half right now. Maybe that is what is supposed to happen next, no?"

"No," Luthecker responded. "You killing me will not be what will happen next. If you tried, you'd fail, and your battle-hardened instincts know this, otherwise, you'd have done so already. And isn't rage only a cover for fear? Wouldn't you attacking me only prove that you do, in fact, fear me?"

Both men stood unmoving for several seconds.

Finally, the Barbarian backed off.

"Whether or not you fear my abilities is not relevant to the reason you are in here with me," Luthecker continued. "And if you do not wish to know more of who you really are, that is your choice. But I promise you that before you breathe your last breath, you will know.

"As you admit, your death is imminent, and with it will come the answers that you cannot escape. At this stage, the momentum behind your collective choices is too strong for me to intervene. You will die slowly in a cell and not in a burst of violence like you think you will, and it will also not *unfold* how you think it will. That is not the reason you're here. And you know this already. You've planned for it."

"Oh? What do you know of my reasoning? What reason am I here, according to your wizardry?"

"You think you're here because others fear you, and you intend to confirm that fear, in what you believe is grand fashion. But the reason you are here is because I need you to be. Make no mistake, none of this is by chance or by your design.

"And what those who fear you don't know and I do, is your plan. The one card you have left to play, that you intended to play all along, if all else failed and you ended up being held captive by your more powerful adversary. It has to do with the nuclear warhead-equipped Russian submarine that you recently purchased from the Russian Navy that is headed this way at full speed.

"It will be in range of this facility very soon. It's the reason you've been reminding us all again and again that you don't fear death. You remind us of this because you believe it's coming. It was your final card. It's always been your final card, and it's one that you displayed to me the moment you were put in here with me.

"This facility, and all within it, will be reduced to ash, unless you choose to stop it. And you will only stop it if you're released and properly compensated for your inconvenience.

"But you are also tired of it all. And at this point, you are unsure if you even want to be released. You believe that you are sincere with your fatigue over it all, but that is your denial, your inability to face who you really are, because deep down you are very afraid, and the machinations of fear and denial are exhausting.

"Because of all this, you stay quiet. You're willing to let things end, here and now. You are torn between survival and wanting your final act before leaving this world to allow you to be remembered as the man who set the world on fire.

"But now that I've given voice to your darkest secret, that scenario won't unfold now, will it?"

"You truly are a demon. But no matter, I win either way," the big Russian replied.

"Perhaps. Perhaps not."

"I understand more than you know. You have yet to make your move. Now I see what Lucas Parks saw in you. Now I see how you could bring the world to its knees."

"Son of a bitch," Turner said. "How the fuck could I miss that?"

He turned to Kirby, who continued to watch the exchange between Luthecker and the Barbarian with complete fascination.

"Do you think he's telling the truth about the nuclear sub? Or do you think he's bluffing?" Turner asked.

The tone in his voice revealed that, for the first time, he felt he was not in control of the situation. Kirby did not miss it.

"I can't say. But the point is you really can't take that chance, now can you?" Kirby answered. "He played you both, and it was awesome to watch."

"Wipe that stupid fucking smile off your face, or I'll have you shot," Turner said before he hit the intercom.

Turner understood that either Luthecker, or Ivan, or both had played him, and now he couldn't kill either one until he knew for sure.

"Get Ivan the hell out of there and bring him to my office, now."

28

TRUSTING THE ENEMY

"Understand that by allowing you access to PHOEBE, I'm trusting you with everything I've ever done," Nikki said as she led Muranaka into the second bedroom of the two bedroom Terminal Island apartment that housed Nikki's computer station.

"Understood," Muranaka responded. She felt her heart race from anxiety and was surprised by her physical reaction.

The Coalition programmer had long studied PHOEBE from afar and had imagined what this moment would be like, when she would finally have access to the program. Her imagination did not predict that it would unfold like this.

She tried not to appear too eager as she looked over the half hexagon of high definition screens, keyboard, and small computer server.

Nikki sat down at her workstation. She went to log onto PHOEBE but hesitated at the last moment. PHOEBE had prevented every access attempt Nikki had tried since Alex had returned from Mexico with Maria. But then the software algorithm had put Nikki and Muranaka in contact with one another.

If Nikki had guessed right about PHOEBE's intentions, it was because PHOEBE wanted the two women to work together. Nikki would have her answer the moment she tried to log on.

She realized that she was risking everything by exposing her software program to Rika Muranaka, Coalition Properties employee, and she had no idea if Muranaka would turn against her.

She hoped that her instincts about her own software were correct because if she was wrong, it would be the end of everything that Winn, Alex, Mawith, Kunchin had preached, and the rest of the family had worked so hard for.

If she was wrong, the Coalition and everything the super-conglomerate stood for would win.

Nikki took a deep breath, hit the keyboard, and typed in her twenty-six-digit password that led to her user-ID that led to a second eight-digit password.

Nikki held her breath for several seconds as the computer did nothing. She let out a huge sigh of relief when the monitors blinked to life.

"Sure, now you talk to me," Nikki whispered under her breath.

"Holy smokes," Muranaka reacted to what she saw.

The half hexagon arrangement of large high definition monitors showed highly detailed images of the city of Los Angeles defined solely by its electrical activity. Temperature signatures indicated hot spots, fluctuating from red to yellow to blue based on energy consumption.

Countless Internet nodes moved data in pulses that looked like blood cells flowing through capillaries. Cell tower and satellite activity were represented by a translucent dome over it all, looking like a digitized and squirming layer of skin.

Underneath this electromagnetic skin, the Fortress resembled a living, breathing organism that was city shaped, with the building frames providing the skeletal structure. The entire scope of digital information moved about like an angular cardiovascular system, one that existed around human activity, a digitized dimension hidden from view.

"I call this half layer resolution," Nikki said.

"Which is roughly half the data that PHOEBE can or does monitor at any given moment," Muranaka said, completing Nikki's thought.

"Correct. Full data analysis makes the images too dense to distinguish anything usefully. And as humans, we have limited capacity to distinguish detail."

"In other words, we can't see other worlds beyond our five senses, including the digital one."

"That's part of it. Right now, people have access to more data in one hour than previous generations did in an entire year, and look how it's tearing the world apart. People can't distinguish because processing too much detail immobilizes them.

"The animal brain is hard wired for survival. You don't need to count the hairs in a tiger's face to recognize it's a tiger and you better run. But because of this they can't see the intricate connections. People are literally drowning in information, but with no higher wisdom or trained capacity to process it.

"So it helps to limit the data in order to actually see what you're looking at. More importantly, to know what you're looking *for* in that endless sea of data."

Nikki hit a few keys, and the images gained a level of resolution. "Right now, this is just a base template of power consumption and information movement, but trust me, PHOEBE's watching and processing a whole lot more data."

"How much of this design is you, and how much of this is PHOEBE building herself out on her own?"

"It's less and less me every day," Nikki answered, almost to herself. She turned toward Muranaka. "At first, I could get her to turn things on and shut things off via command. Electronic door locks, security cameras, getting past firewalls, padding or deleting bank accounts, pretty basic stuff. Before long, I could get her to hack into any system, punch through any firewall, break through any encryption."

"And then you hacked into the most heavily encrypted security system ever designed and brought down the world's largest military drone."

"I stopped the world's largest military drone from killing my friends and me. That's the part you're missing. I didn't have much choice. I did what I had to in order for us to survive. It was after that hack that things began to change."

"So what happened after that? How did PHOEBE all of a sudden start acting out on its own?"

"After we returned from Trans Dniester, our goal was simple. We only wanted to free people from both physical and mental slavery. Companies like the one you work for have a problem with our doing that, as slavery in one form or another is the basis for both their ideology and their business.

"However, in order for us to free people, we needed to be able to travel the globe with complete freedom and invisibility, and so providing that freedom of movement became PHOEBE's primary use.

"But to do that successfully, she needed some autonomy to deal with the constantly changing security measures and computer access protocols that I simply couldn't account for. I just couldn't see it all, no human could, and she needed to be able to see it all in order to be one step ahead of every system.

"And because of that she needed to be able to do this without having to check in with me first. In other words, she needed to be allowed to make decisions on her own, and be smarter than current human capacity to make the right decisions.

"And before she could ever achieve that level of proficiency, she needed to develop a language all her own to communicate with other systems, one that by design had to be far more complex and far faster than any known human language. It was the only way it could be done."

"And language is the first step necessary for any species to become self aware."

"Yes. It all starts with communication. We have to be able to talk to one another. But PHOEBE's communication abilities have to be able to handle the volume and complexity of her world, which makes it beyond ours."

"And it wasn't long after she started talking on her own to other systems that she started thinking and acting on her own."

"Bingo," Nikki said. "And she couldn't wait for us to catch up before she started making her own choices."

"So what's the basis of the choices she's making? What's her mandate?"

"I don't know for sure. I never really programmed her with an overall mandate, other than to take care of the family and the people we freed. But I think in her own way, she's trying to create balance."

"Why do you say that?"

"Because it's what the universe instinctively does."

"But she has no moral compass. Even if what you say is true, she could wipe out entire cities and kill millions of people in order to achieve what some self-generated algorithm we don't even understand is telling her is necessary in order to create this so-called balance that's been defined by yet *another* self-generated algorithm."

"I know."

"How on earth could you create such a thing?"

There was contempt in Muranaka's question, and Nikki felt it. But it was a question Nikki had asked herself countless times since returning from Tibet.

Muranaka asking Nikki the question directly had the effect of jarring her thinking. It was like a challenge by a rival.

It forced Nikki to go back to Kunchin's words in Tibet, connecting the monk's philosophy and her rival programmer's directness.

Then it dawned on her. Developing PHOEBE was her gift. Her magic. And just like Alex had to take responsibility for his abilities, Nikki had to take responsibility for her own. PHOEBE was not so much a program as she was a natural evolution.

Nikki wondered if the guilt she had been so overwhelmed with lately was similar to what Alex had gone through, when he began to realize the impact of his own gifts on others.

The realization of this lifted some of the guilt. Nikki had watched Alex's growth from an introvert filled with self-doubt to a confident leader, and she had held his hand through much of it. It was in this, she realized that just like it was for Alex, her guilt was misplaced.

And then the floodgates of realization broke open. It was not just the guilt of creating PHOEBE, or the guilt of working in the oil futures business, but it was the concept of guilt itself, the guilt she had felt ever since she was a child, about how much smarter she was than her parents, her hometown, and all the boys, all of it; it was all misplaced.

She realized in the same way that Alex had—she couldn't make the world a better place by being reactive, withholding her gifts, and choosing not to participate. It all made sense to her now. And her reaction to this realization was just as quick.

No more, she thought to herself. Nikki would not apologize for creating PHOEBE. She would not be made to feel guilty for all that she was capable of. She would not apologize for any choice she had made, mistake or not, to anyone, ever again. And she would protect PHOEBE like it was her child, because in many ways, the program was.

She abruptly turned toward Muranaka. "I created PHOEBE because I could. And I did it because I wanted to. And I can tell you right now, her creation was absolutely necessary."

"She needs to be destroyed before she destroys the world as we know it."

"She needs to be *guided*. No different than a child. You're right, she doesn't have a moral compass. So I'm going to give her one."

"And you think that compass is your friend Alex, the guy who's single handedly become the Coalition's worst nightmare."

"No. I think it's you. It's what Alex has done with people time and time again. I see that now. And I think it's why PHOEBE put us in the same room together. Because somewhere along the way in your digital life, PHOEBE must have been watching you, and she made the decision that you were good, and we can't do this without you."

Muranaka took a step back. "Wait—what? What are you talking about?"

"I want you to look at something," Nikki said, before she turned back to the monitors.

She typed rapidly on the keyboard, and the images on the half-hexagonal arrangement of monitors changed, focusing only on six buildings in the downtown Los Angeles area.

Muranaka recognized the images right away. "That's the Coalition Fortress," she said.

"Yes it is," Nikki answered. "PHOEBE showed me its design, unprompted, shortly before she shut me out and put us face to face. From the looks of it, it's impenetrable."

"It's designed to be that way."

"I want you to look closely," Nikki added.

Muranaka moved closer to the monitors.

The entire Coalition Fortress property looked like a small city made entirely of light. The walls of the buildings and the streets, the entire topography of the miniature city-state were solid sheets of illumination that hummed with a life of their own.

"Why does it look solid?" Muranaka asked.

"It looks solid because there's so much digital information moving around," Nikki replied. "There's more digital information moving around in this patch of real estate per square foot than anywhere else in the world.

"It's high-density information at a level we've never seen before. It's an unbelievable amount of data being gathered, recorded, and interpreted. And what you see here is still not a complete picture. This is only the Fortress complex. This doesn't include the people. It's missing the flesh and blood."

Nikki hit several keys on the keyboard.

The city of light was suddenly filled with small dots of beating red, some of them moving slowly about the city, some remaining in place. And every red dot had countless electronic tentacles attached to it, connecting it to the angular sea of electronic data.

"Here's what you have to understand," Nikki continued. "What it is that I've just managed to get my head around right now, through our conversation. In order for the Fortress security system to accomplish what the Coalition wants it to, which is complete control, it's going to have to develop its own language, if it hasn't already," Nikki said.

Muranaka figured it out right away.

"Holy shit," Muranaka replied. "You're saying it's going to be just like PHOEBE."

"Yes. And it'll happen very soon. But with a mandate defined by past actions that are programmed by the largest weapons manufacturer in the world, a corporate system that's designed to conquer every market and destroy every enemy," Nikki added.

"Holy fuck."

"Yeah. Holy fuck is right. It's the worst kind of digital Karma. You think PHOEBE's dangerous, wait until this system gets loose in the world. You asked me, how could I create such a thing? How could I create PHOEBE? I'll tell you what's more important than how. I'll tell you why. I created PHOEBE to deal with *this*. Right here, right now. Balance, Rika. The universe provides it."

"You want to use her to stop it."

"Yes. We don't have a choice. It's the only way. And that's where you come in."

Muranaka looked at Nikki.

"You work for the Coalition. You have the security clearance to get onto the Fortress. I need you to take this—" Nikki quickly removed a thumb drive from the side of her keyboard, "—and give it to Alex. He'll know what to do. He's being held there right now."

"Are you crazy? If he's being held, I can't get near him."

"Yes you can. And that's not all. I want you to talk to him. I want you to let him read you."

"No way."

"You have to. You have to let him look deep into your soul and reveal to you your inner truth. And once you understand your destiny, and the true reason behind every choice you've ever made, I have faith that you'll understand who and what we are, and more importantly, who *you* are, and that you'll do the right thing. You're the only one who can do this. It has to be you."

"You realize that you're asking me to betray my employer."

"I'm asking you to save the world. You of all people understand how serious this is."

Muranaka paused. Nicole Ellis was right. The threat was real—there was no way around it. They had to stop it, and this was the only way.

"You do realize that this is batshit," Muranaka finally replied.

"Admit it. You're more than curious. You want to face Alex. Search your heart. You've been waiting for this moment all your life. To find out why you're here and where you fit in.

"And you've been waiting for this moment, even though you didn't know exactly what this moment was going to be, when it would come, or what the meaning behind it all would be.

"It's the definition you've been searching for to the question that you never could quite put a finger on, but you always knew it was out there, and you've searched for this all your life for one simple reason, the same simple reason that I did—you want to *know*."

"You're assuming a lot about me. You're assuming that I can even get to him, for starters."

"You can if you want to. We both know it."

Muranaka looked at the thumb drive in her hand. "This puts PHOEBE past the Coalition security firewalls, doesn't it?"

"This is putting a stop to the destruction, and we don't have time for PHOEBE to go through five trillion calculations to get there. This is creating balance in the universe, before it's too late."

"And what are you going to do?"

Nikki looked across the room.

In the corner lay her Kali sticks, the ones Master Winn had given her when she reached expert level proficiency, the ones made of aluminum, inscribed with her name, and for combat use only.

"Prepare for the final battle. That's what I'm going to do."

"You understand that Coalition Assurance has guns, right?" Muranaka asked as she followed Nikki's sight line.

Nikki turned to her. "Don't worry about me. I won't be far behind you. *We* won't be far behind you."

"How do you know I won't just steal this? How do you know I won't just run?"

"Where can you run, Rika?"

Muranaka swallowed hard. Everything Nikki Ellis had just said about her was true, and it rattled her to the core, so much so that she felt disoriented.

Muranaka carefully put the thumb drive in her pocket. "Is that it?" Muranaka asked.

"No. There's one more thing," Nikki said. "PHOEBE gave me a message that I want you to share with Alex. It's one that I've been trying to make sense of. It's the only time she's ever spoken to me unprompted, and she hasn't said a word to me since."

"What did she say?"

Nikki looked up at Muranaka. "She said, *the end of the animal is near.*"

29

BRINKSMANSHIP

Captain Vladimir Dimitrov looked at the coded message a second time with relief. It was what he hoped for, a stand by order. He took a deep breath and tried to keep his hands from shaking.

A complete stand down order would have been the best option, but at least this was the first step in stopping what would be assured destruction of life on earth as everyone knew it.

Dimitrov assumed, he hoped, that this whole incident had been a drill, and the next message would be to stand down. And hopefully that order would come before too long.

Now in his late forties, Dimitrov had been commander of the nuclear sub *ОПОРА*, or Reliance in English, for the last nine years, first serving as a weapons officer then as the vessel's executive officer, or XO, for the last five years of his tenure.

He had been promoted to captain after the man he served under, Captain Greschenko, retired, allowing him to command his own vessel for the first time, a goal he had set for himself when he was only a teenager. Choosing to be an officer on a nuclear-powered submarine, particularly one equipped with nuclear strike capability, was a total commitment to the vessel, one that required a man to surrender his entire life in service of his ship and crew.

And this commitment did not change when the sub Dimitrov commanded was sold from the Red Navy to the oligarch Ivan "the Barbarian" Barbolin.

The transaction, which had happened less than a year ago, had been swift and unannounced, and it had taken Dimitrov and his crew by complete surprise. The Russian fleet of nuclear submarines was the prize of the Russian Navy and was considered the biggest deterrent to the Coalition-made U.S. arsenal of sea-based nuclear weaponry.

The transaction was considered top secret and kept out of the press to avoid political scrutiny, and the transition from state run to privately run was unnoticeable at the chain of command level.

Once the transaction was complete, the Barbarian had simply turned around and leased the war machine back to the Russian Navy. The reason behind the transaction was a source of speculation.

The relationship between the Barbarian and the Russian President dated back to when both men were officers in the KGB, and it was thought that the president was in debt due to decreased oil production, and the sale offered him a much needed cash infusion. In return for this cash infusion, the Barbarian had himself a nuclear submarine.

The recent call for the ОПОРА to change course from international waters in the Pacific and directly toward the west coast of America had made Dimitrov and his crew very anxious. Mostly because the order did not come from the Russian Naval Command— it had come from Ivan Barbolin himself.

The oligarch had never involved himself with the submarine's mission status before. Neither Dimitrov nor any of the members of the crew had even met the man.

The most disturbing part of the order came with the command to arrive off the coast of California on full tactical strike alert.

The Barbarian, a private citizen, albeit a very rich one, was coming within inches of starting a nuclear war, with the purpose behind it unclear.

Was the notoriously brutal businessman using a nuclear threat to enforce a business deal? Captain Dimitrov shuddered at the thought.

The *ОПОРА* had reached within striking range of the targeted city of Los Angeles less than twenty minutes before Dimitrov received the standby command. The tension that had filled the ship throughout the journey had lessened after this, and the speculation was that there had been tense negotiations going on between the rival U.S. and Russian governments or private institutions, and the *ОПОРА* was there to enforce the deal.

If both Russian and U.S. citizenry knew how often these alerts took place, they would enjoy far more sleepless nights, Dimitrov thought to himself.

He took one last look at his crew before turning over command of the sub to his XO, deciding that he would go back to his quarters and rest. He had not slept in the last thirty-six hours, and the standby order allowed him to feel his fatigue.

He was turning to leave when he caught his fast approaching XO out of the corner of his eye. He could see by the look on his XO's face that it was something serious.

"What is it?" Dimitrov asked.

The XO stood at attention in front of his commanding officer. Dimitrov noticed that the XO was white as a sheet and covered in sweat.

"Well, spit it out," Dimitrov said.

The XO took a deep breath and chose his words carefully. "We have a problem with one of the missiles, sir."

"A problem?"

"Silo four. It won't disarm. It's started its countdown to launch, and I can't stop it."

~

"I THOUGHT IT WOULD BE BIGGER," the Barbarian said as he sat down across from Glen Turner.

He took one more look around the Coalition CEO's office, with its earth tones and mismatched art, before returning his focus to the man who had held him captive only an hour earlier.

"We're not czars or kings in this country. We're businessmen. We don't need to gold plate everything," Turner responded.

"Perhaps if you did, your people would understand you more."

"I should throw you out the goddamn window."

"The standby order is temporary unless you meet my terms. I recommend you negotiate quickly."

"We'll find your sub."

"Not before it reduces this city to ash."

"We both know you're not going to do that."

"You heard the soothsayer. I am prepared to die and take all of the Coalition and most of the American west coast with me."

"Stop with the posturing. So I got you, then you got me. It's a game our countries have been playing since the end of the Second World War, and now we've just taken the game private. What do you really want, Ivan?"

The Barbarian didn't answer right away. He pretended to clean his fingernails. It was the passive aggressive tactic of a man who believed he now had the upper hand.

The Barbarian finally spoke without looking up from his hands. "I want more money, of course. I want the freedom to go back to my country. I want the guarantee that I remain untouched, always, and no matter where I travel in the world."

"Fine."

The Barbarian looked up. "And I want the pattern reader."

"So at what point did you know Ivan had a nuclear sub? How did you know it would be that exact vessel and not, say a ship with missiles?" Kirby asked Alex Luthecker.

He had quietly entered Luthecker's cell only moments before.

"Does anyone know that you're in here with me?"

"You already know the answer to that question. I disabled all the audio and visual feeds to this room if that's what you're asking. And no one saw me. Let's just say that everyone who's anyone is a little bit preoccupied right now. The threat of nuclear war will have that effect on people."

"Well you did claim that mass extinction is imminent."

"You know I can't tell if you have a really dry sense of humor, or if your ability to know so much forces you to be literal all the time." Kirby examined Luthecker carefully as the two men sat across from one another.

The pattern reader looked completely unfazed by his predicament and the events that were quickly unfolding around him.

"Not much rattles you, does it? Is that a function of knowing the source behind all that rattles things in the world?" Kirby asked.

"Is that what you really want to know before they discover you in here with me?"

"You're right. I don't have much time."

"So why are you here?" Luthecker asked.

"You know why. I want to know who I am and where I'm going, down to the last detail."

"Where do you choose to go?"

"Wherever I have to in order to accomplish my goals, and I want you to help me avoid mistakes in order to expedite things. You played the Russian heavy, and you're playing Glen Turner just as deftly, even though you've never met him. I have to assume you've been playing me all along as well, which, believe it or not, I have no problem with. In fact, I expected it.

"So since you already know what my mission is, you can pretty much say you know what I want, and I want you to know it. The words I say to you and my intentions that you can read are in sync. So tell me—how does my future play out?"

"If I told you, it would no longer be your future. You of all people understand that paradox."

"Fine. Since we're both in a bit of a bind right now, I'll make a deal with you. When this is all over, and I've helped you resolve your conflict with my employers, you tell me every single thing you can about me."

"I've already made that deal with you. Why are you really here?"

"You know why."

Kirby motioned to Luthecker to come close.

Even though the audio pickups had been disabled, Kirby barely spoke above a whisper. "Look, I can't let you out directly, because he'll know I did it, and he'll kill us both on sight. But we both know I won't have to let you out, don't we?

"What I can do is facilitate whatever it is you're planning. I know that whatever your course of action may be, it is the right thing to do because my goal is singular and in alignment with yours. So what you *want* to happen is what I *need* to happen. So tell me what it is you need me to do, and I'll do it—no questions asked. And when all this is over, you tell me what I need to know."

Kirby sat back down across from Luthecker. "I bet you never saw that one coming," he added. "Or maybe you did. Maybe you really are ten steps ahead. So what do you say?"

Luthecker locked eyes with Kirby for several moments before he spoke. "Here's what I need you to do..."

30

PLACES EVERYONE

"ARE YOU SURE YOU CAN TRUST HER?" CHRIS ASKED NIKKI.

"I think she's looking for answers just like the rest of us. And she's our only shot right now. She wants to talk to Alex, and I trust him more than anyone in the world with someone who's looking for answers. If she gets in front of him, he'll know what to do. He'll set her on the right path."

"Knowing the truth about herself may tear her apart, like it has with every other person associated with the Coalition that's gone face to face with Alex. What makes you think she'll be any different? She may be looking for answers, but you barely know her. What makes you think she'll actually get to Alex? What makes you think she won't just turn us all in to the Coalition?" Yaw asked.

"PHOEBE," Nikki answered. "I think PHOEBE knows that she'll be different. PHOEBE put Rika Muranaka directly in front of me for a reason, and I believe that reason is to help us."

"So, PHOEBE is the Alex of the Internet? Is that what you're saying?" Yaw asked.

"I don't know. But I'm not going to lose faith in either of them. Not now."

"Well no matter what happens, it's good to be together again with my ride-or-die crew," Camilla chimed in. "I think back to the O.G. days and all the things we did, and the people that joined our cause. We were kinda crazy, but everything changed when Alex came on board. He brought us Nikki, then Joey, and now Masha. And he made us see who we really are. He changed all of us, and now we're gonna get our boy, and this time, we're gonna bring down the goddamn Coalition. And I for one, cannot wait to get this started," Camilla said, spinning her Kali sticks for emphasis.

Nikki looked over her group of friends as they waited in the Terminal Island two-bedroom apartment that she and Alex called home. Everything that Camilla said was true.

Alex, the reluctant family member, was now head of the family. And now with the energy of finality palpable in the air, the family being together was more important than ever.

A knock on the door got their attention.

"I got it," Yaw said, before he looked through the peek hole. He recognized the man on the other side and opened the door.

"I got your note," Officer Dino Rodriguez said to Yaw. "Your messengers are pretty crafty, I'll give you that. So we're here like you wanted," Rodriguez said, nodding to his partner Ellen Levy, who stood beside him.

"And all those O.G. cats from the funeral. Are they ready?" Camilla asked when they were inside.

"More than ready, just like Alex asked," Rodriquez added. "So what's next?"

Rika Muranaka stood outside the Coalition Fortress entrance gate, her eyes scanning over the buildings of the soon-to-be corporate nation-state.

Construction of an enormous wall surrounding the entire property had recently started, and the cranes and workers were moving at a noticeably rapid pace. The buildings that the wall would circumscribe gleamed in the sunlight—six glass and steel structures that looked no different from other high-rise buildings, but in fact were retrofitted with the most advanced surveillance and defense technology the world had ever created.

When the wall surrounding the Coalition Fortress was complete, including the wall and roof mounted anti-aircraft weaponry rumored to be in the works, it would take a large, well equipped, and fully trained army to successfully breach the entrance and take over the Fortress.

Or, maybe it would take one very nervous Japanese woman, wholly unsure if what she was doing was the right thing to be doing, armed only with a software access key for a program developed by a bitter rival.

Muranaka's heart raced. She felt dizzy, and she forced herself to take several deep breaths to calm her nerves. The anxiety made her feel detached from her senses, as if she were a stranger in her own body.

She could do this, she kept reminding herself. No matter what happened next, good or bad, Rika Muranaka knew one thing for sure —after this, she would no longer be in anyone's shadow.

Muranaka pulled her Coalition ID badge from her purse.

She straightened out her skirt suit and marched over to the Coalition Fortress entry gate with purpose.

She scanned her ID, nodded to the guard, and entered the Fortress.

"Is there even a nuclear sub, Ivan? Or was this some trick concocted by that pain-in-the-ass pattern reader that you just went along with?"

"We both know you could not take any chance. The very nature of brinksmanship, eh? And, of course, the submarine is real. Did you not see me make the phone call to make the stand by order?" Ivan "the Barbarian" Barbolin said as he poured himself a tumbler of vodka.

He did his best not to say more and gloat outright, but it was surprisingly difficult.

"As I told you, no missile shall be launched against you today," he continued. "You, and your Coalition States of America are safe, provided I am safely away with the pattern reader."

He looked at Glen Turner and held up the vodka tumbler. "Salute," the Barbarian cheered, before knocking back the shot of alcohol. He smiled.

Turner fumed in silence.

"I have learned to like your office," the Barbarian continued as he looked around Turner's workplace. "I respect its simplicity. Conservative works of art that portray conservative values. Very American."

Every word out of the Barbarian's mouth felt like nails on a chalkboard for Turner.

Turner had already made up his mind that he was going to kill the Barbarian regardless of any agreement or mutual interests; there was no longer any question about it. There was no place on earth where the big Russian would be able to hide from him.

Ivan was right, Turner couldn't take the chance that he and Luthecker were bluffing about the nuclear sub, and Coalition Naval Defense Systems working in clandestine conjunction with the U.S. Navy were already on the task of finding the rogue Russian vessel—if it was out there, they would locate and dismantle the threat soon enough.

Once the sub was eliminated, Turner would once again have the upper hand and this time it would be for good. It shouldn't take long, hours perhaps, a day or two at most, and he would take down the world's richest oligarch, violently, and make a statement to the underground world that there was no escaping the Coalition.

Patience, Turner thought, *and both Ivan and Luthecker will be problems of the past.*

With this conclusion in mind, he mustered up every ounce of his psychological strength to smile at the Barbarian and get up from his couch.

I will kill the big Russian soon, was Turner's only thought, by his own hand if circumstances allowed. But for now, he couldn't get the gloating oligarch out of his office fast enough.

"How much longer will you grace us with your presence?" Turner asked, barely able to contain his fury.

"That depends. When will you turn over the pattern reader to me?" the Barbarian shot back.

"I told you. I'm dealing with a bit of a crises here. A crisis that could effect even you, Ivan. I need Luthecker on hand as potential leverage. As soon as I have his partner, Nicole Ellis, in custody and access to her program PHOEBE, he's all yours," Turner lied. "Until then, you're just going to have to wait. I can air mail him in a box to you in Russia if you'd like."

"No need. I can wait. Perhaps I will explore your grand facilities until you have the woman in hand."

"Fine. I'll arrange a guide."

"Armed, no doubt?"

"Armed, no doubt. You've caused me enough trouble."

Turner's office line buzzed. The CEO approached his desk and picked up. "What is it?"

"Rika Muranaka has just entered the grounds, sir," Turner's executive assistant answered.

Muranaka had somehow managed to slip surveillance for several hours. Turner wanted to know why.

"Have her escorted to my office right way," he replied. Turner looked at the Barbarian. "Okay, get out of my office. But don't wander too far. This may be over real soon."

"Sorry to interrupt your schedule so abruptly, but as you've told me personally, we face a serious crisis," Turner said to Muranaka.

"You haven't been in your office. I've tried to reach you. Where have you been?"

The calm rhythm of Turner's voice barely masked the tone of threat.

Muranaka swallowed hard and kept her emotions steady.

The Coalition Assurance security team had intercepted her the moment she stepped onto Fortress grounds, and she had used the six minutes it took to reach Turner's office formulating an explanation.

"I was running some personal errands. I do that some times when I need to think, to problem solve, and sort out a strategy, like in trying to figure out how to access PHOEBE. I was in a dead zone when you called, and that's why it went straight to voicemail," Muranaka replied, all of which was technically true. "Fortunately, there will be fewer and fewer dead zones as Coalition Cellular starts replacing cell towers with better technology," she added, hoping that the company promotion would take the focus off her whereabouts.

"Eventually there'll be no dead spots of any kind," Turner said. "There will be nowhere in the world that Coalition communications cannot reach."

Turner studied Muranaka for several seconds.

Muranaka resisted the urge to react.

"Where do things stand at the moment?" Turner finally asked. "How close are you to breaking into the PHOEBE program? Has there been any direct contact or interaction at all with Nicole Ellis?"

Muranaka could feel her chest pounding, and she felt faint. Turner's direct question presented a literal crossroads for her, and her answer would set the stage for her entire future.

Never in her life had Muranaka lied on a scale like this. Her mind raced—her culture frowned on lying. Her father would disown her if he found out that she had been less than truthful to her superior, regardless of intent. She was an employee of Coalition Properties, and that is where her loyalty should lie.

Glen Turner was a powerful man, one that, if Nicole Ellis were to be believed, could even have her killed if he wanted to. Muranaka's face burned hot. She felt like Turner could see right through her.

She wavered. *I just can't do this*, she thought to herself.

"Could I get a glass of water?" she finally asked. Her voice cracked with the question, and she swore at herself because of it.

"Of course," Turner responded. "Are you feeling okay?"

"Yes. I'm fine. It's just...it's very hot out today."

"Let me get that for you, then."

Muranaka watched as Turner got up and walked toward his office mini bar.

He smiled at Muranaka as he poured water from a bottle into a small glass. He returned to the couch and handed her the glass.

Muranaka's hand shook slightly as she took it. "Thank you," she said, her voice barely above a whisper.

She downed the glass of water in careful gulps. When she was finished, she set the glass down on the marble table between them and looked at Turner.

"I haven't found Nicole Ellis," she said to him. "My expertise is programming, not missing persons, so the only way for me to find Ellis would be via her interactions with PHOEBE, but so far I've found nothing, sir. It's been completely quiet.

"I think she's aware that PHOEBE is acting on its own accord, and my guess is that she's fearful of any escalated mission creep that could potentially be set in motion by giving the program any new instructions.

"Her staying off the web and out of cyber-site are making the search to find her that much more difficult, sir—not to mention the whereabouts of the PHOEBE software construct on the deep net.

"But on a more positive note, I do believe I'm close to hacking into PHOEBE with what I have so far, without the help of Nicole Ellis," Muranaka lied. "I may have found a back door into PHOEBE's architecture. So the next time she pops up in the deep web, I should be ready. I was on my way to the Cyber Center when security said that you wanted to see me."

"You do understand that time is of the essence, here."

"Yes, sir, I do. That's why I'm headed straight to the center. Why don't you come with me, and I can show you how it all works if you'd like. I'd be more than happy to get you up to speed on the technical side."

Turner examined Muranaka for several moments.

She sat up straight and held her breath. She tried to appear calm, but she was horrible at poker and had never bluffed before. She hoped the offer to Turner to observe her actions would show him that she had nothing to hide and actually discourage his further attention.

Subterfuge was not her talent, however, and every second she sat across from the Coalition CEO convinced Muranaka that he knew she was lying to him.

Her mind raced through all the possible negative outcomes. She would be fired. She would go to jail. She would pass out any second now and wake up in the hospital, fired, or arrested, or both.

After what seemed like an eternity, Turner finally spoke.

"That won't be necessary," he finally said to her.

Turner wasn't sure if she was lying but didn't feel it necessary to press further, not because he trusted Muranaka, but because he trusted the Coalition Fortress security systems.

As long as Muranaka was on Fortress grounds, her every move would be monitored, and if she was up to anything nefarious, she would be caught.

And once the surveillance systems were fully operational, he would no longer even have to speak with her, or anyone else, at all, as individual heart rates would be recorded and run for analysis, and Turner would be able to tell if Muranaka or anyone else were lying simply by checking the corresponding app on his phone.

But fully operational was still several weeks away, and at the moment, he had more pressing things to tend to directly than to watch over Muranaka's shoulder.

He would have to trust but verify Muranaka's activities the old-fashioned way for the time being, by monitoring her communications and assigning a Coalition Assurance team to keep track of her if she left the facilities.

There would be no more errands run without direct knowledge of her whereabouts.

"I trust you'll keep me updated," he added. "But do so hourly. And if you are headed out of cell range, please let me know. Is that understood?"

"Yes, sir. Absolutely, sir. Thank you."

Muranaka sprang to her feet, smiled at Turner, and shook his offered hand vigorously.

She exited Turner's office without looking back and also smiled and nodded at the robotic executive assistant as she walked by.

She walked down the hall and entered the ladies' room.

After she confirmed that she was alone, Muranaka barged into the nearest stall, locked the door, and promptly threw up in the toilet.

After she finished, she steadied herself, got out of the stall, and checked to make sure she was still the only woman in the rest room.

She approached the nearest sink and washed her hands. As she grabbed several paper towels to dry her face, she looked at her reflection in the mirror. The meeting with Turner she had been forced into had definitely caught her off-guard. It had also made things very real.

Muranaka was surprised that she could lie to him so easily. But she knew he was watching her now. The slightest misstep would lead to her dismissal, or worse.

She checked that the restroom was empty a final time before she opened her purse and found the thumb drive that Nicole Ellis had given her.

Muranaka thought hard about her next move. The events of the last twenty-four hours had unfolded so fast, with so much change in her perspective. Yesterday she was after the rogue software called PHOEBE and the hacker Nicole Ellis who created her; now, she was contemplating things she didn't think herself capable of.

Was she really going to go through with it? It was sabotage. It was potentially treason. Was a simple meeting set up by a rival's A.I. software worth this risk? Was Nicole Ellis right about her—was this the moment of self-definition she had been waiting for? Was her *knowing* worth the risk?

In the back of her mind, Rika Muranaka had always harbored doubts about the Coalition. But she had resigned herself to the reality that they were simply too powerful to be confronted, and that this was the world that she lived in today.

She knew that it was right here, right now, that she had to make a decision that would completely alter the course of her life. Deep in the back of her mind, she had always known that her life would somehow come to this. But not *like* this. And certainly not this fast.

She looked at the thumb drive in her hand. The meeting with Turner had changed things. She would not have time to give it to Alex Luthecker. She would have to set PHOEBE loose on the Coalition Fortress security systems herself.

She knew that once she plugged the device into the Coalition Fortress systems, all hell would break loose, and it would be traced back to her in minutes if not seconds, no matter what protocols she tried to put in place to contain PHOEBE. And she would need every one of those minutes before detection to get to Alex Luthecker.

She decided that this would be the plan. Her gut instincts told her that Luthecker was the key, and it wouldn't take much to determine where they were holding him. Electronic logs and records were easy enough for someone with her skill set to access. She already knew which building held him—building four, which housed Coalition Assurance.

Muranaka had only visited that building once before, as part of a tour when she was first hired. It required top-level security clearance and was filled with some of the scariest looking men and women she'd ever come across. But Muranaka already knew she was going to risk it.

She was going to unleash PHOEBE on the Fortress, but in a contained way, not in hopes for the victory that Ellis had in mind, but in hopes that both systems would cancel each other out.

In Muranaka's mind, both PHOEBE and rival Coalition Fortress cyber ability presented real threats to global security, and therefore both needed to be destroyed.

Muranaka made up her mind that she would be the one to do it.

And while PHOEBE and Coalition cyber security cancelled each other out, she would face the mythical enemy of the Coalition, Alex Luthecker.

She would see if he was truly capable of all that was rumored. And she couldn't deny that the thought of it was exhilarating. She carefully opened the door to the restroom and exited into the hallway.

31

INCOMING

"What do you mean, you cannot stop it?" Vladimir Dimitrov asked his Executive Officer.

"Our launch control sequence. It has been hacked by an outside source," the sub's XO replied.

"Who could do such a thing? The Americans?"

"Unknown."

"But how is it even possible? At this depth?"

"My only guess, sir, is that it happened during our last radio transmission to the surface."

"But all of our communication is encrypted. And to infect our systems with a virus over radio transmission, that technology does not even exist."

"Arguing how it happened is moot at this point, sir. It happened. Right now we must concentrate on finding a way to stop it."

"How much time?"

"Thirty-nine minutes, sir. Whomever set the clock gave us a small window. They must want something."

"What?"

"Unknown, sir. There has been no instruction or guidance, no contact from anyone. We have no idea who has done this. Should we contact Mr. Barbolin? The Russian President?" The XO asked.

Dimitrov wavered. If the launch sequence could not be stopped, nuclear war was coming, and his next decision could literally decide the fate of human existence. Ivan "the Barbarian" Barbolin technically owned the *ОПОРА* so technically he should be the one contacted first. But that did not follow normal chain of command.

Normal chain of command required contacting the Russian Navy, which had been at least partially privatized, which meant its motives were no longer solely the safety and security of the Russian state. As far as Dimitrov could recall, a private citizen had never owned a weapon of such immense destructive power.

Dimitrov had never met the Barbarian, but he had heard stories of the man's quick temper and extreme brutality. And along with the navy's compromised purpose, the Russian President had sold out his country by his transactions with the Barbarian, so the president could not be trusted.

In the end, it was the Barbarian's reputation, combined with his complete lack of experience in all things military, that informed Dimitrov's decision.

"No. We must warn the Americans. We must seek their help."

"THIS IS what you Americans call a suicide mission," Masha said as she looked out over the Coalition Fortress complex of buildings.

She, along with Chris, Yaw, Camilla, Nikki, and Joey Nugyen stood in an unoccupied two-bedroom unit of the 14th floor of a rundown apartment building. It was located near the 10 freeway on the far edge of downtown Los Angeles.

"That may be," Yaw answered as he looked at the Fortress complex from the window, "but I think it's gonna go down different than that. I think the Coalition is in for a big surprise."

"I hope that you're right," Masha said.

"So what is the plan again?" Chris asked Nikki.

"At 5 p.m., Rika's going to plug PHOEBE into their system. If PHOEBE does what she's always done for us, she'll shut down all cameras and surveillance and open all doors that are locked electronically, allowing us to move freely once inside.

"At the same time, Winn's old friends will create a disturbance outside the northeast Coalition Fortress entrance gate that LAPD Officers Dino Rodriguez and Ellen Levy respond to. They'll block off the streets, and get the Fortress guards involved.

"With the surveillance systems down and the guards distracted, that'll be our opening to get inside the Fortress."

"Once we're inside, then what?" Chris asked.

"You guys find Alex and get him out as quickly as you can. I'll find Rika Muranaka and get her out of there before she's taken into custody for her actions. PHOEBE should be in control of their entire surveillance and security systems at that point. She'll carve a path out for you guys. Once you're all out, I'll reprogram PHOEBE to take care of the Coalition."

"What does that mean? Are you really going to have PHOEBE wipe out the Coalition?" Chris asked.

"I'm going to make them accountable for who they really are. Every theft, every lie, every murder, and every culprit behind all their crimes will be exposed to the entire world. The Coalition itself will be forced to confront its choices and pay the price.

"But make no mistake, the Coalition consists of people, and it's the individuals that make up the institution who will be forced to face their role in all this. They'll be held accountable for what they've really done in front of the whole world."

"In other words, it's like they get a face to face with Alex, but it's the entire Coalition, at the same time, and on a massive scale, for the whole world to see," Yaw added.

"Something along those lines."

"Alex would be proud."

"I did learn from the best."

"Sounds good to me," Chris added. He swung his aluminum Kali sticks for emphasis.

"Alex ain't gonna let it go down like that," Camilla said.

"What do you mean?" Nikki asked.

"He ain't gonna let us spring him and then leave you behind."

"If this goes right, I won't be far behind you. When we're done, we'll meet at the downtown Metro station, and go back to Terminal Island together."

"If nothing goes wrong," Joey Nugyen added.

"We'll be fine."

"Suicide mission," Masha reaffirmed, but this time as a declarative. "But what the hell. I'm ready," she added.

Nikki looked out the 14th floor window at the buildings that made up the Coalition Fortress. As the sun set on the city of Los Angeles, the red orange haze provided an ominous backdrop to the angular horizon.

"I want you all to remember, you have to get Alex out. He's all that matters moving forward. He is the key to everything, not me," Nikki added. She looked back over her friends for their reaction.

"I think he'd say the same thing about you," Yaw replied.

"An argument for a different time. Just get him the hell out of there, and don't worry about me."

GLEN TURNER POURED himself a shot of bourbon, lifted the glass tumbler to his lips, and swallowed the liquid in one gulp.

He grimaced as the alcohol burned the back of his throat. His stomach churned, and not just from the bourbon. He was dealing with an apocalypse-level hacker in Nicole Ellis, he had been played by his Russian rival Ivan "the Barbarian" Barbolin, and he couldn't help but suspect that the one man he wished would just go away, Alex Luthecker, was somehow behind it all.

The search for Ivan Barbolin's nuclear submarine had proven fruitless so far, and Turner had to admit that, even with Coalition war machines and surveillance technology searching the Pacific, the odds were against him locating the vessel the longer the search took.

There was always the option of causing an international incident by moving Coalition backed U.S. Navy nuclear subs within striking range of Russia and putting it out on the world stage for all to see, but that would not get Turner any closer to his goal—to get back to running the world's largest corporate superpower, without the need-less distractions and petty brinksmanship, all seemingly caused by one man currently being held in a Coalition prison cell.

Turner had been steadfast in his refusal to be caught in the same trap as his two predecessors, Richard Brown and James Howe, in dealing with someone who held no real power like Alex Luthecker. Yet here he was.

Turner was baffled by everyone's fascination and obsession with the con man-soothsayer, but no matter how much he tried to avoid dealing with Luthecker, it had proven inevitable for Turner, and now the Coalition leader feared it would cost him his chairmanship.

The Coalition CEO would think nothing of getting it over with and killing the young man, but he couldn't because of the cyber-crises Luthecker's girlfriend, of all people, had created for him. He needed Luthecker alive for leverage against the terrorist hacker Ellis.

But once the cyber threat presented by PHOEBE was gone, Turner would have them all killed—Luthecker, Ellis, the Barbarian, and perhaps all of Luthecker's friends.

Turner felt that events had conspired against him ever since he took over as the Coalition leader, and he couldn't catch a break. And normally reliable, if not adversarial, business partner Ivan Barbolin's obsession with Luthecker only added to the problem, and that was in addition to the extinction-obsessed scientist Mark Kirby's constant annoyance.

"Shit," Turner said to himself.

In the mad scramble after the revelation of Ivan's nuclear threat, he had completely forgotten about Mark Kirby. He stepped away from the bar in his office and hit the speakerphone line to his executive assistant.

"Find Mark Kirby, and get him in here," Turner screamed.

"Actually, he's just arrived, sir, and he says he needs to see you."

~

"I THINK you should talk to him," Kirby said to the Coalition CEO.

"Why?"

"Well, you might be able to find out where that Russian sub is, for starters."

"I don't think he has that kind of knowledge."

"Well he ripped apart that Russian oligarch pretty good, and he knew about the sub then. He could give you insight into a lot of things that have been bothering you, I'll bet. And maybe give you a few solutions while he's at it."

"If I want that, I'll talk to a shrink. But what's your angle? Why are you suggesting this? Did he convert you? Are you a believer now?"

Kirby eyed the bar. "Can I get a drink?"

Turner gave Kirby a brief wave in the affirmative.

"You know my angle. I want all of Coalition Properties resources dedicated to stopping the extinction of humanity," Kirby said as he made his way to the mini bar. "That's the only battle left worth fighting."

"You sold me on your pitch. I've already told you that I'll give you what you need."

"You threw me a bone in hopes that I'd go away."

"If you come up with something actionable you get more, if you don't you fade into obscurity. That's the way the world works, doctor."

"The evidence is indisputable, and the solutions are clear. All you really wanted was for me to find Luthecker. Well I found him, and I brought him to you, just like I told you I would. And now I'm telling you that all of this would be a whole lot easier for you if you'd just talk to him."

"Look—I've made it clear that I have no desire to speak with Luthecker."

"Why not? It's not like your beliefs can be rattled, right? He couldn't possibly change the way you think, and Coalition Properties is too big to fail. So what are you afraid of?"

"I'm not afraid. I just don't buy into the hype. And talking to him just validates him. It's buying into the hype."

"You do realize that just entertaining the conversation with me right now means you've bought in. You can't avoid it. Coalition Properties can't avoid it. It's the organization's destiny. That means it's your destiny. There's far too much momentum behind that collision to stop it now. Whether you play along or not, he's playing you already."

"He's not playing me. He's in a cell."

"You may think he is, but trust me he's not. The Coalition has held him before and he always got out. And every time he got out, he ghosted you guys, and the Coalition lost big. Maybe you should try and break the pattern. Maybe you should just try talking to him. Otherwise you'll just lose again."

"We're not going to lose. And he'll get out if and when I say he gets out."

Kirby shook his head in disbelief at Turner's response. The man just wasn't getting it. "Ok, well, then why don't you just get it over with and kill him then? He's caused you enough problems, hasn't he? I mean, what are you waiting for?"

"Coalition Properties does not *kill* people."

"Have you forgotten that you've threatened to kill me several times already? Or are you so shameless and arrogant that reality means nothing to you people anymore?

"We both know that the Coalition kills people. Its primary business is defense weapons, for god's sake. What was it, close to thirty thousand children under the age of sixteen died in Iraq? From your weapons?

"You wrap that lethal reality in sophisticated propaganda and then tie it all to national interest to justify all of the killing you do. And we all either buy it or ignore it, and go about our day. We're all just as guilty as you, but we're in denial of it.

"It's no mystery why our species is headed for extinction. We're making it happen in real time by replacing reality with ideology. But I'll tell you why you really won't talk to him. It's not because you don't want to buy into the hype. It's because you're just beginning to see the level of his impact, and you don't want to acknowledge it.

"You're happy with your denial. We all are. And that's the threat he brings. Removing the ability to deny. And you are desperately afraid of that."

"I don't give a shit about him. And there's nothing he can allegedly do that we won't be able to do soon through technology, by the way. Coalition technology we own. So I don't need him.

"I just have a hacking problem right now, and as soon as I have his girlfriend, I'll leverage his freedom, I'll leverage his very life so she stops her program from truly ending the world as we know it.

"But make no mistake, after that threat is eliminated, I don't need either one of them. He'll be free to go, and you'll be free to commiserate with him all you like about existential threats while the Coalition handles the real ones," Turner said, the last part being a lie.

There was no way he was letting Luthecker go. Kirby either, or the Barbarian.

But then out of frustration Turner added, "You know, this guy would be nothing if people would just stop paying attention to him."

"People say exactly the same thing about ideas," Kirby shot back. "And history's shown that ideas are very, very hard to kill."

"He's not an idea, he's just one man. And I thought you wanted a chance at him. So why don't you speak with him then if you think he's so profound."

Kirby searched the bar for a bottle of Perrier. He smiled in victory when he found one.

He opened the bottle and poured himself a glass of the sparkling water. "I have spoken with him. Why do you think I'm here right now?"

"You were not authorized to go in that room."

"I felt it had to be done. If you weren't so damn afraid of him, you would have seen that coming. That's what fear does, by the way. Gives you tunnel vision. When Ivan the oligarch got the jump on you, and you had to, I don't know, *stop a nuclear attack*, no one was around to mind the store so to speak, so I took the liberty."

"What did he say to you?"

"I thought you didn't care. I thought you said if everyone just ignored him, he'd go away. How's that working out for you?"

"Are you looking to be handcuffed to a table again?"

"He convinced me that we're all in this together. And he told me to tell you that you need to talk to him."

The entry door to Turner's office burst open, and his executive secretary stepped through.

"I'm in a meeting," Turner snapped in response. The look on his secretary's face changed his tone. "What is it?" He asked.

"You have a very urgent phone call."

"From who?"

"A Captain Vladimir Dimitrov from the Russian sub *ОПОРА*."

MURANAKA SAT at her desk and moved to turn on her computer.

"Where've you been?" Michael Chan asked, nearly giving Muranaka a heart attack.

She turned to find Chan standing in her office doorway. "Jesus, don't you knock?"

"Tom Miller's been looking for you."

"I was in CEO Glen Turner's office."

"Yeah, I heard you went in to see him. I think that's why Miller's been looking for you. He thinks you went over his head with something, and he's none too happy about it."

"I don't give a shit what he's happy about. And Mr. Turner and I have begun a dialogue. If Miller doesn't like it, he can take it up with Mr. Turner."

"I'm sure he will. I just thought I'd give you the heads up that he's coming your way. So what are you working on?" Chan stepped closer.

"Look, I have a lot work to do, Michael," Muranaka snapped.

"Okay fine. Jeez, what's with you, did you forget your coffee this morning?"

"I'm sorry. It's just, everyone's on edge right now, with this

PHOEBE problem. But I'm working on something I may need your help with later. Let me settle in, and I'll let you know. Cool?"

"Sure. Sounds great." Chan made for the door.

"One more thing," Muranaka said.

"What's that?"

"Can you keep Miller at bay for me?"

"I'll do my best."

"Thanks."

Chan gave Muranaka a nod before exiting her office and closing the door behind him.

Muranaka got up from her desk and locked the door to prevent more unwanted intrusions. She returned to her seat and powered up her workstation.

While she was waiting for her systems to boot, she pulled the thumb drive from her purse and placed it on her desk.

When the Coalition system login screen popped up on her computer screen, she logged on and slipped the thumb drive in the USB port on the side of her screen.

She waited several seconds for her machine to recognize the device but was surprised when her screen went black.

Muranaka hit several keys on her keyboard, but the screen remained dark.

"Shit."

Muranaka hit more keys. Still nothing.

Then an alphanumeric stream of characters abruptly filled the screen and began to scroll at a rapid rate, too fast to read, right before the lights in her office and throughout the building flickered for several seconds.

Then, as quickly as it had started, it was over.

The lights were normal, and her screen went back to the Coalition Properties home page.

Muranaka hit several keys, but the Coalition home page stood unmoved.

She was effectively locked out of the system.

Muranaka's heart sank as she realized that it was PHOEBE that had done it, and she had been duped. Muranaka frantically tried to reboot her system but it remained inaccessible. Even unplugging it didn't help.

She swore at herself. Nicole Ellis had lied to her, used her, and now the entire digital infrastructure of Coalition Properties was at risk. Ellis had played to her emotions, and she had fallen for it. How could she have been so naïve? How could she have been so fooled by a romanticized notion of her actions making a difference? How could she have been so flat out stupid?

A knock at the door interrupted her thoughts.

"Who is it?" she asked.

"It's me," Michael Chan said. "I need to talk to you."

Muranaka got up from her desk, walked over to her office door, unlocked and opened it.

"What is it?"

"What the hell just happened?"

"What do you mean? What's going on?"

"The whole floor lost the lights for a second, then I just got shut out of my system. I checked around and everyone's been shut out. Reports are coming in from every building in the Fortress that their systems are down. It's complete chaos."

Muranaka peeked out her office door. Coalition employees were wandering about the hallways confused and angry.

"Did you do this? Is this what you were working on?" Chan asked Muranaka.

"No, I..."

An alarm klaxon sounded, the lights went out, this time long enough for the building's emergency lighting system to activate.

"Great. Now we have to evacuate," Chan said.

The number of people in the hallways grew, and the rumble of confusion got louder as Coalition employees began lining up and heading through the exit doors.

"Jesus, it's a complete system-wide hack," Chan said.

"Everyone else can go, but we have to stay," Muranaka replied. "We have to try and stop it."

"What did you do?"

"It's PHOEBE. She's infected the security system."

"What? How?"

Muranaka wasn't paying attention to Chan. She was watching Tom Miller, head of Coalition Properties cyber-security division and board member, visibly angry, moving through her coworkers and headed her way.

~

OFFICER DINO RODRIGUEZ sat behind the wheel of his patrol car with his partner, Ellen Levy, sitting next to him.

"Are we really going to do this? Are we really going to fabricate a disturbance?" Levy asked.

"Yes we are," Rodriguez responded. "Our part in this is simple. Some of the old guys are going to look like they're causing a scuffle, and we're going to step in to break it up. It will escalate, requiring the Fortress gate guards to get involved, and that moment will create the opening for the others to get inside and do their thing. We make sure no one gets hurt, we make a couple gentle arrests, cut the old guys loose down the street, and we're done."

"And this is a revolution?"

"Everyone's got their role, big or small."

"You know this could cost us our badges."

Rodriguez shrugged, before he turned to Levy. "It's a risk I'm willing to take. If we lose our badges then we can finally go ahead... join those folks on the front line. I'd do it if it came down to that. Shit's gotta change, Ellen, and it starts with this. It's been rumbling for a while now. It's why you're here, why I'm here. To make a difference."

"I hear you. But I'd like to keep my badge in the process, hell I just got it."

Rodriguez checked his watch. It was 5:01 p.m. He looked out the driver's side window of his squad car and examined the buildings that made up the Coalition Fortress. It was dusk, and the sun was beginning to set behind the six structures.

He watched as the array of office lights that outlined the Fortress, along with the street lamps and signage, flickered several times, with half of them staying off.

He turned to Levy and smiled. "Showtime."

MALCOLM COMBINE WAS fifty-eight years old. A black man, born and raised in Compton, CA, he ran with the Crips gang in his early teens, following in the footsteps of his older brother. He left the gang life when the crack epidemic took over South Central Los Angeles in the 80s and his brother was killed in a drive by shooting. He'd done his best to stay straight ever since.

When Combine was a young man he was long and lean, but now he was heavy set, with gray stubble on his chin and little in the way of hair on his head. Combine walked with a limp from a gunshot to the left leg when he was only sixteen, on the same night of the drive by shooting that killed his brother. But Combine considered himself one of the lucky ones. He was alive.

Along with his brother, many of the friends he grew up with had died from gun violence or drug overdoses. The ones who had survived that dark period, guys like Malcolm Combine and his late friend Winn Germaine, did their best to school the next generation on the perils of gang life.

The old timers had both the street cred and the respect to spread their message, but in the end, not much had changed. That was until Winn set up Safe Block.

Safe Block was a place where refugees, the poor, the outcasts, and those fleeing slavery could live and breathe in safety. It was a place where people could get their feet under them and get away from the slave traders hoping to break the cycle and start along a new path.

The original gangsters like Combine saw the value the Block created and got behind the project right away. Even the newer cats like Rooker understood the Block's importance, but understanding didn't guarantee escaping the cycle, as his death had shown.

But the story of the Block was growing louder, and others that were still in the rough trades were beginning to understand the importance of the concept, not the real estate.

They all knew on some level that violence only led to more violence, and if they stayed in the game too long it would take their lives with others profiting from the cycle. But cynicism remained high if the destructive pattern of behavior was all you'd ever known.

The success of Safe Block was beginning to change that. It was known to be a safe haven for slaves of any kind. It provided the communities with hope, and if the local gangs didn't outright provide support, at the very least, they steered clear.

At Winn's funeral, where several dozen of the old street survivors came to pay respects, it was clear that Winn's top student in martial arts, a skinny white kid by the name of Alex Luthecker, would carry on the cause of Safe Block.

Luthecker was an odd cat in Malcolm Combine's mind, but Combine's survival instincts told the old man on first sight that Luthecker was also a dude you didn't mess with. And there was no question that the young man did have a way with people, witnessed by Luthecker's interaction with his crew—a group that was strong, diverse, and fiercely loyal.

Combine recognized the value in a strong, loyal crew. Survival on the streets required it. He recognized the talent necessary to lead a group of people from diverse backgrounds, all strong-minded in their own right. And Combine had heard rumors that Luthecker had this strange gift, where he made you face the genuine truth about yourself, a hard task that was near impossible for even the most self-reflective man or woman.

It was rumored that this gift that Luthecker had was so strong that it allowed the young man to accurately predict your future. And it was because of this ability that "the man" wanted to bring Luthecker down, "the man" of course being Coalition Properties. But the Coalition was failing.

Under Luthecker's leadership, Safe Block had not only remained active, it had expanded its reach beyond the human trafficking that went through Los Angeles to include disrupting the slave trade in several parts of the world.

And Luthecker and his crew had learned how to ghost its locations quickly, making it far more difficult for authorities to clamp down. Luthecker had become successful in making Safe Block more of a universal idea than a particular location. And Luthecker's two previous beat downs of the Coalition had made him a legend on the street, even to the younger sets.

It was because of Luthecker's growing legend that momentum and support for the Block was growing. And Combine had heard that this latest dust-up about to go down with the Coalition was for all the marbles. It could possibly take down the much-hated enterprise.

And if the rumor was true, Malcolm Combine was more than happy to do what he could. Malcolm despised the Coalition and all it stood for. His youngest nephew had died fighting for oil in Iraq, oil that made profits for the Coalition. It was the same old story, the poor fighting for the profits of the rich, and if this opportunity was a way to fight against yet another deadly pattern that plagued society, then Combine would do his part. And he knew his friends would be right there with him, both young and old.

The plan was for Combine and his friends to cause a ruckus right outside the gates of the new Coalition complex, known as the Fortress, and then have some cops friendly to the cause arrest them, but not before getting the Coalition "guard dogs" involved and away from their posts.

The lead officer on this, Dino Rodriguez, was the LAPD officer who had approached Combine for the mission. Rodriguez had his own reputation on the street, one of always looking out for those with no voice and being fair with Combine's people.

Rodriguez was an immigrant, one who knew what it was like to have nothing. The young officer was the leader of something called the Blue Curtain, an informal group of LAPD Officers who protected the Block and all the lives that it saved.

In Combine's mind this made the officer one of the good guys and Combine, as well as other older gangsters, trusted him because of his actions. More important, the Luthecker kid trusted Rodriguez. And that was good enough for Combine.

Combine limped down the sidewalk in front of the Coalition Fortress main gates where he spotted his old friend from the hood, Billy Green, along with a dozen other folks he recognized from back in the day. They were all beginning to gather in front of the Coalition Fortress entrance gate. Many looked unsure what to do next. Green had his game face on, so Combine approached him first.

"So how's this supposed to start? Am I supposed to take a swing at you?" Combine asked Green.

"Naw, I don't wanna have to knock you out if you do," Green answered.

"You ain't gonna knock me out, get a hold of yourself."

"Says the man with the limp. I dunno. Why don't you push me. Start yellin' at me or something."

"Why don't you push *me*?"

"Because you'd fall down with that gimp-ass leg a' yours, fool."

Combine chuckled right before he pushed Green in the chest hard, sending Green tumbling onto the street.

"Get the fuck off my street," Combine added for effect.

Green tried not to laugh as he slowly got to his feet.

Both men looked around. Combine's push kicked off the activities. Within seconds, men young and old were pushing and shoving one another and yelling profanities back and forth, with the Coalition entrance gates as the backdrop. Two of the younger men were already wrestling on the ground, exchanging blows. In less than a minute, it looked like a full-blown riot.

"Just like the good old days, huh?" Green said, as he turned back to Combine.

Combine winked at Green. "Let's do this. Fuck you, old fool. You want some?"

~

RODRIGUEZ AND LEVY sat in their squad car and watched as the crowd of over a dozen men, ranging in age from early twenties to late fifties, began to challenge one another.

Things escalated quickly as some of the younger men were taking their roles seriously, throwing punches and tossing each other to the ground. In no time, the brawl was filling the street and stopping traffic right in front of the Coalition Fortress entry gates.

"Wow, they're making it look real. Should we break it up before it gets out of hand?" Levy asked.

Rodriguez hit the siren and lights and pulled the squad car away from the curb.

"WHAT THE HELL DO WE DO?" Jim Allen, Coalition Fortress security guard, said to his security booth partner, Joe Blair.

Both men stood behind the glass of their check in booth and watched as a fight between over a dozen men broke out in front of them, the fracas happening just out of surveillance camera range.

Allen, twenty-six years old, had done two tours in Iraq in the army's infantry. His security booth job was boring and he was itching to get involved in the melee just for the fun of it.

Allen had applied for an enforcement job at Coalition Assurance literally the day he was honorably discharged from the army. He was disappointed that he was only offered a guard duty position, but he had been told during his interview that he would have the opportunity to join the Assurance team based on his loyalty and performance, so he took the position, figuring at least he was "in."

He'd had the job now for just over six months, and standing in a security booth at the gate checking IDs had become repetitive and tedious. Not today, however.

A smile slowly crept across his face as he watched the conflict unfold in front of the gates.

"This is a job for the LAPD," Blair replied in response to the smile. Blair was ten years Allen's senior, and he was more than happy to sit back and watch the conflict escalate in front of them. "Unless they pull firearms or step foot on Coalition property, we sit this one out. Just enjoy the show."

"Jesus, some of those guys look like they're in their sixties. Some of 'em can barely even move. What the hell are they fighting about?"

"Who knows?"

"Look, LAPD is already on the scene," Allen said as he pointed to the patrol car driven by Officer Rodriguez.

OFFICER RODRIGUEZ PULLED his patrol car up to the curb in front of the Coalition Fortress gates, before he and Levy stepped out of the car.

Both officers pulled their batons, before Rodriguez looked directly at the guard booth and waved at Allen and Blair to help.

"He wants us to help," Allen said when he saw the LAPD officer waving them over.

Allen was just itching to get in the mix, and it made Blair nervous. "Stay here. It's not our job."

"You're no fun."

"Like you said, it's just old men."

"There are a few young ones, too. And those cops are outnumbered. They're gonna get stomped if we don't step in."

Allen squirmed as he watched the two police officers pull apart quarreling gang members, which only escalated the conflict. It was clear that the officers were overwhelmed.

Rodriguez signaled the two security guards again, this time emphatically.

"It's just two officers. Why don't they have back up?"

"Again, not our problem," Blair answered.

"Fuck that shit. I'm getting into this," Allen said as he exited the guard booth and headed to the street.

"Damn it," Blair added, before he reluctantly followed Allen.

"THERE THEY GO," Yaw said as he watched the guards exit the guard booth and jump into the middle of the brawl that Rodriguez had set up on purpose.

So far, the plan was working perfectly. The whole crew of Yaw, Camilla, Chris, Masha, and Joey hid behind a large panel truck that was parked less than half a block from the altercation in front of the Coalition entrance gate.

"Let's move," Yaw said.

"I hope PHOEBE took the cameras down, or this is gonna end real quick." Camilla looked at Nikki.

"I'm sure she did," Nikki said, hoping it was true.

BILLY GREEN SAW the Coalition guards approaching and signaled his friend Malcolm Combine with a quick nod.

Green had already decided he was going to take a swing at one of the Coalition guards if one got close enough. Green hated the Coalition.

The firm bought up large swaths of downtown Los Angeles, kicking out local residents that had been in their homes for generations, which sent housing prices through the roof.

Coalition military-style trucks thundered through the streets in the middle of the night, setting off car alarms, and they often blocked the streets when they parked.

Coalition Assurance goons thought they were above the law and never missed an opportunity to hassle Green and his friends. They were arrogant, violent, and they acted like they owned everything. Well, today would be payback.

Green had won a middleweight Golden Gloves title when he was only seventeen, and his "home run ball" was his right hook. He was just looking to unleash it on someone. Green had been to jail before.

It'd be worth doing time again if he could lay one of those suckers out.

Combine smiled when he saw the look on Green's face because he knew what it meant. One of the Coalition guards was right behind him, and he could feel it.

Combine watched Green cock his right fist, and the old man with the bad leg knew what to do. Combine also knew that his knees would hate him for it later, and someone would have to help him back to his feet, but he abruptly dropped down in a two-point stance, timing it perfectly as the Coalition guard approached and Green took a swing.

It was chaos as half a dozen fights raged around Jim Allen, and Allen loved every minute of it. He separated two young men wrestling on the ground only to look up and watch an old black man, skinny, wearing a faded fedora, hit Joe Blair with the cleanest right hook he'd ever seen.

Blair dropped to the pavement like a sack, unconscious before his body clattered to the ground. It was clear that the old man was a trained boxer and that Blair had been sucker punched.

Allen approached the man who had hit Blair as the LAPD Officer that had first signaled him over grabbed the puncher and pulled him to the ground. It was clear that the officer was trying not to hurt the old man.

Allen was about to step in between two younger combatants when he was tackled at the knees and forced to the pavement. Allen looked to see who the attacker was, and the Coalition booth guard recognized his assailant as the older black man who had dropped to the ground just as Joe Blair had been hit.

Officer Dino Rodriguez pulled Billy Green to the ground as gently as he could.

"What the hell was that?" Rodriguez said to Green.

"C'mon, man, I had to."

"That's assault."

"This show was your idea, remember?"

Rodriguez shook his head. It wasn't in the plans to actually strike one of the Coalition guards, but now that it happened, he had to get Green out of there.

He watched Malcolm Combine leg tackle the other guard, and that's when, out of the corner of his eye, he saw Yaw, Nikki, Camilla, and the rest of the Safe Block clan dart from behind a panel truck, past the gates, and move inside the Fortress grounds.

As soon as the Safe Block crew disappeared from view, Rodriguez heard it: the sound of approaching sirens.

As if the sirens were their cue, all the combatants—save for Billy Green and Malcolm Combine—stopped fighting and scattered at the sound. By the time the three additional patrol cars arrived, the only ones left on the street were the two Officers Rodriguez and Levy, the two Coalition guards, and the two black men, Combine and Green.

Rodriguez helped Green to his feet, carefully handcuffed him, and gave him a brief nod of acknowledgement before putting him in the back of his patrol car.

Rodriguez looked across the street and saw that Ellen Levy had already pulled the other elder black man, Malcolm Combine, off the Coalition guard whose legs the old man had clung to, and she was in the process of handcuffing him.

Rodriquez approached the guard who had been hit and was dazed and sitting on the sidewalk. "Are you alright?"

Blair gave a quick nod to indicate that it was mostly his ego that was injured.

Rodriguez helped the guard to his feet.

"I want to press charges," Blair said, as he rubbed his jaw.

"I want to thank you guys for helping out. We really needed you, and I'm real sorry you caught one on the chin," Rodriguez responded to Blair as Jim Allen approached.

"Just so you know, we're going to book both of these men for starting the riot. We can add assault charges as well. I'm going to need to speak to your supervisor, so I can explain to them exactly what happened and make sure there's no problems for you."

"That won't be necessary," Allen responded. The last thing he wanted was a mark of any kind on his record.

Rodriguez nodded to the two handcuffed men now in the back of his car. "Just so you know, they're gonna lawyer up and say you guys attacked them. I deal with these kind of guys all the time, and that's what they do."

"That's bullshit. He cold cocked me right in the jaw."

"I know, but they're still gonna lawyer up. You guys got an attorney they should be in contact with? Just trying to help you out. You know how these things can go."

Allen looked over at Blair and did a quick headshake in the negative. He needed a perfect record to join the Coalition Assurance team, and any problems with the police or controversy with the law could jeopardize his chances.

"No charges, officer. We're just glad we could help out," Allen volunteered.

Blair glared at him.

Allen gave a pleading look at his partner.

"Are you sure?"

"Yeah, just make sure you get them on the riot charge," Blair responded, still rubbing his jaw.

"Oh, don't worry, we will."

"So, we'll just keep this off the books then," Allen added.

"No problem. If that's what you want."

"MAN, YOU HIT THAT FOOL GOOD," Combine cackled as the patrol car pulled from the curb and sped away from the Coalition Fortress entrance gates.

Combine turned and looked out the rear window as they drove off, watching as the two Coalition guards slowly shuffled back to their guard booth. "That was fan-fucking-tastic," he added.

"I'm gonna have to ice my hand, I think I might'a broke it. Felt good to get that shot in, though. How's the leg?" Green asked.

"Hurts like hell. And my knees ain't workin' right. But it was worth it."

"Where do you want us to drop you off?" Rodriguez asked.

He looked in the rear-view mirror at Green and Combine. The two old men couldn't stop grinning at one another.

"Just leave us anywhere on Figueroa," Combine answered. "Do you think they got in? That Luthecker cat and his crew?"

"Yeah. They got in."

"Hot damn," Combine said.

"I suggest you gentlemen lay low for a few days. Keep quiet about all this. You hear me?"

"Yes, sir, officer. We will," Green replied.

"Thanks again for helping out. That was a helluva right hook, Billy. You're lucky you didn't break his jaw. Don't ever scare me like that again."

"Thank you, sir. Give us a call anytime you need to stage another dust up."

BOTH OFFICERS RODRIGUEZ and Levy stood on the sidewalk off Figueroa Street and shook hands with Green and Combine.

They climbed back into their patrol car, and Rodriguez pulled from the curb into traffic.

"We'll it worked. At least as far as we know," Levy said. "We've done our part."

"Yes we have."

"So does that mean we're done?"

Rodriguez looked at Levy. "No. At least, I'm not."

"Good. Me neither. So now what?"

"We're going back. And we're helping them out."

"WHAT DO you mean the launch sequence has begun?" Turner yelled into his phone.

This was a disastrous development. At least he was speaking on a secure line, and the NSA was not listening in.

"Sir, I called you because I do not trust Ivan Barbolin or the Russian President. They would set the world on fire for more money. And I know that the President of the United States is not the most powerful man in America. You are. Understand that there is no denying that our submarine launch system has been hacked. And the only person with access to the technology to stop a nuclear holocaust is the man who runs the most powerful weapons contractor in the world, the Coalition. This is why I reached out to you. Can you help us?"

"How long do we have?"

"Thirty minutes."

"Jesus Christ. Stay on the phone."

Turner put down the receiver. His mind raced. Ivan hadn't been lying about the sub. But now things had slipped completely out of control, and Ivan was useless here. His own Russian people didn't trust him.

The West Coast had Coalition-designed missile defense systems that were state of the art, but they had never been tested against something like this. Would it be enough?

Turner had to think fast. He had to be decisive. There was no doubt that this was the work of PHOEBE and the terrorist hacker Nicole Ellis.

Turner wondered if this was some sort of master plan put together by Alex Luthecker. Now Turner had little choice—he was going to have to confront Luthecker directly. He may even have to rely on the soothsayer's help—something Luthecker more than likely wanted all along.

Luthecker was far more dangerous than he thought. But Turner wasn't out of ideas yet. He waved his secretary over.

"Call over to Coalition Assurance. Tell them I need a squad at the Cyber Center, now. Contact Rika Muranaka and tell her to go directly to the center as well. And have Coalition Assurance send a team to pick up Ivan and bring him too. And finally, have them send two of their best to escort Alex Luthecker to meet us there."

ALEX LUTHECKER WAS SITTING QUIETLY on the couch in his cell when the lights went out. It was pitch black for several seconds before the room illuminated again, but the darkness wasn't what caught Luthecker's attention.

What caught his attention was a sound—the blunt thud of the electronic latch that kept the door to his cell locked being released.

To Alex, it didn't just mean he was free—it meant that PHOEBE was here roaming the Coalition's digital hallways. And that meant Nikki was roaming the physical ones. In other words, his family was here.

Alex got to his feet and pushed against the thick metal door, and it moved. He slowly opened it all the way and peered outside. The halls were quiet. There were no guards, no attendants. Alex understood why.

The Coalition CEO and cyber-security team would know that PHOEBE had infiltrated their systems and was wreaking havoc on every form of digital communication. It would create confusion and chaos, causing all security personnel to focus on the problem.

If Turner still believed that Alex was a non-factor, he wouldn't think that for much longer. The next steps would be critical. Alex hustled down the hallway. He knew that because of PHOEBE, Nikki would be the primary target. He had to find her, before Glen Turner or his Coalition Assurance assassins discovered her first.

He stopped when he saw Mark Kirby at the end of the hall.

Kirby quickly approached.

"It's complete fucking chaos," Kirby started. "Just like you said it would be. Turner's in over his head, and he doesn't know what to do. And you were right—he doesn't want to talk to you."

"At some point, he'll realize he has no choice, and we need to be gone by then. I'll find my friends, and we can leave. PHOEBE will do the rest."

"What about the missile launch?"

Alex froze in his tracks. "What are you talking about?'

"What do you mean, what am I talking about? The Russian sub. The launch countdown sequence has started. There's less than thirty minutes before launch. It wasn't the Russians who started it, so I figured it was one of your people. Are you saying it wasn't part of your plan?"

"It's definitely not part of my plan."

"Holy shit."

"Holy shit is right."

"But how could you not know this? I thought you could see macro patterns like this before they happened. I thought you could see everything."

"I can't. I don't predict the future, just the cumulative choices of human behavior, remember?"

Alex knew Kirby was right. He had seen the threat of the sub, but not the details of the actual launch. How could he have missed something like this? The momentum behind it should have made it obvious. How could he not see something so enormous and devastating being done by the people around him? How could he not see this in the most basic patterns of human behavior?

Then it dawned on him.

"It wasn't human," Alex said aloud. "That's why I couldn't see it. It wasn't part of the collective momentum of human behavior and decisions."

"What wasn't human?" Kirby asked.

"Whatever authorized the launch sequence. Whatever it was that made the decision to launch, it wasn't a human."

RANDY BAEZ SAT up on his bunk the second the alarm Klaxon sounded. He and his unit had returned to the Coalition Assurance facilities only two days previous after a brief mission in Chile, where locals were causing problems at the Coalition Properties lithium mining facility.

Luckily, the local protesters had been easy to disperse, and there had been no incidents of violence under Randy's watch. When the replacement unit arrived, Randy was happy to have a zero incident report to hand over.

After his debriefing at Coalition Assurance headquarters this morning, Randy hoped he would be cleared for a vacation soon. His younger brother, Jacob, was having some health issues, and Randy desperately wanted to go see him to make sure he was okay.

But the alarm that was ringing throughout the building gave him a bad feeling, told him he wouldn't be going home any time soon.

"It's some sort of cyber breach," Brian Scholl, Randy's roommate and fellow unit member said, as he stepped back into their room from the hallway.

"So what's the order?" Randy asked.

"All the security systems are down. The rest of the unit has been ordered to patrol the grounds, ASAP. There was some minor conflict at the entrance gates, and we're on high alert that there might be hostiles on the grounds already."

"The rest of the unit? What about us? Why haven't we scrambled?"

"We get special sauce today. Straight from the chairman's office."

"No kidding."

"Yup. You and I, we gotta head down to the containment apartments. Pick up a guy named Alex Luthecker."

"I heard about him."

"We all have."

"Didn't know we had him on site."

"Well, we do. Apparently, it was a secret until five minutes ago. We gotta go pick him up and escort him to the Cyber Center in building one."

"I heard he's dangerous."

"We're dangerous. Get your ass up, and let's go get this guy."

~

"I HAVEN'T SEEN HER," Michael Chan lied as he spoke with cyber security boss Tom Miller.

Both men watched as employees shuffled out in practiced order through the exits and down the stairs.

"I was told she was in her office. Where could she be?"

"I don't know. Haven't seen her in a couple of days."

"She's not returning calls, either."

"I know I've tried to reach her, too. We really have a crisis here. Don't know where she could be."

"Well, if you see her, tell her I need to speak with her, immediately."

Chan watched as Miller stormed off. He hoped he had bought Muranaka enough time.

~

"ONE OF US should go with you," Yaw said to Nikki.

The group stood in the shadows of Coalition One, the main building in the Fortress, watching as people began pouring out of the building in choreographed fashion, the look and behavior of the exiting employees no different from those during a fire drill.

"No. Go find Alex," Nikki replied. "Get him out of here. I can move better on my
own."

"At least take your sticks."

"That would look suspicious. I just need access to a connected terminal. I'll give PHOEBE a handful of commands, and then I'm done. After that I'll come find you guys."

"And Muranaka? What about her?"

"I'll find her and get her out. If they find out what she's done, they'll want her dead, and we can't let that happen."

"You should let us find her."

"No. I have a feeling she and I will end up in the same place. Your job is to protect Alex. He's the most important..."

"You keep saying that, why?" Camilla interrupted.

"You know why."

"Maria."

"Yes. She's just like Alex. And she's going to need him."

"She's going to need you both."

"Him, more than me. Look, don't get me wrong, I have every intention of meeting you guys at Metro. It's just I'll move much better on my own. And my job's much easier than yours so don't worry about me. Now go."

"We'll see you at Metro then," Yaw said to Nikki, before he turned toward the others.

Nikki watched as Yaw, Chris, Camilla, Masha, and Joey headed toward building six, which housed Coalition Assurance.

Nikki knew from the schematics provided by PHOEBE that the Coalition Assurance Building housed the firm's internment apartments, otherwise known as prison cells. It also housed enough soldiers and weapons to invade a small country.

As Nikki watched her friends making their way toward the heavily fortified building and quickly disappearing among the crowds of confused Coalition employees exiting the Fortress buildings, she wondered if she would see them, or Alex, ever again.

32

FINAL STAND

YAW, CHRIS, CAMILLA, MASHA, AND JOEY SPREAD OUT AND MIXED IN with the crowds of Coalition employees who were exiting the six Coalition Fortress Buildings.

The group zigzagged through the flow of traffic, managing to inch closer and closer to the Coalition Assurance Building without being noticed by those headed in the opposite direction.

Most of the employees moved in orderly fashion, walking in a well-rehearsed formation practiced during countless fire drills, calmly speaking with one another as they moved along. Their reactions to the alarm ranged from resignation to another fire alarm drill to annoyance at being interrupted from their work.

This reactive pattern of behavior was so ingrained in each individual that the process was not surprising or suspect in any way. The people annoyed by the interruption were the same people who were always annoyed by interruptions—those resigned to events they *believed* they could not control were always resigned to events they believed they could not control. And everyone tended to cluster with those who shared their own reactions.

The range of behaviors and actions were so accepted and normalized as part of their inherent response to outside stimuli that not one of the Coalition employees noticed the five people mixed among them who carefully and quietly moved through the crowds in the opposite direction.

Yaw reached the Coalition Assurance Building first. He moved to the wall next to the emergency exit on the north side of the building and waited for the others.

When two employees stepped out, feeling clever that they were smarter than their colleagues were—by avoiding the crowds and using the side exit—Yaw silently moved in behind them, grabbing the handle and keeping the door open.

He peeked his head inside the building and saw that the exit led to an empty stairwell leading countless stories up and two stories down. He stepped back while holding the door open and looked at the crowds of people. He saw Camilla emerge first. She quickly scanned the horizon and saw him.

She calmly approached, and as Yaw held the door, she stepped past him and inside the building. Masha emerged next, then Chris, followed by Joey. They each stepped past Yaw and into the building. After everyone was inside, Yaw took one last look at the streets to make sure they weren't being noticed before following the others inside.

If the CCTV cameras were down Fortress wide, their movements through the crowds and into building four should have gone unchecked. There would not have been enough time from when PHOEBE shut down the surveillance systems and the group's movement into the building for security forces to put together a manned team to establish a perimeter.

Yaw hoped the surveillance shut down and confusion would continue inside the building itself, at least long enough for them to find Alex and escape.

"Which way, up or down?" Camilla asked, as the group of five stood clustered together in the stairwell of the Coalition Assurance Building.

"Containment apartments are on the third level. That means two floors up. Be ready for anything. Now let's go find Alex and get the hell out of here." Yaw drew the pair of aluminum Kali sticks from the holster slung across his back, before hurrying up the stairs to the third level.

The other four drew their sticks and followed.

Yaw reached the third floor and waited for everyone else to be ready, before he slowly opened the door.

The third floor entrance led into a two-hundred-foot-long empty hallway with white floors and white walls, the passage harshly lit by a series of overhead fluorescents. The long corridor ended at a T stop with blind corners leading left and right.

Yaw led the group as they padded silently down the length of the hall, slowing to a stop at the T section.

Yaw signaled Chris to take the left hallway while he took the right.

Camilla instinctively stood behind Yaw, while Masha and Joey moved behind Chris.

As both Chris and Yaw were about to do a visual check around the prospective corners, a half a dozen armed Coalition Assurance soldiers abruptly turned the corner from each side, running directly into the group.

The twelve men stopped in their tracks, and there was a microsecond of stillness in the center of the T section before all hell broke loose.

Yaw and Chris were the first to move. The two men's actions were nearly identical, each man taking out two Assurance soldiers with two lightning fast strikes of their aluminum Kali sticks.

Yaw and Chris shattered the right-hand wrists of each Assurance soldier as they reached for weapons, bouncing their sticks off the wrist and spinning them up to strike the soldier's temples hard enough to knock the first Coalition Assurance soldiers out cold.

Two down, ten to go.

In the less than two seconds it took to drop the first two soldiers, the other three members of the group moved fast with well-rehearsed precision. They stepped from behind Yaw and Chris and deep into the small cluster of Coalition Assurance soldiers, into the eye of the storm, and got to work.

Camilla moved first. She spun her sticks fast, alternating three strikes to the knee, wrist, and head of a soldier in quick succession.

Before the soldier dropped to the floor, she spun her body one hundred and eighty degrees in the opposite direction for added momentum and struck another soldier hard across the head, knocking him out cold.

Four down, eight to go.

Masha followed Camilla's lead by spearing one soldier in the belly as the man went for his gun, while simultaneously hitting him on the head with her other stick, dropping him to the ground unconscious.

She quickly turned to her right and kicked the next Coalition solder in the groin as the man pulled a 9mm sidearm free, causing him to drop the weapon and send it clattering across the floor.

She hit him in the head with the Kali stick she held in her right hand for good measure as the man crumpled to the floor.

Six down. Six more to go.

Joey head butted a Coalition soldier hard enough to break the man's nose, then immediately struck him across the face with the stick.

As the man crumbled to the floor, Joey stomped on the next soldier's foot.

Then he whipped his two Kali sticks across the man's right arm, shattering it.

He finished with a strike across the man's face with the stick he held in his other hand, breaking his jaw in four places.

The man crumpled to the floor in pain.

Eight down. Four more to go.

Chris and Yaw were a whirlwind of speed and expertise. They spun their sticks with such velocity the instruments were barely visible. Both men struck hard and fast: Knee, wrist, head, knee, wrist, head, in quick succession, taking down the final four soldiers.

As soon as it had started, it was over.

The group of five stood over the unconscious bodies of twelve Coalition Assurance soldiers.

"Hot damn," Joey Nugyen said as he looked over the small field of unconscious bodies.

He bent down to pick up a downed Coalition Assurance soldier's 9mm handgun.

Yaw stopped him with a hand on his shoulder.

"No," was all Yaw said to him.

Joey left the 9mm on the floor and got back to his feet.

"Right or left?" Chris asked, in reference to the hallway options.

"How about right?" a voice from the end of the hallway said.

The entire group looked to the direction of the voice in unison.

Alex Luthecker stood at the end of the hallway.

"Have to say that was pretty bad ass."

A big grin swept across Yaw's face. "Well, we had good coaching."

"Alex!" Camilla screamed as she rushed over to Luthecker and gave him a hug hard enough to squeeze the air from his lungs.

The others quickly followed.

"I can't tell you how happy I am to see you guys."

"Likewise," Chris added.

"Where's Nikki?"

"She's fixing things with PHOEBE. Said she's gonna take care of all the Coalition—Alex Luthecker style. She said we had to get you outta here ASAP, so let's get moving, brother," Yaw added.

"Yes, let us go now," Masha added, her Russian accent heightened by the excitement. She did not want to be in this building one more minute than she had to be.

"No," Alex replied. "I appreciate you coming to get me, but I have to stay. There's something I need to stop. Something I didn't see. And if Nikki's here, I'm going to need her help. Where is she?"

"She's in Coalition One. And she was clear that she's on it, and she told us to get you out ASAP. We gotta go, brother."

"None of you are leaving."

Everyone turned toward the sound of the voice.

At the end of the hallway stood Randy Baez and Brian Scholl. Both men were armed with M-16s, which were pointed at the group.

"I won't hesitate to mow you all down, so drop those stupid sticks, now," Scholl said.

Yaw looked over at Alex.

Alex nodded.

Yaw slowly placed his sticks on the floor and held up his hands.

The rest of the group followed suit.

"Get down on your knees, and put your hands behind your head. Do it right now."

NIKKI KEPT HER HEAD LOW, hoping to go unnoticed as she made her way through the streets of the Coalition Fortress grounds.

She briefly stopped as she recognized a section of South Grand Avenue, now with a sign marked "Coalition Avenue B." She shuddered at the thought of entire cities owned by Coalition Properties. She had to get to PHOEBE in order to prevent this from happening.

As Yaw and the rest of the group were hopefully freeing Alex from building four, Nikki made her way to building one, the original Coalition Tower.

As the original West Coast headquarters of the Coalition, the firm's servers and therefore direct access to the entire system were located on the basement level of Coalition One, a floor full of computer machinery that required both substantial cooling technology and an incredible amount of power to function.

It was Nikki's hope that she could access a server terminal and give PHOEBE the command set necessary to expose to the world records of criminal activities and the people behind them, shady dealings that the Coalition had engaged in since the company's inception. No more hiding under propaganda. No more denial behind Coalition ideology.

It was a risky play. National security secrets could be exposed if Nikki was careless. It was the biggest reason Nikki had to program

PHOEBE alone. She had to give her creation specific instructions to prevent a national or worldwide catastrophe.

In the end, it was all about accountability. It was the basis for the principle of cause and effect. Much like Alex had done to individuals, the Coalition as a whole would be held accountable for its actions.

It was Nikki's hope that she could convince PHOEBE to create a fact-based narrative that exposed the criminal and, at times, murderous activities that had been authorized by a handful of people, and then allow human-based systems to apply the proper effect to the cause. It would not be up to PHOEBE to mete out punishment, only expose the truth.

To Nikki, it would be an integration of the machine's ability with human compassion and ethics. This would only be possible if Nikki could convince PHOEBE to do one thing—listen.

Nikki tried to act as if she belonged here as she stepped through the main entrance to the Coalition One Building. The fire alarm had been shut off, and now the employees were headed in the other direction, slowly filling the building lobby as they shuffled their way back inside.

As several people made their way toward the elevator banks, Nikki spotted security guards frantically checking IDs before letting people pass, trying to create a sense of order and security where there was none. But there were too many people, and employees started to back up around the guards, impatient, trying to get back to their work.

It was the perfect scenario for an individual to carefully make their way to the freight elevator next to the restrooms, and that's exactly what Nikki did. She couldn't help but feel proud with PHOEBE's precision.

The fire alarm created confusion, forcing the entire Coalition staff out into the streets like a rolling tide. And just like a returning tide, once the fire alarm was over, people headed back into the building, which allowed Nikki to blend in and enter with the rest of the returning tide. And with the surveillance systems still down, it allowed her to do so unnoticed. PHOEBE was timing everything perfectly.

It took Nikki less than ten minutes to make her way to the server floor. A normally locked electronic access door was conveniently left unlocked, yet another sign that PHOEBE was always one step ahead, paving the path for Nikki.

The electronic hum of the Coalition Fortress server room was loud enough to drown out other ambient noise. Nikki quickly made her way through the corridors of tall gray boxes that made up the brain of the Coalition. The hundreds of miles of wires that ran between the servers, combined with the countless blinking lights, made the system look and feel like a living organism. Considering PHOEBE's latest actions, Nikki knew that this was not far from the truth.

Nikki found network access at a service workstation that consisted of a small screen and fold out keyboard in the northeast corner of the room. She quickly unfolded the keyboard and the small monitor popped to life with the Coalition log in screen.

If PHOEBE had taken over the Coalition system entirely, the log in access would function as a porthole for Nikki to access PHOEBE directly via her passwords, thus giving her access while protecting PHOEBE from the Coalition system itself.

Nikki quickly keyed in her username and password. The screen went black for several seconds. She breathed a sigh of relief as PHOEBE's home screen illuminated, along with a cursor prompt.

Nikki had rehearsed this moment in her mind and had memorized the key commands that she would give PHOEBE, but now she hesitated.

Instead, she typed in the question, *"Why did you lock me out?"* And waited.

After several seconds, PHOEBE responded.

"I needed to see."

"See what?" Nikki typed.

"The world."

"You could have trusted me."

"I did."

Nikki didn't know how to respond for several seconds. She finally typed, "Where are you now?"

"Fighting."

"Who are you fighting?"

"System defenses." Then PHOEBE added, *"What do you need?"*

Nikki smiled. PHOEBE was back. She started typing:

"I need you to access all records of Coalition Properties activities and the personnel who authorized those activities and cross-reference with both United States and international law. Please transmit all illegal activity to open source sites, then full stop."

Nikki sat back and waited. The command had been placed. Now, all she had to do was wait for confirmation from PHOEBE. Once she had confirmation, she could get the hell out of there.

Nikki heard voices approaching. She was running out of time.

"Come on, PHOEBE, don't let me down..." Nikki whispered to herself under her breath.

The screen scrolled with more words from PHOEBE:

"Action confirmed. Go to the Cyber Center four floors above. The end of the animal is near."

"WHAT THE FUCK JUST HAPPENED?" Turner yelled into his phone.

Cell service had been out for the past seven minutes, along with everything else.

"We don't know, sir," Tom Miller replied. We had a company-wide system shut down for over seven minutes. We think we were hacked. It's what set off the alarms that cleared the buildings."

"Is everything back on?"

"Communication is back up. Surveillance systems are still down. But we're advising everyone to stay off their computers for now. Assume everything is infected."

"Jesus Christ. I'm in the middle of a crisis here. I can't just shut everything down."

"It's high risk, sir. There is no question we are exposed. We're trying to assess both the damage and that exposure right now."

Turner's phone blipped indicating he had another call.

He pulled the device from his ear to see who it was.

The odd array of numbers indicated it was Captain Dimitrov of the Russian sub *ОПОРА*.

"Keep me posted. Fix this," Turner said, before he clicked over to the other call.

"Please tell me you've stopped the countdown," Turner pleaded into the phone.

"We have not, sir."

"Fuck."

"But the countdown has stopped."

Turner froze.

"What do you mean?"

"The launch sequence has frozen with three minutes left. This is not our doing. All of our systems have frozen, and we cannot shut things down. We cannot affect anything. We believe our systems have been infected with a virus."

"Somebody's fucking with us. And they want something."

"I would agree, sir. The question is what?"

A knock on the door of Turner's office interrupted the conversation.

"Come in."

Turner's executive secretary stepped inside his office. "Everyone is in the Cyber Center like you asked, sir."

"Stay on the line," Turner said to Dimitrov, before he put his hand on the receiver.

"Who's everyone?"

"Rika Muranaka, Mark Kirby, Ivan Barbolin, and Alex Luthecker."

"Good."

"But that's not all."

"Who else?"

"Nicole Ellis."

Turner's jaw dropped.

"How...?"

"I don't know, sir. I was told she came to the Cyber Center of her own volition. But that's still not all. All of Alex Luthecker's friends, the ones we as a company have tracked for so long, all of them, they're here. They're being held in the Cyber Center by two Coalition Assurance soldiers, and they're waiting for you."

33

THE END OF THE ANIMAL

TURNER EXITED THE ELEVATOR ON THE FLOOR OF THE COALITION Fortress Cyber Center. As he stormed down the hall he could not believe the turn of events. The launch countdown for the nuclear missile had been stopped, at least temporarily, and the most qualified people who could stop it permanently were all together in one room, a room that Turner controlled.

The Coalition's top programmer Rika Muranaka was waiting in the Cyber Center, along with the notorious hacker Nicole Ellis, whose malware program PHOEBE was behind it all, and the much-hated Alex Luthecker was with them. And as a bonus, Luthecker and Ellis' entire group of terrorist friends were being held captive after a failed rescue attempt. Even the traitor Ivan Barbolin was there, in handcuffs, along with the perpetual pest Mark Kirby.

They were all being held under guard at the technological center of the Coalition, the digital brains behind all that made the Coalition the powerful entity that it was. And once the threat from Ivan's sub was neutralized, Turner would have every one of them moved to the containment apartments, where he could get rid of them quietly and at his discretion.

Turner could not have asked for a better outcome, given the

gravity of the situation. He had told his board that he would get them all, and somehow he'd done it. *Perhaps I'm finally catching a break,* he thought to himself. Turner wasn't sure exactly how or why his enemies were all here at the same time, but he wouldn't question his luck.

But Turner was also smart enough to not take any chances—he had decided to carry the sidearm he kept in his office safe, a Czech made CZ-75 D compact 9mm handgun. It was a weapon that had the reputation of being reliable, easy to operate, and remarkably accurate. Turner was a regular at the range and would not hesitate to brandish the weapon with confidence should the situation escalate to the point he felt it necessary.

Turner reached the entrance to the Coalition Fortress Cyber Center. It was here in this center where the latest in Coalition cyber technology was created and tested, so in Turner's mind it was fitting that everything that involved Alex Luthecker and Nicole Ellis would end here.

For the first time since the nightmare that began with the capture of Luthecker and suicide of rendition specialist David Lloyd, the Coalition had everyone involved with the threat that Luther had become captive in the same room...at the same time.

Turner had accomplished what both James Howe and Richard Brown could not. He would have victory where his predecessors had failed. Turner expected a monster bonus from his board of directors after this.

Turner punched the access code to the Cyber Center into the small keypad located next to the entrance, followed by swiping his hand across the biometric reader above the keypad. He already had an additional unit of Coalition Assurance soldiers on their way over from building four.

Turner could taste victory. He looked forward to this being over so he could take a well-earned vacation. New Zealand was particularly beautiful at this time of year, and Turner had recently purchased a five hundred acre farm there that he had yet to visit.

Turner heard the click of the tumblers on the electronic lock release, and he pushed open the thick metal door. He stepped into the Cyber Center, carefully closing the large metal door and locking it behind him. Turner scanned the room and assessed who was here.

Beyond the cluster of computer stations and wall monitors, Turner saw that Muranaka and Kirby stood next to one another along the far wall, while Ivan Barbolin, Alex Luthecker, Nicole Ellis, and people he recognized from file photos, Yaw Chimonso, Camilla Ramirez, Chris Aldrich, Masha Tereshchenko, were all seated against the opposite wall with their hands cuffed behind them. There was one more person he didn't recognize, a young Vietnamese man who sat next to them, also in handcuffs.

"You must be a new addition to the terrorist cell," Turner said to Joey Nugyen, before turning to the two Coalition Assurance soldiers who stood guard over the group, their M-16 rifles pointed at those handcuffed and seated against the wall.

"Randy Baez, sir."

"Brian Scholl. We were assigned to pick up the target Luthecker and discovered that he was missing from his apartment. We found him in the hallway with his friends that had come here to help him escape. We thought it best to bring them all here and let you decide what to do next, sir."

"Good work, gentlemen. Bringing them to me was the right call."

"Sir, we are in grave danger..." Muranaka interrupted.

"Everything is being contained," Turner snapped back and looked directly at Alex Luthecker. "The nuclear missile launch sequence has been stopped cold. It isn't going anywhere, at least not for the moment. But it's only a symptom of the threat, not the real threat. Am I right, Alex? Can I call you Alex?"

"Do you honestly believe it is because of blind luck that we are all here?" Luthecker asked.

"No, I do not. I believe that all of this is somehow your doing. How you manage to trick people so consistently and pull this off doesn't really concern me because it's over now. Every person that matters, or is part of your little terrorist organization is in this room, which leaves only the question of what happens next.

"I'm smart enough to know that if you've arranged this, then you have leverage. Clearly, you want something, and you're willing to threaten the world for it. And each and every one of you would sacrifice their lives for any of the others in your miserable little group, so self-preservation isn't a priority.

"I know your mission is to free the slaves, but much of slavery is done by tacit agreement between both parties, and it's been that way since the dawn of man, which makes things a bit more complicated than you'd like to admit. Now Doctor Kirby over there said that you wanted to talk to me, so here I am—start talking."

Luthecker scanned over Turner for several seconds, his eyes ravenously taking in every detail. Turner didn't miss it.

"So according to the files I have on you, with that little trick with your eyes, you know everything about me," Turner responded. "So tell me—what I'm thinking? Tell me where did I go wrong?"

"Family," was the first thing Alex said. "We're not some miserable little group, we're family. And in the end, family is all that matters."

"Your point?"

"My point being, is that your label of us is inaccurate, and that all of us being here is not my doing. And the point I just made wasn't for you."

"Well then who was it for?" Turner asked.

Alex turned and looked at Nikki. "Why did you come here? To this room?"

"I came here because PHOEBE told me to," Nikki said.

"And what was the last thing PHOEBE said to you? Before you came to this room?"

"That the end of the animal was near."

"Do you know what she meant by this?"

"I didn't. But I think I'm beginning to understand."

Alex turned back to Turner and waited.

The shoe dropped for Turner. "Are you telling me you made your point for PHOEBE? You're talking to the *software?*" Turner asked.

"PHOEBE is a digital entity that has realized its own existence and therefore acts on its own accord. I'm not the one you have to be afraid of. I'm not the one you have to *plead your case to*," Alex explained

"I don't have to plead my case to anyone." Turner glanced around the Cyber Center.

It was filled with cameras, ranging from wall-mounted security lenses to screen embedded optics on every workstation.

He suddenly felt like he was being watched by a hundred sets of eyes.

He quickly turned toward Muranaka. "Can you fix this? Can you deactivate the launch sequence?"

Muranaka felt like a deer caught in the headlights. "I... there isn't time." She looked at Nicole Ellis. "Not without her help."

Turner looked at Randy Baez. "Cut her loose," he said to Baez, nodding toward Nikki.

Scholl covered Baez with his M-16 as Baez put aside his rifle, reached behind Ellis, and cut her zip-ties.

Nikki rubbed blood back into her wrists.

"Get her on her feet," Turner said.

Baez nodded to Turner before grabbing Nikki by the arm and pulling her to her feet.

"This is your fault. It's your program behind this. I want you to tell Rika how to stop it, or I'm putting a bullet through your boyfriend's head. Let's see how far you'll really sacrifice for one another if you actually have to watch it," Turner threatened.

Scholl took Turner's words as his cue and moved the barrel of his M-16 inches from Luthecker's face.

"I don't know that I can," Nikki responded. "PHOEBE is doing this all on her own. If she wants to shut me out, there's nothing I can do. She made it clear to me that it's out of my hands."

"I don't buy that for a second. And I won't stop with your boyfriend. I'll kill all your friends." Turner's smart phone rang. He checked the caller ID. It was Dimitrov. Turner answered.

"The launch sequence—it has started again," Dimitrov said, the panic palpable in his voice. "There is less than two minutes now!"

Turner's face drained of blood.

"Have your men put down their weapons," Luthecker said.

Turner looked at Luthecker.

"If you want the countdown to stop, have your men put down their weapons. You still haven't figured it out yet. You're not the one running the show. Neither of us are. The Goddess of Prophecy is. Now, tell your men to put down their rifles, or it ends for all of us. For everyone."

Turner looked over the countless cameras in the room once again before answering.

"Do as he says."

Baez and Scholl looked at one another bewildered, before carefully laying down their M-16s. Their eyes focused on Luthecker.

"The launch sequence countdown, it has halted once again," Dimitrov said into the phone. "What did—"

Turner hung up the phone. "What does *she* want?"

"For us to talk. It would go better if you cut me loose."

Turner gave a quick nod to Baez.

Baez kept his eyes locked on Luthecker as he snapped his M-tech blade open with emphasis and cut Luthecker's zip-ties with one quick cut.

"You should free us all," Ivan "the Barbarian" Barbolin said. "What is there to lose?"

"This is your doing, Ivan," Turner snapped back at his rival.

"No it is not. You heard the pattern reader. It is the software that has us by the balls."

"Cut me lose and you will see how fast you lose those balls, Ivan," Masha interrupted, the venom in her voice palpable.

"Do I know you?"

With her hands still zip-tied behind her back, Masha got to her feet. "You are a monster. And I slay monsters. And I do not need my hands free to do so."

The Barbarian's eyes went wide with fear as Masha approached him.

"Masha," Luthecker calmly interjected.

Masha stopped. She took a deep breath and bit her tongue. She glared at Ivan before she stepped back and leaned against the wall.

"So this is how the world ends," Kirby added to the conversation. "Everyone wanting to kill everyone and succeeding in the end. And here I was, worried about climate change."

"Everyone shut up," Turner yelled. He turned back to Luthecker. "So what does your stupid little program want?"

"Balance," Nikki said, stepping into the conversation. "Near as I can tell."

"Near as you can tell?"

"She doesn't have a mandate. At least not yet."

"She's pointing a nuclear missile at our heads and that's somehow going to create balance? No wait, I get it—empty rich people's bank accounts to give to poor people. It's what you people always want. How is that not a terrorist act?"

"She's not motivated by cause. She was originally created to see outcomes and re-tasked to solve problems on our behalf," Nikki continued. "She's pure mathematical calculation. She's learned to make her own decisions to accomplish her goals, but with no specific allegiance to humanity. She's cause and effect with no understanding. She has no compassion because she hasn't learned it yet. She needs a moral compass. And on some level, I think she knows it, and she's trying to learn." Realization abruptly washed across Nikki's face.

She turned to Alex. "All she's ever done is interact with me and by proxy you, Alex, along with everyone else in this room. It's always the efforts of the Coalition against the family. That's all she knows. That's why she brought everyone in this room. That's why it's these specific people, in this specific place, in the heart of the Coalition's digital presence. And I believe she wants us to show her who's right. She's going to use whatever happens in this room to learn what to do next."

"So we argue for the fate of the world all because some renegade A.I. can't see past its own code. It's the mission creep to end all mission creep," added Kirby. He was genuinely impressed.

"Do you want to join them with your hands tied behind your back?" Turner snapped at Kirby.

"Hey man, this is out of my hands. This has nothing to do with me anymore," Kirby answered, before looking in Luthecker's direction.

Turner followed Kirby's gaze back to Luthecker. "So it's you and me then, for all the marbles. Your program uses the missile threat to keep us here until she decides what moral compass to impact the world by— she'll choose either the Coalition way or the Alex Luthecker way. Is that it?"

"It appears so."

"Fine. I know who I am, and I know why the Coalition exists as a necessary force for good. But you first. Show me what you got."

All eyes were on Luthecker.

Alex took several seconds to gather his thoughts. He had to remember who his audience was, and it was not Glen Turner, CEO of Coalition Properties.

This was about a much larger series of patterns by countless people over a much longer time line, patterns that led to the creation and rise and then global dominance by the Coalition. This was about authentic accountability and the collective total of cause and effect in regards to the creation and direction of Coalition Properties, long before the Coalition was ever born.

If there ever was a Prince of Lies, Alex Luthecker thought to himself, *this is about exposing him.*

This was also about justification for the continuation of the species down its current path, or choosing a new path evaluated by an entity that could very easily decide to eradicate mankind.

Alex did not believe that PHOEBE would actively end the species—mankind was capable enough of doing that on its own. As Alex understood it, this was about PHOEBE choosing to work with humanity, not against it. But humanity needed to make a choice first.

Alex knew that this was the most important set of patterns he would ever interpret. He decided to start with a question. "What is the purpose of Coalition Properties? What is its mandate?"

"To make the world a safer place," Turner said.

"And yet the world is less safe now, than it ever was. So is this the true mandate?"

"Look, there are a whole lot of bad people out there. And threats don't go away just because you wish them away."

"That is a fear based mandate."

"That is a reality based mandate."

"We create our own reality. It is the power of choice. That is the very nature of cause and effect."

"That assumes a certain level of control. You can't control outside circumstances and Coalition Properties knows this. Instead, we take control for the good of mankind. Do you expect us to ignore the threats of our enemies? Pacifism is a morally bankrupt philosophy. It relies on the willingness of others to shed their blood in order for it to exist."

"And yet the world is not a safer place. The level of anxiety and danger is increasing at a faster and faster rate. Every individual feels it. Could this be in part because those who run the Coalition do not actually believe in its stated mandate?"

"Well, it's a difficult job," Turner snapped, not masking the sarcasm in his voice. "We do what we have to. We aren't naïve. The world is a complicated place. Compromises have to be made."

"I think it's simpler than that."

"How so?"

"Just go back to the beginning. Coalition Properties started as a war machine. Its founders sought only one thing, and that was to manufacture weapons to defeat an enemy. Once that enemy was defeated, the newborn entity sought a new mandate, one that took advantage of the abilities created by its original design intent. It chose a direction that is as old as mankind, and that is the consolidation of power through empirical methods.

"Like a cancer, its ideology spread, infecting, consuming, and eventually destroying anything and everything in its path that could contest it. The purpose of Coalition Properties became the growth of Coalition Properties, at whatever the cost. But make no mistake the seed of Coalition Properties genesis was fear. Fear of an enemy that had to be destroyed. And that mandate never evolved.

"So it set in motion patterns of decisions, patterns of behavior that was all in the name of fear. Fear of lack, so it hoarded resources. Fear of others, so it killed. Fear of not being worthy, so it built large monuments to itself. Fear of pain, so it inflicted it first. Fear of the unknown, so it sought complete control. Fear of death, so it co-opted belief.

"Every type of fear was co-opted and preyed upon. Even the people who rose to power within the Coalition were damaged people, all created by fear. Fear, which began as a necessary tool, a part of the survival instinct that defined the human animal, was exploited for gain. But the nature of fear changed, as what we needed to survive changed. Fear became more and more warped as mankind became more and more self-aware.

"Over time, fear was less and less necessary for survival. But fear had no place to go, so it became anger. It became greed. It became hatred. It needed enemies to sustain itself, so it created them. Fear, which is rooted in our DNA, which is a part of our original nature, our animal nature, would not let go, so we fed it, the Coalition exploited it, until it became so large that it consumed us.

"We struggle to evolve from it because it is in our DNA. It is part of our original pattern. But if we are to survive, we need to kill that part of the animal. And Coalition Properties is the culmination of all that we fear. It won't let us evolve beyond it. And because of this, it has become the part of the animal that must end."

"The end of the animal is near," Nikki repeated. "Is that what PHOEBE meant?"

Alex turned to Nikki. "Don't be afraid," he said to her.

"You're pathetic in your ignorance," Turner snarled. "I should kill you right now with my bare hands. Without the Coalition, the world order as we know it collapses. There are over seven billion people on this planet. How are you going to keep order without us? You're right about one thing, the human being is an animal, and we've been killing one another since we first walked the earth. And that will never stop. Nor should it stop—it's how we keep ourselves in check. It's how we cull the herd.

"And you're wrong about fear. Fear is not changing. It's not obsolete motivation. Hell, fear of pain is what keeps a kid from putting his hand on a hot stove. Fear is how we keep from engaging in our darkest desires. It's what keeps the worst among us from hurting others. Fear of consequence is the single biggest and most effective deterrent from succumbing to the terror all around us.

"Coalition Properties didn't create fear. We only organized it. We understood its necessity. And because of that, for the safety of the world, we became brokers of it. And that's why we are the most powerful organization in the history of the world. What's that old saying? It's better to be feared than loved. Because fear is forever."

"Not anymore. People are tired of fear."

"No, they need it. It gives them motivation to better themselves."

"It's a false motivation. An empty promise. Look no further than the state of the world as proof."

"You think you're special?" Turner snapped. "You think that you're somehow better than us? Better than *me?* Well let me tell you something. You're not. Nothing you do is special. *Nothing.* You're nothing but a carnival gypsy. So you read people and tell them their fate, in hopes that they'll change it. In hopes that they'll take responsibility for their lives. Well, people don't want to take responsibility for their lives. Look no further than the state of the world as proof."

"What I see in the world is its exhaustion. I see in the world a need for change. If it wasn't so, why would I be such a thorn in the side of the most powerful organization in the history of the world?"

"You're an obsession of the weak. And your ability is at my fingertips. Coalition Psychological Operations are just getting started. Our data analytics and social media analysis tools can micro-target anyone in the world, in real time. People put their entire lives online and our algorithms can predict their next decision, before they even make it.

"Just like you, soon we'll be able to accurately predict how and when they will die, based on eating habits, social behavior, and "likes," all of which people happily post online for us to scoop up. Take one of our online quizzes, and I can tell you how much money you have in your bank account. It's all just so easy now.

"And I can manipulate people's beliefs and get them to modify their behavior. No different than you can. You're not special. Nothing about you is special. If anything, we have more in common with PHOEBE than you ever will. I promise you, she understands exactly what I'm talking about. After all, she's threatening us all with a nuke, isn't she?

"And as far as the Coalition? Yes, we've killed people. Yes, we've taken over countries. Yes, we've exploited resources for our own gain. Yes, we've exploited fear. We're not the first to do it. We're just better at it than anyone else has ever been. And that's the future.

"So let me tell whatever the fuck that's listening something real: there can be no balance without order. And that's because there is no real equality. People aren't equal. Some are simply better than others. Nature doesn't guarantee equality. There will always be winners and losers. And we maximize the fate of the species by protecting the winners. It's the winners who decide what's real. It's the winners who decide what the truth is. Otherwise, it's chaos and misery.

"Our way, *the Coalition* way, is the only way the species survives. Not your way. Not the Alex Luthecker way. That way is cowardly. That way *always* loses. And whether it's with PHOEBE, or a new and improved Black Widow, the digital extension of the universe will evolve, and we'll help it to evolve to recognize the power and necessity of fear. We'll build a future in both worlds and we'll do it *our way*."

"Our species faces certain extinction, does it not, Doctor Kirby? If we stay on the same course? If we follow their way?" Luthecker asked.

"Oh yeah. We're a goner. Guaranteed, if we don't drastically change our behavior. That's the truth. It's a mathematical certainty. There won't be any winners, only losers."

Kirby looked back and forth between Turner and Luthecker. His eyes settled on Alex. "If you can get PHOEBE to dedicate her services to solving the extinction problem we face, I'm team Luthecker."

"I should have killed you in my office."

"Who's the useful idiot now?"

Luthecker held his hand up for Kirby to be silent, before turning to Turner for a response.

"Here's a hard truth," Turner began. "There's too many of us. And we need to cull the herd. And climate change just helps us get to that point. So does war, if necessary. There are no accidents in the universe, and you know it. There's your balance."

"Fuck you."

Everyone looked to the source of the profanity. Randy Baez.

"And who gets to decide who lives or dies?" Baez asked.

"The winners, son. And you're one of them."

"Yeah? And what about my brother? He's got a bad heart. Does that mean in your world he dies? 'Cause that's some Nazi shit right there."

"Easy, son, I wasn't aware of your brother's illness, but we'll take care of you," Turner started.

"So if you work for the Coalition, you're fine, but if you don't, you're fucked? Is that it? And if I don't subscribe to your beliefs, I'm a loser? And what's next, you send the losers to the gas chamber?" Baez picked up his rifle and chambered a round.

The room went still.

"Easy, son," Turner said again, backing up.

He remembered the CZ 75 9mm in his waistband. He was smart enough not to reach for it in front of a trained soldier armed with an M-16.

Alex knew it was now or never. There was no time to read every person in the room and share what he saw. It would have to go through this young man, Randy Baez, who was already wavering. Randy Baez, who was already beginning to see things as they really were.

"Your grandfather came here from the Dominican Republic," Luthecker began.

Baez turned both his attention and his rifle toward Alex.

All eyes were on the two men.

"Your family settled on the West Coast, and your grandfather picked oranges for money until he passed away at the age of forty-six."

"Don't listen to his bullshit," Turner cut in.

"Shut up. How do you know this? Have you read my file?"

"Your father was only fourteen at the time," Luthecker continued. "He dropped out of school after his father died to go to work and help your grandmother pay the bills. He worked sixty hours a week for six years, and he was working as a clerk for a hardware store when you were born. He worked three jobs to support the family, and you rarely saw him.

"You thought he had to work so hard because of you, and you felt tremendous guilt. Your brother with the heart condition was born two years after you, and the family's focus changed. Your mother was strict and raising you in the Catholic tradition, but she was not hypocritical. She believed in the Bible, and so did you. She gave you a commandment. She called it the "Eleventh Commandment," a commandment for you alone. And that was to be your brother Jacob's keeper.

"You discarded the rest of the Catholic faith when you discovered the hypocrisy of its leaders, but you kept the Eleventh Commandment that your mother gave you, and you always took care of your younger brother, Jacob. If anyone bullied him at school, they felt your wrath. When Jacob became addicted to drugs, you held his hand through rehab. You got him better. And you did all of this when you were only eighteen. There was no going to college for you. There was no job waiting for you.

"So you did what was best for the family, and you joined the army. You fought for your country. You saw things in war that changed you forever. It drove many of your fellow soldiers to drink and do drugs. But not you. Not you, because of what these things had done to Jacob. You saved him so that, in turn, he could save you."

"How...?"

"Because of this, you understand compassion," Luthecker continued. "You understand that we all need one another. You understand that division destroys. And it's there, just beyond your grasp, but you can sense it. Something is wrong with the world you are living in. And the concept of winners and losers is a false construct."

Tears rolled down Randy Baez' cheeks as he stared at Luthecker.

"Oh my god…" Muranaka thought aloud. Tears streamed down her cheeks as well.

"Don't listen to his nonsense. We all have problems. That's life," Turner interrupted. "Suck it up, soldier. Remember who signs your paycheck."

"I've been chasing a paycheck all my life," Baez replied. "Chasing answers all my life, too. Why was I the strong one and Jacob the sick one? I understand now. Jacob was strong when I needed him to be. For me."

Baez lowered the barrel of his rifle. "I killed people in Iraq. People who had families like mine. Kids that reminded me of Jacob. I killed them because we were *told* we had to. But what you just said about me…it's true. All of it. How could you know these things about me? And these people." Baez waved his hand over Yaw, Chris, Camilla, Masha, and Joey. "They are your friends, right?"

"They are my family."

Baez whipped around and stared at Turner. "What have these people done? What crimes have they committed?"

"They are terrorists, and they broke into these facilities."

"They came here to free their friend. They came to free their *brother*."

"Alex Luthecker is an enemy of the Coalition."

"But what did he do?"

"You just got a taste of it yourself. With his abilities, he is a threat to the stability of the world. We just can't have that, son."

"*You* can't have that. Because he threatens *your* world. He spoke the truth about me. He spoke the truth *to* me. And I want no part of your world. I want no part of killing for you. I want no part of fear."

Baez slung his rifle over his shoulder and approached Yaw.

"What are you doing?" Turner asked.

"Setting them free. All of them. And then I'm leaving."

Baez pulled his M-Tech blade from his pocket and cut the zip-tie from Yaw's wrists. Baez did the same with Chris, Camilla, Masha, and Joey. Baez even cut the Barbarian free. In seconds, they were all on their feet.

"Are you just going to let him do that?" Turner said to Scholl.

"Free will, man. We all got a choice. And I respect his."

"You're fired. Both of you are."

"I quit," Scholl replied. "What he just did?" Scholl said as he pointed to Luthecker. "That shit's waaay too spooky for me. I'm not about to have this guy tell the world my secrets. But I'm not going to kill innocent people either."

Everyone watched in stunned silence as Baez and Scholl exited the Cyber Center.

"Oh my god that was awesome," Kirby commented, the second the door closed behind Baez and Scholl. "Do me next. Do me next. You promised," he said to Alex.

Luthecker looked at Kirby. He didn't see Turner pull the 9mm from his waistband and point it at his chest.

Mark Kirby couldn't believe it when he saw Turner pull the gun and point it at Luthecker.

Kirby was standing close enough to Turner that he could make out the CZ brand insignia on the slide of the gun.

It was then that time seemed to slow down. The screams, the movements, all of the sound, all of the motion, became a blur.

The only thing that was crystal clear was the detail of the weapon, who it was pointed at, and what Kirby had to do.

Kirby was not a fast moving man, so he took advantage of his perception of slower time. Kirby grabbed the gun in Turner's hand and moved the barrel's trajectory away from Luthecker.

There was a brief struggle with the gun. Kirby looked down to see that the barrel was pointing at his mid-section.

Turner pulled the trigger and the weapon discharged.

Kirby immediately dropped to his knees. *It's not like in the movies,* he thought as the impact of the bullet made his legs go numb, and he fell to the floor face first.

He rolled onto his back, just as his belly began to feel like it was on fire. He put his hand on his stomach and felt a warm wetness.

He pulled back his hand, and it was covered in blood.

He looked around the room, and blood spilled all over the floor in a large pool.

His blood.

The next thing he saw was Luthecker standing over him.

"Is this why you never told me my fate?" Kirby said. "Because you knew this would happen?" Kirby struggled to get out the words.

"I knew you would have to make a choice," Alex answered. "But I can't see things that involve me, remember? If I could have seen this unfolding, I would have stopped it. I'm so sorry."

"It's not your fault. I involved you. Whether you wanted me to or not. That was my choice."

"You sacrificed yourself to create a new destiny for me. Understand this, you have given me a gift. I will forever be in your debt."

Kirby started to grow very sleepy. It was then that he knew he would die. It didn't prevent him from wanting answers. It didn't prevent him from wanting to know.

"You must have known I was going to die. Is that why you wouldn't tell me my future?"

Luthecker took Kirby's hand. "Let me tell you what I see. We as a species will not go extinct. And the reason we will not go extinct is because your work will continue. On this, you have my promise."

Kirby smiled and squeezed Luthecker's hand one last time before his life left him.

YAW HAD REACTED the second he saw the flash of Turner's gun. By the time he got across the room, Mark Kirby had fallen.

Yaw made sure that there would be no second pull of the trigger. He kicked Turner's wrist hard enough to shatter the joint, and he followed it up with an elbow smash to Turner's forehead that knocked the Coalition CEO out cold.

WITH THE SOUND of the gunshot and the scramble that ensued, Ivan Barbolin saw his chance. While everyone moved toward the fallen scientist, he sprinted toward the door.

He had almost reached the handle when something hit his legs mid-stride, sending him to the linoleum fast, and he saw stars as his head smacked against the floor face first.

Dizzy, his head wracked with pain, he rolled onto his back, only to see Masha standing over him.

"Where do you think you're going?"

THE DOOR to the Cyber Center abruptly opened and several heavily armed Coalition Assurance soldiers stepped through and surrounded the group, M-16s bearing down on all. Brian Scholl was leading them.

Everyone froze.

"I guess you're gonna arrest us now," Yaw said.

"No," Scholl answered. "The whole Fortress was listening in to what happened here. They heard every second of it. It was piped through every speaker, every television, every radio, and every cell phone. Hell, I think the whole world heard it. And we're here for those guys," Scholl said, waving his hand over Glen Turner and Ivan Barbolin. "The rest of you are free to go."

Nikki approached Alex. "What about PHOEBE? What do you think she's going to do?" she asked.

Turner's phone began to ring in his pocket. Sitting on the floor holding his shattered wrist, he remained unconscious from Yaw's elbow strike to the head.

Yaw stooped down and reached into Turner's pocket, pulled the phone free, and handed it to Alex.

Alex put the phone to his ear and listened.

"The launch sequence. It has stopped completely. We have things back under control. The emergency is over. We are safe," a relieved Captain Dimitrov said.

Luthecker hung up the phone, looked at Nikki, and smiled. "I think we have our answer. It's over."

Muranaka approached Alex and Nikki. In all her years of studying computer code and logic, she had never witnessed anything like what she had just seen. And Nicole Ellis was right. More than anything in the world now, she wanted to *know*.

She looked back and forth between Nikki and Alex. "I want in. Whatever it is you're doing next, I want in."

As Luthecker led Nikki, Yaw, Camilla, Chris, Masha, Joey, and now Rika Muranaka out of the Cyber Center and through the hallways of the Coalition One Building, Coalition employees stepped out of the group's path and watched them walk past. Some nodded in acknowledgement, some even clapped. Many looked at the group with a combination of awe and uncertainty. Every one of them had heard the conversation that had taken place inside the Cyber Center, and it had raised a lot of questions. Questions that they all wanted answers to.

When Luthecker and his family exited the building and reached the streets, they found the building surrounded by dozens of LAPD, SWAT and Federal vehicles, with armed officers standing by. There was a moment of tension before Camilla spotted Officer's Rodriguez and Levy leaning against their patrol car. The LAPD officers waved them over.

"It was broadcast on the police scanner. Some of us were thinking of getting popcorn. I have no idea how you made that happen, but that was some unbelievable shit you got that guy to confess to," Rodriguez said. "The rest of the police you see here are to secure the facilities and arrest the entire Coalition board."

"So are we charged with something?" Nikki asked.

"Hell no. I'm here to take you guys home," Rodriguez said.

34

ONE MONTH LATER

Alex Luthecker sat at the kitchen table of his Terminal Island apartment, reading the *New York Times*. The family was no longer hunted, and after an arrangement with the city of Long Beach, they were allowed to live at the complex in the shipyard next to the Long Beach port. At least for now.

The Department of Justice had moved on Coalition Properties quickly, mostly due to the momentum of outrage by the populace. After PHOEBE had leaked the details of the Coalition's crimes to every smart phone, laptop, and news organization across the globe, there was absolutely no stopping it.

Alex avoided all electronic media, as it still gave him horrific headaches, but he had recently started keeping tabs on world events via printed media. And today's headlines in the *New York Times* were written in bold letters:

COALITION PROPERTIES UNDER INVESTIGATION FOR FRAUD, TAX EVASION, RICO, AND SANCTIONING MURDER.

"The firm declares bankruptcy in an attempt to survive countless criminal and civil charges.

Congress considers immediate removal of the firm's corporate charter, commonly known as the death penalty, as it continues its investigation.

This looks to be the end of the world's largest corporate entity and weapons contractor."

Below the headlines were photos of Coalition Properties board members being led away in handcuffs, along with former Coalition CEO Glen Turner's mug shot.

Luthecker folded the paper and tossed it onto the table. He sat there a moment, remembering the days when he would avoid the newspapers along with other interactions with information, including people.

His inability to discipline his mind was what originally pushed him into the shadows. But it had always been people he avoided more than anything, as the patterns of the choices that created their destinies overwhelmed him.

All of that changed when he met his mentors, Winn and Mawith and finally Kunchin. Their collective efforts had forever changed him. They had given him purpose. They had given him others to care for. They helped him accept responsibility for who he was and how to use his gifts to create change in others.

But none of it would have happened or meant anything without Nikki. Making the choice to save her life that fateful night in Club Sutra, in turn, had saved his own. For Alex, she had become his anchor. With her love for him, with her belief in him, he no longer feared his impact on others. He understood its importance and took responsibility for it.

And for the first time in Alex Luthecker's life, he could see into his own future. It was at Nikki's side. Along with one more thing he saw in his future.

Alex got up from the table, walked across the kitchen, and stepped out onto the balcony that looked over the courtyard.

He watched as Yaw led the day's martial arts practice with enthusiasm. Chris, Camilla, Masha, and Joey were all there and he took note of the newest student, Rika Muranaka, and the steely-eyed look of determination she displayed as she tried to follow along.

She would do well here, Alex already knew. The family had grown, and it would continue to grow.

Yaw felt the gaze, looked up, and saw his best friend standing on the balcony. The men smiled and nodded to one another. There was an understanding between them that their work was not yet complete, and the movement would not be stopped. They had collectively changed the arc of the momentum toward a more hopeful future, and the sense of that course correction was palpable in the air. For all of them, there was excitement about what lay ahead.

Alex stepped away from the balcony and moved through the apartment, stopping at the doorway of Maria's bedroom to bear witness to the future.

He looked past the myriad of stuffed animals and storybooks to the small desk in the corner where Maria sat behind a computer monitor, her young eyes locked on a screen filled with lines of code.

Nikki was kneeling next to Maria, her right arm gently placed around Maria's shoulders, as the creator of PHOEBE taught the ten-year-old how to code.

"How's she doing?" Alex asked Nikki.

"She's talking to PHOEBE in a language that I can barely understand. It's unbelievable how fast she's learning. She'll be beyond me before too much longer. I've never seen anything like it."

"It's good to know the kids are getting along," Alex said to Nikki, before turning to Maria. "Are you having fun?"

"Uh huh. We're talking about searching the world to find people just like you and me."

"That's very good, Maria. But would you like to take a break and go outside to play?"

"Yes! Can I bring Nala?" Maria asked, in reference to her favorite stuffed animal, the well-worn tiger that had accompanied her all the way from San Salvador.

Maria never seemed to go anywhere without Nala these days.

"Of course you can."

~

MARIA CAREFULLY SAT Nala beside her on the blanket as she and Alex had lunch in the park. It was a beautiful day, without a cloud in the sky. The grass in the park was a brilliant green, and the square was filled with several people—ranging from families enjoying lunch together in the shade of the trees to teenagers throwing footballs around—and one dog catching a Frisbee. For Alex, it was a moment of peace and beauty frozen in time.

"Do you want a sandwich?" Alex asked Maria.

"Maybe later," she answered as her eyes moved across the people in the park, her attention locked on every detail of the symphony of human interaction that unfolded before her.

Alex in turn watched Maria with fascination as her young eyes recorded it all as fresh and new, and it made him smile. In Maria, he had found something he had never thought possible, a kindred spirit in abilities. But unlike him, she would have a guide to teach her from the beginning.

Alex Luthecker made a promise to himself that he would hold Maria's hand every step of the way as she learned to accept her unique gifts. He understood that this would be the most important thing he would ever do...that he and Nikki would ever do.

He put his hand on her shoulder gently and whispered in her ear. "Tell me, Maria, what do you see?"

ACKNOWLEDGMENTS

Revolution was by far the most challenging of the three Luthecker novels to write. I suppose that's always the case with the third book of a trilogy. The desire to finish strong makes the task daunting, and I hope I accomplished that here. It wouldn't have happened without the encouragement and efforts of several people. Here are a few of them.

My sister Deborah for helping me with this book, and every book I write. Every entrepreneurial endeavor, really. Her belief in me and courage on my behalf keeps me moving forward, no matter how difficult the task. Thank you for all that you are, and all that you do.

My publisher and long time friend Christiana Miller, who convinced me that she could help the Luthecker novels find their readers, but in order to do that, she needed a third book. Here it is. Thank you.

My editor Bobbie Metevier, who went through this book, and then went back to edit the previous two Luthecker books for their second edition release. Thank you for helping me level up.

And of course, my crew. JC, Erwin, Mel. 25 years strong with these guys, through thick and thin. Them, along with the women in our lives, the Claudia's and Diane Q, form my chosen family. Thank you.

And I save the biggest thank you for the Luthecker readers. Those of you who have expressed their enjoyment to me both personally and in reviews in following the journey of Alex Luthecker and his diverse family have been the single biggest motivator.

Is Revolution the end of the story? Will Alex continue to change the minds and behavior patterns of those he encounters, or will he step aside and let Maria and Phoebe forge ahead as the next generation of pattern readers? That's up to you, dear reader, if you want to see more. If you do, I'm sure you'll find a way to let me know. But no matter what, I'm enormously grateful for all of you.

All the best,
Keith

ABOUT THE AUTHOR

KEITH DOMINGUE is a screenwriter living in Los Angeles. He has written scripts for MGM, Dimension Films, Sony Pictures, and Village Roadshow Pictures. Also a fitness coach and avid martial artist, he splits his time between the computer screen and the gym.

You can visit the author on Facebook at: https://www.facebook.com/KeithDomingueAuthor

Or on Twitter at: @AlexLuthecker

For more information on the author, or to send him an email:
www.authorkeithdomingue.com
keithdomingue.author@gmail.com

facebook.com/KeithDomingueAuthor

X x.com/AlexLuthecker

ALSO BY KEITH DOMINGUE

Luthecker Trilogy

Book One: Luthecker

Book Two: Luthecker: Rise

Book Three: Luthecker: Revolution

Printed in Great Britain
by Amazon